The War for the Tree

M.A. Fitzgerald

First published 2023
Published by GB Publishing Org
Copyright © 2023 M.A. Fitzgerald
All rights reserved

ISBN: 978-1-912031-19-1 (paperback)
978-1-912031-05-4 (eBook)

Cover Art © Morganico

GB Publishing Org
www.gbpublishing.co.uk

CONTENTS

Prologue

*W*ho am I?
    Eyes stuttered and darted.

They found a floor, a white floor – a snowy floor. Then her feet. They shuffled seemingly of their own accord, one, then the other, ploughing through the snow until becoming lost beneath it. To watch their slow lumbering progress was hypnotic. She found herself having to wrench her view elsewhere.

Her eyes clouded. She blinked.

Was that a hand?

It was, she decided.

But hers?

It didn't look like hers. She tried to focus but it made her dizzy. Thin, smoky tendrils lined up before her eyes. She tried to make a fist, but her fingers merely puffed away. She gasped but no sound came. Her voice was gone. Fear tumbled through her as she fell to her knees, then to the floor. Again she glimpsed her hands, scrabbling and clawing at the snow. Her fingers dispersed like a breeze through cloud as her face followed into the cold floor. Yet she couldn't feel the cold; she felt nothing. She got up and staggered on.

What have they done to me?

Branches and trees came at her as she walked. She passed through some and got snagged on others.

I must be dead.

Her eyes rolled in their sockets, fighting to stay level. She glimpsed an ocean of snow before her vision spun and again she stumbled, her strange hand trying to prevent her fall on a tree trunk. Her hand dispersed upon impact – her face followed hard into its side.

Blinking, she woke.

A dull pain throbbed on the left side of her face. The pain sharpened as she moved her jaw, twisting into a grimace.

For a time she lay on her back, shallow breathing her only movement. Her eyes tentatively opened and began to dot around the gloom. The collision had

1

somehow stilled them. Blurs began to darken and form into shapes. Something was swaying above her.

A branch? In the wind?

She raised a hand into the air and her fingers blew sideways, like snow from a mountain's peak.

Yes.

Her arm lowered to her side, the effort exhausting. Though her vision was black and white, something further off wasn't. A pinpoint of colour. A foreign body in this dream. Her eyes narrowed curiously. She could not remember the name of this colour. Her eyes trembled as she traced this blur within a blur, the tip of a brush that moved across a page, undecided where to begin. A sound travelled with it.

A song?

It had been too long to know any songs, to *recall* any songs.

The sound was irksome and unwelcome. She closed her eyes but the sound remained, blooming and swelling and filling her ears. She tried idly to remember her name, but her mind laboured. Soon, the soft black of her eyelids began to glow – with this colour that wasn't black or grey or white. She knew something was before her. *Over* her.

Be gone. Be gone!

She tried to scream, suddenly enraged, but the sound only echoed in her mind.

Opening her eyes, she flinched and tried to shrink away from the colour that was everything now. Her eyes creased. Though painfully, she could look upon it, bright as it was. Something... something was looking at her. She put a hand to one ear, trying to block that cursed noise, raising her other hand.

In defence? No.

The hand shielding her eyes began to curl.

Get... away!

Her hand struck at the thing, and suddenly she was transported. Like the breaching of a dam, memories began to spill, then wash, until they poured over her.

She knew what she had been.

She knew what they had done.

As her eyes rolled, her body convulsed. She screamed again, but this time she felt it. Heard it. Liquid filled her eyes. She could see clearly now. The colour was dying, the face in it dead. Her hand fell away from it. A solid hand she noticed, opening long white fingers.

She smiled somewhat.

She had remembered her name.

A distant light

Henry Best was not a hero. Nor was he an adventurer.

His teddy 'Bear' though was most certainly a hero, and an adventurer; at least Henry liked to think so.

Adventures though were largely imagined by the eight-year-old boy. In the Victorian terraced house Henry shared with his father in London, sofas would become boats and carpets became oceans. Shark-infested as standard. On occasion he might run into a many-eyed and many-tentacled sea beast who could be sent back below the waves with a couple of whacks from an oar, and back beneath the floorboards.

Adventures of that sort were not on the cards this evening. Christmas had come to Henry's house, and to every other house in London. It was Christmas Eve.

Henry was loping around, a paper crown on his head, his teddy 'Bear' in tow. His father, Harold, was busy entertaining a gathering of friends, customary for this time of year. They sat around a large dining table, drinking and laughing, sometimes so loud it made Henry jump.

He placed Bear down, pulled at the neck of his thermal vest, and re-tied the knot on his dressing gown.

Henry peered from beneath his crown to count their guests, nodding a curly brown mop of hair as he did so.

Brian and Jackie. Phil and Sandra. Julie and Michael. And Henry's father. All adults. Though he'd had a royal fuss made of him when the guests came through the door, he generally felt a bit left out. He had hoped to see Julie and Michael's twin girls, the same age as him, but they were staying with their grandparents.

The only other absentee was Henry's mother, Annabelle. Two years gone, lost to pneumonia.

At the time, Henry had never heard such a word. He wished a word like that had never been invented. Perhaps if it hadn't, his mother might still be here.

A thought snagged his mind. Like a hook on a line, it pulled him from the waters of his conscious present and into a memory. It was a memory he often visited.

'...to me?'

'What?'

'I said: are you listening to me?'

'Oh. Uh, no. Sorry.'

Henry's eyes brightened.

His mother's rolled.

She leaned across the bath Henry sat in and pumped the shampoo dispenser once, then twice, working the gloop to a lather before sitting back onto the toilet lid. She sighed, giving Henry a reproachful look. He returned the look with innocence, to which his mother inclined her head, pushing a loop of her auburn hair over one ear, careful not to get the soap in her hair.

'Why were you up at the crack of dawn? Your father said he came downstairs to find you jumping around on the settee and whacking the floor with a broom handle.'

Before Henry could answer, his mother continued.

'There are marks all over my cream cushions.'

Dropping his chin to his chest, Henry avoided his mother's gaze by staring at the bubbles surrounding his midriff. He blew a few away before meeting his mother's eyes again, assuming as serious an expression as he could.

'I don't know,' he shrugged.

'Well, I certainly don't,' said Annabelle as she worked her busying, motherly hands over his head, creating a great foaming hairdo. Sitting back, she went to speak. Henry's sorry expression, coupled with a towering, soapy quiff led her to laugh instead.

'What?' asked Henry.

'Look,' said Annabelle, reaching for the shaving mirror.

Henry offered his face forward. Smiling, he watched bubbly sideburns slide down his cheeks.

'Close your eyes.'

Warm water cascaded over his head, poured from a jug. Finished, she gave him a towel.

'In all seriousness though, Henry, this has got to stop.'

The towel over Henry's head parted. He considered his mother through its curtained opening, perhaps to gauge how serious she was being. His mother again pushed a loop of hair from her thin but pretty face and frowned.

'Do you mean the cushions or the banging?' Henry asked from beneath the towel.

'Both,' she said, lifting it from his head. 'And the super-early mornings too.'

'I'll try not to wake so early,' Henry resolved, sliding himself back into the water.

'Perhaps,' she started, standing and pausing to think, 'we could keep you up another half-hour in the evening. You do seem to take a while going off.'

'Yes!' cried Henry. He shot upright, creating a wave that rode up the bath's far end, just shy of the rim.

Annabelle huffed and extended the towel she held.

'Come on. Out now, please.'

Henry stepped from the bath and wrapped himself in the towel. He thought to follow up on his mother's idea. 'It takes me *aaaaages* to get to sleep, Mum. Please, can we do another half-hour?'

A smaller towel came over his head. The scent of apple and cinnamon – from a detergent his mother used – filled his nostrils, as busying motherly hands towelled his head dry. It was Henry's favourite part of bath time. Pyjamas were placed in the boy's hands.

'We'll try the later time tonight if your father agrees,' said Annabelle as she helped her son into his top. 'But don't think it will all be TV.' Henry's head popped through the crew-neck of his pyjamas. 'You can do some reading.'

'Will Dad read to me?'

Henry parted his curly brown mop of hair.

'I expect so.'

The part of the memory that Henry could still recount in detail followed. First his mother hugged him, then she held him away.

'I'm off to stay with your aunt Gracie this weekend. Leaving this Friday.'

'*Gracie?*' repeated Henry, a little sour-mouthed. 'She smells of cat food. And she doesn't like Dad.'

His mother smiled sweetly. 'Yes and yes. But you're not to say those things to anyone. It's only to help her out with a move.'

6

'So it'll just be me and Dad then?'

'Just you and Dad.'

'Cool. We'll miss you though, Mum.'

Smiling, she knelt to hug her son. 'I'll miss you both too,' she breathed. 'Just look after your father when I'm gone, okay?'

*

Henry, not for the first time, reflected on those words his mother had once said.

Look after your father when I'm gone…

Those words instilled something in him that day. Had she meant them to?

Now he looked over to the table, sidestepping the view of Brian's back to see his father, slumped and easing the cork from another bottle.

Life since his mother's death had been a blur of confusion and tears. He'd taken it hard, naturally, as had his father. But with a child's resilience, he'd somehow gotten on again, perhaps forced to by his father's seeming inability to move on, and with a strange reversal of roles, Henry had almost become the rock between them.

But that's not to say Henry felt anything like a rock. He would always sorely miss his mother and would need comfort himself. Sometimes he'd wake crying in the night, but had mostly given over trying to rouse his father, who was slipping further into the drink and would only wake in confusion. His father wasn't a bad man. He'd lost his way, wrapped entirely in his own grief, forgetting his fatherly duties and barely speaking of Annabelle. But Henry wouldn't give up. He'd come through soon.

Henry had instead turned to his Bear. He would listen, never interrupt and would lay all night with him. Some people thought eight was perhaps a bit old for a soft toy, but Henry couldn't let his old friend go.

If only the twins were here.

As if she'd heard his thoughts, Julie flashed Henry a broad but sympathetic smile and began to rummage around in her bag. Leaning back from the conversation at the table, she opened her phone and passed it over.

'The girls are always playing the games they have on these things. I'm sure you'll find one.'

'Thanks!'

Henry straightened his crown and took the phone. He walked back to the sofa, eyes scanning the screen, and dumped himself down. Bear placed beside him. He crossed his feet, noticing his tartan slippers were threadbare.

The best seat in the house. Before him stood their Christmas tree.

He held still for a moment, his face lit by the screen's glare. It was one of the special things they'd all done together as father, mother and son.

Now just the two of them, Henry thought that tradition would slip, but it was one of the few things that hadn't changed. His father still had the ability to select and dress a tree and add that touch of magic.

You see, when a Christmas tree is decorated, when the finishing touches are added, when the Fairy is placed carefully atop her perch and the lights bloom through the deep green, a world comes to life within a tree. A world unseen to a human eye, at least, to an eye that wouldn't know what to look for. To an eye that wouldn't know where to look, for a world that doesn't want to be found.

Now, whether Henry was destined, or whether he just got lucky, he glimpsed a tiny part of this world, but not that he knew it.

*

After several failed attempts at a driving game, Henry lost interest. Placing the phone aside, he massaged life back into his fingers and paused. Something caught his eye. A flash? Something... in the tree?

What was that?

Henry rose from the sofa, holding Bear by a limb, and shuffled closer. Blinking and craning his neck, tip-toeing and bobbing, Henry found its origin.

There? No. *There*.

A light. But a *different* light. Nestled in the dark branches.

A fine pinpoint of light, almost entirely hidden. Unlike all the other lights on the tree. It seemed so far away. A faraway star.

Henry was enchanted. So much so, he barely heard the sound. A distant sound, not from the room or its chattering guests, but coming from the light. Gently at first, it whispered, gathering and building like a quickening wind. The light pulsed and started slowly towards him, burning brighter and brighter, and yet brighter still, along with the sound of the growing wind until the light was so bright, the wind so great, it was all he could see and hear.

8

The room around him was gone. His feet left the ground for a moment and then again, like he was floating slowly upward, towards the source of the light growing all around him. Floating became flying. He tried to grab on to something, but grasped only air, almost losing Bear. He called out to his father. Again. Louder! But the winds took his words and scattered them.

Can't they see me? Or hear me?

A breeze picked up and stayed, flapping his pyjamas, making him squint. It brought with it a wintry mist.

Henry was swallowed through it.

Toe-tapping music

Waist-deep and head-first in something cold and soft, Henry came out of a brief concussion and gasped. Freshly fallen snow had taken most of the sting out of a nasty landing. He was buried for all but his legs at the peak of a snowy hill. He kicked and bicycled until something grabbed them. And he screamed.

A brief struggle and Henry was plopped from the hole and onto his behind. He swiped his face clean to reveal the silhouette of a creature, reaching to grab him a second time.

With his back to the ground and nowhere to go, Henry did the only thing he could and kicked the foul creature low. The thing dropped with both hands (paws?) clasped between its legs, a low moan escaping it. Henry turned and leapt, but hit the snow again - the creature quick - a paw claiming his ankle. And then to add to the horror, it spoke his name.

It wanted *him*.

A case of mistaken identity was perhaps his last defence. But the voice sounded oddly familiar. This time he looked carefully at the creature holding him. Its face was familiar too; large amber-flecked eyes, great big ears and furry.

A rub of his eyes revealed Bear – his teddy – stood hands on hips laughing. He was bigger than Henry now, maybe even as big as his father.

'OK?'

Henry pushed himself upright. 'What the hell…?'

'Hey! Don't swear!' said Bear, waving a paw.

'Swear? Are you kidding? Hell isn't swearing. Swearing is… well, that doesn't matter. Are you Bear? Am I... dreaming? *Is this real?* It feels real. This snow,' said Henry, feeling his cheeks, 'feels cold.'

Bear couldn't keep up.

'Am I... small?' asked Henry, in a small voice.

'Well,' said Bear in his low, easy voice. 'I feel tall. Quite big, actually.'

'But Bear,' said Henry, quite matter-of-factly. 'How are you talking? And moving? Are you... friendly?'

'Don't worry,' said Bear, scratching himself and glancing around. 'I won't eat you.' He paused. 'Then again, let's see what's here first.'

Henry's sudden silence brought laughter from the stuffed toy. He smiled. 'I'm just fooling around.'

Henry flicked a handful of snow at Bear. 'Well, *don't.*'

They stopped talking for a moment and gazed around in awe.

'You know what?' asked Henry, standing and brushing down his pyjamas. 'I think that this *is* a dream. A very strange dream. How else am I here?'

'I'm not so sure.',' pondered Bear scratching just behind his shoulder, 'but I tell you, I've been waiting a long time to get that spot.'

Ignoring Bear, Henry began to tune in to their surroundings. He trod his slippered feet around the hole he'd made landing, before settling still at the top of the hill they stood on. The landscape was a winter desert. In every direction were rolling, snow-draped hills, ranged by an echoless silence. Filling his view above was a black, cloudless sky, frosted with innumerable stars. There was no visible moon. Bear padded through the snow to Henry's side and threw a thick arm around the boy's shoulder.

'I've no idea what this is, Henry, but if I'm alive to your eyes, then I'm happy.'

'I'm glad you're here, Bear,' said Henry from beneath the woolly comfort of Bear's arm, 'but we need to get out of here.'

Bear looked over his shoulder. 'Then there can only be one way.'

Henry turned to follow his teddy's gaze. A hazy light challenged a part of the sky on the horizon behind them.

'Ready?' asked Bear.

The boy turned up the collar on his mustard-striped dressing gown and doubled the tie at his waist. 'Ready.'

*

Rounding the top of probably their fourteenth hill, Henry and Bear were met with the now all-too-familiar sight of yet another downward slope, leading off to the foot of another snowy hill.

What was unfamiliar, however, was a snowman at the foot of it. It was dressed just as a snowman would be: top hat, scarf, pipe. *Everything.*

'A snowman,' said Henry, waiting for Bear's agreement.

Bear mouthed the same.

11

'Who would make a snowman all the way out here?'

Bear's wonder turned to excitement. 'Come on,' he said, starting downhill, breaking into big bounding leaps.

'Hang on!' cried Henry, peeling after him.

The snow suddenly became fun, making the cold and weariness disappear. Even the snow spraying up from Bear's heels into Henry's face made him grin.

He was almost alongside Bear.

Bear turned to laugh, but tripped, and in an explosion of powdery snow he was gone – left in Henry's wake. Henry couldn't resist watching Bears tumble, and given he was now running forwards but looking backwards, he suffered the same fate.

Then Henry found his feet and set off again at the same reckless pace.

Bear arrived just after Henry, who was now inspecting the snowman, and hands on knees and breathing hard, asked between breaths. ''Well?'

'It's definitely a snowman,' concluded Henry. 'But...'

'But?'

'He looks... *nervous.'*

Bear got up and plodded over to take a look. Henry broke from his wonderment and reached up to touch the carrot nose. The snowman leapt backwards and raised a pair of snowy fists.

'Who in Treelights are you two?!' he demanded in a stricken, muffled voice.

Henry was startled straight. Bear had been knocked onto his behind with the shock. He scrambled up to his paws.

'State names. State names!' said the Snowman shaking a fist before their faces.

Henry, sir. Henry,' said the boy, straightening further still.

'And the Beast's?'

Bear turned to look behind himself before he realised. 'You mean *me*?'

'Course I mean you! Up on your feet and give me a name!'

Bear rose slow and steady, his paws raised in appeal. 'How about we all calm down a bit? I'm Bear, this is Henry. We're lost.'

'We don't mean any trouble,' said Henry. 'We'd just like to get warm.'

'And maybe something to eat,' said Bear, lowering a paw to his belly.

12

The snowman kept his beady coal eyes on Henry, darted them to Bear briefly, and back again to the boy. Eventually he blew a heavy breath and dropped his arms. 'Well, you don't look like one of *hers*. Is that all you want?'

'That's it,' said Bear, bringing his arms outwards, reaffirming they were just a Teddy Bear and a boy.

'Well in that case,' said the snowman, 'you'd better come in.'

The snowman reached backward toward the hill, felt around a bit, then brought forward a snow-covered door. A neon-blue light lit the opening. The snowman stood framed in it. 'Quickly now,' he said glancing left to right. 'Don't worry. It's safe.'

The door, it appeared to the pair, led straight into the hill. Bear stepped forward and placed his hands either side of the frame, peering in like a suspicious cat. A corridor of the same neon blue led to another door further down. Bear turned his head. 'Henry...?'

Henry shrugged, then nodded.

'We'll follow you in,' said Bear to the snowman.

'Okay, okay. Just hurry inside. He replied, chasing the door shut behind them.

The neon blue around them was mesmeric. An endless depth of colour with no visible wall or floor line. A muted noise buffered against the far door. They followed the snowman along the corridor of light, stopping just short of the door. The snowman gave them a last look.

A wave of sound and light – *many lights* – warmth, scents, and more washed over them, assaulting their senses. They stood mouths agape. It seemed they'd stumbled into a party. A fancy dress party beneath a great, domed ceiling. The costumes were mind-boggling. The initial noise they'd heard rearranged into chatter and music as the components of a band struck up; a Big Band sound of lively, infectious, toe-tapping music. Henry's wide eyes followed a walking stick; no, a candy cane. Red and white-striped, hopping off onto a dancefloor.

Bear's eyes were drawn to the far wall where a gingerbread man was snaking biscuit-like hips in time to the bass guitar he was playing. The drums had an elf – *an elf?* – in smart green garb with a belled hat, bent over the kit, tap-tap-tapping a symbol before travelling over the skins with his arms a-blur, his face furious with concentration. There was too much to take in.

'Enjoy yourselves,' called the snowman over the music. He draped a cold arm each around their shoulders and nodded towards the bar. 'First drink's free.'

'Thanks,' said Henry, but the snowman had already left. Both tried to look as if everything was normal, that this party was just one of many. Henry tried to look nonchalant.

Just how out of place could they be in a place like this?

After a few more glances, and a nudge from Bear, they sidled up to the bar as casually as they could. Two Christmas puddings, their outfits oddly cake-like and moist – even smelling like puddings – were sat sipping drinks at a glass table beside them. Both had dark, white-less eyes, blinking as they spoke. One leaned into the other, and their eyes fell upon Henry.

Henry's eyes darted elsewhere – to a variety of dates and clementines, talking loudly and dancing, surprisingly well, given their bandy legs were stick-thin. 'These aren't costumes,' said Henry, turning stiffly to Bear.

'You've only just noticed?' said Bear from the side of his mouth, his attention on the elven barman he'd been trying to hail. The elf, dressed as a shabby, tired Santa, sauntered over and climbed a stool to their height.

'What's it to be?' he asked in a voice an octave higher than Henry's, tossing a tea-towel over his shoulder.

'First drink's free?' yelled Bear over the music.

The elf nodded then turned an ear toward them.

'Well, we're looking to get something warm in us. What's recommended?'

With mild irritation, the elf gestured towards a variety of bottles, vials and jugs behind him.

A large glass bowl of steaming red liquid sat on the bar to their left, a ladle rested on its rim. To their right was a broad glass cylinder of bubbling orange gloop, rising twice Bear's height. For fear of causing offence, Bear motioned to the red bowl.

'And your friend?'

Henry puffed up, tall as he could.

'Just a warm milk. Please.'

The elf grinned and jumped down from his stool to get their drinks. Henry gave Bear a look and winked.

'There ya go,' said the elf, returning to view above the bar, and slid their drinks toward them. 'Enjoy.'

Henry and Bear felt a little more comfortable and confident now. They leaned on the bar and began to survey their surroundings. Bear began tapping a paw to the music.

'Whoaa,' said Bear, pulling the drink from his lips. 'That's spicy. How's the milk?'

Henry didn't hear Bear. He was busy guzzling his hot milk. Bear guessed it was just fine then. Bear leaned closer to Henry's ear.

'How about a sit down?'

Henry nodded. With the back of his hand he wiped the milk from his chin. Bear pushed slowly through the busy gathering, having to keep excusing himself as he weaved through fluttering angels, whooping snowmen and pogo-dancing candy canes among other oddities, until he found a spot in-between some clapping bow-tied parcels sat in a semi-circle around a table. They had simple pencil-drawn faces that were always changing, as though constantly being re-sketched.

Also enjoying the band were a group of elves necking a dark liquid, laughing and occasionally linking arms to dance.

Henry began to think like he'd entered a theme park, and was deciding which ride he wanted to go on. Glancing up he saw gold, green and red tinsel draped from a ceiling he struggled to find an end to, with a variety of baubles suspended in mid-air, each rolling a dazzling reflection of beautiful lights. Every now and then a laughing star would fly across the decorations above, trailing a line of twinkling, winking dust. Nobody seemed to really notice; they were all too busy drinking and dancing.

'Okay?' yelled Bear to Henry, a big grin across his furry face. Henry nodded enthusiastically and looked back up at the ceiling, following another star off into nowhere.

Bear leaned in close. 'D'you need the toilet? I do. You want to come with me and find it, you know, stick together?'

Henry placed his drink down, his mouth full, and nodded. 'I'm bursting!' he gasped. and then belched.

Bear raised an eyebrow.

15

He considered asking for directions but thought better of it. 'Let's try over *there*.'

Bear started off around the dancefloor toward a busy corridor of warm light just beyond it, declining as politely as he could a dance with a very lively and sticky-looking date along the way. Stepping up the few steps into the corridor, there came a commotion of noise beyond the slow-moving queue, causing the mass in front to divide.

Two snowmen were frogmarching a clementine by his little arms, his feet running in mid-air, and the three of them were coming straight at them.

'Unhand me! This is harassment!' the little fruit yelled, fighting to free himself, causing the trio to lurch unpredictably left and right. Bear wheeled, grabbed Henry off his feet and threw himself towards the wall to avoid the pair of them getting run over in the melee. But the wall they hit did not hold them. It hinged and swung open, throwing them through and to the floor, before easing shut again, muting the noise outside.

'Bear – you're suffocating me!' cried Henry, fighting to free himself.

'Sorry, Henry, sorry. Just let me...' Bear rolled himself off to rise, only to find a walnut and a Christmas pudding glaring down at them. They shot a final disapproving look before turning back around, re-joining a group, all quiet chatter and tinkling glasses.

Bear pulled Henry to his feet, nodding apologies as he did so.

Looking around, the pair realised they were in a smaller domed room, a bit like an igloo, and bathed in a faint red glow that seamlessly changed from green to purple, then back to red again. Low, plump-looking seats played host to several groups of strange folk, very much the same mixture as the other room. Here, though, the atmosphere was much more low-key and with no music, all until a beautifully wrapped parcel threw a pair of string-like arms onto the keys of a piano and walked its fingers up to the high notes – managing at the same time to throw Henry and Bear an odd look.

'The other room was better,' said Henry under his breath.

There was scattered applause as the pianist started into a tune. Henry and Bear obliged too, before Bear suggested quietly that they should leave. With a fixed smile and a nod, Henry slid his hands into his dressing-gown pockets and followed after Bear, hoping to find where they'd entered in from, but this proved difficult. There was no visible door in the wall. They turned, smiling, nodding along to the music as they looked carefully around for another door.

'I see nothing,' said Bear.

'Me neither.'

And then the music tailed off and stopped. Heads turned to the pianist, and then to an out of breath elf who had just entered the room, clutching his throat. 'They're here!' he gasped, stabbing a finger to where he'd entered. 'It's a raid!'

Pandemonium erupted.

All present turned heel and broke toward Henry and Bear – who'd have been trampled themselves had they not bolted too – away from the riotous noise of shattering glass, stifled screams and upended chairs.

Henry and Bear, being farthest from the trouble had a small head start, running towards a wall on the far side as the galloping herd were closing fast. A candy cane hopped past, followed by a gingerbread man, making good ground. The gingerbread man tripped hard on a chair, snapping a leg clean off – scattering crumbs everywhere.

The scattering of biscuit managed to up-end a snowman, briefly holding third place, but he was held up, frantically searching for his missing head.

Bear steadied Henry, bumped sideways by a gift-wrapped parcel running blindly, its string-like arms flailing. He managed to keep him upright and moving. A Christmas pudding drew so close behind, they could smell the butter brandy it was smothered in.

Another larger snowman strode past with an elf on his back, with the little fellow kicking his heels as though he rode a slacking racehorse, his face fixed backward in fear. By now, some of the party had reached the far wall and were running hands across it like demented mime artists, trying to find an exit.

To their relief, they watched a cane disappear through a hidden door into the darkness outside, followed by the snowman-elf partnership; the elf ducked under the door at the very last moment. The pudding was next, though it lost its holly and twin berries it wore topside as it shot through the door like a bullet from a gun.

Henry and Bear were neck-and-neck with the parcel, who had lost ground through weaving and dodging, and a walnut blowing hard to their right.

Henry choked for breath, losing the ground beneath his feet, as Bear collared the back of his pyjamas. He was pulled through the air and out the door, just in front of the closing rabble – who clattered into the entrance – before landing in a heap on the snow.

The most notable casualty was the bow-tied parcel, slightly crumpled and cradling a tear on its side.

Another door of solid ice opened along the snowy hill they had come from, followed by another a way down from that, spitting noisy lines into the cold and dark outside.

Bear straightened Henry to make sure he was okay.

'What was that all about?' asked Henry between breaths. 'What was going on?'

'I don't know,' said Bear, casting back to the melee, 'but we'd best get away quick as possible. Let's go where the leaders went.'

They looked to the cane, pudding and snowman (who'd dumped his elven passenger and was now sporting a limp and a fresh coating of snow). They were running towards what looked to be a log lean-to, sheltering an assortment of boxes and animals.

'Sleighs!' gasped Henry, now jogging alongside Bear. 'Sleighs, with reindeer too. Look, Bear, you see?'

Henry picked up the pace, jumping excitedly when he saw the first sleigh leave the shelter carrying the candy cane, followed by the snowman, then the pudding, arguing with the left-behind-elf, trying to force his way into the same carriage.

'L-I-TT-L-E H-E-LP-E-R SLE-I-G-H COM-PAN-Y...' panted Bear, straining to read the staked sign ahead.

'Little Helper Sleigh Company,' confirmed Henry. He slowed to a walk, now near enough to see the surprised but happy faces of the remaining elven drivers. Kitted out in matching green outfits with belled hats, each sat atop a deep red sleigh, harnessing a pair of reindeer. They were pulling upwards on their reins and hoofing the ground as though impatient.

'Well,' said the first elf, hopping down to open a door on the side of the sleigh, 'you don't see many Bears and... *young* around these parts, but it is a pleasure all the same. Hop in and don't worry. There is a fleece blanket to warm yourselves into once we get moving, and moving we shall be, as I sense it'll be a busy night ahead.'

The elf looked out beyond Henry and Bear as he spoke, spying more custom heading his way.

They nodded thanks as they climbed in and sank into the worn, high-backed leather seat.

'Treelights?' asked the elf, reaching to light a lantern.

'Guess so,' shrugged Bear.

'GIII-D-I-UP!'

The elf cracked the reins and they slid off from the line toward the dancing lights on the horizon with a great sense of relief.

Into the Tree

Henry and Bear were on the move again and were quite happy about it too. They had escaped the melee and were now travelling – in some style – taking in the wintry world beneath a very cosy blanket. They rode uphill and downhill, around trees, sometimes having to duck branches, and into icy passages bearing great, long-toothed icicles that bridged small valleys. Henry would lean over the side and watch the ground fly by, while Bear held him – until they received a stern finger-wagging from their elven driver.

The stars above bathed a silvery-blue glow across the landscape near as bright as a full moon, creating shadows from the trees, and the valleys became deeper the further they travelled. It was in the darkness of these deep cuts through the landscape that they were grateful for the meagre glow from the sleigh's lamps, illuminating the rising icy walls either side of them as though they travelled the belly of some giant frozen whale.

As their candles flickered, their travelling shadow jumped around the walls; racing alongside them, reminding them that without their delicate light, darkness would engulf them. But with every valley entered came a climbing slope back out, and relief. With every hill rounded came a feeling they were getting closer and closer to their destination, still just a hazy arc of colours on the horizon, silhouetting the elf perched upon his seat like a spectator at a firework display. In time, Henry started to settle a little and, after a quiet spell, his nodding head finally came to rest on Bear's shoulder and he was asleep.

Bear would not sleep though.

He was relaxed and warm, and although their driver seemed to know where he was going, he felt he should remain cautious.

Where were they going?

What was Treelights?

If he asked the elf, it may make him wonder why they didn't know, and where they came from. These were questions Bear would struggle to answer. Fresh from one risky situation, he didn't want to enter another. And, as he mulled it over, he too succumbed to sleep.

*

The uneven ground woke Henry with a jump. After a quick double-take, he found to his surprise he still inhabited this strange new world.

How hard had he bumped his head?

He struggled upright, easing the slumbering Bear from him and saw through disbelieving eyes what they'd been heading towards. Advancing from the horizon was a pathway to the heavens; a pathway of branches and lights – a tree, his watery eyes decided. It rose into the night sky like an ice-white flame, its sheer scale staggering. Lights like a million crystals ebbed and winked along dark, snow-laden branches.

'Bear!' cried Henry. 'Look at this!'

Bear grimaced and rubbed his eyes. He followed Henry's arm down to a pointing, shaky finger. Lights reflected in his big amber eyes.

'Oh my. A tree. A giant... *Christmas tree*? It's – it's beautiful!'

The elf glanced back over his shoulder.

'It's – it's more beautiful than I've ever seen it actually,' said Bear, back-pedalling beneath the elf's scrutinous gaze. 'It's been a while, I guess.'

The elf gave a dismissive shrug and re-gripped the reins.

'I don't want him to think we don't belong here,' said Bear quietly to Henry. 'I don't want us getting any unwanted attention, understand?'

'Good idea,' said Henry.

As the tree grew closer, they noticed its base was obscured by a fast-moving mist, like a whirling snowstorm. It blew in all directions, billowing and turning, over and over, cold and hostile, quite unlike the tree itself. The Elf in answer to this reached down and grabbed an old leather jacket. He buttoned it from top to bottom, turned up the collar and shuffled into his seat.

'Get comfy under that blanket and hold on!' he shouted, and with a whip of the reins, Henry and Bear were jolted back into their seats. 'Treelights here we come! *Giii-d-i-up!*'

The elf's sudden enthusiasm buoyed Henry and Bear. Fear had given way to enjoyment; nerves had turned to smiles.

'He's taking us through that storm,' said Bear.

As quickly as he had spoken, mist started streaking past them like fleeing ghosts, as if trying to escape the very thing they were heading into, with greater regularity until, as a cloud, it swallowed them.

Their candlelight died.

Henry gripped Bear's paw and didn't let go. The snowy hills and night sky, the brilliant light from the tree had all disappeared, replaced with a cold and dark winter storm, blowing violently as if attacking them, showering them with snow in waves. The wind fought them for their blanket and Bear and Henry fought to keep it, trying to see through squinted eyes where they were going. When the wind changed direction they sighted the Elf, who'd disappeared in the storm up until now - still in his seat - but low to the wind and fighting too.

'BEAR!' shouted Henry, his voice carrying off. 'I DON'T THINK I CA-'

But Bear couldn't hear him. He just ran an arm tight around Henry and held on. They closed their eyes and huddled, for it was all they could do. Then something hit them hard, knocking the wind out of them.

'MY SINCERE APOLOGIES!' yelled the elf, sprawled across their laps, his eyebrows thick and snowy. 'IF YOU'LL EXCUSE ME, I MUST GET BACK TO MY SEAT.' And with that, he staggered back up to clutch the reins. The storm battered them for what seemed an age.

And then it was gone.

The wind died instantly, Henry and Bear's blanket suddenly heavy. They rose cautiously out of their seats, looking around.

They were inside the tree.

Sprite

The first thing to hit them was a smell of pine – fresh and strong, an all-encompassing scent of Christmas. The second was a sensation of being dwarfed. Broad, dark canopies of wild, woven branches, thick-set with needles – needles as big as Henry – hung over them, creating a tapestry of deep green.

Nestled in the branches were a multitude of lights; a galaxy of colour, lighting pockets in the dark of the tree, illuminating the way before them.

The ground was virgin snow, lit with a faint luminescent blue glow. In the near distance, running up from the ground and rising through a long steady slope, was a snow-covered path, four times the width of the sleigh they rode. It wore long icicles along its sides. The path travelled off into the branches, up and out of sight.

More and more paths came into view, each riding off in different directions, up through the ceiling of green. Apart from the hiss of the sleigh's runners and the slow thumping of hooves on the ground, there sounded almost like a distant hum; possibly singing from far above them, so faint it might only have been imagined.

'Quite a ride, eh?' The elf rubbed his gloved hands together, snapping Henry and Bear out of their trance-like state. He flicked snow from the bell on his hat. 'Funny, I've never gotten used to it.'

Henry let out a long breath as though he'd held it for the storm's duration.

'So, tell me,' continued the elf, the reindeer now cantering, 'what was the big rush earlier? Place got raided, right?'

He hung on this last question, looking back at his passengers, passing an eye between them, waiting for an answer. Henry tried to look occupied. Bear decided it was time to finally come clean – at least *half*-clean.

'Look, we're not from these parts. That's to say we... come from a bit further out.'

'Further out,' repeated the elf blankly. 'From another tree, right?'

Bear picked up the slack and nodded.

'Knew there was something about you. You both...' – the elf again leaned back to look them up and down – '...seem different.'

'That's us,' laughed Henry. 'There's not many of us.'

23

'Well, not here at least,' said Bear, his eyes warning Henry. 'Back in our tree we are commonplace.'

'And not a big deal,' said Henry a little too loudly.

Bear gave Henry a sharp nudge.

'So, which tree-' said the elf, but he didn't finish. Something had caught his attention. He brought the reindeer to a halt, lifted his hat from an ear and listened. There was perfect silence. They sat there waiting. Henry and Bear looked around them, then at the elf, then at each other. More waiting. Until...

'YAGGHH!'

The elf cracked the reins. Henry and Bear flew back as the sleigh shot forward. They scrambled upright and looked about like frightened animals.

'What's happening?' asked Henry gripping the carriage side. 'I can't see anything.'

'Hang on!' shouted the elf, now low, almost arched over the reindeer, coaxing and urging the same thing over and over: 'Come on girls... come on.'

The reindeer were galloping hard now. Snow flew as hooves thundered. The chill wind began to bite.

Henry turned to kneel on the back seat, looking back at where they'd travelled from. Though everything looked as it had when they'd entered, something was changing. Something in the air. He shuddered. Something was coming. He could feel it.

Bear pulled Henry down and threw the blanket around him. The tree's lights in their wake began to dim, light after light. The darkness was moving toward them. It was chasing them, extinguishing light as it rolled forward, like some creeping black hole.

They heard a wailing, far off but clear enough to tell it travelled with the darkness. They dared not look back, frightened witless and willing the elf on as he stood rolling and lashing the leather. They veered a sharp left, losing speed and took an age to build it again. The wailing became clearer, louder; their surrounds darker and darker. They would surely lose this race.

The reindeer suddenly rose up in front of them and they followed, their stomachs dropping hard as they veered onto one of the frozen paths upwards. The elf struck a fearful look back as they climbed up and up. Eventually the coloured lights began to brighten as the wailing grew fainter.

'Well done girls, well done,' said the elf. His reindeer were slowing now and snorting, billowing mist from their nostrils. He turned to Bear and Henry, frozen and gripping their blanket, eyes wide, and chuckled as he turned his attention back to the path ahead.

Bear came round, easing his grip. 'Henry. Henry?'

Henry blinked, suddenly animated. 'What *was* that?'

The elf swatted the bell on his hat from his eyeline. 'That's the second time that's happened, though the first wasn't as close. Let's hope whatever it is moves on, as I don't think my girls here can run that fast every day.'

'You don't know what that was?' asked Bear.

'No,' said the elf, rolling the reins. But his face implied otherwise.

He steered the sleigh carefully around a sweeping bend of the frozen path, passing through a tunnel of branches as they climbed. They rode close to some of the lights as they went higher, hearing a distant tuneful sound for a moment. They basked momentarily in the light, and then into near darkness again as they passed by.

After a while the path levelled, allowing them to sit up and look over the sides. Branches overlapped below them, forming a dizzying maze of green. They saw baubles too. If the lights were stars, then these were planets. Huge, glazed balls of different sizes. Henry watched their reflection in one as they passed by. Onwards they went, further upwards and inwards until, rounding a hill, they stopped upon a wondrous sight.

*

Somewhere, not far away, something screamed in tortured rage. It held out a smoky, ghost-like hand and curled it into a fist.

'STOP!' it screamed. The ride slid to a halt. Her name was Phaedria.

She placed her arms to the sides of her carriage, threw her head back, closed her eyes and drew a long, steadying breath. Now still, her lids opened to reveal dead, black eyes. They rolled to the creature who served her. He laughed – quickly stifled it – and shifted uneasily. He held his head low, swaying it from side to side, avoiding her stare. Reluctantly he raised his gaze.

He didn't know if he was smiling or not, and part of his mind didn't care.

The creature then flipped violently over and writhed in the snow, greatly pained, before passing out.

She looked away, indifferent.

Stowing her wand, she peered ahead. Upon her head she wore a tiara, but its shine and splendour were gone. Wings, light and translucent that once grew from her back, were now just blackened stumps. A black robe adorned her length. It had a skin-like texture, like a bat's, and was tied at the neck with a thin white snake. She had been banished, cursed to live in ethereal form. No more than spirit. A smoky blackness ran through her, tumbling and turning, defining her outline like trapped fumes. There was only one goal in her cursed life and that was the pursuit and capture of lights.

The lights that lived in the tree.

Also in her employ were two black wolves, very much a mirror of herself. Their eyes were shot white, like lamps, giving no clue as to where they looked. Both had muscular, haunched shoulders. Their fur was matted and wild; dried blood stained their paws. They were tended by no one, existing only to serve their master. Their devotion was unflinching.

This left her dangerous servant now unconscious.

He feared and hated his master, her charges too.

Sprite, as he was known, was two feet tall, grinning and ice-white from head to toe; from his hair, grown upwards like a flame, to his feet, long and bare. He wore little clothing, just a tattered pair of trousers, shy of his shins. His face was narrow with large, dirty yellow eyes and little black pupils that were never still, seemingly chasing imaginary things. With his eyes closed, though, Sprite could blend into the snow or dangle among icicles and become hidden from view.

A long time ago, not long after she lost her physical form and a great portion of her powers, Phaedria -cast-out, nurtured a plan.

She realised she needed someone; someone she could impose her will onto. After all, she was unable to physically interact with anything living.

That someone became Sprite. In her banished and outcast state, Phaedria went into hiding, far from everything and everyone, and by chance had stumbled upon a strange white creature, deep in the darker parts of the tree. Watching from the shadows, she followed and observed his movements. He was wiry, quick and agile.

He was just what she needed.

26

Firstly, though, she would need to trap him, but she would need more than just herself to challenge him at this time. He would realise in her weakened state that she would be no match.

A fast and unpredictable creature with, it appeared, some magical ability. She would leave and return with help.

*

The tree didn't hold what Phaedria needed.

She realised she had to brave the Storm Ring at the base of the tree and look beyond, in the sloping hills of the surrounding lands. Within one of the dark valleys in the snowy hills, far from the tree, she found what she was looking for.

They approached her from the dark walls, their eyes appearing first, and began to circle her, taking her for lost. They were in no rush. They had this one. Stalking, growling, snarling, the wolves found their positions either side of her and poised. They leapt in unison, jaws wide, but their bared teeth passed clean through her, tasting not flesh but foul air before crashing together like sacks of bones.

Phaedria didn't move. She simply observed the wolves scrambling back up, shaking their heads. They measured her more carefully now and resumed stalking, a little more hesitantly.

One wolf arched and hacked, trying to bring something up, then returned its stare to its prey. It wretched again, twitched, then convulsed on the floor in a fit. The second wolf watched this with some alarm, and then found itself hacking too.

In moments, both were laid out on their backs, legs askew, eyes rolling, heads lolling. Phaedria remained watchful.

A noise of splitting, cracking bone broke the silence, accompanied by a pleading, trembling whimpering from the wolves, both shifting and scratching at the ground. Their shapes were changing; their fur was darkening. They twisted and convulsed and grew until they were near twice their previous size. In unison, they rose slowly from the ground and padded together, side by side, until they stood before their new master. Their pupils dissolved away as their eyes washed white.

Phaedria's face twisted too, into a cold smile.

*

Sprite scuttled around, hopping from branch to branch, foraging. His usual business. Occasionally he'd pause to rummage amongst the needle and twig, his head shaking every now and then, seemingly to free itself of thought.

He dropped soundlessly to the snowy floor beneath him and rolled out his neck.

All was quiet, barring a distant whistling wind.

The creature stopped momentarily and sniffed the air, catching something different – and they were upon him. He moved just in time – one of the beasts grazing his shoulder, trying to gore him with its teeth. It missed and tripped, rolling to a halt.

Sprite quickly found his feet, managing to dodge the wolf chasing him by launching over it, close enough to brush its fur as it lunged. As both animals shook the snow from themselves, Sprite noticed another figure stood motionless in the dark. He could hear the wolves behind break towards him again, but he kept his darting eyes upon the new figure. The growls grew louder as they powered through the snow, but still he stood transfixed by the dark figure. It moved into the light, slowly revealing its awful face.

Sprite somersaulted backwards, dragging sharp fingernails across one wolf's back, drawing blood. But the other wolf caught his ankle in its jaws, pulling him out of his turn and hard into the ground. He flicked snow at its eyes; its grip loosened, and Sprite scrambled free – but hurt. Again they came. This time he managed to leap and grab a low branch, unsettling snow onto them. He climbed onto it and stood facing Phaedria, the Fallen Fairy.

She returned his gaze with interest. Sprite kept his eyes on her before scampering around the branches like a skilful monkey, stopping sharply above her. She looked curiously upward and saw the creature wave a hand before him. Small droplets, like mercury, fell from Sprite's open hand. They exploded, combusting, chiming, each birthing a miniature creature. These creatures – summoned replicas of Sprite – landed on the branch below and began to animate wildly, seeking a target. Spotting the fairy and wolves, they leapt, cascading through the air in numbers. The first wave was vapourised by a blast of light from Phaedria's wand; the second landed on her face and shoulders, scratching and tearing in a frenzy.

They were able to touch her!

She cursed, swiping and swatting them off, and fired a volley at the next wave.

Phaedria scrambled and staggered, her shoulders heavy with the little creatures, until from a sound of shattering ice, the assault stopped.

Brushing herself, she saw her wolves, bloody and covered in shards of ice. The summons' brief lives had ended.

The wolves began growling, howling, wanting more than anything to get hold of this demonic monkey and leaped in turn in an attempt to pull him down.

Phaedria strode forward and fired a shot from her wand, then another in quick succession. Sprite dodged the first, but was flung backwards by the second, and landed awkwardly in the snow.

He struggled to rise, but couldn't.

The wolves bore him down, ready to tear him apart, but stopped just short upon Phaedria's command.

She wandered over to assess the creature. Sprite motioned his hand again, but his magical pool was low. He could manage only two summons. They raced from his palm toward Phaedria. She kicked one clear to be fought over by her wolves. The other managed to clamber up Phaedria's cloak, but was caught between forefinger and thumb.

She brought it eye-level, marvelling at the feeling of life in her hand.

Soon, the manic movements slowed until it hung looking at Phaedria, bewitched.

She eyed it intensely and brought her lips close to whisper. A dark smoke snaked from her mouth and absorbed into the small creature, turning it ice-white to black.

The little creature was lowered and released. It turned and broke into a run towards Sprite. He was still laid-out, clutching his ankle, a deranged grin across his face. That expression disappeared as the summon tore over Sprite's body and forced its way into his mouth, passing as smoke through his teeth. And then it was gone. A moment passed.

Sprite jolted from the ground, mouthing mute screams and tearing at his chest, as though a fire had been lit within him.

The wolves moved quickly under order, seizing Sprite by his arms with their jaws. They pulled him flat onto his back. His eyes opened to see Phaedria stood over him.

'You serve *me* now.'

He passed out.

Treelights

T he tight branches that had enclosed them for so long suddenly bore
sharply outward, opening out onto a vast, green-ceilinged hollow, rising
dizzyingly above them. Below them, a snow-covered slope ran down and away
into a bowl, mirroring the depth and width of the ceiling above. Shrouding a
great part of this ceiling was a cloud, and falling from it was snow.

On the branch walls of the hollow around the outside were openings, just as
the one they had just passed through, spaced evenly around the lip of the
snowy bowl with each leading downwards.

As they peered over the crest of the slope, they saw that far down through
patches of forest and hills was a picturesque winter village, at its centre a vast
tree trunk that travelled from the floor, upwards through the cloud and out of
sight. Random windows were cut within the trunk, glowing warmly golden.

Dotted around its base were many tall and thin houses, all draped in snow.
Smoke trailed lazily from a few of the chimneys. A large grey stone tower
stood to the right of the trunk within a kind of town square, clock faces on two
of its visible sides. They could see movement in the narrow streets and
alleyways of the village in the form of dots milling around like busy ants and
could almost feel the warmth and vibrancy of the village below them.

'Treelights,' announced the elf, pulling a halt and seating the reins. He took
a pipe from his jacket and began knocking it out on the sleigh's side. 'You
want taking anywhere in particular?'

Bear threw a paw to his mouth, whispering sideways to Henry. 'He'll want
paying of course! We don't have *anything.*'

They stared at the elf's back as he concentrated on his pipe. The elf hadn't
asked for any payment, but given that they'd travelled a way, they supposed he
didn't do this sort of thing for free. Henry patted his pyjama pockets. He
rummaged his hand in and pulled out a large golden coin. Bear's eyes
widened.

He took the coin to examine it.

'It's just a chocolate coin,' conceded Bear, his hope deflated. He turned to
their driver. 'The square?'

31

'Very well, sir,' replied the elf, his pipe sending up smoke as they shifted off slowly downhill.

Bear again cupped his paw and leaned into Henry.

'It might be best if we come clean and tell him we have no money.'

They looked back at the elf, hoping he might be a reasonable chap.

'Well, we might as well carry on to where he's taking us,' resigned Bear, quietly. 'It makes no difference now.'

They settled back into the blanket, with still plenty to look at and still a small way to go.

*

The sleigh passed out of the last patch of forest, sliding into the grooves of a well-worn track until the village presented itself.

Toy soldiers, snowmen, Christmas puddings and elves all made up the busy bustle moving up and down the narrow street. Tall, rendered houses with twisted timbers huddled closely either side, throwing golden light from their windows onto the snowy ground. Candlelit lanterns hung above their doors.

Looming behind it all was the imposing figure of the great trunk, rising high into the cloud way above and then out of sight.

Thick snowflakes danced in the air.

No one seemed to take notice of the elf pulling the reindeer to a halt. Placing his reins beside him, he jumped down from his seat to the ground. A younger elf ran to them from a waiting point, hopped up and opened their door.

'Well, we managed to get here in one piece, gentlemen,' said the elf with a chuckle. 'It has been a pleasure, might I add, escorting you both to Treelights, and I hope you enjoy your stay.' He took the door from the younger elf and hooked the latch. 'My fee of course will be-'

'We hoped to talk to you about that,' interrupted Bear.

'Oh?' said the Elf, slowing the folding of their blanket.

'We probably should have... said something when we noticed. You see-' said Bear pulling at a tangle in his coat, '-we might be a touch short of the fee you're asking.'

The elf finished the last fold abruptly, before looking them up and down.

'You're not explaining yourselves very clearly, friends.' His tone lowered. 'My fee is five pieces. No less.'

Bear paused, then made to look as though he were searching himself for the money, stalling for time to think. Henry extended a closed fist.

'I wonder if this would do,' he said.

The elf stared at Henry's hand. His apprentice craned his neck for a view too, and as Henry's fingers fell outward, the colour drained from his face.

'Her seal,' blurted the young elf. 'You're one of *hers!*' Stumbling backwards towards the sleigh door, he disappeared from view.

Henry and Bear looked over the sleigh's side to see the elf laid out on the snow, frantically trying to get to his feet. They jumped down and attempted to help him to his feet, but let go as he screamed: 'Get away! Get – *get off me!*'

The elf found his feet and headed for the first thing he saw – the sleigh's front seat. Flooring the elven driver on his way, he sat bolt upright, eyes wide, and cracked the reins hard.

If the folk of Treelights hadn't noticed the sleigh's arrival, then they would certainly notice its departure.

The reindeer broke suddenly forward, forcing all in their way to clear a hasty path to allow the sleigh through, which under the control of a panicking young Elf, and growing faster by the second, required increasing urgency to dodge. The crowd parted as though the elf, now frozen in fear, was divinely parting a sea.

Snowmen dived, gift-wrapped parcels ran, and fellow elves flew rag-dolled over the top of the runaway sleigh. Barber shop canes were quick, but two furiously plodding Christmas puddings were knocked flat before the dangerously listing sled – now trailing scarves, tinsel, and one or two extra passengers – sped out of sight leaving a trail of destruction. And all chased by its furious owner on foot.

'I think we'd better disappear,' said Bear.

Everyone was too busy dusting off and checking others were okay in the wake of the elf's exit to stop and wonder what had caused the sleigh to speed off in the first place. Henry and Bear slipped off unnoticed into an alleyway.

'What was all that about?' asked Bear, rubbing a paw over his furry head.

Henry opened his hand again. 'It was this coin, I think. He just flipped when he saw it.'

Bear came closer, seeing nothing more on inspection than a golden, foil-wrapped chocolate coin.

Henry frowned. 'She said something about us being "one of hers".'

'Well,' said Bear, looking back up the alley, 'we have to get rid of it before anything like that happens again.'

'I know a good place to put it,' said Henry, smiling. He peeled away the foil and ate it. 'Let's go,' he said between mouthfuls.

Turning out of the alley into another street presented a far calmer scene, though the houses and shops looked very similar.

Peering in through the snow-steeped window frames as they passed gave glimpses of a variety of shopkeeping; folk passed in and out of doorways, announced by tinkling bells, waving hellos and goodbyes, laden with goods.

They passed a shop full of snowmen, jostling around display cases sporting all manner of fancy carrots to try on, as well as some very expensive looking top hats hung on the walls.

The promise of *Three Free Coals with every Carrot* appeared to have drawn a crowd. They passed the steamed windows of a drinking house, its inhabitants swaying and clinking tankards in high spirits, seemingly in celebration, with a great roar going up as someone up-ended.

The third shop they looked into revealed three elves toiling over a very large Christmas cracker, one cutting a glossy ribbon, the second securing the ends, and the third, bespectacled, sat at a table, perhaps penning jokes on pieces of parchment.

They stopped to watch a Christmas pudding through another window, sat in a barber-styled chair. A fresh layer of butterscotch was being applied to its head by a hovering angel, piped from a bag, while another two waited, holding a fresh sprig of holly with a shiny pair of berries, ready to place on top.

Some brandy was splashed around the happy pudding's face and, sheet off, it was finished. The last shop on the corner drew the most interest; born not from curiosity, but from want. The place was having a promotion: sample tasting of some delicious new wares with an option to *Try before you buy*.

'Come on,' said Henry. Without another word, he and Bear stepped in and passed along a line of trays holding baked, iced, sugared, buttered and drizzled foods.

Little hands and paws darted over each, making sure not to miss anything, each of them sure that what they were currently eating was the nicest thing they had ever tried, before tasting the next and then the next, announcing just

34

the same thing each time. At the end of the line was a large steaming bowl of 'Wild Berry Juice' guzzled so quickly that possibly half of what they drank ended up down their fronts. Dragging a paw across his mouth, Bear turned to the elven cook, still in stunned surprise at their enthusiasm.

'Thank you kindly, but we are undecided. We shall let you know.'

Full to bursting, the pair waddled out.

'Delicious!' announced Henry, cradling a swollen belly, his mouth smeared with chocolate.

'Agreed,' agreed Bear.

They stopped to rest against a wall, breathing laboured but satisfied breaths.

'You know,' said Bear with a furry grin, 'I'm beginning to like Treelights. Come on, let's go explore some more of the Town.'

And with a groaning Henry, they set off up another street towards the towering trunk.

This street was a lot quieter, with less light bathing the snow and only a handful of lanterns lighting their way. They trudged past a cluster of closed shops and another drinking house, but it didn't seem as popular as the first. It was dark inside and its windows were murky. At first they thought the place empty, until silhouetted figures cast by a backroom lantern drew closer to the window as they passed. A snowman's face lit red as he pulled on his pipe, watching them intently.

Bear shepherded Henry onwards with a sinking feeling that they had walked into the wrong side of town. Quickening their pace, they turned another corner, repeatedly glancing behind to see if anyone might be following. The tree's trunk now was lost from sight, hidden behind the crooked, leaning houses.

They heard a hushed voice from somewhere. Movements.

Then, passing a dark alleyway, Henry and Bear were plunged into darkness.

Something – *Sacks?* thought Henry – was pulled over their heads, and before they could fight or even shout they were hauled up and carried off.

All they could hear were running feet and shallow breaths as they were carried for what seemed an age until, after many twists and turns, they were bundled roughly onto what felt like a seat.

35

'HENRY,' yelled Bear just a sack away.

'BEAR. I'm here. I'm here,' said Henry between gasps.

'Can you breathe?'

'I'm... okay. I... I can breathe... I-'

'QUIET IN THERE UNTIL WE'RE OUT OF TOWN!' came a threatening voice, followed by a boot aimed at Henry. Instead it winded Bear, and they shifted off on what felt unmistakably like a sleigh.

All remained quiet as they rode out of town; only the swish of the sleigh's runners on the snow to be heard. Once the hill they'd climbed had levelled off, the sacks were removed.

Bear, eyes wide, looked immediately to Henry and was relieved to see he was okay – just a bit hot and bothered.

'Well, well,' said a strangely familiar voice. 'If it isn't my free-loading chums.'

Turning, they saw the elf they'd hitched into the tree with, but with a swollen lip and a scratch on his cheek. He was sat among a bunch of surly elves. Surly by elven standards at least.

'You boys sure chose the wrong side of town to be making an escape through,' continued the elf, grinning. It became apparent at this point that he was also missing a tooth.

'We tried to explai-'

'Just you shut up!' he growled, looking down a gun-barrelled finger.

'What are ye gonna do wit' 'em, Seamus?' asked another elf, a bit younger than the rest, his voice rising with excitement.

'I'll tell ye what I'm gonna do with 'em.' Seamus' eyes narrowed. 'I'm gonna... gonna take 'em to see Rory.'

'The king o' the elves?'

'The king o' the elves,' confirmed Seamus with a nod. 'That's what I'm gonna do.'

A collective 'oooh' rose up.

Henry and Bear looked at each other.

'But before I do, we are gonna make a little stop somewhere – jus' to see what kind o' stuff these boys are made of.'

Bear knew this meant a roughing-up of sorts, and might've laughed at the thought of being worked over by seasonally dressed midgets, but these seemed to mean business.

'Oh, oi am likin' the sounds o' this,' said the younger elf, rubbing his hands, his eyes alive.

'You boys jus' settle yourselves in and enjoy the view, eh?' finished Seamus with a wry smile.

Henry and Bear blew a weary breath. They were far from the town now, riding one of the narrow paths down through the snow-laden branches, twisting and turning as the path dictated, as stars and baubles wound past.

Onwards they rode, giving the pair time to get a better look at their captors. The main aggressor – the elf they had travelled into the tree with – sat central to three elven accomplices, two either side, and a driver, making four. Each wore belled hats and tan leather waistcoats, with old and worn leather boots.

Seamus kept a close watch on the captives while the others, well-drilled in looking for danger, scanned the tree.

They banked a last corner before starting a steady slope downward, picking up speed. Henry and Bear gripped the sides, feeling uneasy about racing along a thin slope of ice as the path ahead unravelled from the darkness.

In time, the path dove, then levelled onto a broad snowy floor before disappearing entirely. Bear gazed and wondered. It didn't seem to be the base of the tree where they'd entered; perhaps another tier, slightly higher.

The lookout elves relaxed their watch now and took their places either side of Seamus, telling Henry and Bear they were perhaps drawing close to their destination, filling them with dread. Henry's head dropped.

Bear nudged him. 'Chin up, Henry. We'll be okay.'

Henry sighed and looked up. He gazed across the canopy of branches high above, enveloping them, and forgot his troubles for a moment, taken by the beauty of the twinkling stars. But two twinkled a little differently. They flashed gold for a second and began to fall, spinning toward the ground until they landed with a light thump in front of the sleigh.

Their ride stopped. Every head craned to see.

A pair of golden coins with sinewy arms and legs were rising from a crouching position. They were as big as Bear and were pointing strange knives their way. It seemed to an astonished Henry that they were just like the chocolate coins he'd hung in net bags at home on the tree, but instead of a happy impression on the coin faces, these wore a look of aggression.

'Get down from your vehicle,' barked the larger of the two. 'Now.'

The elves froze. They looked to each other, and then in panic, someone grabbed the reins and attempted to run the sleigh right through them. The coins leapt aside and brought their swords down on the reins, cutting the galloping reindeer loose. The carriage shuddered as two more coins fell from above, landing amongst them. Blades were held to the throats of two terrified elves. Nobody moved. One of the coins approached the door and opened it, still holding out his sword, which Henry now recognised as a rather sharp looking pine needle.

'Shall we finish them here?' asked a coin from the carriage, his blade held to a whimpering elf's throat.

The coin at the door paused. 'No. I think she might want to take a look at these herself.' He nodded towards Henry and Bear. 'Okay. Round 'em up and let's get moving. Come on, she'll be back soon.'

A hapless star

'SEEK!' screamed the Fallen Fairy as her sleigh ground to a halt. Sprite, silently cursing, launched out of the sleigh and pulled himself up into the overhead branches, scrambling quick as a squirrel in pursuit of a fleeing star. He could hear Phaedria's screams of 'DO NOT FAIL ME!' echo after him as he wound swiftly through the branches. He would have to claim this one.

He was getting closer.

He could hear the star just ahead, cutting blindly through the foliage, and then he spotted it: its light extinguished, camouflaged, translucent, whipping left to right. This star was quick.

He halted his pursuit. His head inclined. A hand was extended and turned, palm down.

Droplets of silver fell from his palm, solidifying and chiming as they burst, birthing miniature Sprites. Their numbers grew steadily more numerous until there was a mob of them, bending the branches they stood on, their heads a blur of movement.

Sprite extended an ice-white finger, signalling their route of chase, and off they went.

If Sprite was fast, then his summons were faster.

They flew through the foliage, barely touching it, leaping ceaselessly onward. It would only be a matter of moments before their short lives would end. They were gaining now. One managed to fire itself forward, landing on the star's upper point, and clambered around to its face, scratching and gnawing. The star tried to shake it off and in doing so slowed, enabling two more summons to land upon it, each clawing and pulling.

More and more boarded until the star, blind and heavy, spun out onto a bough of pine needles, smothered point to tip. The summons then seized up, their manic movement gone. A ping. Multiplied; and a chorus of tinkling and shattering, like a great xylophone dropped, and their little lives ended. The star lay flat and motionless. Its faint, dull, oval eyes opened to see Sprite peering from a branch above, a wicked grin across his face.

He pounced – but fell straight through where the star had been, not expecting it to dodge him at the last moment. He caught another branch as he fell through, swinging upwards with the momentum and hit his head.

Landing, he winced and hissed. The star had gone.

He knew that through failure he would soon be feeling pain.

Slowly and reluctantly he started back towards his master. And then, just by luck, Sprite caught sight of something, near hidden. He gave no outward indication he'd sighted it and carried on lolloping downward, casually passing its hiding place.

Springing like a spider, he gripped the hapless star in his long hands, its efforts to flee pointless. One had escaped him, but this one had been foolish not to have flown while it had a chance.

He would escape punishment today after all.

He dropped silently out of the canopy beside the sleigh, holding what she wanted. Both wolves growled their disappointment.

'Excellent,' said Phaedria, her eyes widening. She reached into her cloak and pulled out a satin bag, tied with a piece of string.

Opening the bag presented a cloud-like lining of miniature lights, caught like flies in a web. Stars.

She held it out to Sprite. He duly held the star over the bag, where it drew away and shrank into its opening.

'I began to think you'd failed me, Sprite,' Phaedria said, pulling the strings tight.

Placing it back in her cloak, she cracked the reins. Sprite sneered and bounded over the snow after them.

This one is different

Heavy-legged and weary from being poked and prodded, Henry, Bear and the elves plodded on, herded in a line behind the marching Coin Captain.

Nobody spoke except the coins patrolling up and down the line telling them to 'Stay in line!' or 'Keep up, elf scum,' but Bear still managed to voice quiet encouragement to Henry every so often.

They had trudged after the ever-alert captain for what seemed a very long time before he finally halted.

He raised his pine-needle sword, indicating the party stop. Two patrol coins kept watch on the group while the captain and another scanned their surrounds.

They had reached a particularly dark part of the tree, barely lit by distant stars, and were stood before a broad branch that stooped down from above to meet the ground. It was blocking their path.

Happy that the coast was clear, he reached into the branches before him, searching them. He wrestled with something out of sight and eventually stood back, looking left, then right, as two great boughs scissored open, revealing a huge, upended, hollowed-out tree. The group were prodded to get moving again, and under close guard they stepped inside.

Two lanterns hung from the walls. They were taken down and lit with flints, throwing a golden ring of light around them. One was taken to the front, one walked to the back.

'Move,' said the captain.

Their collective footsteps rang in echoes around them as they shifted off in a line, each of them straining to see as far up the tunnel as the flickering lanterns permitted. Henry noticed the walls seemed old, looking as though something enormous had once been dragged down here, resisting with its great claws, as deep gouges ran its visible length.

Further and further they ventured, with the light barely repelling the darkness, and only turning up more tunnel. They took a downward shift, going deeper until at last, and to the relief of the captives, a circle of faint light appeared way off up the tunnel. Eventually they were stood before it, realising it to be a doorway.

The door was circular and golden, maybe eight times the height of Henry. To the captives it appeared as a coin, a giant coin, but its face was not embossed with an image, only scorched and blackened by the heat and smoke of the many torches that had passed by.

The captain stepped up and inserted a key, causing the door to swing steadily outward. With the hinges complaining, the cupped-eared captives took a step backward. A welcome glow now lit the opening. The coins filed everyone in at needlepoint until the captives were huddled inside, shoulder to shoulder.

They now stood within a vast, dark underground cave. It felt to Henry like a tomb. Beneath their feet was a long, stilted wooden walkway which ran away from them towards a wooden fort, fenced on either side by sharpened stakes. The fort sat upon a black stone hill which rose out of the darkness beneath. In each of the fort's corners were turrets, and within these stood coin guards. Now and then a burning torch along the walkway provided a spitting crackle of light, faintly illuminating the stone ceiling high above them.

The captain fixed his eyes briefly upon each captive before sheathing his needle.

'Keep moving!' he ordered, and spun on his heel toward the fort. The weary band trudged on, shuffling over the straining planks. Henry tilted a little sideways, peering down the shuffling line to see the captain throw up a signal to one of the turrets.

A coin guard dispatched there returned a nod and disappeared.

Before long they met with a portcullis. Chains clanked and spun as the gate was raised.

The first elf in line was shoved roughly through the doorway - a push designed to floor him - but as he fell forwards, he somehow stayed on his feet, carrying himself in a stooping, staggered run and eventually over the edge of a logged platform. There was a dull thud, then a groan.

Relieved to hear him hit solid ground, the rest of the party hurriedly stepped in, not wanting to be the next to make a dramatic entrance.

They looked over the walkway's side to check on their counterpart, but their eyes were quickly drawn to what lay before them instead.

Running around the fort's high-staked walls was a logged platform, patrolled by coin guards, leading down at intervals into a courtyard.

The courtyard was divided by staked fences into areas, each alive with activity. At the very centre of all this was a craggy stone hill with a hole in the top, like a small volcano. A wooden frame was built around its opening. Every now and then something was hoisted up from it by some coins taking the strain on a rope.

This operation seemed to be overseen by an animated figure in black, screeching and shouting above the constant din, urging them on. It had a strange shifting creature at its side.

'This way!' yelled the captain, jolting the dumbfounded group from their daze. With a shove they were herded around the walkway. The party's eyes remained right as they passed the first enclosure, watching the action below them. There were coins pumping a variety of weights in and out and up and down. Coins performed sit-ups while others bench-pressed impossible looking weights. Some jogged around the yard's perimeter, while another group were climbing and swinging around a framework of apparatus.

They slowed as the captives filed past, following them with their eyes. Once the line had passed, they resumed as normal.

The group's wide eyes, still fixed upon the enclosure they had passed, now switched to see what was happening in the next. The coins there were paired off and squared-up to each other. Others were up on their toes, switching pine needle swords from hand to hand, their partners parrying and blocking.

Five or six coins were being taught the correct method for ensnaring an opponent in a net.

None of the combatants took any notice of the line passing above them.

Rounding the fort's corner, they approached the final enclosure. This one didn't contain many coins, at least not in large numbers.

Instead, it was occupied mainly by hard-toiling mice who were sifting through piles of rubble. There was no noise or chat, barring the chinking sounds of tools striking stone.

Only one or two noticed the party, but quickly dropped their heads and got back to work. Central to all this was the stone hill opening. A line of coins pulling a rope hoisted a mouse in a cage out of its opening. The door was then opened, allowing the mouse to carry a heavy bucket of rubble down into the yard. Weaving through piles of rubble, the mouse would dump the bucket on the floor for other mice to sniff and sift through, then return to the top of the hill to wait to be lowered again.

Henry, Bear and the elves finally stopped at the ramp leading down. More mice, but on stilted platforms, stirred a thick brown liquid inside a great cauldron beneath them. It hung over a fierce fire, heating the thick ooze, causing wispy fumes to drift from its bubbling surface which dallied in the air before ghosting upwards into the darkness.

Henry caught a whiff of something sweet and familiar, like chocolate, and realised it was exactly what the mice were being made to stir.

From the order of a supervising coin, the stirring stopped. The mice regimentally moved either side of the cauldron, while another group beneath hefted over a large stone block. It was positioned below the cauldron's spout.

The mice above took the strain and carefully poured its contents into what Henry now saw to be a cast. Once full, it was wheeled away while another was brought over to take its place.

The dark figure caught Henry's eye. He could now see that this was a kind of woman, but her skin was murky and appeared to move, as though she were formed from smoke.

The captain looked to her, then to the captives. 'Single-file, heads up. Only speak when you're spoken to.' He looked his troop up and down and drew breath. 'Move,' he said.

Phaedria was turning a piece of rock in her hand while questioning a coin. He was stood straight, his golden lips moving quickly, when the conversation tailed off upon her seeing the arriving captives.

Her black eyes narrowed.

The captain strode over and clicked his heels.

'My Queen,' he said with a short bow, sweeping an arm toward his captives. 'We caught these travelling at speed through the tree.'

She tossed the rock sideways, raised her chin and took the few steps to meet them. The coin troop hurriedly formed them into a line.

Her eyes dragged across each of the elves, one by one as she walked, until she stopped in front of the final elf, Seamus. She lifted the belled hat away from his face with her wand, and his eyes came up to meet hers. Walking on, she met Bear. Her eyes widened with interest.

44

'Now, there's a sight,' she said. Her head crooked as she followed his outline before giving his ear a squeeze. 'I remember... remember something like you in a past life. But-' and she nearly laughed. 'Look at the size of you.'

She looked to his arms. 'Are you strong?'

The coin captain stepped forward, took a paw, and pushed a thumb into his bicep. 'Feels soft to me.'

Phaedria's eyes fell upon the coin and he took a step back. She turned to resume, but her eyes caught on the boy beside the Bear. They widened lidless with interest.

'*Very* interesting,' she said, extending a hand to touch the boy's face. She stopped short and withdrew it, bringing it back to her side.

'Shall I make arrangements for their lives to be ended?' asked the coin captain.

'This one,' she said, eyeing Henry, 'this one is different.' She leaned back, looking Henry up and down as though admiring a dress she held. 'Now, where might you be from?'

Phaedria applied something like a smile, but the effect was unnerving. Henry shifted on his feet. 'Another tree,' he spoke softly, remembering their conversation with the elven sleigh driver. 'We are from another tree, Bear and me.'

Phaedria raised her eyebrows and made a little hole with her mouth. 'You are both... together?' she asked, her wavering hand gesturing towards Bear.

'That's right,' said Bear. 'Together. We got lost in a storm and came upon this tree.' He placed a paw on Henry's shoulder. 'We don't want any trouble.'

'Trouble,' she echoed. 'Why would you be in trouble?'

Henry looked to the hill to witness a mouse receiving a lash across its back.

'We just want to get home,' conceded Henry.

'Home, meaning... another tree?'

There was a pause of silence, barring the sounds of tools striking stone.

'Correct,' said Bear, his paw leaving Henry.

Phaedria brought her wand to her lips and tapped once, twice, thinking. 'Well, we could just let you leave,' she reasoned. She walked in a circle, looking to the ground in thought. 'But what's the rush? Left something cooking on the stove?'

The coin captain chuckled. Phaedria, back turned, ignored him.

'Why don't you hang around? We could use a big, strong teddy bear and the wisdom of a human young.' She hung the question in the air, awaiting an answer.

At that moment, the young elf who'd entered the fort via a dive from the upper walkway was brought over. His arms were draped around two coins, supporting him. They dropped him in a heap to the floor. 'You want him killed?' asked the larger coin, his hand hovering over a pine needle hilt. The elf looked up at him, pained at the question, and began whimpering.

'Killed? Are you some blood-thirsty savage?' asked Phaedria, throwing the coin off-guard. 'Get back to what you were doing!'

The pair took off, almost running.

She looked after them, shaking her head. 'Get him up off the floor, Captain.'

The coin strode over and hauled the elf up. Seeing he was able to stand, the coin stepped away and watched the elf dusting himself off.

'What's your name?' Phaedria asked.

'Beansprout, m'lady,' he replied, checking the bell on his hat still tinkled.

Seamus's eyes rolled upward.

'*Beansprout*. Why don't you come on over and join the rest of your band, eh? It looks like you've had a tough old day.' She guided the limping elf into a space in the line and took her place to face them.

'Aren't we a sorry bunch?' Phaedria smiled.

The line stood still, waiting.

'I think I have a plan,' she said, signalling the coin troop. 'Take the teddy bear to the mine. The elves can break rocks, but the boy stays with me.'

A pair of golden hands fell upon Bear. After much protestation and a brief skirmish, the group were herded off.

Henry broke and leapt onto a coin's back, pleading for his friend to be left behind. The soldier shrugged him off.

'Whoa, whoa,' said Phaedria, guiding the boy away. 'It's only for a short time. As soon as I can arrange transport,' she reasoned, 'I'll have them straight out of there. It's only to make up the numbers.'

'Liar!' said Henry.

'Liar?' echoed Phaedria, feigning hurt. She lowered to one knee in front of him. 'Help me to help you,' she said.

'What does that mean?' said Henry, his eyes following Bear.

'Well, I need you to do something for me.' Phaedria pushed a brown lock from Henry's forehead.

He recoiled, but she remained at his level. 'If you do as I ask, well, then your furry friend can go.'

Henry was listening now. 'You promise?'

She placed a hand over her swirling, blackened chest.

'I promise.'

A swift escort

Henry knew what he had to do.

All things considered, what choice did he have?

Two sombre-looking coins approached him. One turned, lowered to a knee and Henry clambered onto its back like a rucksack.

Ready, the coin escort, along with Henry, climbed the ramp and made its way around the walkway. Although Henry had no interest in the goings-on below, his eyes were drawn to another planked walkway, exiting the cavern over the far side.

Coins, many coins, marched along it towards another opening.

The portcullis approached.

As the gate thundered upward, the second coin took a flaming torch from a wall.

Over the planked walkway they went. Henry wriggled to get comfortable, his eyes peering over the top of the coin's casing toward the exit tunnel.

Here, the second coin broke away through the great golden door and into the darkness of the tunnel's opening.

Henry's ride picked up the pace. Following the flaming beacon before them, they ran into the opening.

Up the tunnel they flew, so quickly that the deep gouges in the wooden walls were all just a blur of dark wood rushing past.

Henry clung on, hearing only breaths and footfalls in his ears. Something lit up in the distance.

Henry realised it to be the hidden opening, granting splintered shafts of light. The coin with the torch, silhouetted, stood in the opening. He signalled the path was clear. Henry and his ride continued at speed out of the tunnel. After a spell of cross-country navigation, as brisk as the sleigh he'd ridden with Bear into the tree, the coins finally slowed. Henry was dropped from the coin's back onto the snowy floor in the centre of a clearing. The coins scanned the area.

'Our job's done,' said the carrying coin, rolling his shoulder. 'You're on your own now.'

And with a turn of heel, they were gone. Everything became strangely silent, so much that it resonated in Henry's ears. He suddenly felt terribly alone but shrugged off the feeling. He had an important job to do and very little time to do it. Looking up, Henry began his search of the tree's lights and in no time noticed a twinkle of blue nestled in the greenery above, standing out from the other colours.

It had to be the first star and his starting point. He searched the cluster around it, trying to find the second. And then there it was. The white star. Winking in the distance.

His directions had come from Phaedria herself. He had to trust her now.

Henry was given a small supply of chocolate to eat, though the coin guards had been loath to see it taken. It would be just enough, he was told, to keep him going until he'd reached his destination.

Henry drew breath, steeled himself and headed toward the blue light. As he switched between watching the lights high in the tree and the snowy ground beneath his feet, he recounted the deal he'd made with Phaedria.

In his mind he spoke of what had been said between misty breaths.

Follow the lights. Climb the tree. Find the fairy. Present the gift to her.

If this was done within the time she'd allowed, Bear would be freed. If the time limit were exceeded, Henry would lose him.

Henry choked up a little and found himself thinking of his father. He'd have known what to do, problems and all, but he wasn't here. Henry drew in his dressing gown and quickened his pace. He had to be strong. Just like at home. The white star he'd sighted so slightly earlier, was now almost a constant glow in the rich, green foliage, eclipsed now and then by the gently swaying branches, but still enough to get a bearing on.

Unknown to Henry, he was being watched. Up above the ceiling of foliage, Sprite crept like a spider. He stalked Henry quietly with keen eyes. It had been little trouble tailing him from the Coins' Domain. As Henry and his escorts had left the tunnel, he'd slipped behind them, staying low in the darkness, keeping his distance.

As they'd exited, he'd snaked silently around the tunnel's lip and up into the branches. Now, with Henry alone, it was his job to follow and make sure he didn't abandon his orders and try to escape. But, and at great personal risk, it would be Sprite who would abandon his orders.

He stopped and let the boy slowly slip out of sight and through his fingers. Blinking his big dirty yellow eyes, he twisted left and clambered off.

*

Henry had been making good ground but had begun to slow with fatigue, steadily progressing into exhaustion. His legs had become heavy, making the route evermore zig-zagged. Continually looking upward had caused his neck to ache and his eyelids had become heavy and tired. He had passed from his first waypoint, the blue light, to the white light, and was certain he'd glimpsed the third.

A pinpoint of gold in the distance.

Given his poor neck ache wasn't going away, he memorised a path to his destination across the snow. Watching the floor, he followed it.

Time passed. Before long, Henry could go no further without a rest. He mustered another three steps to reach a small mound of snow and dropped heavily onto it. He ran his hands down his legs, trying to massage some life back into them when he thought he should take another look up.

The third star? Where was it? He had been heading straight for it.

Sure, he'd strayed a little, but he'd corrected that by straying back again, hadn't he? But now it was nowhere to be seen. The colour fell from Henry's face and he felt sick. What was he to do? He blew a defeated breath and struck at the snow.

How could he have let his concentration slip when so much was at stake?

He decided he would correct it. Jumping up, he paced a circle, searching the dark canopies above, but as he trod ever more circles he just couldn't find where the star once was.

Time was pressing on. He would have to make the best guess he could and keep going.

Henry made an estimation of where he'd come from and where he was going to and headed off again. This time he ignored the pain, searching ever upwards in the hope of suddenly spying the golden star.

Darker parts of the Tree

It was over.

The path he'd chosen hadn't turned up the third star and, if it was at all possible, he was more lost than before. Henry stopped, allowing himself to abandon hope for a moment and began to cry.

He decided he would turn back and somehow rescue his friend, if he could.

Henry wiped his tears with his sleeves and stamped the snow from his feet. But although he had stopped crying, its sound continued to echo very faintly around him. It was coming from somewhere else altogether and didn't sound like Henry at all.

Moving quietly, he crept closer to the source of the gentle sobbing. Climbing a small, snowy hill, Henry peered through the gap of a low-slung branch.

Rubbing its eyes and sat upon its behind was a small colourful box, tied on its top with a bow. Its eyes were pencil-drawn and cartoon-like, but they moved as though they were constantly being re-drawn by an invisible pencil.

Henry's curiosity drew him further into the gap until he found out too late that he'd overreached and fell through it to the floor, causing the gift-box to leap up and scuttle off in the opposite direction.

Sprawled on his side, Henry watched the box losing momentum as it desperately tried to plough its way through a deep drift of snow, struggling like a fly on sticky paper.

He got up and went over, stopping short, and bent down before it. The box had stopped struggling. It flashed Henry a sorry look with its big eyes before throwing tiny hands over them. It was bawling from a small, torn mouth in its paper facing.

'Whatever is the matter?' asked Henry. The little box just wailed louder.

'Hey, come on now. What's all the crying about? What's wrong?'

Lowering its trembling, string-like arms, the box stopped crying. Between some sharp intakes of breath and much snuffling, it looked slowly up at Henry.

'Who are you?' it asked in a tiny voice.

'I'm Henry.'

The box looked up, and resumed rubbing its eyes and sniffing.

'Are you lost? Could you use some help?'

The box lowered its hands and glanced up again, its eyes re-sketched as sore and red. 'Yes. Yes, I am lost.'

'Well,' said Henry, now lowering to sit cross-legged, 'we shall have to see what we can do about that.'

The box, covered neatly in a light green wrapping with gold stars and a crimson bow, looked a bit more cheered by this and managed the beginning of a papery smile.

'Come on,' said Henry, offering a hand. He pulled the box from the snow and onto its feet.

'Now, where is it you came from?'

The box, with a finger to its mouth, looked randomly around.

'Well, if I were to lift you, then you might have a better view of things. Here, hop up,' said Henry, holding out his arms. The box jumped up. Henry held it at arm's length in the air and shuffled a small circle.

'See anything you recognise?'

'Uh, maybe... maybe over there. That gap in the trees,' said the box a little uncertainly. 'Try over there?'

'Okay.' Henry lowered the box to his waist, then headed for the gap.

'Do you have a name?'

The little box, legs dangling, looked upward. 'Is there a name on my box?'

Henry took the box and turned it, checking its top and sides.

'Here,' he said, taking a label to read. 'Only *TO* and *FROM* and *HAPPY CHRISTMAS*.'

'Well,' said the box, peering curiously around, 'that's because I haven't been given away yet.'

'Oh,' Henry was still no clearer. 'How did you come to be so lost?' he said, ducking through the gap in the trees.

'I was playing near the edge of the forest, turned around and here I am. I never meant to run off or get lost.' And then something distracted the little gift, its stringy legs pedalling excitedly. 'This is the way back home!'

'Shall I put you back down now?' asked Henry.

'Oh, yes. Here is just fine. I know where I am now.'

Henry stopped and put the box down gently. It zoomed off, plodding tiny feet through the snow as though it were a clockwork mouse let loose. A few yards away, the box stopped and turned.

'Hey, why don't you come with me?'

Henry brightened for a moment, and then remembering what he'd originally set out to do, deflated. 'I have to go. You see, I'm lost myself. I was trying to find somewhere, but I'm having no luck.'

The little box pondered this for a moment and then skipped quickly back to Henry and began tugging at his pyjama bottoms.

'Come and speak to my family. They know almost everywhere in this tree and I'm sure they'll help you find your way. Come on.'

The box pulled Henry's reluctant legs forward, one, then the other, until he gave in and followed. Once off, he had a task keeping up as the box wasn't bothered by the branches that Henry had to duck under and around to keep pace. It was only when the box struggled up the small hills that Henry caught up, giving the little gift a nudge.

After a while, Henry noticed his surrounds becoming darker as the pine branches above swooped lower and lower, thinning out the light from the stars. He had to make himself smaller to avoid getting caught on the needles and, straining his eyes forward, noticed a white light radiating through a hole in the foliage. The box ran ahead and stopped in the opening.

'Come on!' it yelled before disappearing through it.

Henry had to get on all fours and crawl to follow, although once through he was able to straighten up.

But with the sight that had met him so suddenly, he almost fell back down.

Within a great clearing were many gift-wrapped boxes, all running and playing around the toe of what Henry recognised to be a very tall and broad, red and white stocking.

Little boxes launched out of its top like popping popcorn and would slide down its length until they'd land on the floor and climb its back, to do just the same again. From what he'd assumed to be a tear in the stocking, near its frayed top, came a big chuckling laugh, but a second glance told Henry it was a mouth, with a pair of creased button eyes above it. They widened into big circles at the sight of Henry.

The stocking cleared its throat, and with a shake it sent a ripple down its length, causing all the sliding little boxes to bounce from its side to the floor.

The stocking then assumed a serious manner, but given its jolly appearance and being surrounded by cute little boxes, the effect wasn't really achieved. Nevertheless, it addressed Henry in a deep and authoritative tone.

'Who are you?' it boomed. 'And what *are* you doing here?'

'My name is Henry,' he said, just loud enough to be heard.

'And?' continued the stocking with growing annoyance, 'What do you want?'

As Henry started to explain himself, the stocking broke off, distracted by something below. Henry saw that the little box he'd followed in was tugging at its heel. He couldn't hear what was said, but the stocking's severe look lightened the more he listened, until he lit up, cheerful once again.

'Henry!' said the stocking as though hailing a long-lost friend. 'What is this I hear? Children! Where are your manners? Clear a way for the young to come through.'

Henry took a moment, then made his way slowly between the dividing parcels until he stopped at the foot of the stocking.

'My dear fellow, I am indebted to you. For returning one of my own, you may ask of me anything.'

Henry had to tilt backwards to take in every part of the stocking's face.

'I'm actually lost myself,' he confessed. 'I was trying desperately to get somewhere, but I'm ready to give up.'

'From where have you come and to where are you going?'

Afraid to tell his story to the stocking and the tightening crowd of parcels, he opted to give them a shortened version.

'I got some directions from a friend. I was following stars.'

'And in what order are the colours of these stars?'

'Well,' said Henry, eyes drifting to one side. 'I started at blue, then white. I was on my way to gold – then green. I'm afraid I've forgotten the rest.'

The stocking mapped this in its mind, mouthing the colours in turn until eventually its face sat still. It peered down at Henry.

'Starting that path will have brought you here from one of the darker parts of the tree.'

Henry said nothing.

'Tell me now. Are you in trouble?'

Henry shuffled uncomfortably. 'No sir.' he replied, but his voice almost broke.

The stocking gave him a long, measured look before settling back into itself. Looking beyond the gathering at nothing in particular, the stocking spoke again, but with a distance in its voice.

'Taking that particular path would have led you in the direction of our Governing Fairy.'

Henry dropped his gaze to the floor and pushed his hands into his pockets. He could feel the stocking watching him. Lifting his head, he met with the large button eyes.

'I... I guess so. Yes, it would be going that way, I suppose.'

The stocking's gaze lingered on Henry. A small shift produced a ripple all the way to its toe, clearing its throat.

'Very well. Your business is your own, but my offer still stands. If you like, I can steer you back onto your path, but via a much faster route. Would that be of use?'

'Yes, sir. Thank you,' said Henry, lifting. 'Can you show me? Now?'

'Whoa there. You are in a hurry now, aren't you?'

'I am sir, I am.' Henry hopped from foot to foot.

'Well, then we shall have to make haste.' The stocking cast his big eyes over the gathered boxes before him, muttering to himself.

'Now I'm sure that somewhere here is something that could be useful. Now if I could only remember where... *ah!* Little Bobby, please come forward.'

A rectangular box fought eagerly to the front, and once clear of the crowd, began jumping up and down.

'Very good, very good, settle down. Come on, settle down. Good. Now then, who would be looking after... Gordon! *Gordon?* Where are you?'

The boxes looked around themselves. Too small to be seen among the crowd, Gordon wound his way slowly through the legs of the mostly larger boxes until he appeared from the line at the front looking a little flustered, but happy.

'Excellent!' said the stocking. 'The two of you unwrap yourselves as quickly as you can. Hurry now.'

They didn't need a second invitation. Both tugged at the bows on their tops as though it were a race. As the ribbons fell to the ground, so the tops of their boxes opened like mechanical doors.

Both gifts, pleased with themselves, gazed round at the other parcels who were a mixture of awe and envy.

'Come forward and take what's inside, Henry.'

Henry cautiously stepped up, feeling a little awkward at the keenness of the gifts to reach him first. Deciding, he placed a hand inside the smaller box.

'Go on, take it then,' said the stocking.

Henry lifted out a woolly hat and some gloves. 'Thank you,' he said.

The larger rectangular box bumped his brother aside and leant forward, offering his open top to Henry. Henry again reached in, having to lift out what was inside with both hands. 'Whoa. A sled!'

There followed much excitement and shoving from the remaining parcels, hoping-upon-hope that Henry might open *them*. They settled down at the Great Stocking's bellow from its deep, craggy mouth.

Now, with the sea of boxes backing off, the stocking kinked its midriff to roll down to Henry's level. Leaning into Henry, the stocking poked forward its black button eyes and turned them toward him too.

'Henry, my boy,' it whispered, 'go careful. There's danger afoot in this tree – mark my words. Now listen carefully, or this place will become a maze to you.'

And so Henry listened, and learned the way to a place named Winter's Cut.

A ride on a snowflake

Henry thanked the stocking and bade quiet farewell with the promise he'd visit them another time, before slipping quietly back out the way he'd come. Before long he'd struck clear away.

He was grateful for the woolly hat and gloves – the warmth made him feel safer somehow – and pushing his hat straight, he took the stocking's directions (something he was even more grateful for) and got back to his task.

After a long haul, and as promised, Henry found the downward slope of a hill.

He took the sled from his back and planted himself down.

He leaned forward, trying to find an end to the slope, but there wasn't one. It just ran off into the darkness.

Henry sat back, leaned forward, and sat back again. Stalling, he blew a long breath and darted his eyes around the tree. He had to go now.

He hopped his bottom forward, moving the sled an inch. Another inch. Once more, and the sled see-sawed on the snowy lip. He was off.

Over the hiss of rails on the snow, Henry's heart trying to exit his mouth, came the buffeting wind, numbing his face and ears. He brought himself low and gripped the wood for all his worth. Excitement and fear merged into one.

Through his screwed-up eyes, Henry watched for any mounds or tree stumps that might spill him as the ground flew by underneath. Ahead, he spotted a snow-covered log in his path. He dug a slipper into the snow, leaning as far as he could and steering just wide enough; the kicking sled nearly spilling him.

Henry gave a cheeky laugh.

He chanced a glance up at the tree, the stars, then back to the quickening floor.

Thoughts of Bear brought his mind back, and in an attempt to gain more speed Henry brought himself low.

As he raced further down the hill, so the snow either side of him began to rise, guiding him into the middle of what was fast becoming an ever-deepening gully. Up and up the sides rose, like gathering waves, threatening to crash down any second, seemingly waiting for the right moment to do so. But they stopped just shy of enclosing him, leaving the lights of the tree still visible through the gap above. They stained the snow with beautiful colours as they passed overhead. Henry sat up, trying to see what lay ahead of him. To his sudden horror he realised he was heading for a big white wall of snow.

It was too late to bail. He clung on, braced for the worst, one flinching eye open.

Instead of impacting, he rode up the wall, pinned to the sled as he banked hard into a turn he didn't see. Henry rode it back down to the ground in a new direction at terrific pace. He saw another bank coming and readied himself.

Again he rode the wall, crushed into its side and as the bank fell away he was shot in a new direction. Onwards he flew, gasping for breath, ever watchful, but the sloped walls gradually dropped away and Henry was spat out onto an open snowy plain.

As the sled wound down its speed over the snowy ground, Henry sat up exhausted but relieved. Up ahead, a dark horizontal line appeared across the snow. It grew longer and wider as Henry slid toward it.

It revealed itself, to his horror, as an icy chasm with a sheer drop on either side. Henry straightened bolt upright, and drove both heels into the snow, gripping the sled. He drew closer, the shed quivering, and with one final heave he came to a halt – mere feet from the edge.

Still gripping the sled's rails, Henry gasped and then blew a long, ragged breath.

After a time, and still shaking, he rose gingerly to his feet. Moving carefully up to the edge, he peered in. Great craggy blue cliffs of ice coursed down to a barren, snowy bed. An icy wind funnelled between the steeped faces, attacking the ground as it tumbled its length, lifting flecks of snow and ice from the floor and dragging them along in its wake, whipping them higher and higher.

As the snowflakes wove around each other, so they grew in size, so much so that as they passed level with Henry he could see the crystallised patterns that made up each one.

By the time they'd travelled out of sight, they were near the same size as Henry.

He'd certainly arrived where he was meant to, but the stocking hadn't quite conveyed just how vast this place was.

Henry abandoned the sleigh. Walking near to the sheer edge, he followed the course of the wind between the faces and the dancing flakes below. Somewhere further along would be his chance – if the stocking was right. It was up to him to get back on track.

He had to succeed.

Henry clapped his gloved hands together, rubbed them warm and headed off. In time, the flakes to his left began to rise and dive from the ravine like dolphins racing a ship. The walls of the cut were waterfalls of powder and ice where skewed and bumped flakes had crashed into its side – casualties in this maddening race. Henry fumbled in his pocket and brought out a smooth, spherical stone. He brushed a thumb over its surface. In his mind he travelled back.

It had been part of her deal. Phaedria's deal. Away from the coins in the cavern, she had knelt to his level and as she did so, her cloak had parted a little. A fist was there. It fell open, holding a stone. 'This is for Lilly. Our tree's governing fairy. It's hers.' She inhaled and her very being seemed to swirl.

As Henry followed the dark trails, his eyes were brought back to the stone.

It shot from beetle-black to white. 'Make sure she receives it. Before it blackens again. There will only be so much time. Nothing is more important.'

Right now, it was definitely a shade of grey.

He placed it away and quickened his pace, trying to see as far along as he could and straining to make sense of what lay ahead. A ghostly line flowed up from the ravine in the distance, streaming through a torn black hole in the branched canopy way above.

It had to be the flow through the tree he was told about.

Spirits lifted, Henry began to jog. Such a strange sight kept his eyes from the ground and more than once he stumbled or upended over an outcrop or drift, but he managed to reach his destination, just short of the skyward turn.

The turn, Henry found out, was due to the cut's abrupt ending.

It had been rounded out over time by the battering of the wintry elements, forcing the flow to exit upward. It was as though a tap had been turned over, running millions of gallons of snowflakes up through a black plughole.

Henry knew one of these was his ticket to the top of the tree.

He just hoped it wouldn't mind a passenger too much. Watching and waiting, he figured his best bet was to approach the snowflakes from behind where the cut ended.

Positioning himself, he tried to ignore the constant crash and hiss of the flakes being diverted. His eyes followed random flurries upward.

He tried to control his breathing.

He would jump on three.

One... two... th-

Henry stalled.

He rolled his neck and bounced on his toes, transfixed by individual flakes.

Ready again, he stepped forward.

One... two... two...

Henry overbalanced, flailed, and caught himself. He paced away, turned a half-circle and closed his eyes. Opening them, they narrowed as he broke into a run.

Henry jumped into the cut, arms open. Stretching, reaching, falling, bumped by a flake, into another. His gown got caught by the neck, choking him, until it snapped and again he fell.

But he landed on another, this time managing to secure something of a hold.

It dipped, spun and then rose on the wind.

To his breathless relief, it held him. He secured a hold and whispered thanks. Like a balloon released into the wind, the flake swirled upwards, a little slower than the others with Henry's weight, but enough to ensure the chasm below steadily disappeared. The tree disappeared from sight too, lost in the misty flurries of snow circling him.

He had joined the great race.

Henry whipped in and out, up and down and around and around hundreds of snowflakes. He chased after flakes while others chased him, and he laughed with excitement into the wind. But the wind, it seemed, took offence.

It whipped up a lively gust and took Henry, pulling him sideways. One after another, the flakes bumped and crashed into him, showering him in ice and snow, threatening to knock him off and send him tumbling back down. Henry held fast, his fingers numb. And then, the barrage stopped.

Covered in snow, Henry opened his eyes.

He had been blown clear. He shook the snow from his shoulders. The sensation in the pit of his stomach convinced Henry he was still rising through the tree, though he couldn't see further than a few feet. The swirling snow had been replaced with a thick, whirling mist. Occasionally snowflakes came like visitors out of the fog, but they appeared less and less until they called no more.

Was he still heading in the right direction?

The eerie cold air made no sound. Then the silence was intruded; a blowing wind whipped up from nowhere around Henry, circling him, turning the fog as it did so.

Through guarded eyes, he could see figures in the wind; wispy, thin white streams, coursing and intertwining. They took turns in diving towards Henry as though taking a closer look, and as they drew near, he thought he could make out thin, curious faces looking at him.

Eventually, the streams dove back out through the mist, linking end to end, joined as one, until the last wispy streak at the end of the tail was pulled past Henry.

It reached out to the snowflake, and he shot off with them.

Now a part of the chain, Henry held on. Rather than floating, he was flying. He struggled to see below through his watery eyes, but there was only grey mist streaking past at speed. There was nothing to do but hold on.

In time, the fog began to break up and Henry could glimpse the faint line he was a part of. It weaved and swooped, until it dove and drew level above a broad expanse of cloud – close enough that Henry could reach down and touch it.

The cloud stretched out ahead; at its end, it met with an imposing rock face.

Speeding like an arrow, Henry followed their projected course and saw they were headed towards a small dark opening in its side.

One after the other, the pale strands passed through the hole and disappeared. He clung to the snowflake, watching helpless through a gap in its pattern.

With seconds to probable impact, the last of the ghostly line let go.

The flake downed onto the cloud and tangled gently as it hit, somersaulting Henry off its back to enjoy a very cushioned landing indeed.

Dizzy, he scrambled up onto the cloud on all fours, having to keep moving to prevent himself from falling through.

He sighted the snowflake behind him, upright but dipping, until it slowly downed into the cloud like a sinking ship.

Henry too felt himself dropping, and began something of a desperate doggy-paddle toward the rock face. For every advancement he made, he fell the same length down.

Summoning his remaining energy, he scrambled as quick as he could over the impossibly soft puffs until he managed to get hold of the rock face. He clung on, exhausted. Gaining a foot-hold on the rock, he pushed himself up onto a ledge and rolled onto his back.

Seconds later, Henry opened his eyes.

There was no sign of the ghostly winds. To his side was the cave-like opening. He got up and cautiously approached the opening. Silent in his slippered feet, Henry peered in.

Winter

T he surrounding stone was roughly hewn, with a smooth, granite floor. Henry looked around, then took a chunk of chocolate from his pocket and ate it. The tunnel appeared to be his only path onward.

He had to duck a little to choose a route in, mindful not to cut his head on an overhead rock. He paused, claustrophobia setting in, but stilled it. His eyes drew back to the opening where he'd entered, knowing that soon he'd be without its light as the tunnel ahead was growing darker.

Resolved, he kept both hands trailing the ceiling and trod further in, the light behind dimming as the gloom before him deepened.

Before long he was in near darkness, fumbling along, reasoning that the streaking winds had to have taken a route out of here somewhere. How he longed to have his torch from under his bed at home.

With just the sounds of his shuffling feet and his heart hammering in his chest, Henry pressed on, his eyes wide and searching.

Until, though a mere pinpoint, he spied a faint white light ahead. Focused, unblinking, Henry trod more confidently now as the light grew larger and began to bloom around the tunnel walls until he could make out a room of sorts in the distance. With his hands free of the ceiling, he stepped toward it.

Clear of the tunnel, Henry found himself in a chamber of solid ice: wall to wall, floor to ceiling; no doors or windows. The only way out was the way he'd come in.

Where had the winds gone?

Stepping carefully to the far wall, Henry peeled off a glove and ran his fingertips along the face. *Cold and smooth.* Replacing the glove, he stepped back to look around and at the same time heard a crack. Several splits, central to the wall he'd touched began appearing, like laddered lines from the floor upward.

Cracking sounds echoed around the chamber. Henry skidded back to the tunnel's mouth, worried the room would collapse. The laddered lines deepened. The wall itself rumbled and shook, and then tumbling, it began to fall backward to form steps. The room stilled to a deathly quiet.

Henry crept to the foot of them, peering upward.

'Hello?' he called, the sound reverberating around him. 'Anyone?'

He patted at the stone in his pocket and pulled it out. The grey was darkening. He gave it a brief polish and replaced it before deciding to press on. With great trepidation, he began treading the steps, his ears alert to any sound, his eyes alive to any movement, again calling out, hoping the tree was just at the top.

Climbing the final step, Henry found himself in a broad corridor. The walls and high ceiling were still ice, but they gave way to stone and then a flagstone floor. As Henry pressed on, he noted the ceiling drew higher and before long he was stood at the threshold of a pair of monolithic timber doors.

They ran from the floor, stretching right up to the top of the high ceiling, which could only be seen if Henry tilted his head right back.

He began to approach the doors, unaware he was tiptoeing, probably afraid to awaken whatever lay beyond them.

His mind imagined a lair of dragons lain lazily across piles of treasure and pretending to be asleep. But they lay in wait, in wait for a lost, wandering boy who could be charred with a little flame and eaten leisurely, the memory of Henry just a belch to the wind.

Searching, he could find no handles, though they wouldn't be of much use anyway. The doors looked too much even for a dozen men to move.

He stepped up and leaned an ear in the hope of hearing something. Extending a hand, he touched the door. *Nothing*. Then a resounding boom attacked the silence high up behind the door, like a canon crashing backward. The doors shuddered, moaning low and deep as they dragged themselves inward and thudded open, showering the entrance with snow and ice, like a great ship colliding with an iceberg.

When everything settled, he saw what lay beyond them with wide, swivelling eyes. Something like a huge cathedral presented itself. Majestic and magnificent. Immense stone columns, as wide as old oak trees, lined uniform either side of a flagstone floor, leading down to what appeared to be a throne set up on a raised platform.

The columns raised up to support a ceiling; a complex framework of huge timbers carved with designs, so high that Henry wondered how on earth they could have been put there.

Looking back to the throne, he noticed three large steps leading up to it. Its size implied its owner was probably a giant. Henry swallowed.

As he crept slowly forward, Henry's eyes couldn't help wandering around his surroundings. Tall stone walls stood beyond the columns to his left and right. Peppered along their length from top to bottom were dark holes like the mouths of cannons, long redundant. Henry's eye line was distracted. A commotion appeared from the throne.

Something hovered above it, something like a small ball. Its surface flowed around itself like storm clouds in a planet's atmosphere. They rotated and pulled, turning grey winds and flurries of snow in tight circles, all the while gathering in size and energy until, with a tearing sound of lightning and a flash of blue light, the whirling maelstrom of weather tore open, throwing out a blizzard.

Henry threw up his arms to shield his face, his body doubled to the wind and snow. He braved a look forward and saw ice creeping over the floor toward him. It travelled faster than Henry could retreat. Though he hopped in panic, it sealed around his feet, one, then the other, freezing him in place ankle-deep.

At this, the raging wind and snow became less fierce, allowing Henry to at last look to the source of the storm. A figure, central to the concentration of weather, could be seen through the turbulent flurries. The snow dallied and slowed its pace like wind dropping out of a sail, but continued to orbit the figure.

On the throne and stood quite still was something quite remarkable. If a comparison were to be drawn, then Henry thought the figure resembled a small wizard, robes and all. Small, meaning he was around half the size of Henry. Quite the opposite though was the size of the little fellow's beard.

It was an extraordinary statement of sweeping loops and curls, spanning as far out as his shoulders and came sharply down to a point just above two bare blue feet. It looked like a coat of arms and appeared entirely sculpted of ice. Peering through all this and from beneath a sagging wizard-styled hat was a glacier-blue face with great bushy eyebrows and an equally bushy moustache. Both looked preserved by the cold. His eyes watched Henry, now crouching, a hand painfully down to steady himself.

The ice around Henry's ankles shrank back. Cracking and tinkling, it receded towards the throne.

The wizard opened his mouth to speak but no sound came. Instead his uttering lips sent a great billowing breath into the wintry air; it shaped and twisted and formed something in the mist.

Hanging before him, defying the circling wind was first an image of Henry, and then a question mark. It hovered there briefly then dispersed like steam. The figure remained motionless, watching Henry from behind the orbiting snowfall.

Henry knew the question. 'I'm Henry,' he said, his small voice carrying up to the rafters. 'Henry Best.'

The figure didn't move or reply, but the weather around him intensified and swelled, threatening to engulf Henry.

'I'm... looking for the tree's fairy – Lilly,' he added quickly.

The storm stayed, then subsided. The little blue wizard seemed to digest this, though he gave no indication.

Henry decided to tell his story – almost in full. He began by telling of his friend Bear, the trouble with the Fallen Fairy and his quest to reach the top of the tree. The figure seemed to listen, waiting until Henry had finished.

Apparently satisfied, the storm subsided and quelled to just light snowfall around the throne. The little figure began muttering silently again and from his breath another image was eventually realised, though the particles created something more like a painting.

It was the tree, but free of snow as though springtime or summer. The image changed rapidly as the wizard's lips worked, blowing, altering the picture. Snow began to fall and sit heavily on branches. The tree darkened, looking bleak and thin. Henry turned over what he'd seen in his mind and looked to the throne.

'Winter?' he asked. 'Is... that your name?'

The figure nodded slowly, the first movement Henry had seen him make.

'Please, don't keep me here. Don't you understand what I've got to do? I've told you everything.'

Winter remained motionless.

'I don't have much time. Can't... can't you help?'

Winter gave no sign.

Then, the snowfall petered out until just a light dusting remained. Another single nod.

Choking back emotion, Henry smiled. In fact he beamed.

A sound from nothing began to well up then, from behind the huge columns. It rose up the walls, all the way to the ceiling, building into a spiralling rush of noise. Something was coming at a great speed. Henry readied himself, eyes darting around. Then from the dark holes in the walls spat stream upon stream of ghostly white strands, looping and weaving up to the high ceiling before diving in numbers to the floor.

Henry, squatted with his hands over his ears, watched as the ghostly winds pulled up one by one, hovering above the flagstones, each blowing and swaying as they presented themselves before their king, Winter.

An army of winds stilled and waited. Winter blew a huge breath into the cold air around him. Controlled, crafted, the mist began a series of images depicting instructions for the gathered to follow. They changed and moved so swiftly, Winter mouthing so quickly, that Henry couldn't keep up or comprehend what he was seeing. At last the breaths died away.

The winds, acting on the instruction, turned to face Henry, each wavering face fixed upon him. Their features - ever changing - were never fully realised. And without warning, one rose into the air, followed by another then another. Before long there were nine blowing winds suspended in a ring above Henry.

Two of the winds dropped either side of him, taking a hand each to lift the boy into the air, his dressing gown whipping around him. The winds rose to the ceiling, towing Henry by his arms as they drew a figure of eight between the cross of beams. They dove at the floor before pulling up, shooting over the heads of all present.

Winter, stood on his throne, was the last thing Henry saw as he rocketed out through a hole in the wall.

Everything went black. Sound blasted in waves against his ears as he hurtled through the inky darkness. All he could see through his squinted eyes was the faint glow the winds traced as they snaked ahead. Then there was suddenly

light. Just splintered shafts at first, and then enough to blind him. Like a human cannonball, Henry shot free of the tunnel.

The clouds he'd flown over previously fell away as he climbed ever higher, away from the rocky face, a passenger again to the chain of winds. He sighted the river of snowflakes, flowing in an upward column through a break in the tree.

It was a destination they shared, as the line wound towards it. Once close enough, the winds pulled upwards and rode parallel to the channelling flakes.

Henry's role was merely to hang on – a task made easier by the virtual weightlessness the carrying winds granted him. He was free to enjoy his ascent through the tree. Surely for all his setbacks he might regather the time he'd lost.

His thoughts strayed to Bear. Would he be okay? What if he wasn't?

Henry shook his head, annoyed he'd allowed such thoughts to court his mind, and suddenly felt the rushing wind around him again, the sound constant in his ears. With the mist clearing, he could see the stream of flakes puncturing the broad canopy of branch above, the many lights dotted there each a beacon of colour breaking up the dark boughs scattered across the ceiling.

Close now, the line slowed. Rogue flakes played across their path. Some followed, caught in their wake; then a part of the flow, they broke through the opening. A new snow-laden tier stretched out below them as they rose higher.

The line of winds coursed up and away from the flow of flakes and into the crisp night air, so sharp and fresh that Henry realised he was now out in the open, the sky spread out above him.

A hijacked bauble

T he air was peppered with lazily falling snow, the fallout from the river of flakes finally ending their upward journey and beginning a new one back down.

The winds with Henry in tow climbed upwards and outwards, banking into a slow wide circle that skirted, to Henry's surprise, the most outwardly branches. As they passed over the pine needle tips poking out from the snow, Henry peered over the edge and saw with dizzying awe the tree dropping sharply away as though he were looking over the edge of an immense green mountain. Each layer of the tree jutted out from under the branches just above, all frosted with the flakes that tumbled down through the air. From up here, everything seemed wonderfully at peace. A secret, magical world, free from worry or danger.

They seemed to be heading for the tree's great trunk.

Its enormity increased the closer they flew, until the winds, keeping a level distance, circled it.

The tree's lights in its boughs shone like spotlights, turning shafts of multi-coloured lights through the air. A dazzling red haze engulfed Henry then, blinding him – a jolt that would certainly have unbalanced him were he not held by the last of the winds that pulled him. The winds snaked, then levelled, and pursued a straight line toward it.

Henry saw they were heading towards a logged balcony that wrapped around the trunk, and it appeared to be populated. Henry couldn't tell by what.

As they flew closer, another light found them. Its beam was blue; combined with the red it became purple, creating a lavender-like glow.

The lights, Henry saw, shone out from the tops of hanging baubles, guided by a silhouetted figure stood holding the fierce light.

The platformed ring around the trunk could be seen clearly now. Stood watching their approach and central to the platform looked to be an angel, complete with a halo and white robes, though ill-fitting due to an ample waistline, making them strain across his gut.

Stubby little wings sprouted from his back, but they looked too small to be of any use. He held a clipboard and was tapping it impatiently as he observed their descent.

Henry tensed. Rounding the side of the huge trunk were two pairs of coin guards, pine needles sheathed at their sides. They settled alongside the angel and watched the line approach. The winds banked and drew up before floating down to the platform, affording Henry the feel of something firm beneath his feet again.

'The Winds of Winter,' announced the angel in a bored voice. His eyes ran down his clipboard, his halo illuminating the page before him. 'And,' he glanced up, 'escorting an unknown passenger.' He scribbled something. The winds broke their line and hovered over the platform, facing them. 'We were offered no advance warning of your arrival. What is your business here?'

The winds parted either side of Henry. One of them motioned a wispy arm toward him. The angel lowered his clipboard and looked at Henry, who was fidgeting awkwardly.

'Well?' he asked, raising his eyebrows.

'I... I don't mean to be a problem-' started Henry. The angel raised a hand, stopping him short.

'I'll ask again, perhaps a little slower this time. What... is... your... business... here?'

Henry was lost for something to say, and made more urgently to give reason, but the Angel again raised a hand. 'You have already wasted enough of my time, which given my busy timetable is far more precious than you could imagine. Now, I am in no doubt as to the only reason you are here is to pester our good *lady* with the granting of some selfish wish, and you hope that you may too waste her time. I'm afraid,' he continued, raising his quill, 'that your little journey has been in vain. You should be grateful that I don't report you for time-wasting. And so,' he said loftily, 'I bid you good day.'

The angel turned on his heel and wobbled past the coin guard. Being wholly inexperienced in dealing with rude angels, Henry was lost. He'd come all this way only to be told to go away. This wasn't supposed to have happened.

An image of Bear and the others toiling under guard in the mines flashed in his mind. The sound of the angel's tutting faded away, replaced by the sound of his heart pounding in his ears. Something like anger rose in Henry's chest. He calmed the swell inside himself and in a clear and measured voice he called out.

'I had important news for the Fairy Queen,' said Henry brightly. 'News that could save lives.'

The angel slowed in his tracks. His back turned, he cocked an ear. 'What kind of news?'

'Oh... information about Phaedria,' said Henry, feigning great interest in the tips of his fingers.

The angel's face fell as he took a step toward the boy. 'Phaedria?' he said, his composure forgotten. 'But she... are you *sure*? I mean-'

He quickly straightened, suddenly aware that the guards were watching with eyes that told of a failing respect. Remembering his position, the angel cleared his throat and rested his hands upon his belly. He looked upon Henry.

'So, you claim she's... *alive*?'

Henry looked up from his fingertips. 'And she has an army.'

The angel's face changed quickly from a look of shock to one of growing outrage.

'An army,' he laughed. 'An army! Now I really shall have to report you. I had heard rumours of missing stars, so your tale of Phaedria naturally took me in for a moment, but to now hear that she has an army too? Preposterous! Tell me then; of what does this army consist? Hmmm?'

Henry said nothing for a moment and then pointed to the gathered coin guards. 'She's making *them*,' he said, 'from chocolate mixed by mice.'

The coin guards were suddenly a mixture of confusion and surprise. The angel took another step forward. Narrowing his eyes, he considered Henry for a time. 'Very well,' he said. 'I'll grant you entry.' Pinching his quill between his chubby fingers, he began to scribble again. Finished, he stabbed a full-stop, then motioned an arm towards the trunk where a golden light began to play. It burned brief and fierce before melting away to form an opening; a doorway in the wood.

The top of the Tree

'Good luck,' said the angel scornfully. 'If you're lying, you'll need it, and as for you all-' he said, turning abruptly to the winds, 'you have more than outstayed your welcome.'

Blowing and swaying, the winds turned to Henry with something on their long faces that resembled a smile and began to move off one after the other, spiralling upward.

Henry raised a hand in goodbye, and then quite unexpectedly the winds gave a sharp turn and dove straight at the angel. He ducked, but bore the full force of the winds rushing past him – his robe blowing up around his ears and revealing far more than he'd liked.

As he huffed and puffed on his knees, his hand automatically went to straighten his halo, but it wasn't there – it was hung from a small branch quite out of reach in the wake of their disappearance. All he could do, though it would be of no use, was to shake a fat fist after them.

'Now would be a good time to go,' said a pleasant voice behind Henry.

Henry turned to meet with another angel, though this one was remarkably more angelic than the other.

'Come on,' she urged, smiling, 'before he storms upstairs to complain.'

Henry followed after the angel. She floated just above the ground, her legs trailing backwards, her toes pointing to the floor, as though being pulled through water.

On her back were two graceful wings, fluttering gently. On her head was a halo, though it seemed a part of her, not like the weighty, unbalanced ring the other angel wore like an oversized crown. And it glowed softly gold, not dazzling and shiny, but a fine warm light. She fluttered into the golden hollow and waited to one side, watching the scene beyond Henry.

Stepping in beside her, Henry turned. Through the closing door he could see the chubby angel feeling at the top of his naked head while the guards, at a loss, scuttled aimlessly around him. The door sealed shut.

Henry looked around. There didn't appear to be any visible walls. No roof and no floor, but instead a golden glow that seemed to pass into nothingness.

It reminded Henry of the neon corridor the snowman had guarded.

The angel seemed happy to wait while Henry took it all in. Hung in the air to the angel's right were three red buttons with small white writing on them.

The topmost read: *TOP OF THE TREE*; the one below it *ALMOST THE TOP OF THE TREE*; and the last said simply *ALARM*.

'Going up?' asked the angel.

Henry nodded.

The angel leaned over and pressed the topmost button. She joined her hands in front of her and gave Henry a polite smile, to which he blushed.

A second later and the golden glow jolted, seeming to melt downward.

The angel turned to Henry. 'So, you're here to see Lilly?'

Henry brought his eyes from the golden streaks flying past to meet her. She had warm, smiling eyes. Her face was pale, her blonde hair resting in curls upon her shoulders.

'Why haven't we stopped?' asked Henry.

'Well, from an outside view the Fairy Queen's kingdom would appear relatively small, but,' she said with a gentle laugh, 'it may just surprise you. She doesn't just balance all day on the end of a twig, you know.'

'Oh,' said Henry in muted surprise, feeling a touch foolish. 'No, of course she doesn't. Sorry, yes. I *am* here to see Lilly.'

'Don't worry. We'll be there before you know it. She's a wonderful lady, you know.'

Henry pondered this for a moment. The blurred walls that were falling all around them melded back to a golden haze. All was still again.

A *ping* announced itself and the button that read *TOP OF THE TREE* lit up. There was a shudder and the door slowly parted.

'I don't think I mentioned; I'm Gabriel, by the way.'

'Henry,' said Henry, unsure of whether to offer his hand.

Gabriel extended an arm outward and smiled. 'Welcome to the Top of the Tree.'

Henry looked forward and blinked. He could see only two things. The first was a rickety wooden bridge, just wide enough to allow passage for Henry and Gabriel, though given the terrible state it was in and the fact it adjoined only to thin air surely meant it was a path they wouldn't be taking.

The second was the clear night sky. It was a night more beautiful than Henry had ever seen, powdered with brilliant white stars, seemingly so close Henry might almost be able to reach out and pocket handfuls of them. But, he thought, he must be in the wrong place.

Confused, Henry turned to the smiling angel.

'Have we come to the wrong floor?'

Gabriel looked blissfully forward. She eventually noticed Henry.

'Sorry. This way.'

She drifted out of the lift and began to pass over the bridge. Stopping, she looked back. 'I thought you needed to see our fairy urgently?'

Henry went to speak but his words fell short.

'It's quite okay,' she offered in place of Henry's silence. ''Come on.'

Henry blew. Slowly, gingerly, he walked onto the bridge, a ready hand hovering just shy of the handrail to his left. He drew level with the angel.

'Well, you have more than a measure of bravery, young Henry,' said Gabriel. 'Especially as you have no idea you are completely safe. Anyway, let's not dally. We have a bauble to catch.' Slowing her wingbeats, Gabriel landed barefoot on the planks. They creaked and swayed.

From a step, she was at the bridge's end, peering over, seemingly occupied with finding something below.

With a brisk flutter of her wings and a clap of her hands, it appeared she'd found it. Drawing a silver horn from her garments, she placed it to her lips.

As Henry made to her side, he gave a start at the sudden sound. A note, bright and regal sounded through the crisp night air. It held, then died – the horn replaced. Gabriel turned to Henry and smiled. 'Don't worry. Our escort is on its way.'

Curiously, Henry shuffled up to the edge, his fingers bloodless from his grip on the rail. He followed Gabriel's eyes downward, past an infinite curtain of stars. Where Henry expected to find ground, albeit far below, there was none – just the bridge's timber supports running back toward the trunk.

'Please,' offered Gabriel. 'Just be a little patient. Ah, never mind. Here comes one now.'

Henry followed Gabriel's line of sight downward but saw nothing different. Then a skittering movement – a star?

74

The star wobbled left and right, taking the appearance of a red ball, growing steadily bigger. After a time, Henry could see it was in fact a glittering red bauble and not a star at all. And coming at quite a speed.

It became dreadfully evident that the thing would not be stopping – if that were its intention – and it was headed straight for them.

Henry, frozen, heard a disapproving 'tut' beside him.

'You'll have to mind I'm afraid,' Gabriel said, placing a hand on Henry's head and guiding him to a squatting position. A second later and the giant red ball smashed through the rotten wooden rails, just missing their heads.

'Why do they insist on using such inexperienced young pilots?' she asked, splinters and dust falling around her.

Henry didn't look after the careering bauble, so afraid were he of the strength left in the creaking bridge's remnants, that to move a muscle, perhaps even his eyeballs, might just bring the last of it down.

Beside his squatted figure stood Gabriel, following the bauble's arcing run, her bare foot tapping the planks with impatience.

The bauble began a listing, whining sound, as though it were doubling back.

'Is it going to do that again?' cried Henry.

'Judging by its speed and the angle of its approach – I'd have to say yes,' said Gabriel, following it with her eyes.

With panic coursing him, Henry looked back to the lift. Perhaps they could chance a dash back to the door. But to his dismay there was no door. Only the tree's narrow trunk.

'Someone's going to be in a lot of trouble,' muttered Gabriel to herself.

Henry wasn't really listening.

His eyes tore back to the bauble now screaming toward them.

Gabriel took his hand. 'We'll have to board it ourselves.' And leaping from the bridge, she took Henry with her.

A moment later the bauble smashed clean through the bridge, reducing it to a cloud of woodchip. With Henry held tight around her waist, they tumbled through the cold night air until, broadening her wings, they swooped upward through the downfall of debris.

'I suspect our pilot is very young,' gauged Gabriel from beneath the glow of her halo. 'Unqualified too. Come on Henry. Let's go find out who it is.'

And with a wide-eyed Henry clinging on, they took after the bauble. With a few flaps of her wings, the pair were soon in the bauble's slipstream, pestered by the trails of dust and splinters it tailed.

As they mirrored it left to right, Henry could now see that there was indeed a small angel, stood bolt upright behind a wheel, not unlike the wheel of a ship. Even from this distance the panic in the pilot was evident.

'Hang on!' cried Gabriel. With a series of movements from her elegant wings, they dove at the bauble to touch down just behind the pilot who hadn't seemed to have noticed.

She placed a hand on the young angel's shoulder – hair wild and tangled with woodchip – and a shrill scream went up, forcing Henry to his knees and covering his disbelieving ears. Their pilot, he realised, was female. He grabbed at Gabriel's ankles, his eyes turned upward for answers.

'Great treetops, be silent!' Gabriel clapped a hand over her mouth. 'Here, let me take the wheel now. Come on, young Pluck, loosen your fingers a little... that's it... just a little more. Okay, good. Come on now, stand aside... there we go.'

And then Gabriel was behind the wheel. The young angel stood dazed. She turned slowly and saw Henry lying prone. Her expression changed from fear to bewilderment, before stopping at plain curiosity.

'Who are *you*?' she blinked.

Henry was a little taken aback. Coming as close to death as he ever had, his breath hadn't quite returned.

'*Hello*?' said the young angel, moving closer and lowering. 'Can you hear me?'

As Henry was about to speak, the young angel turned back to Gabriel.

'Is he hard of hearing?'

Gabriel gave a quarter turn of her head.

''He can hear you perfectly well, young Pluck. I think it's your flying technique that has the poor boy in a muddle. Which begs the question: how is it someone as young and inexperienced as yourself is behind the wheel of a red class bauble?'

'Well,' said Pluck, siding up to her senior, 'it's funny you ask that. You see, Cherubim and i-'

76

Henry's interest in the conversation slipped away as he looked around. The swift flight of the bauble buffeting downward on the chill wind was causing the starry night sky to blur and rotate.

He clambered up onto all fours and began to inch his way across the top of the bauble until he was able to peer down over the side.

Rising up from below was a great area of snow-covered land. It was like descending onto a wintry model landscape that someone had painstakingly modelled, making every detail perfect, but the swooping-turning motion of the bauble made it hard for him to focus on anything.

What are you doing down there?

The bauble broke through a cloud and its flight slowed and levelled, passing the ground far below at an easier pace, affording Henry more time to explore the landscape.

There were great snow-laden hills needled with dark-spired trees that swept down into icy valleys where they surrounded frozen lakes that appeared to have never seen thaw. As the ball they rode swooped at ease between the hills, Henry could see wispy balls of light below, weaving between the trees, darting and chasing as though trying to keep up with the bauble overhead. Henry followed them until they were lost from view.

The trees became less numerous now as they flew on, and the patches of snowy ground between the trees in the valley began to open up to snow-drifted plains. Straining, Henry could see dots of movement below, milling and circling, leaving tiny prints in the snow as they ran. From this distance it looked like a bird's eye view of a playground. Henry longed for a moment to be back with his friends at school.

The little figures passed away as the bauble wove on. Henry wondered how much further they had to go, but as far as his eyes could see there seemed no end to the wintry expanse. He would just have to ask.

Henry eased himself up onto all fours, shuffled back from the edge and adopted a squatting position. From there, still close to the surface, he shuffled towards the wheel.

'What are you doing down there?'

Henry looked up to see Pluck stood over him, apparently mindless to the danger she was putting herself in by standing completely unaided.

'Uh... I've never travelled by bauble before,' said Henry meekly, feeling a touch foolish at being sprawled at the feet of this young angel who couldn't be much older than himself.

'The bauble will allow you to stand, silly. It has its own "gravity field" – or something like that. You would have to be doing something pretty stupid to actually fall off one.'

'Just watch who you are calling silly, young Pluck,' interrupted Gabriel, 'and I think if anyone's been stupid round here, it's the angel that hijacked this bauble!'

'Hijacked?' gasped Pluck. 'I heard the call from the horn but there didn't seem to be any pilots around at the time to-'

'Even so,' said Gabriel. 'It's far from your duty to just jump onto a bauble, especially a red-classer, and go whizzing off into the sky-'

'But I've always wanted to be a pilot,' cried Pluck in protest, walking back to the wheel. Gabriel fixed Pluck with a look, perhaps to determine whether it might really be this young angel's ambition – or if she was just trying to fool her.

She turned away undecided, her focus back on flying. 'Go make yourself useful she said with a flick of her head. 'Help young Henry find his feet, and while you're there you can be his guide.'

There was a moment of silence. From his view from the floor, Henry thought Pluck might defy her, but she eventually turned, looking a little hard-done-by.

'You'd do well to apologise for almost turning him into a woodchip!'

A huff followed a shrug. As Pluck's eyes rolled up into her head, they stopped short and focused on a thought way off somewhere.

'I'm sorry,' said Pluck finally. She crouched and offered a hand.

'That's okay.' Henry took it and got up. 'You're sure I can stand on this thing?'

'Sure. Even absolute beginners can.'

Henry smiled. He peered down over the side and would have to agree. He felt as though he were stood on something quite solid and that the movement of the bauble was just a pleasant, swaying motion.

'You see?' said Pluck following his face.

Henry nodded, grinning.

'But flying them is just a little bit trickier. Now then-' said Pluck in a more business-like tone, 'if you were wondering what that huge blue circle down there is...'

Henry followed her line of sight.

'...then I can tell you – a little closer please Gabriel – it would be one of the best ice-skating spots you will find. Gabriel, please... you're passing too fast-'

'Henry is actually on some urgent business, young Pluck, so you'll have to make do with my low flying for the moment.'

Pluck turned to Henry with visibly mounting interest. 'Important business? Ah! Given our course, you must be off to see our fairy. So what's *that* about?'

'That's Henry's private matter,' said Gabriel, looking back from the wheel. 'He might be able to tell you something of it later.' She corrected her flight, noted a waypoint and pulled back a gear on the steering column.

Dejected, Pluck huffed again. And then with a thought she leaned into Henry's ear.

'I mean it, Pluck,' said Gabriel, her eyes still front. 'Leave the poor boy alone.'

Pluck struck an outraged expression. She was about to protest her innocence and then thought better of it.

'Anyway,' she said, glancing back to Gabriel, checking for eyes in the back of her head, 'as I was saying, if you look down – *ah* – it's gone now... well, never mind. If you look a little further along you'll see-'

'Our docking point,' said Gabriel, turning the wheel so the bauble began to swing a slow circle.

'You can come with us to see our fairy,' she added to the sudden delight of Pluck, 'and explain why you've been piloting baubles.'

'What?'

'No arguments, Pluck. Now come up here and help.'

Reluctantly, the young angel took a coiled line from an anchor point and began to unwind it. Henry saw they were backing into a thick canopy of branches where many other baubles were hanging.

With a soft crunch, the bauble pushed into the hanging pine needles while Pluck leapt off onto a near bough. Gabriel tossed the line over a branch and Pluck looped it several times before tying it off. Done, she gave a thumbs-up.

'Here,' said Gabriel, offering her hand. 'You'd better hold on.'

Gabriel pulled a lever on the wheel's column and the bauble dropped as the line pulled taut, creaking them back and forth.

Henry could feel the bauble was back to being an ornament.

'Henry?' Gabriel offered her hands. Taking them, he was flown to a snowy expanse of branch.

Gabriel pondered. 'This way I *think*.'

And with Pluck jogging to catch up, they set off.

The three of them trod towards one of the many rope-bridged paths leading into the dense pine foliage.

After passing many (now familiar) inhabitants at forks and passes on the bridged walkways, a bustling crowd had begun to congregate and jam up at one of the exits down to ground level.

Bauble pilots here were required to form an orderly queue and produce their pilot's licence to a pair of studious-looking elves, although the 'line' had become more of a mob.

'This way,' said Gabriel, side-stepping the crowd as she led them to a sombre-looking angel who was watching the herd of pilots with disinterest.

'Why so bored, Raphael?'

Broken from his trance-like state, the angel turned with surprise. 'Gabriel! What in Treetops are you doing all the way over here?'

'Oh, the three of us have some business with Lilly.' Gabriel presented Henry and Pluck by her side. 'So I'll need a favour.' Gabriel motioned her eyes to a side gate just beyond.

'Oh, whatever, old friend. You got time for a quick catch-up?'

'I'm afraid I have to keep on.'

'Shame.' Raphael's dull eyes surveyed the crowd. 'I can't tell you how long I've been stationed here, but it feels like a lifetime.'

Raphael took the few steps, unlocked the gate and stepped aside. Gabriel showed Henry through, followed by Pluck who'd adopted a pumped-up strut and an air of importance.

Raphael couldn't help but laugh. 'Be sure to catch up with me soon,' he called.

'Will do,' said Gabriel with a backward wave.

The three made off briskly, winding their way through the exiting pilots. The wide floor of woven branches beneath their feet bore away from them over a hill, eventually turning off downward toward a long-tunnelled run. A line of overhead tree lights lit the way down with each singing the faint, mournful song Henry recognised as always hearing on his journey through the tree.

He could see little faint eyes and mouths within the stars, watching the travellers pass. Up ahead was an arched exit.

Before long they'd reached its mouth where, with a hand shielding his eyes from the bright light, Henry looked out and beyond.

'Duck!' said a voice from somewhere and Henry found himself brought down by Gabriel's hand. Something fizzed over their heads and disappeared.

'Damned stars!' yelled a gift-wrapped box holding its bow-tied top. It rose to give chase, but the stars hadn't noticed. They morphed quickly from a giggling swarm into a sleek line and droned off over the crest of a hill.

'Young stars,' explained Gabriel while everyone slowly rose to their feet.

'Don't worry,' she said, noticing Henry looking strained. 'It won't be long now.' Henry felt a little doubtful.

The three, along with assorted bauble pilots and passengers, began the steep trudge up the snowy incline. It was here that Henry noticed a young gingerbread boy dragging his father up the hill, insisting all the while that their destination was 'just over the top'.

Henry surveyed the area. It seemed there were small family groups everywhere, each laden with luggage of some sort and each keen with anticipation; all apart from one Christmas pudding. He was plodding a ragged path upward and looking very much worse for wear.

'Bauble flight sickness,' whispered Gabriel.

Some of the young had run from their groups to reach the crest of the hill where they pulled up side by side and stood quite still.

Then, an eruption of noise; some jumped and whooped while others scraped up handfuls of snow so it came down in powdered showers.

Pluck snatched Henry's hat and tore off up the hill, laughing. The snow was almost up to her knees.

Henry looked to Gabriel. She raised her eyebrows and smiled. He peeled off after her, leaping as he ran to stay on top of the snow. He was laughing too. He found her at the top, gasping for breath and wearing his hat. Henry swiped it off her head, checked it over and put it back onto his.

'Behold!' announced Pluck, her arm sweeping a half-circle. 'The Fairy Queen's kingdom!'

Still catching his breath, Henry gasped. He'd made it, he breathed. He was here.

Pluck threw an arm around his shoulder and grinned. 'So what do you think?'

Treetops

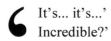‘It's... it's...'

‘Incredible?'

‘Yeah... incredible.' Henry blinked. ‘I can't believe I'm finally here.'

Gabriel had caught up with the youngsters. She looked between the Kingdom and Henry and smiled.

It spanned as far left and right and beyond as he could see. The hill he stood upon dropped away into a huge sunken valley. Its land was alive with life. Everywhere, the snow-draped land softly glittered with tiny jewel-like lights playing upon its surface.

The young from the crest were now racing down the hill, tumbling into virgin drifts and producing ghosted rainbows; so delicate, they were never really there. ‘The Great Star,' said Gabriel, leaning into Henry so he could follow her gaze.

Henry drew away and had to steady himself. An immense silver star hung way in the sky above them, central to all below it. Strangely, it seemed near and far at the same time. Its surface turned like the sun, but it was cool, white and depthless.

Each of its five points bristled, like a heartbeat, and as the star pulsed it shed a fine, sparkling dust. Its glow was calming and comforting.

Henry dragged his eyes from it and let them venture over the land. A line of overhead lanterns tied at points to pine trees lit a path down the hillside, the same on every side of the valley until the web of lights met in the centre below.

The valley was surrounded by mountains. Far up, their crooked peaks were shrouded in cloud, each sowing flurries of snow down their steeped sides. Henry looked up and behind him to find they were stood in the shadow of a mountain themselves – the tunnel they'd travelled through had led them clean beneath it and almost to the foot.

Wisps darted between the branches. They traced shimmering trails, stopping only to hide as another line of racing stars tore around the trees. Henry watched them downhill until they were gone.

Gabriel gave their surrounds a brief scan. 'Let's go find our fairy, Henry.'

Henry nodded with vigour. The trio joined the others who were beginning to shift off down the hill into the valley. They took a well-trodden path down.

Henry wondered at the line of lanterns strung between the trees overhead, zig-zagging the route they were to follow.

As the hill levelled off, so the pines rose and became more numerous, bringing the excited chatter of the party down to a whisper, as even the Great Star above couldn't penetrate the dense foliage, making the wood appear dark and foreboding.

The delicate lanterns above provided the only light now and as they jangled and swayed, they created long, leaping shadows.

Henry looked to Gabriel. 'Why are there no stars in here?'

Gabriel pushed down a hand, quieting Henry. 'They've gone to fill gaps elsewhere,' she whispered, her eyes shifting. Just a temporary measure.

Henry walked on, pondering this.

Ahead, and to the delight of some of the young, including most of the adults too, lunar shafts, like spotlights, were penetrating the branches. The Great Star was beginning to make more and more appearances through the canopy until, with an audible sigh of relief from all, the trees parted out onto a broad frozen lake.

Henry paused to straighten his hat and looked around the gathered mountains.

Stood out from the sheer face of one, set high into its side, was what could only be a castle.

It appeared half-buried, due to the relentless fall of snow from the clouds crowding its peak, and so its true size remained hidden. Steep walls of stone grew up and out of the mountain's side. Upon each of these were tall towers of stone; crooked fingers with snow-spired tips.

In each of the walls were windows. Only one was dimly lit. Strange, Henry thought, as the place appeared long deserted.

At its base was a door preceded by a cliff-face of steps zig-zagging a path to its threshold.

Though its demeanour was one of neglect, it still managed to look beautiful – yet menacing – at the same time.

'Is that Lilly's home?' asked Henry, dismayed, figuring it would take a huge effort to reach.

Gabriel shook her head. 'It was Phaedria's.' And perhaps deciding better of an explanation, said simply; 'Lilly doesn't live there.'

Henry drew in his dressing gown before giving it a final look.

'We won't have to go that far,' said Gabriel, turning him. 'Our fairy is over here.'

'Really?' Henry brightened.

'Yes, really.'

Gabriel turned Henry towards a copse of trees.

'I don't see her.'

'I do,' said Pluck, pulling Henry sideways. 'There. No, not there. Just... over... *there.*'

Henry's eyes sparked. Surfacing above the trees were fluttering little wings; blurs of white, like butterflies disturbed.

'The young of angels,' said Gabriel with a fondness to her voice, 'being taught to fly. This is the School for Angels.'

'The School for Angels...' marvelled Henry, and then a thought struck him.

Bear's plight. Fumbling, shaking, Henry found his pocket and withdrew the stone.

Dark grey. He pocketed it again and exhaled.

'Come on.' Gabriel took Henry's arm. 'It's high time you met her.'

The journey felt to Henry like an age; or perhaps his mind had aged, his thoughts racing. Would Lilly believe him? If she didn't, then what of the stone? Would she simply dismiss it? Could he convince her?

Henry was so preoccupied, his hat caught on a low branch as he arrived at the copse. He picked the needles from it, turning it over in his hands.

'Look, Henry. There's a lesson in progress.'

Ducking low-slung branches, Henry made quietly to the edge of a large circular clearing and peered up.

'Good,' came a voice. 'Good. Steady. *Steady...*'

Henry edged his neck out further.

'Now try passing back through. Oh dear.'

And then a little more, trying to locate the source of the voice. Henry somehow knew it was Lilly. Perhaps it was the brightness of her voice – light and lively – but also graceful and familiar.

And then Henry saw her with the briefest of glimpses. Like a rabbit startled, he quickly hid beneath the trees again.

'Class, we have a visitor,' came the voice. 'But don't let that affect your concentration. I don't want to see anyone showing off.'

Pluck laughed.

Henry burned scarlet.

Gabriel eased back a branch and manoeuvred Henry to look through it. The 'class', Henry realised, really were small angels; each smaller and younger than Pluck.

They were stood about the snowy floor, disorganised and tired. Some were whispering and others giggled while some just looked bored. One fought to hem in some oversized robes. Clearing her throat, the fairy caught their collective attention. 'Now, you've all been doing so well, I won't be keeping you much longer. Our last exercise before you go will be some hoop training.' There were a few groans.

Henry's curiosity drew him from beneath the shelter of the branch to stand at the edge of the clearing. Looking up, he saw her quite clearly.

From the delicate beat of feathered wings she hung airborne, slight and beautiful. Her face looked kind, her hair parted either side of her face. She wore a dress that flowed as though it swayed in the current of an invisible tide. Her feet, Henry saw, were bare.

One slender arm was held aloft in an act of conduction, as the other pointed a wand. Deft flicks sent small, cloud-like hoops from its tip.

As they sailed off in different directions, they grew in size, slowing and stopping at different points in the air.

'Okay, class,' she called, restoring some order among the chattering. 'I want you all to pay attention. Following my lead, I want you all to test your wings as so...'

The fairy flapped a wing left, then right, making her sway in the air. The gathered angel young attempted the same, though more than a few appeared to have trouble using just one wing at a time. Henry wondered if it was a bit like learning to wink.

Looking mostly satisfied, she went on. 'Now, in something like an orderly fashion, ascend as best you can up to the first hoop.'

Three young angels fought to head a hasty line.

'Elijah, Jophiel, Uriel. This isn't a race! Back up a little. Come on now.'

Reluctantly they dropped back, shuffling into position.

'Elijah,' said Lilly, folding her arms. 'Let's see what you can do.'

'Come on; up, up, *up*!'

The young angel flashed into the air, buzzing her wings, only managing to fly sideways and then downward, skidding into the snowy floor.

'Okay?' asked Lilly.

Elijah, crestfallen, patted himself free of snow and trudged off to join the back of the queue.

'Who's next?'

The line bobbed their heads in eagerness.

'Uriel. Come on, show us how it's done.'

Uriel gave his friends a wink and took wing to hover in front of the first hoop. Five coins stood around the perimeter positioned themselves at various points below the targets.

'Begin, please.'

Without further ado, young Uriel flew forward, expertly negotiating the first hoop. A flap here, a twist there, and he was through the second. Getting a little ahead of himself, he dove rather too quickly for the third, and adjusting too late, his wings caught, slowed by the cloud. Henry gasped, watching the angel plummet. On cue, a coin ran and dove to catch the hapless angel effortlessly.

With only his pride dented, Uriel grumbled thanks, straightened his halo and joined the others.

Lilly heaved a sigh. 'Very good for the first, too swift for the second and so the third arrived too quickly. One day you'll fly for Treetops, but not until you've learned to pace yourself.'

A little crestfallen, Uriel joined the back of the queue, his friends laughing and patting his back as he went. Lilly then noticed the young boy, now stood out in the open.

'Um... I'm terribly sorry to disturb your class, Miss Lilly, really I am, but I must tell you something.' Henry bowed awkwardly.

Gabriel and Pluck hadn't noticed Henry leave their side. They stood open-mouthed.

So too did the class. To interrupt the Fairy Queen was one thing; a human young in their midst was another.

Lilly, however, remained impassive. 'One at a time, class,' she called, before hovering over to the boy.

Gabriel quickly joined Henry's side to bumble out an apology, but was cut short by Lilly's upturned hand.

'Please, Gabriel, let the young speak.'

A gift for Lilly

Henry gazed around, suddenly aware that all eyes were upon him. The class had slowed to a stand-still. Even the coins' sharp composure had slackened.

Gabriel nudged Henry.

'I have met another fairy,' he said, looking into the depthless blue of Lilly's eyes, 'but she isn't like you. In fact,' and Henry winced a little, 'I think she's planning bad things.'

Silence came like a pause in time, broken by a rise of gasps and whispers. Lilly only had to look back to her class to restore complete silence again, and then with a number of flicks from her wand, each of the airborne clouds popped and vanished.

Looking troubled, she stowed her wand and clapped twice. 'Class will finish early today. Gather your things and head straight home.'

She watched after the line, guided off by the coin guard until they were gone. Turning to Henry she lowered herself to his level. She took his hands and fixed him with warm, yet sorrowful eyes. 'I know you tell the truth,' she whispered. 'She is alive – or something close to it. I can feel it.'

She ran her thumbs over the backs of Henry's hands, then let go to stand. 'I need everything you know,' she said more clearly now, 'but you give me cause to hesitate. I sense...' Lilly turned her head slightly. 'You have something... something to show me?'

Henry's relief was visible, as though the burden that weighed heavily upon him had suddenly grown wings, it lifted and left. He placed his hand into his pocket and looked Lilly square in the eyes. 'I have this for you.'

Henry's held out an upturned fist. All eyes fell upon it. He looked from face to face, then opened his hand.

He revealed the stone, scorched and darkened, grey like a storm cloud – although Henry's hand didn't sway, it gave the impression of something very heavy.

Heads leaned in to look more closely; Pluck went to take it from Henry's hand. 'Be careful, Pluck,' Lilly warned. 'And everyone else. Don't touch it. Move away... give the young room.'

As the gathering backed away, Lilly angled closer. She looked around the stone very carefully, her breath stilled. Her coin guard closed, looking at each other. She drew closer still – and then spoke urgently in a foreign tongue.

Pluck and Gabriel were lifted and carried a dozen paces clear before they realised there were coin guardians beneath them. The remaining coins rearranged themselves, readied. Henry's hand trembled.

Lilly drew her wand, her eyes only on the stone. 'What's your name?' she asked.

The boy's widening eyes fell to his palm. He felt very much alone. 'Henry,' he said, his brain suddenly rebooting. The stone's surface began to swirl.

Grey stretched over grey, turning over and over, the repetition quickening. It shot black and began to tremor.

'Ready when I say, Llorn!'

A coin guardian flexed his fingers. Lilly drew an arc with her wand and bounced once on her toes. 'Now!'

The dark sphere shot from his hand and flew at Lilly. Henry flew sideways, clear of the melee in Llorn's grip. As he fell, Henry saw Lilly stop the speeding ball with a blast of white light from her wand, buffeting the ball to the floor. It landed with a muffled thud.

Lilly looked pained. She rolled her neck, her features determined.

The ball sat motionless, buried in snow. Though Henry lay prone, shielded by Llorn, he could still see from a gap beneath the coin's body.

All were still, though alert, all eyes to the floor. One coin looked to another and received a nod. He turned on his heel and fled. Nothing seemed to be happening.

Henry wondered for a moment if the whole thing might have been a slight overreaction and thought the group might stand down. And then from the hole in the snow, powder lifted and scattered, as though the ball were a furiously burrowing rodent.

The coin who'd fled returned with the means to do battle. From his laden arms he sorted spears and nets, pine blades and staffs, tossing them one by one to his team who caught them, their eyes unmoved from the ground.

Lilly drew her wand through the air and spoke loud and clear. 'Protect the young. Protect yourselves! Do not disobey me!'

Gabriel buzzed over to Pluck, her arms wrapped around her. The highest ranked coin cast a solemn look to Llorn, then another, and received a nod from both. He then turned to the others and thrust a pine needle sword skyward. 'Protect our fairy at all costs!' As his order echoed, the floor erupted. All were momentarily blinded.

There was a sound of shattering glass and then a sickening, cracking noise. Some regained their sight to see a darkness swelling in the fallout. The form skitted a quick circle before it stopped.

With the crystal mist almost gone, Henry could see with mounting horror that the thing was a monstrous spider; beetle black, hairless and three times taller than anyone present.

It faced Lilly, bared its fangs and wound low. Its path was suddenly blocked by two light-footed coins – one twirling a pole, the other a pine blade. The eight eyes on its head passed from one to the other.

The blade-wielding coin leapt forward and slashed, aiming to sever a leg. The target limb rose just out of reach. Again and again came the blade, each dark leg silkily avoiding it.

A call went up for the coin to pull clear, but the spider had manoeuvred him to the perfect point. A leg came down like a javelin, skewering the coin upright, clean through its gold casement.

The guardian's mouth opened and hung. His eyes rolled to his captain as though in apology, and his body fell limp.

As the leg retracted, the coin blackened and flaked away like burnt paper. The spider turned to the next coin, only to meet with a blast from Lilly's wand. Knocked from its feet, it flew backward, curled like a dead flower, and was set upon by the remaining coins.

The creature tried to rise, but a staff swept away its footing and it lay sprawled on its back, legs writhing. Netted, the spider began taking blows, its movements minimal. A coin leapt on the black parcel, a pine blade between his teeth, looking to finish, but it was to be the coin's final action.

Venom spat upwards in a violent fountain, searing a hole in the netting and melting the coin. The remaining guards backed off as the hissing spider rolled upright, free of the net and assessing its next target.

Lowering, it sprang at the coin between itself and Lilly, fangs poised, but it thudded into a transparent magical barrier thrown up from Lilly's wand. It scuttled upright, two legs from the ground, wounded.

Henry saw Lilly had expended a lot of her strength. She looked jaded and drawn, but her resolve hadn't wavered.

'Go and help,' said Henry beneath Llorn.

The coin tensed but remained shielding Henry.

'Llorn. Please.'

The coin assessed the battle. It wasn't going well. 'Stay low,' he barked, rising. 'Don't move.'

The spider meanwhile was fighting two coins, one thrusting a spear, the other a trident. Another coin leapt in and clipped a leg tip with his blade. The spider let out a shrill scream and danced as though stood on a hotplate. It lunged reactively at its assailant, scoring the coin's casement with a black fang. The coin fell wounded, but was pulled clear by his captain before a second attempt.

A standoff began to play out, but the coin's battling efforts were no interest to the spider. Its many eyes turned to its true target.

Wound, it sprang at Lilly, legs open to envelop her – but Llorn had anticipated this. He dove at the same time, drawing his blade. 'Now, my Queen!'

Lilly thrust her wand forth; from its tip came a ghostly hand that grabbed the spider mid-flight. The spell held just long enough for Llorn to arrive beneath the spider and drive his dagger into its swollen black gut.

The spell broke. The spider fell hissing and spitting onto Llorn, smothering him.

It twitched horribly and then became still. For a moment nobody moved, then the coins were upon it, dragging its heavy corpse from atop their brother.

Lilly parted the fearful gathering and crouched over Llorn, looking
him over.

Henry was first to speak, though his voice was near stolen. 'Is he... okay?'

Lilly creased her eyes shut. 'I'm afraid,' she said softly, 'that it would take a whole army of ball spiders to finish this coin off. He'll be just fine – barring some minor burns.'

The party exhaled as one.

92

'My thoughts are with our fallen,' she said, following a charred piece of ash off into the air. 'But my concerns lie with our foolishly brave comrade.'

They'd almost forgotten their wounded brother being cradled by his captain.

'How is he, Arorn?'

'He's taken some poison. Maybe enough to kill him,' he conceded.

Henry found space among the gathered coins, each wrought with concern, and saw the fallen coin huddled and shivering. His lower left side had blackened. Lilly crouched and looked the coin over.

'Magic can't help here,' she said, pushing a lock of her hair to one side. But she drew her wand anyway.

She stood and popped a pearl-white flare into the heights. 'I've called a bauble to take him. We must place our faith in others now.'

Within moments, a whipping white bauble coursed its way down. Landing, two angels hopped off and fluttered to the floor. They looked the coin over and prepared him to board. His captain bade him farewell along with the rest, saying he expected to see him soon.

'Half chocolate, half gold, and a bellyful of fight, eh?' said the captain, mustering a proud smile. 'And don't worry, we'll keep your blade sharp.'

Once up on the bauble, the captain had a quick word with the angels, then let them go. The group watched as the bauble shrank away over the mountains.

All was quiet, but for a small voice, barely a whisper. 'I'm sorry,' said Henry, clutching at his dressing gown. 'I'm so sorry, I-'

'Didn't know,' said Lilly, stepping toward him. 'I'm afraid you were tricked, Henry, and I'm angry at myself for not sensing so.' Her features lowered to convey concern. 'What was promised to you?'

Henry struck open-mouthed. 'Bear,' he said, dazed. 'My Bear!' And he broke from the shock stealing over him. 'She has him, Lilly! She has him!'

Lilly frowned. 'This "Bear" is a friend?'

Henry nodded several times.

'There is a chance you May not…' Her eyes left Henry to follow the floor she now paced, '…may not see-'

'No,' said Henry weakly. 'We must go and get him. She promised…' His voice rose. 'You were supposed to...' Henry stood right before Lilly, his hands just shy of clutching her dress. He stopped talking, as though the penny dropping had taken his voice with it.

'It was an assassination attempt,' said Captain Arorn across him. 'She never intended to keep her promise. In your determination to save your friend she knew you'd reach here.' Arorn took Henry's shoulders. 'You must tell our fairy what you saw.'

Henry took a breath and then another. He focused.

'She's making an army. An army of coins.'

All were stunned into silence. Lilly was the first to break it.

'Henry, I promise we will do everything to find your bear. You must tell us where she is.'

Henry searched her eyes. He found nothing but sincerity. 'You promise?'

She placed a hand to her chest. 'You have my solemn word.'

His eyes glazed. He closed them. 'She has a cave. A huge cave deep down in the tree, and a fort on a rock.' His eyes opened and widened. 'There was a tunnel.'

Lilly took his hand. 'Was this army ready? To march?'

'I don't... I don't think so.'

Lilly cast around, still holding Henry's hand. 'Does anyone know this cave? Or the tunnel?'

Most shrugged. All looked blank. Satisfied none did, she looked back to Henry, holding his hands firmer. Her features softened.

'Could you show us the way?'

Henry thought for a moment. 'I might be able to, but it would take a very long time to reach.'

Feathered friends

'I will send you, along with company, if willing, to find where this cave is. I sense with the timing of all this that her army may have started marching out. There's no time to lose. Gabriel, Pluck, and... ' Her eyes passed over her guardians. 'As part of my promise, Llorn will accompany you.'

She looked to each as she spoke. Pluck gave a little clap and buzzed her wings. Gabriel brought her back to the ground with a reproachful look.

'You will need to be swift, silent and unnoticed. Flying by bauble is then out of the question. However, flying is just what you will be doing, provided you agree to it.' She looked between Henry and the excited-to-bursting Pluck as she said this. Pluck nodded furiously.

'I'll do it,' said Henry.

'Very well. Then the three of you shall each become birds. Small, quick birds. Robin redbreasts to be exact. The fourth, Llorn, shall need to be aggressively quick and shall become a bird of prey. A jayhawk would be best, I think.'

Henry looked pained with confusion.

'You will instinctively know how to fly as a bird,' said the fairy matter-of-factly, 'although the initial sensation will take a short while to get used to. The spell should have duration enough for you to fly around the breadth of the tree twice, though I hope Gabriel will be back far sooner than that with the exact location of Phaedria's army and its headed course.' She parted her hair and looked to Henry.

'As for you, I want you to simply lead Llorn and Gabriel to the cave's entrance, if possible, nothing more. And Pluck,' she said, rounding to find the bouncing young angel. 'You will stick to Henry like a sticky date. You will have the important role...' – she raised her voice authoritatively – 'of making sure that Henry gets back here safely. And please, do stop bouncing.'

She looked to each of them to see that they understood, then turned to Llorn. 'You'll transform for a shorter duration. As soon as you find the entrance, get in. Scour the cave and find the captives. You shall unfortunately be unarmed. See the Captain for a briefing. Are we all understood?'

There was a general murmur of agreement.

'One last thing before you become one of our many-feathered friends. Do not be tempted to snack upon anything you might spy along the way. The wrong foodstuff and our plans could be scuppered.'

Drawing her wand, she smiled. 'May the luck of Treetops be with you.'

And with that she pointed her wand at Gabriel, then in quick succession passing between each of them, each time a blazing orange light morphing the recipient instantly into a bird.

Gabriel, just as a robin might, chirruped and flew to an overhead branch. Llorn screeched and, as though impatient to get on, soared upward, circling the clearing. The remaining pair floundered on the ground.

Lilly crouched close to Henry and Pluck. They were having a spot of bother righting themselves up and onto their new three-toed feet.

'Nice and easy, come on,' she said, offering her wand for the pair to perch on.

Henry felt the wand gently correcting him until he found his feet. A test waddle and all seemed okay. And it really did. Though everything had grown vastly in size, and his arms, chest and head were strangely feathery, he felt quite at ease being a bird. He flapped a left wing, then a right.

Pluck too looked to be taking all this in her stride. She looked to Henry and sang happily. Of course, he'd understood everything she'd said, but he wasn't sure he was quite ready. 'Give me a moment,' he trilled, but she wasn't about to wait and took off.

Like a wet kite, she laboured up and down, falling this way and that, but her determination won through. She remained airborne for a whole lap of the clearing. Not wanting to be left behind, Henry steeled himself, gritted his beak and leapt from the ground flapping. He arced and crashed – his bird head buried. Suddenly his legs shot backwards, followed by the rest of him. He was promptly dusted off by Lilly's giant hand.

'You are a bird,' said the fairy to his ear, 'so you must think as a bird.' Finding a comfortable perch upon her forefinger, Henry concentrated and let his mind go blank.

He felt his stick-thin legs bend a little and instinctively sprung. Flapping for all his worth, he managed to climb a ragged path upward. He tried to relax and cleared his mind. His wings immediately assumed a new shape, drawing dynamically and thrusting with more span, allowing him to flap less.

A turn here and a swoop there and Henry suddenly felt as though he'd flown all his life. Spying Pluck from on high, he sang out and dove down to follow.

She slowed beside him, looking equally adept. For a moment they looked at each other, both sharing the most wondrous experience. Llorn, as a jayhawk, swooped in and told them in a rising shriek to come back down to Lilly.

Eventually the four alighted on a log just before her, each flapping and adjusting.

'Well I couldn't have hoped for a better display than that,' she said, smiling.

Pluck twittered thanks. 'Now, remember.' Lilly looked to each in turn. 'Fly naturally once you are closer. We must assume that Phaedria has regained most of her powers and could be able to send something of her own in pursuit of you. Try to remain hidden and keep to the plan.'

Her light expression gave way to concern. She came near and took a knee. 'While you are gone I shall gather our greatest force, but for us to succeed – for the Tree to go on – you must *all* succeed.' Smiling eyes dissolved her concern. 'Go on now, be away with you.'

Llorn cawed the order along the line and in turn they followed him upward, circling the clearing. Below the coins waved; the captain saluted.

Cries of 'good luck!' rang after them as they flew one by one through a gap in the pines. Llorn held the line, climbing powerfully, high over hills and then the diminishing sight of Treetops.

The four were on their way. Llorn led the formation with purpose. He banked steep slopes, twisted paths through thick pine and soared over valleys. Henry noticed that they'd flown clear of the dark forest that had held him in such awe and he could see the mountain they'd travelled through with its tunnelled pass just ahead. But they didn't dive to meet it.

Instead, they rode up its face and banked into a roll, just disturbing snow from its very pinnacle, and headed down its opposite face.

Eventually, Llorn drew in his wings and arrowed, heading for a cave-like opening in the snowy floor far below. His heart in his throat, Henry did likewise. The group hurtled into the deep crag with Llorn as the foremost spike in their trident, attacking an ever-increasing darkness.

Eyes streaming, ears deafened to all but the roaring wind, Henry held his speed. The dark relentlessly pressed in around them until with a last fading look to Llorn, Henry's sight was extinguished. There was nothing now but the force of air against his frame, the wind billowing in his ears.

Henry felt panic striking his senses. He counted to calm himself, occasionally looking left to right, eyes as wide as the wind would permit, but the others couldn't be seen.

All until a speck of brilliant white appeared below him. It began slowly, dressing their surrounds in a pale, faint glow. It was their exit, and throwing his neck forward he made a bid to catch his friends. Looking around himself now, he could see walls of thick branch rushing upward, a funnel of foliage with a welcome escape at its end.

Llorn called back for all to slow. With each in turn opening their wings, they began a wheeling descent. The exit was upon them. Henry narrowed his eyes to the light, though with his vision halved he clipped an overhang and tumbled branch over branch and out of the hole.

Talons swooped from the darkness and took him, crushing his frame so hard he could make no sound. Then gasping, he fell – *released* – onto a broad, flat branch.

Looking up, Henry saw an angry Llorn stood over him. 'Do you want us all killed?'

Henry coughed, choking for breath, hoping he wouldn't require an immediate answer. He wouldn't need to. Pluck touched down, followed by Gabriel.

She hit the ground running and got square up in Llorn's face. 'Get away from the bird, go on! He is only a young, Llorn-'

'Young. Human. It doesn't matter,' he said with equal aggression. 'We've got a job to do. We can't afford any mistakes.'

Pluck came close to Henry, still laid out, and began to look him over. She ignored the argument behind her, but for all her fussing, Henry found she only served to obscure his view.

'And might it be an idea to keep him in one piece?'

98

Henry fluttered upright. Ignoring Pluck's attentions he jostled between the pair, interrupting something about 'acting naturally'.

The pair stopped for a moment and looked at the young robin before them, flapping its wings and chirping excitedly.

'Please don't argue. I wasn't thinking.'

Llorn scowled at Henry. Gabriel scowled at Llorn. The pair looked set to go again. Pluck arrived, pushing Henry out of the way. 'Are you both stupid? Four birds, stood around. Arguing?'

Gabriel's frown stayed, then lifted. Llorn remained unmoved. He puffed up his chest and scrutinised the surrounding foliage. Apparently satisfied, he looked to the three. 'We were lucky. Stay quiet and wait here.'

The jayhawk's talons gripped a path over the branch. He stopped where the greenery thinned. Motionless but for his darting yellow eyes, Llorn looked every bit the predator hunting his next meal. A time of tense quiet passed.

Pluck was halfway through whispering mutinous grumblings into Henry's ear when Llorn began making his way back.

'I've found a run of stars and beyond, I'm certain, is Winter's Cut. That,' said Llorn, his eyes falling on Henry, 'is where you take over. Don't make this a waste of time.'

'He found his way to the very heights of Treetops,' said Gabriel, stepping up, 'right up from the White Plains and the Storm Ring. I think then,' she added coolly, 'that we are very lucky to have Henry.'

Llorn raised what could have been an eyebrow. 'Follow me now,' he said dismissively. 'And be sure to keep fair distance from each other; the exception being Pluck and Henry who'll fly together. Let's not forget,' he said again addressing Henry, 'to fly *naturally*.'

And with that he took flight, swooping low across the bed of lush pine needles, alighting far across. His head disappeared through a hole below.

Pluck huffed and pecked. 'Who does he think he is?'

'Come on,' said Gabriel, expanding her wings. 'If I could choose anyone to lead us on a mission it would still be Llorn. Now let's go.'

The three caught up with the jayhawk, his head still below level. The group waited. Llorn's head reappeared. 'Give me a minute,' he said, clicking his beak toward Gabriel, 'and you robins shall wait another minute after that before following me. We take the route orange by green by yellow by white. We'll regroup somewhere after that.'

Before they'd voiced agreement, Llorn was gone. Henry thought Gabriel might complain, but there was no word. She mimicked Llorn by passing her own head through the open hole in the foliage.

Again silence. Henry looked around, keeping his own check on any movement, but they seemed very well covered in this part of the tree. It was also a moment of peace, allowing him to realise again the beauty of the tree and its spiced, sappy fragrance. Gabriel re-emerged, bringing Henry back round.

'I have a few seconds. You remember the sequence of stars?'

The pair looked at each other before nodding.

'Okay,' said Gabriel, shifting and ready to drop. 'If you spy anyone, don't panic. Just keep flying. Llorn and I will be waiting.' Gabriel gave a final look below. She winked at the pair before disappearing.

A vacuum of silence followed. Though Henry had Pluck for company, he couldn't help feeling a little lost.

'Well,' said Pluck, stepping around the opening, her eyes scanning the void below. 'How're you feeling?'

'Good,' said Henry, though his demeanour said otherwise.

'Just remember,' she continued, her little round eyes dotting sideways, 'exactly why you are here.'

A quiet followed as Henry digested this. He thought of Lilly, his quest, the spider and Bear. But most of all he thought of his father. A small fire lit within him.

'Are we done waiting?' Henry joined Pluck's side. 'Is it time yet?'

'On the count of ten, we'll go. And Henry-' She placed a wing around him. 'Relax. It's not every day you get to be a bird, so let's try to have a little fun.'

And with that she fell forward into a long swooping dive. Henry, buoyed, followed her.

On the move again, the pair swiftly traversed the oncoming boughs and branches, flitting this way and that as only small birds can. Henry found tailing Pluck to be something of a discipline. As his skills in flying improved, so his appetite to race grew, but he managed to hold back, instead watching as casually as he could for movement around them.

Baubles swung past and distant lights played upon their surrounds. Still, Pluck flew on, a little erratically, but nevertheless she seemed to know where she was going. Henry followed over a great arc of rolling pine before they levelled into an open straight.

Pluck slowed to Henry's side. She spoke from the side of her beak. 'You see it?'

Henry couldn't miss it. In the darkness, the star burned like a setting sun. Gold, honey and amber. For a moment, Henry imagined a warmth that wasn't there. The pair drifted, freewheeling towards it, bathed in its splendour.

'She's beautiful,' said Henry.

Pluck nodded blissfully. Though danger wasn't far away, the pair could claim to be carefree; at least for now. They passed it reluctantly by, enjoying for a moment the faint song it sang.

Pluck flapped her wings double-time. 'That's one down. Come on,' she said, glancing back. 'I think I see the Star of Green.'

A pair of eyes followed from the shadows.

A perilous flight

Henry and Pluck found the Star of Green to be just as remarkable as its orange sister, as they glided a course through the expanse of limbs. It shone as a beacon of emerald, a green jewel set upon a cushion of lush foliage, saturating its surrounds.

Henry looked to Pluck, still flapping industriously, the green glow alight in her eyes. 'You've done well so far,' he said between breaths, but Pluck didn't answer. She seemed agitated.

They altered course to avoid an overhang; a bauble swayed gently across their path. Pluck slowed, falling back. Henry pulled into a turn and flapped a slow circle back to her. Pluck was hovering when he reached her, her left stained green, her right in shadow. She began to look urgently around. Henry drew up. He too began to feel instinctively edgy.

'Can you feel that?' she asked between wingbeats.

'I can't explain it,' said Henry, holding level. 'I feel... threatened?'

Giving a last look to their surrounds, Pluck dove off. 'Don't delay. Come on!'

The colours of the tree faded as the dark began to grow. In time the pair became shadows. They slowed, their eyes keen, threading a path as best they could.

It made Henry nervous.

He felt the tree was tightening around them, that each shadowy limb they passed was trying to grab at him, so his flight was interjected with a lot of jumpy manoeuvring. Pluck might've complained were she not lost in concentration.

The sound of their beating wings seemed amplified two-fold, echoing back from the darkness.

Whap-whap-whap-whap.

They altered course, light now a priority, and a great, dark bauble loomed out of nowhere. Twisting, they dove to avoid it. The bauble carried past leaving the pair unnerved. They moved on, slower, too spooked to make light of the situation.

Whap-whap-whap-whap.

The dark fingers of the tree bore into a bank and a tunnel of sorts, affording less room, the sound of their wingbeats coming back off the walls.

Whap-whap-whap-WHAP.

Henry was startled; his flight interrupted. Everything wound down to slow motion. Something flew with them.

Whap-whap-WHAP-WHAP.

No need to voice warning, both robins' wings became a blur. Something was upon them and it sounded big. His discipline discarded, Henry propelled like a bullet, matched by Pluck. Neither looked back – neither dared to – for to do so would cost them. Branches flayed them, needles spiked, the sting unnoticed.

WHAP-WHAP-WHAP-WHAP.

In Henry's mind, the nightmarish talons of some great, winged creature were beginning to open over him. Eyes closed, he beat those wings for all his worth, his lungs on fire. The chasing beats began to lessen. His eyes opened, but the fierce light of a star blinded him. Painfully, Henry adjusted to the shafts lancing the thinning branch. They gave Henry hope. They were near the third star.

And then it struck Henry. Pluck wasn't in front, nor behind. A tumbling crash of noise broke out from behind. Henry pulled up sharply and spun, looking randomly around.

A shriek of pain came up from a torn hole somewhere back. Without further thought, Henry made his way back to the opening and flung himself headlong through it. Twig and branch, broken and severed, followed needle and feather in freefall. Another cry went up, but it came from the pursuer, a tearing call of attack.

Henry shot clear out of the thick cover and into the open below. He looked around, blinking against the star's glare, and spied the desperate chase playing out. A snowy white bird of prey was closing on Pluck, twisting and mirroring its fleeing target. Henry made for them, arrowing his flight. Each time the attacker gained it threw forward its claws, but grasped only air, causing shrieks of rage and frustration.

Again and again the creature was upon Pluck, only to narrowly miss due to the robin's skill, but it wouldn't be much longer. Tiredness was overcoming

Henry's friend. Seeing his chance, Henry cut across their path and flew at the huge bird's head. Its eyes only on Pluck, the attacker saw Henry too late.

The robin's beak glanced a cutting blow, enough to spin the bird and make it reel in rage. Its target had changed.

It was enough to relieve the exhausted Pluck temporarily. Grabbing a branch, the ragged robin fought for breath, her wings leaden. It was time for Henry to fly, and with an enraged bird of prey on his tail he would have to be swift. With little time to think, he worked his wings as fast as he could. When the chasing beat of wings became all he could hear, he'd turn and dive, and fly hard away.

But it was little more than a delay, and twice he'd almost been caught. Spying his chance, Henry detoured back into the thick branch.

Up and down, left and right, Henry tore a reckless route; behind him was the crash and hiss of branch and twig – the closing sounds of his pursuer. A turn and then another unwittingly led Henry back into the open, and this time his wings had just about given as much as they could.

He beat a path toward the branches of pine far across, but the growing sound of wingbeats told him he wouldn't make it. An angry shriek rebounded around the clearing, but it hadn't come from behind. Henry opened one of his tight-shut eyes to see Llorn driving hard toward him.

This time the snow hawk saw. It let the chase go and diverted to meet Llorn. The two collided hard. The crack of feather and bone died beneath the bird's cries as they drove at each other, leading with their razor beaks and fearsome talons.

In the time it took for Henry to regain breath, the fight was done. The wounded hawk turned tail and fled, its foe too much, a fall of down-winding feathers in its wake.

Llorn let it go, the clash only slowing their mission, and alighted upon the nearest branch. He looked his wounds over and then turned to meet an anxious voice coming through the greenery. 'Pluck! Henry! Where are you?'

Llorn went back to tending a wing as the excited robin shot into the clearing looking frantic. Pluck called out, and then Gabriel was beside her.

'What happened? Are you okay? Where's Henry? HENRY?'

Henry raised a wing to indicate his position.

'We were chased,' gasped Pluck excitedly. 'And I would've been gobbled up like a raisin if it wasn't for Henry showing that snowy idiot a thing or two about flying-'

Henry shrugged.

'And then Henry became the raisin, but Llorn turned up just in time and sent that dumb bird packing. He'll still be hurting next week.'

Gabriel looked to Llorn, his head poking around his plumage.

'You got lost then?'

Henry fluttered down beside them.

'It wasn't exactly easy to follow, was it?' protested Pluck.

Henry agreed. 'We did our best.'

Gabriel eyed the pair with annoyance. 'I think the pair of you should thank Llorn for coming when he did, don't you?'

Before they could agree, Llorn landed heavily onto the branch the three shared, causing it to bow and sway.

'Fools!' he squawked, his glare hopping between the robins. 'The fate of Treetops lies in our hands, and all you do with that honour is take detours and play games with snow hawks!'

Gabriel didn't care what Llorn had to say. She was just pleased the jayhawk had been to hand when he was most needed. With nothing said in return, Llorn swept a long, lingering look over the group, and then he was up and away again, circling them overhead.

He called down. 'Time has been wasted; we must abandon caution. Follow me now and quickly!'

Gabriel nodded to the robins. 'Come on, let's go!'

Henry sprung off with Pluck just behind, muttering darkly. As the four flew, Henry gave a backward glance to the Star of Yellow. With his eyes accustomed to the light and the threat of death passed, he could appreciate its warm golden charm, if only for a few moments, as the four beat their wings toward the final star: the Star of White.

Phaedria's monster

All eyes were front. None strayed. The Coin Army stood ready, ready for inspection. The cavern was a sea of gold. Stalking their lines was a coin; a captain, overly busy with making sure that each shone, that each held a weapon, that none might cause problems. He cut back to the front, tucking a baton beneath his arm, hoping none noticed the stench of fear seeping from his every pore. The thick air in the cavern seemed to still. All present held their breath, for the Fallen Fairy could now be seen.

She stood at the far end, partially in shadow, her black robes lapping like snakes in the breeze. As her face entered the torch-lit gloom it drew darting glances from the ranks. Though her physical form was stabilising, her deathly white face jarred and moved. With each movement her eyes changed direction, making each coin under her gaze wobble slightly. She walked forward, a perverse delight upon her livid face. The Captain looked unnerved. He kicked his heels, swallowed, and took the few steps to meet her.

'My Queen, your army awaits-'

Phaedria stopped and stared at the Captain, who quickly side-stepped and stood to attention. It was only when she'd passed that he dared to dab at the chocolate secreting from his top. He hurriedly tucked the wipe away and scuttled to his master's side, though out of her immediate reach. Unconsciously, he closed his eyes and engaged in silent prayer.

As the Captain furiously whispered, he became suddenly aware of an ominous silence. He flicked open a startled eye and quickly realised he'd been foolish. But it was far too late to be undone. She ran a black tongue over her lips, the colour of dried blood. 'To whom do you pray?'

The Captain cleared his throat and fought to compose himself. 'My lady,' he blurted, dragging the dirty wipe across his face. 'I was asking only for safe passage and good luck on our march to Treelights.'

He looked at his master with wretched anticipation.

She took her eyes from him and let them preside over her awaiting army. Stepping forward, she stopped and brought her wand low. The ground tremored and swelled. Earth began to rise. She stepped to its rising centre until it settled as a hill. High enough to see all.

The Coin Captain joined the last of the tumbling earth at its base. Other than the spit and hiss of torches around the walls there was silence.

Drawing an unnaturally long breath, Phaedria appeared to grow. Her body elongated and her midriff thinned until she stood, near twice her usual height. Her arms, now thin and mantis-like, swung open. She spoke in a voice that sounded split between two people – one a rising shriek, the other dull and deep.

106

'Coins of the tree,' she cried, her fingers spidering the air. 'A new time is upon us!'

Her white-less eyes swept the cavern. 'The time of the Fairy Queen shall soon be at end, and we are many. And we are strong,' she continued. 'I now have powers that cannot be matched. They easily surpass anything Lilly has knowledge of, and still,' she roared, 'they grow!'

The approval of stamping feet and jostling weapons was interrupted by Phaedria's thrust-out arms. As the silence resonated, she looked along them to her fingertips. They twitched in response and she began to reduce back to her normal form.

'Such is the size of this army, so is the need for strong leadership.'

Like a black light, her eyes once again roved over all present. 'I have no doubt,' she said, sweeping an arc with her wand, 'that I have a Captain here who can command like no other.'

The Captain's chocolate-streaked face was a snapshot of horror – until he realised what had been said. He blew, and dragged the rag over his head, smearing his dark sweat, and unwittingly fashioned himself a kind of parted hairdo.

Straightening, he saluted. It took a huge collective effort from those who could see him not to laugh. One coin succumbed. The wand quickly switched hands. From a fierce blast, he exploded.

'As I was saying,' continued Phaedria as chunks of chocolate and gold rained down around the cavern, 'my Captain here has everything I seek. He is brave.' She leaned forward. 'He is fearless!' She straightened. 'And he is utterly heartless!' she cried, throwing her arms upwards.

The Captain, a little abashed, smiled. Then, remembering all the qualities his Queen saw in him, he quickly reverted to eyeing his troops with a steely gaze.

'But,' she said, holding a slender finger aloft, 'we have new blood among us. How can I be sure that my faithful Old Guard, my guard of a handful who joined me long ago, is still the best?'

The Captain, watching his troops, gave a jolt and looked to Phaedria. 'My lady-' he began, but she continued unhearing.

'As I look out tonight,' she bellowed, 'I see many. Strong. Smart. Mean. Come, captains-in-waiting. Show yourselves. Come show your mettle.'

At first there was no movement from the ranks, but then as one came forward, so did another, until four burly-looking guards had pushed through the many present and were stood waiting at their Queen's request.

She passed an eye over them. 'Four?' she asked. 'Only four with the ambitions of a Captain?'

The company of one group parted then, and a nasty-looking cock-sure coin came to the fore. He was batting the flat of a pine needle on his palm.

'Just five of you? Taking on the might of my Captain? Well, I'm afraid it's a non-contest.'

The Captain, who'd watched the mean rabble congregate before him, had been fearing the worst. But at hearing 'non-contest' he quickly feigned disappointment and swiped a fist through the air.

Phaedria blinked slowly. When her eyes opened, they rested upon her Captain. 'If we'd had six to face you, I'd have counted that a fair fight.'

The Captain shrugged.

Disappointed, Phaedria raised her head to speak, but a thought stopped her. She flicked her wand at the air, but nothing happened.

And then a strange, tinny, tearing sound lit the air and all eyes were drawn to beside her. To her Captain's horror, his golden casement was peeling away from him – top first, down and onto the ground, where it creased into a ball and rolled off. There he stood, not a scrap of armour upon him. His shock and bewilderment kept him rooted. His eyes swivelled to his master, begging an answer.

'Almost done,' she replied. From a pulse of her wand, she melted his right arm to a dripping, chocolate stump. 'There,' she said satisfied. 'Now the playing field is a little more even. My champion shall be unarmed, so to speak, such are his skills.'

She drew deeply in through her nose and cocked her head back. 'Let the challenge begin!'

The Captain didn't move. It was more of an execution than a battle. A hard-thrusting sword from the cocksure coin ended the Captain's life and career.

As he wiped the chocolate clean from his weapon, he looked down at the broken body of his former Captain and spat. The four gathered, stood back, affording him some room.

He looked up at his Queen. She studied him with smouldering delight. Stepping down from her platform, she walked among them. 'Four Captains,' she said. Flicking her wand, she bestowed a new mark of rank upon each coin as they stood.

Each regarded themselves with hushed reverence. She lowered her wand and continued pacing, eyeing the fifth. She stopped before him and cocked her arm awkwardly. As it shook, she closed her eyes and began a long-drawn breath. Anticipation built across her army. She forced her eyes so wide they were lidless, then thrust her wand forward. The coin fell to one knee, wracked with pain, his face contorting. He cried out – then screamed – but the scream became a bellow, in guttural defiance at the change coursing through him. His golden armour began popping and splitting as his bulk began to increase.

Pieces fizzed and pinged into the air until he was doubled, naked and breathing hard, knuckles clenched in the dirt. He suddenly looked up, causing all around him to gasp. His features, once the same as every other, were now mutilated and twisted. His once rounded body was now misshapen and disfigured; his eyes were shot a pale red.

He slowly rose, drawing more gasps. His size was more than twice what it was before. He stood, heaving, learning to breathe through his new frame while studying his powerful new arms.

Phaedria dropped her wand arm and slumped. When she eventually raised her head again, her features were hateful and joyous. She moved slowly towards him, inspecting her new monster. Nodding approval, she eyed him with lustful admiration.

Turning, she faced one of her new Captains and raised her wand tip, causing him to flinch.

'Take two guards and go rally those lazy mice in the mines. Have them gather enough gold to forge armour for my new champion.'

'Yes, my Queen.'

'Once they are done,' she added, 'kill them and the bear.'

The coin clicked his heels and nodded. 'Very good, my Queen.'

109

Grimm, Scrim and Eddy

The journey to the Star of White had been uneventful, though tough going. Llorn had set quite a pace. Henry was sure Pluck would've griped the whole way if her lungs hadn't been in such dire need of breath; in fact, all three were blowing hard when they finally came upon the silvery-white bloom of light.

It broke through the pine toward them like moonlight reeding through water, a welcoming lighthouse in the darkness.

Its wonder was partly lost on Henry, who'd been trying nervously to recount his journey up through the tree and was now wondering just how much use he'd actually be.

Llorn led the group to a shaded branch where they gratefully touched down. After scanning their surrounds, his eyes settled on Henry. 'This, human young, is where you take the lead. The upward flow from Winter's Cut begins over there.' Llorn indicated with his wing. His great feathered head came close until it filled Henry's vision. 'Don't mess this up.'

Gabriel held and Pluck bustled her feathers, but it was Henry who spoke first, clearly and unhurried. 'My name is Henry,' he said, meeting Llorn's piercing eyes.

Llorn's composure might've faltered for a moment. Henry wasn't sure, but his words drew no reprisal, and eventually Llorn turned away. Pluck was still smarting, and from a hop the little bird drew up behind Llorn and gave him a good peck on his behind.

Incensed, Llorn spun, one of his fearsome talons poised to strike, but Gabriel stood between them. Llorn froze, his leg held ready. Gabriel's expression wasn't so much one of anger or surprise, but sadness. 'Is it only now you've become a powerful bird that we see what a bully you've become?'

Llorn's eyes lost focus, as if pondering this for a moment. A weighty silence fell over the group. Showing a glimpse of what might've been regret, he slowly lowered his leg. His eyes narrowing, he addressed all as though the scene had never happened. 'My will is only to serve my Queen. I don't care for any friendship, and nor will I care if we ever meet again once this is done.'

Llorn's words fell on silence. Henry was a little saddened. As Llorn looked between each to see they'd understood, Henry had hoped that Llorn's attitude might've softened a little, that they might've all become good friends. He had, after all, saved his life.

Pluck broke the silence. 'That's fine with us, you big idiot,' she spat. 'I'll be glad when I can finally stop taking orders from you... you big chocolate dummy!'

Llorn merely looked at the little robin sour-mouthed.

'That's enough of that, Pluck,' said Gabriel, holding a wing across her chest. 'You will do everything Llorn commands without question. Do you understand?'

Pluck fought to articulate her feelings of injustice, but her beak eventually closed wordless, a look of simmering disquiet on her face. Gabriel folded the wing back to her side and looked coldly at Llorn. 'Let's get on with our job.'

Llorn kept his eyes upon Pluck. He turned to Henry, his eyes eventually following, and spoke. 'You will follow me down. We will skirt the upward draught until we draw level with Winter's Cut. From there you will lead. And you two,' he said to Pluck and Gabriel, 'keep up.'

Llorn leapt, his wings a flash, and propelled upwards. Henry had time only to roll his eyes before springing off after him.

'He's unbelievable,' laughed Pluck, shaking her head with exasperation. 'Really. How can one coin be such an idiot? Is he taking lessons?'

Gabriel said nothing as she watched Henry go. 'You'd better keep up,' she said sideways to Pluck, 'or I'll strip you of feather and make you walk home. Now come on!'

Henry, meanwhile, was doing his level best to keep up. Llorn had taken a route around the perimeter, staying with the shadows, soundlessly winging between the hanging green limbs. Every so often he'd disappear, causing Henry to panic, but he'd glide back into view, albeit briefly. It was only because Henry had a fix on Llorn that he knew where he was. To a casual observer he wouldn't have been there.

Just as things were looking up, Llorn vanished. Henry's little black eyes scanned. Llorn wasn't ahead of him, nor behind. He dove and rose, scouring the green needles, but found nothing.

Chiding himself, he was pulled into the darkness and gagged by a wing. As his widening eyes swung round, he was told with a look not to make a sound. Maybe Llorn had snapped, Henry thought. Perhaps they'd brought Llorn to the brink.

As Henry wildly pondered his final moments, he felt his head being forcibly turned to see something. Llorn eased his hold on Henry as the pair leaned forward to peer through a gap in the branch. From their vantage point they observed a star. It was so pale and pink in colour and light that it barely lit more than a few feet around it. The star was also moving fast. It looked desperate as it cut a weary route through the boughs of needles, obviously blindly fleeing something.

Henry's eyes, average for a young boy, wouldn't normally have penetrated the darkness following it, but with the eyes of a bird he saw the swift movements of three figures; each bounding, diving and leaping. Henry inched forward and squinted.

The three were coins – one with a dagger between its teeth and the other two with nets. As they sprung skilfully from limb to limb, Henry could clearly hear the complaints of one coin.

'How much longer is 'e out on recon?' griped the centre-most coin. 'E's no fool. I'll bet e's laid out on a bed o' green, catchin' *zzzz*'s an' takin' 'is time.'

The coin at the back of the group flew forward and struck his griping counterpart with the butt of his dagger smartly across his head. The coin stopped, pain and outrage across his golden face, but before he could voice complaint a voice carried back to him.

'I'm sick of your whining. If you don't personally net this one, then that star will be the end of you. I'll make sure of it!'

It didn't take long for the coin to choose from his options. He shook off the pain and leapt after them, cursing.

The weakening star, Henry saw, didn't really stand a chance. It broke out of the foliage and into an opening, covered by overhanging pine. Without the cover of branch they would soon have it. Henry looked to Llorn who was watching the scene with vague interest.

'We've got to help,' implored Henry, looking between the faltering star and Llorn. Llorn made no move. He continued watching as though he'd not heard.

'Aren't you going to help?' Henry cried, his eyes darting between Llorn's, searching for some semblance of concern.

'Help? Of course. My Queen owns these stars. They are her young.'

Henry followed his words and his heart warmed. 'I'm waiting for the right moment.'

Henry became more animated now as he watched the chasing coins closing on their prey.

'Stay here,' said Llorn. 'Oh, and Henry... make sure you do.'

With that, Llorn sprung through the hole and took swift and silent flight. Henry watched after him. He knew he couldn't keep his promise to stay put. He climbed out through the opening. Too much was at stake here; besides, Llorn could use an experienced pair of wings. Leaping, Henry took off after them.

Llorn, meanwhile, was making good progress. Though the three just ahead were leaping around like fleas, the scent of a star in their nostrils, his timing had been pretty good. He upped his speed to attack.

So close now, the coin with the dagger was nigh upon his prey. With its energy near spent, the star just ahead wasn't dodging anymore. It had only enough left to keep clawing forwards. It had become almost too easy.

A sudden gust howled through the tree, bringing the leading coin around, his bloodlust diluted. He stopped.

The coin cocked his head and sniffed. There was something else with them. The coins with him bounded past. He called for them to halt, but only one heard.

'Wassup?' the coin called back.

'Something is here,' he said, darting his eyes. 'Call Scrim. CALL SCRIM!'

But Scrim was deaf to everything, the threat of failure and death blotting all his senses. This star was his.

He leapt onto a broad bough. A quick look ahead told him he had a clear run of branch. Faint pink needled up through the blades just ahead. It was almost beneath him. He leapt after it, his net readied. The overhang would end soon, and timed right, he'd only have to release the net and *capture*! The star would be his! He smirked as he drew almost level above the pinky glow. Any... second...

He threw out his arm, but it pulled back the other way. And then there was pain. The coin turned and saw his arm caught in the beak of a great bird. Before he could voice a word or even register surprise, he was rising rapidly, hung by his useless limb.

The last thing he saw before he slammed at speed into a thick, unyielding branch were the vengeful yellow eyes of Llorn, watching him drop all the way.

The thud echoed back to the remaining two coins, who were ambling at a far slower pace, the chase out of their hands.

'You 'ear that, Grimm?' asked one, his voice a whisper.

Grimm didn't answer Eddy. He was watching the darkness ahead intently.

'I don't like it,' whined Eddy. Grimm drew up his dagger and looked along its edge. He turned it over as he spoke, the light catching its side. 'I don't think it's an angel we're dealing with,' he warned. 'Be on your toes.'

The pair sprang from sight, hidden among the green. Henry, meanwhile, was doing his best to find Llorn, but as he was learning, Llorn wasn't always easy to find. With no one in sight, he pulled up and alighted upon a small branch. The tree, he noticed as he adjusted his wings, was silent. There were no stars close by, and so there was no song, though faint colours dappled the surrounds. Henry wondered about Llorn. Would he be okay?

From what he'd seen him do already, Henry was sure there wouldn't be a problem. He thought to turn back. It was probably a good thing really that he hadn't caught up. If he went back, then Llorn would never know his command had been disobeyed. He'd probably have got in the way anyway. Consoled, Henry took off, retracing his route.

From beneath a dark overhang, two coins were waiting. Both were breathing as quietly as possible. A fluttering noise was coming toward them.

'This could be it,' breathed Grimm, fingering his blade. He cautiously eased back the branch and spied the small bird.

'Well?' hissed Eddy, his net poised.

'No,' said Grimm, allowing the branch to return. 'It's just a robin. Now keep quiet. Whatever it is will be along soon.'

Sure enough, as time passed the quiet was broken by another sound. It was another bird, only this time the wings sounded heavier. Grimm again eased back a part of the branch and held his breath. Through the narrowest of gaps he spied a jayhawk.

This bird was the one. Perfectly positioned, he readied himself. Grimm raised a hand to Eddy and began a countdown on his golden fingers, his eyes only on the bird. Almost beneath them, the last finger fell and the coins leapt from their perch to attack – but they stuttered. A shrill tweet from somewhere behind startled the pair. It was enough to alert the bird and upset the coins' timing.

Llorn pulled up as the net sailed by and the dagger missed – and he watched the pair plummet, grabbing frantically at the air. As one disappeared, amazingly the other became snagged, tangled in a branch far below.

The coin panicked and again fell, but his fall was stopped by the ends of four fingers. Henry joined Llorn's side.

The jayhawk's eyes followed down to the coin below. Just as Henry poised to ask what they'd do, Llorn spoke. 'Let's go and see,' he said, as though to himself, 'what our little friend is up to.'

Llorn wended slowly down, followed by Henry. They landed just over from the coin. Looking across, Henry fought to hide his surprise. The coin dangled still as a windless night from his left arm. His fingers were barely visible over the top of the branch that had prevented his fall. Henry saw the branch had split where it forked. It was a wonder it still held. Henry waited for Llorn's lead.

The large jayhawk, meanwhile, was making himself comfortable. He took a little time adjusting his talons around the branch they held, feathered his plumage and then rolled his head lazily round. Finally his eyes settled on the coin. Unblinking, the coin stared back.

'Well, well,' said Llorn.

Henry noticed Llorn now spoke English. It sounded bizarre. The effect seemed lost on the coin, who remained still, his eyes unwavering.

Llorn held them. 'What's a coin like you doing in this part of the tree?'

No answer. Llorn waited. He leaned further forward and continued. 'It looked to me as though you were... *chasing* something?'

Dangling from one arm, the coin said nothing. His eyes narrowed slightly. He adjusted his fingers, but it was obvious he couldn't pull himself up. The coin returned to his motionless state. A silence grew.

A creak – then a crack like a rifle – sounded. The coin dropped a few inches. Henry saw the branch wasn't stable. It would go sooner or later. The coin seemed to know this. He smiled miserably at Llorn.

'You see,' said Llorn, 'I can't let you go.'

The sickly smile left the coin's face. He measured Llorn and then spoke in a low growl. 'Think again, bird.'

Llorn couldn't help a little laugh. Dropping his head, he sighed. 'You know things that I need to know.'

The coin's features, Henry noticed, were faintly lined with curiosity but gave quickly to anger. 'What makes you think you can stop me, *bird*?'

He spat the last word as though it were an insult. 'I can fall a lot faster than you can fly.'

'That might be the case,' said Llorn, 'but I'm not your average bird.'

'Oh?' said the coin, his features spiteful. 'You look bird-like to me. I'm a dead coin anyway. I'll take great pleasure from denying you what you want. In a way I 'ave a dyin' wish.'

Another creak. Grimm's eyes drew to the fork. He lowered an inch and for a moment his eyes danced. Henry saw Llorn's eyes steel.

'You didn't catch any stars today, did you?'

Grimm eyed Llorn curiously. 'In fact,' he continued, 'you couldn't even catch that young pink one between... now how many was it?' Henry noticed Llorn raising the toes on his left talon as he counted. 'Three of you?'

The coin spat. Llorn followed the spittle down into the darkness. Bringing his head back, he went on. 'What's she like to work for?'

The question stung the coin. Henry knew Phaedria's operation was meant to be built on surprise. He could only guess how the coin felt, wondering how these two birds knew of his master.

'I've heard,' Llorn said, as though confiding a secret, 'that she won't tolerate failure. *Of any kind.*'

For the first time, Henry noticed the coin look at him, though just briefly. Doubt flickered in his eyes.

'Three stripes.'

Grimm looked at his arm. Henry could almost see his mind working. 'What would the punishment be for a Captain, I wonder?'

Grimm looked increasingly uncomfortable.

116

'I would guess,' pondered Llorn, rolling his eyes thoughtfully upward, 'that death would come very, very slowly to the Captain who'd lost two soldiers as well as turning up empty-handed.'

Grimm's arm began to shake. He glanced a look down, and then back up at his hand.

'I'll admit,' pressed Llorn, glancing down, 'that death in this way seems a far more attractive prospect.'

Grimm was slowly abandoning his show of defiance. Henry watched him grip and re-grip. He looked to the break in the branch, his breaths shallow.

Llorn had stopped talking.

Henry guessed correctly that the coin had finally made up his mind. Grimm held his breath. He went limp, closed his eyes, and let go. He didn't fall more than six feet before he had the wind knocked out of him.

The jayhawk had struck perfectly, having orchestrated the moment, his talons imprisoning the coin. They plummeted into the darkness below. Henry froze and held. *Silence.*

Then through his wide, black eyes he saw Llorn soaring back up, his claws clasping Grimm. He swooped low over the branch Henry stood on, threw open his wings and landed, releasing the coin. Grimm cowered. The sight of Llorn over him was truly fearsome.

'I told you-' said Llorn in enraged tones, 'that there are things I *need* to know.'

The coin, witless, could only manage a whimper. He looked a million miles from the defiant coin before. He stared up at Llorn and shrank away. 'Wuh... what makes you think I'll tell you anything?'

Henry was sure he'd formed the word 'bird' to go on the end of the sentence, though it was too softly spoken to hear if he had. Llorn's eyes began to widen. He inhaled long and hard, his chest swelling. Grimm looked like he was shrinking. His beady golden eyelids creased closed.

The jayhawk's head coiled back and his beak opened wide – only to exhale. Grimm's eyes rolled. Henry thought he might faint.

'You know,' said Llorn, airily observing the tree. 'I never tire of the fragrance of pine. Funny that.'

Grimm, his face screwed up tight, opened an eye. The coin struggled with himself to revert back to who he was. 'Enough!'

117

Llorn, who'd been vacantly gazing around the tree, stopped whistling. He had been pleasantly surprised to find that he could. He looked back at Grimm, having momentarily forgotten he was there.

Grimm grimaced and continued, albeit in a much quieter tone. 'What,' he eased carefully from his mouth, 'are you plannin' to do... with me?'

Llorn gazed down at the coin. Grimm smiled weakly. 'I thought that was clear. I want you to tell me where your Queen is, what she is up to, and how many her army numbers.'

'I... I don't really know anything.' He wrung his hands in apology.

'Really?' said Llorn, his expression rising.

'Yes.' Grimm's reply was unconvincing.

Henry thought of Bear then. He'd been quiet up to this point, letting Llorn deal with the coin, but he wouldn't have him lie, especially as his friend was in danger.

Chirruping, he told Llorn he was lying. The coin was startled at Henry's outburst. He looked worried and confused for all he had heard were tweets and twitters. 'What did he say?'

Nodding, Llorn listened, all the time eyeing Grimm. 'He agrees with me,' said Llorn finally.

'So...' said Grimm, eyes flitting between the birds, 'what does that mean exactly?'

'It means,' said Llorn, 'you are lying.'

Grimm gulped. 'If I was lyin' – not that I am, mind – what would 'appen to me exactly?'

Llorn considered the coin for a moment. 'It would mean you'd be coming with us.'

Grimm looked like his brain was aching. He held his head in both hands. '*Where* would you take me?'

Llorn's eyes smiled. 'To see your Queen of course!'

Henry saw a bead of chocolate running from the top of the coin. It coursed between his furrowed brow and dripped off the end of his broken nose. His eyes had darkened. 'Why would you do that?' he croaked.

'Oh, I'm sure she's keen to know how your little mission is panning out,' said Llorn distractedly, observing his wings. 'You could fill her in.'

118

Grimm was a sight. Chocolate dripped from his brow. His eyes blinked away the thick runs; his mouth opened and closed. Although Grimm hadn't responded, he didn't need to – his appearance was doing it all for him.

Llorn straightened up. The time was right. He stepped over to Grimm, and as he did so Henry saw he appeared far less fearsome.

Llorn lowered to speak. 'You know, we don't have to take you to her.'

Grimm looked up at Llorn, his eyes hopeful, his face a mess of chocolate. 'Really?'

'Well,' said Llorn, looking between the coin's eyes, 'you would have to do something for us.'

'What's that then?'

Llorn's expression hardened. 'First, three answers to three questions.'

Grimm's head dropped. He raised it again. 'What would the birds 'ave me tell?'

Llorn leaned forward. 'You know the questions.'

Grimm pondered. His frown told of a warring mind. His features receded.

Decided, he spoke. 'Phaedria ain't... well, she ain't complete. She needs stars. To 'elp 'er, you see.' Grimm paused. 'She's got a base,' he continued. 'She made us. Brought us alive with magic.' He looked up to Llorn. 'She controls us.'

'Where is this base?'

The coin scanned his surrounds. 'Deep down in the Tree. Beyond Winter's Cut. There's a sequence... a sequence of stars.'

'Is he telling the truth, Henry?'

Henry came over. 'Ask him about Bear,' he said.

The coin looked less startled this time. His eyes rolled up to Llorn resignedly. 'What's 'e askin'?'

'The bear,' said Llorn. 'Is he alive?'

Grimm rubbed his chin and thought. 'He was alive when last I saw 'im, but-'

He paused, throwing a sideways glance at Henry. 'I couldn't say for sure what e's doin' now.'

'Where is she now?' Llorn continued.

'You swear you won' take me to 'er?'

Llorn nodded. Grimm spoke, his eyes dark. 'She's about to lay siege to Treelights...'

Llorn and Henry exchanged urgent looks. The jayhawk pressed on. 'How soon and with how many?'

The coin made a face. 'Probably a day away. Maybe two, and with too many to count.'

Llorn came quickly round. 'Henry, meet the others as fast as you can. Fly in that direction.' He brought a wing back. 'Fly for a short while; they'll be there. Tell Gabriel what you know; only the facts. Then do as she says, understand?'

'Got it,' he said, turning to fly. He held, struck by a thought. 'But how would you find the base?' His round little eyes were vacant. 'And Bear?' Henry rounded on Llorn, animated.

Llorn's made calming motions with his wings. 'Don't worry,' he said coolly, indicating to the coin.

'I have myself a guide.'

Captain Bale

'Okay, Grime,' said the freshly-appointed Captain Bale. He placed a hand upon his opposite's shoulder. 'You're relieved.'

The coin gave a mildly surprised grunt, then a nod. He rose from his stool and stretched. He gave a last glance to the workers as he prepared to depart the low, dry tunnel, and wondered if it would be his last.

He bent and picked up a half-finished mug of something and shuffled off, muttering a farewell to a pair of coin guards on his way out.

Captain Bale stepped forward into the crackling torchlight, the flames liquid gold in the sheen of his casing. His eyes swivelled from mouse to mouse, until they stopped upon the one who was different. They narrowed and stayed so.

Bear, tatty and dirty, blackened around his eyes and looking worn almost to his stuffing, met the look.

The Captain motioned the guards to him. There was a hushed conversation and nodding. With the meeting concluded, the pair marched briskly to the mice, who'd begun to cower, and waded into the pack. Two were selected. The coins dragged them into a wavering pool of light at the feet of their superior. The mice rolled their eyes upward, expecting death, but they were wrong.

They survived the brief flaying, though it brought squeaks of protest from their fellows. Captain Bale quelled the noise with a fresh bite of his whip. He took a step forward, casually coiling the length to a hoop, his eyes passing over the weary crowd. Most tensed when he finally spoke.

'I am not a coin to make speeches, and I believe actions speak louder than any words, so I'll keep this short; mine me enough gold to encase five... no, six coins. If you haven't by the time I return...' His eyes pulled left to right. 'Well,' he laughed. 'You'll find out.'

The mice looked sick. Captain Bale spun smartly and strode to the stool. An hourglass was produced and placed on the seat for all to see. 'You have-' he said, turning the timer and motioning his hand, '*so* long.' He smiled, stepped into the cage and departed for topside.

There was a heavy silence as the crowd of two dozen or so mice studied the tumbling sand. The guards settled either side of the exit. Many mice now cradled the groaning pair in the dirt and carried them over to a nook in the stone wall.

Bear watched with concern. His eyes ran to the guards, then the hourglass. They finally rested upon the wretched and weary mice all around him. In his time with them he'd earned a deserved respect. He'd produced the work of three mice consistently, covered for those who'd fallen from exhaustion, and had kept their spirits up. They'd seen him as a kind of leader and if ever they needed one it was now. With raised paws and with an urgency in his voice he spoke. 'Mice, we have work to do!'

The mice mobilised, scampering off into the gloomy tunnels. Bear worked them like a ship's captain. He streamed orders, grouped teams and helped organise the distribution of tools. They'd never moved so quickly or been so keen. On occasion, Bear would return to the opening, his eyes straining to the stool and the hourglass.

As he guided a group to their station, he held back one of the mice. He'd become a confidante and a friend. His name was Morris.

'Morris,' said Bear, holding the shoulder of the mouse. 'We've got to talk.'

Bear led his friend off through one of the low winding tunnels, ducking here and climbing there. He slapped the backs of mice as he passed, spurring them on, until much further on, and holding a torch he'd taken from a wall, he stopped his friend at a break in the passage.

'Here,' said Bear. He checked behind to make sure they were alone.

'Why are we here?' asked Morris, confused.

Bear turned to him, bringing the torch up, his furrowed brow lined in shadow. It did nothing to settle his friend.

'Bear?' asked the mouse. 'Why aren't we working?'

Heaving a sigh, Bear spoke. 'What's been asked of us is impossible.'

Morris's paws at his side began clasping. He fidgeted uncomfortably trying to form a question, his mouth pursed. 'But if we work – harder than we've ever-'

All the time Bear was shaking his head.

Morris advanced and grabbed his fur. 'Are you sure? There's no way?'

Bear said nothing. Just the gentle lapping flame and the dull knock of rock-fall intruded the silence.

'We have to talk alternatives,' said Bear, running his eyes over the tunnel's roof as though hoping to spy a huge chunk of something golden.

'Alternatives?' yelled Morris, gulping like a fish. '*What* alternatives?'

Bear leaned back to look up the tunnel, hushing his friend at the same time.

'Bear.' Morris re-gripped Bear's fur. 'What else could we possibly do?'

Bear ran a paw over the back of his neck. 'We could rush the guards,' he suggested.

Morris frowned, releasing Bear. 'That would be suicide. And you know it. We could,' he said, rubbing his whiskers, 'overpower them if we rushed them. But we'd never get beyond the last of her army.'

Bear lowered his torch and stared hard at the wall.

Something ran through his stuffed head that made his big amber eyes light up. A grin stole over his face. 'Tell the mice to stop.'

Morris's features rearranged to dark concern. 'Bear?' The mouse searched his friend's eyes. 'What are you talking about?'

Bear played out a scene inside his head. Morris groaned.

'Tell the mice to stop mining,' said Bear, patting his friend on the shoulder. 'We are going to dig our way out of here instead.'

Morris struck blank. Then his mouth pulled to a mischievous smile. 'Y'know,' said the mouse, shaking his little white head, 'for a toy with a headful of stuffing, you can be quite bright.'

'Let's put those little noses to work,' said Bear. 'Sniff out soil. Roots too-'

'And we'll keep up the pretence of mining,' said Morris. 'We can post lookouts.'

Bear replaced the torch in the wall. 'Get the message to every-mouse. Come on, let's get to it.'

And they worked their way through the tunnels, the new instruction quietly passed on. Bear agreed to create as much noise and diversion as possible, by way of shouting orders and drumming up work-song to cover anything unusual from the tunnels. Mice barrowed piles of rubble to go topside, as all the while the guards merely laughed at their enthusiasm.

All seemed well for a time, but time came forward at a quickening pace. The tumbling sands fell. They took up more and more of Bear's attention as he helped unload the rocks.

No call had gone up from the mice. No signal had been given. The songs had left Bear now. He made off up the tunnels, and at their endings he found mice scampering, climbing, sniffing and digging. Barrows carted rock, hefted by mice, straining and shuffling towards the entrance, as Bear hurried them along, helping here and there.

Taking a barrow, he jogged back to the mouth of one tunnel to find the guards easing their backs off the wall. Bear upended his load and took a look at the timer as the final grains slid off the glass walls and settled below.

The guards were conversing. Their eyes weren't upon each other, or the work going on before them. Both were instead scrutinising the hourglass through squinted eyes. One crouched to draw level, announced something, then rose. Bear watched with dread as the guard turned, nodded to the other and signalled up for the cage to be lowered. Time, it seemed, was up.

Some of the mice had noticed the occurrence and ground to a halt, then more and more slowed and stopped. Bear gathered them back up the tunnels, waking them from their daze, pushing them off in different directions, telling them to abandon their carts.

'Come on!' said Bear, clapping his dusty paws and fixing all with blazing eyes.

He began pulling rocks from a pile as the mice swung little picks, until Morris tugged at his fur.

He led his friend back to a dark point of the tunnel. 'I've seen the hourglass,' he said, his eyes lined with dread. 'You must know in your heart-of-hearts this is pointless now.'

Bear looked to the mice, then to Morris, and he slumped. Time had forced Bear's final option. Taking Morris with him, they walked back to the tunnel's opening to spy the guards watching the cage descend, their fingers drumming on the hilts of their blades. Bear's eyes lowered and he began pitching around.

A pickaxe lay in the dust. He picked it up and turned it in his hands to familiarise himself with it, gauging its weight. He looked back to the guards, now holding the cage, guiding their captain inside to a halt.

Bear looked at Morris, his mouth a grim line. The mouse gave an eventual nod.

'We'd best get everyone together.'

The pair took the walk back up the tunnel, ushering mice as they went. Morris diverted into other openings, calling for all to come at once, and many scampered here and there rounding up the workforce. Eventually satisfied all were present, Bear broke the news.

'Mice,' he said over the heads of the many gathered. They were tightly packed, sardined into the rocky tunnel. An occasional mouse held a torchlight high, lighting dusty, tired faces, all rising and twitching, trying to see and hear what was going on.

Bear raised his paws, Morris close by his side. 'Your efforts have been valiant,' he began, his eyes roving over them. 'But I'm afraid it was all for nought.'

There was a lot of uneasy movement. Most looked confused. Some conferred.

All awaited Bear's address.

'We've really got no choice now.'

'Just what are you trying to say, Bear?' squeaked one mouse, her little paws to her throat.

Morris came forward and clambered up onto a pile of rubble up to Bear's height. 'We have to fight.'

From a brief silence came gasps and open mouths. Some put their head in their paws while others flatly refused. Just a few seemed resigned to what had been said. Bear ordered silence and got it.

'Any left in the tunnels,' he said to the nearest group, 'go and bring them out. And bring back every tool you find along the way.'

The mice padded off over dust and rock to summon the others from the tunnels.

Then came the sounds Bear feared the most; they were the sounds that made every-mouse's head pop up and turn to the source. It was a clamouring sound that quickly built to a raucous din, rolling and echoing off the walls. Great circles of shimmering golden light rode over the ceiling, lighting up the tunnel.

Every-mouse looked carved from stone.

125

Bear strode off to the tunnels, calling for all to come quickly. Morris did the same. As the mice returned with pickaxes, they stopped open-jawed. Bear and Morris pulled them through, shaking the shock from them, telling them to arm everyone.

With near every tunnel clear, Bear wended his way through the crowd to the fore with Morris eventually joining his side.

Bear cast around the crowd, perhaps hoping to see an army straining at its leash, perhaps to inspire himself, to kid himself that they might stand a chance. But all he saw were the frightened and disorganised bodies of some bedraggled and dusty mice. A few held weapons but they held them low, like heavy bags of shopping.

And there they were: as wide as the opening would allow and as deep as the passage was long, all gleaming gold, all ready to deal death. Stepping out from the front line was Captain Bale.

He sauntered into the breach between the two groups, making only brief eye contact with the miners until he stopped at the stool and joined his hands behind his back. He bowed a little, observing the hourglass, then continued down until he could see it clearly. He feigned surprise and gave a little laugh. Rising casually, he held the glass and looked into it, tapping its side. His eyes swung over to the meagre efforts of the mice's work before tossing the hourglass onto the dusty ground at Bear's feet, where it spun before stopping. Bear looked up to see the captain cocking a leg onto the stool. He unhooked his whip and turned the handle over, feeling the leather with his fingers. His interest seemed elsewhere. It made for a good show.

'You didn't quite succeed,' he said, his eyes leaving the whip. He smiled thinly. 'Pity.'

Bear drew a leg back. 'You never wanted us to succeed!' he yelled. Kicking the hourglass, he sent it flying. Captain Bale had to duck; the glass smashed off the roof of the tunnel, showering his cowering entourage.

'Steady now,' said the Captain, brushing fragments from his person as he brought himself upright. 'We don't want any nasty injuries... well, not *just* yet.'

'What are you waiting for?' demanded Bear. 'We know your intentions.'

Turning on his heel, Captain Bale turned to face him. His troop were having fun. He creased a smile, but his eyes didn't follow.

'I like you, Bear,' said the Captain.

'I'm afraid I can't return the compliment,' sniffed the furry toy.

'Most of all though,' he continued, eyeing Bear with a slant, 'I like your *coat*.'

Realisation dawned on the mice. Some gasped in disgust, some darkened with anger – Morris in particular. His shoulders were hunched, his breaths shallow. Bear, however, remained impassive.

'Now, you'll probably have guessed why we are all here,' continued the Captain, lazily running a finger over the low tunnel's ceiling.

'Well, I don't recall asking for any spare change, so no.'

Captain Bale laughed theatrically and then resumed his line of questioning – his face deadpan. 'You want to be a comedian?' he asked. 'Perhaps we could have you entertaining the troops, or...'

A torch spat and flared, dispelling the silence.

'Why...' asked the Captain, stepping forward, 'not be a "hero" instead?'

A mouse two lines back sided a paw to his mouth. 'Don't even consider it, Bear. Don't you dare!'

Bear's eyes strayed a little sideways. He was thinking.

'Come on, Bear.' Captain Bale took another step, his arms spread in appeal. 'The others won't have to suffer.'

He came close enough to touch Bear; in fact, his hand started forward but it stopped and returned, shaking slightly. It made every-mouse stir with unease. Instead the coin leaned forward, his lids halving his eyes. He spoke as though intoxicated, in a quiet faraway voice.

'It would look so nice draped over me. Set me apart from the other captains. I wouldn't want it torn, no, no.' He stepped carefully back two steps, his senses seemingly returned. 'Think about it. I'll give you one minute.'

A strange, gurgling cry wrought the air. It was coming from a broad mouse named Charlie – a respected and hard-working tunneller. His eyes glazed, his chest full, he stepped robotically forward and shot an arm into the air.

It held a pickaxe.

'Think about this!' he yelled, swinging the axe into the chest of Captain Bale who had watched him thus far with strange amusement.

127

The coin rocked back onto his heels. He grabbed at the air and then steadied himself, aided by the coins behind him. Time stilled. The flaming torches licked and lapped.

Captain Bale's eyes slowly rolled up into his head. He fell backward where he spun a quickening circle, until he lay flat and still. For a moment, nothing happened. Then, many whips cracked the air, cutting Charlie. He stayed upright but tottered; a gust of wind would have felled him.

Bear and the mice stood aghast. A twig spear was finally run through Charlie, finishing the mouse before any could reach him. He upended, skewered, resting awkwardly on the twig. He was gone.

The sight of one of their own, a mouse of standing, impaled halfway to the ground brought a mixed reaction. Some fainted, some squeaked. Some just stood numb. In others though, it brought the fight straight to them. Some charged forward, blind rage flaring their nostrils, but they were quickly stopped.

Bear stood in the breach, shoving them back, holding them off. He calmed them, telling them he had the solution.

When the commotion had stilled enough, Bear turned to face the coin army. If their captain had meant something to them, it didn't show. If anything, their mood was improved. A hateful glee stained each of their golden faces; perhaps now because there were no rules. No order.

Bear considered their fallen comrade. With great restraint, he straightened and faced them. 'Take me,' said Bear, stepping forward, 'but please-' he implored, his paws wide in appeal, 'don't harm the rest.'

A second passed, then uproarious laughter filled the cavern. Coins propped against each other, aching with laughter. As the last of the groans died, a common soldier coin spoke out. 'You think you could stretch to clothing us all?' More laughter. 'Oh no,' he said, wiping a chocolate tear. 'We want you all.'

The last of the hubbub died down. Bear's eyes flashed to the pickaxe lying spiked through their captain. A heavy silence grew. A soft padding sound intruded, coupled by short breaths.

'Roots!' a voice gasped.

Every head turned.

128

Stood at the mouth of one of the lesser-mined tunnels was a blackened, weary mouse. He leaned against the tunnel's wall, blinking, his eyes adjusting to the glow of gold. 'I've found...' He couldn't finish the sentence. Instead his bloodshot eyes widened with disbelief.

'Roots...' he muttered. It was the spark that lit the powder-keg.

Bear lunged at the axe, unseating it, and swung wildly at the first line of coins. 'GO!' he bellowed, slashing across a coin's face then bringing it hard into another. The mice gathered quickly and made for the tunnel mouth, taking the dazed root-finder with them.

Around half a dozen stayed to join the fray, charging the line, blindly scything the air with whatever tools they held. The surprise and speed of the attack caused the coins' frontline to retreat, almost comedically, but they could go nowhere. They were packed so tightly that some were cut down.

The coins behind them were trying to push forward. As the frontline broke and fell, so the oncoming rush began trampling the fallen, their casings buckling and creasing underfoot.

A new line hastily formed. The fighting opened out. A coin fell. A mouse was halved clean by a blade.

'Back,' yelled Bear as he striped the eye of a coin, partially blinding him. 'Head for the tunnel. Now!'

The remaining handful, still fighting, began backing up until they could turn and break for the entrance. Bear followed last, holding two coins at bay before turning heel to run after them. A roaring monster of noise crashed around the walls after him. Puffing hard and torn in places, Bear swiped a torch from a wall and plodded hard for the entrance. Two of the mice he'd seen battle with were stood in the tunnel's mouth, willing him on.

As he neared, they disappeared inside. With hell on his heels, Bear ran into the opening but stopped and turned, wildly brandishing his pickaxe and torch. Amazingly, the surging coins came to a clattering halt.

For the second time another breach was formed, only this time Bear was all that stood on the other side, his face fierce and resolute. He shoved and pushed the mice back, telling them to go on, not to join his side. A moment of confusion fazed the coins, but it quickly passed.

Their prize stood before them. Bear's intent was all too obvious. They grinned at his foolishness and they came on as one, firming grips upon their weapons.

'Not on your own, Bear!' yelled a mouse trying to round him. 'We'll stand with you!'

'There isn't time to dig our way out!' shouted another, trying to edge past. 'You can't hold them!'

Bear spun and roared, his eyes wide with a madness. 'Go! Leave me and dig!' he snarled.

The coins' grins widened. A whip-crack and the torch was loosed from Bear's paw, where it guttered on the dusty ground and died. The tunnel's darkness intensified. Shadows lengthened.

In the half-light of the opening, Bear switched the tool he held from paw to paw and readied himself. He gave one last look to the advancing army and brought his pickaxe back.

'Goodbye,' he said simply – and then heaved his axe upward into the rocky overhead lining. It gave just as the coins arrived, too late to stop the tumble of boulder and rock sealing the opening.

Questions

Dust rose as the avalanche of rock finally settled. Every coin doubled, sputtered and coughed.

From the fallout Phaedria appeared, her eyes protective slits. She surveyed the wheezing sorry mess and snarled. 'What happened?' She wrenched a coin from the floor, his feet dangling. 'I asked a question; answer me quickly if you want to live.'

The coin drew breath, but the air was dusty and he spluttered and drooled. She'd heard enough.

Dropping the coin, Phaedria stepped back. 'Kill him,' she ordered to a dusty, blackened coin who had only just recovered. A moment came and passed.

The blackened coin spied a pine blade and clasped it, before raising it to examine its edge. His shadowy eyes slithered to the protesting coin now sprawled on his behind. 'At once,' he replied.

It was from the third blow that the coin on the floor stopped moving. The cavern immediately silenced with only a few still retching or choking, their watery eyes vivid from what they'd just witnessed.

'I'll ask again.' Phaedria's dark, blazing eyes hopped from coin to coin. They stopped and stayed upon the nearest soldier. On cue, the coin quickly spoke. 'The mice seem to have escaped.'

'Kill him,' said Phaedria again to the coin, who seemed to be taking to his new role of executioner with relish.

It took a while for the writhing Coin to die, a single wound deep and eventually fatal ending his career as a soldier. The dust-blackened coin stepped back and wiped his sword clean, taking a moment to admire his handiwork. He returned to her side, his eyes wild and alive.

The coins began to rearrange themselves backwards as discreetly as possible. Some turned slowly sideways in a bid to become invisible. An air of expectancy could almost be touched. There were more questions that needed answering.

'Tell me,' demanded Phaedria, scattering the silence, again to the coin nearest to her. 'Where is the Captain, the Captain I appointed?'

The coin wrung his features. He looked left to right before meeting her weighty stare. 'Me?' he mouthed, a trembling hand at his chest.

Before the nod of confirmation came the heavy flat of a sword on his head, knocking him unconscious. It continued to batter him until it withdrew, straightened, and finally pushed through his casing. Stepping back, the blackened coin wiped the chocolate from the sword onto his thigh. He glanced at the body before turning to his master, like a dog seeking approval.

Phaedria sighed, confounding her luck. She raised her wand and reduced him slowly and painfully into a molten, golden-brown heap.

'Once more,' continued Phaedria, side-stepping the bubbling puddle. 'What-'

'But my lady!' gasped a coin bowed desperately low, interrupting her. 'By the time we've managed to tell you what happened, more than half of us will be dead.'

Glowering hatefully, the Fallen Fairy approached the kneeling coin. She rose up, her wand tip between forefinger and thumb. 'A good point,' she noted wistfully, letting the wand go limp in her fingers. She twirled it, mulling things over and then pointed the wand at the coin. A mark of rank seared into his chest.

'We have ourselves a new Captain,' declared Phaedria. 'But...' She moved close to the coin. 'Make another unprompted suggestion and I shall peel you from your casing and feed you piece by piece to my wolves. Other than that, I wish you luck. I only hope for your sake that you outlive your predecessor.'

The Captain digested this and bowed his head.

'I think,' said Phaedria after a brief assessment, 'that that shall do for loss of life today.'

An army of shoulders relaxed.

Stowing her wand, Phaedria's eyes rested on the walled-off tunnel entrance. 'I see now what has happened,' she said, nodding. 'Consider yourselves fortunate as my mood is improved. Any other day and a river of chocolate and gold would run through this tunnel. I'm confident you won't fail me again.'

She turned to leave, but paused and raised a finger. 'Just one more thing. I have need for just one more coin, their armour clean. Shining, in fact.'

Not needing any further encouragement, a coin began shoving his way through the ranks to stand gleaming and proud before his master, a broad smile upon his face.

'Yes,' she said, looking him up and down. 'You'll do.'

She pulled her wand and melted him into a buckling, screaming heap until he lay as liquid, a puddle within an increment on the floor. 'I think five casings should be enough. Captain, have them stripped, melted and forged. My champion will need armour.'

She strode off, but paused and turned. 'Oh, and Captain. Have that tunnel cleared for his arrival. You have some mice to catch and a bear to bring before me. Don't make me have to go back on my good word again.'

Her new Captain, hand shaking, saluted as best he could.

*

On the other side was silence, but for a cough. Bear coughed again and tried to move, but every part of him was pinned and trapped. In the small gap around his head, he could see nothing and hear nothing. His taste though seemed to be working perfectly, as his mouth spat in disagreement with its dusty, dry content. He strained to move again but only his head could. Bear lay and groaned with resignation.

There was a sound. Again. A muffled, hollow sound of rocks knocking over one another. It was growing closer.

Air vacuumed around his face and suddenly there was an orange glow and noises. The noises grew into voices with the words: 'Found him! Found him!' recurring louder and louder. Eventually all he saw were the faces of many mice.

'It's lucky you've got no bones to break,' said a voice with a squeak of laughter. 'Though you may need re-stuffing,' offered another, earning a small cheer.

Carefully, Bear was brought back to his feet, shouldered by two mice acting as crutches.

'We thought we'd lost you,' said a mouse Bear remembered as Tom – a worker of real note in the mines. From beneath the spit and hiss of a torch Tom held, the tunnel came into view. Beyond the small party around him was fevered activity. A chain of mice shifted rocks. It looked as though they'd been busy.

'The roots,' mumbled Bear. 'Are they digging towards them?'

'We've had reports of a damp smell of soil,' remarked one. 'It shouldn't be too long now.'

Bear tried a step forward. His head was a bit wobbly.

'Easy now,' said the mouse propping him up. 'We've got this part in hand. You take a seat by this wall and rest. Dorothy here will patch you up as best she can.'

Bear was eased down as a slight but kind looking mouse approached and began tidying some loose stitching behind his ear. She dusted and fussed – and then laughed with exasperation. 'Are you sure you're a teddy bear? Out there you looked more *grizzly* to me.'

Bear sighed. 'I do hope Henry is getting on okay,' he said more to himself than anyone else.

Start the damn engine!

An old song was struck up by one and then all. They cared not that the coins might hear; such a sound could only dampen their spirits and it lifted around the walls and ceilings. The song sang of better times, of loved ones and home. Bear might've sung too but he could make no sense of the high, warbling notes drifting into his ears.

The song helped morale and kept up a good tempo. Even the rocks that bobbled from mouse to mouse had been progressively shrinking. And then the line stopped and so did the song. Each looked to the mouse beyond. The rocks had stopped coming. Anxiety grew. The tunnel in turn echoed silence. Torches, dotted here and there, were raised.

And then with a start every-mouse turned, hearing the sound they'd all but forgotten, their faces long with dread.

A chink. Another chink. A rock falling. Voices. Coins. They were close. But another noise sounded, and it brought every head back round again.

Three mice were struggling to stop one of the few heavy work carts laden with soil and rock, now rolling and gathering pace down the tunnel. Those in its path scampered clear, while others threw rocks beneath it, but to no effect.

With four timber wheels squealing, the cart pitched, listed and grazed a wall, losing two passengers with just a final mouse clinging topmost.

With whiskers blown back and through the scattering soil he spied Bear, made a decision, and leapt – flattening the soft toy. Both slowly raised their heads to watch the cart thundering toward the rock-sealed entrance. At that moment, a part of the blockade fell.

A coin appeared to be scrambling through a hole on his hands and knees. He heard the deafening noise and looked up quizzically – just as the cart struck a boulder, somersaulted and ejected its load at the coin, burying him instantly.

Every-mouse held their breath, each a statuesque depiction of what they'd last been doing. Bear peeled the mouse from him and slowly rose to survey the silent wreckage.

'Seems their hole is plugged again,' he said to the gathering rodents, all twitching and sniffing around the soil and rock.

'It appears so,' said Morris, sidling up. 'But that won't hold them for long. C'mon,' he said, nudging the other mice with his nose back up the tunnel. 'We've got work to do.'

Bear skipped around the ragged exodus headed back up the tunnel with Morris in tow, harrying the mice and urging them onward until they were each alive with urgency.

A call came down, faintly echoing around the walls.

'Not long,' said a mouse, appearing in a pool of torchlight before them. 'Not long now.'

He raised onto his hind legs and worked the soil and dust from his paws before lowering again, trembling and exhausted.

Bear hurried past him, unseating a torch from the wall as he went. At the far end, the mice were gathered, each doing their part to clear the ejection of soil scuffing out of a small hole in the rock.

Bear pushed through the furry bodies and brought his torch to the opening. 'Are we there yet?'

A mouse barely recognisable to Bear from her caked and matted fur emerged from the dark. She brought herself and her paws before the flame. 'The soil's cold,' she said, briskly rubbing them. 'That means the snow's maybe feet away.'

'Good, Katie, good,' said Bear, leaning sideways to look beyond her. 'You got enough paws up there?'

'We're a good team,' she said, meeting his eyes. 'We'll get it done.'

Bear brought the stuttering flame a little lower to his midriff. 'Will I be able-'

'To squeeze through?' the little mouse finished. She rolled her eyes around the opening and looked Bear up and down. 'We'll find out, won't we?'

Katie turned away and padded back off into the dark. Bear watched after her before turning himself and brought his torch high. 'We're there,' he announced to the huddled nervous faces, 'so stop what you're doing and listen. I need a fast pair to go snuff out those torches down the tunnel.' He shook the torch in his paw. 'And another three to gather any picks. We'll be leaving one by one, with the youngest and females first.'

Morris cast around and picked out a couple of faces. From a flick of his paw, they were off. Another selected three more mice who gathered up what tools they could.

Paths cleared in the crowd as mothers and young began hopping up into the hole. A lot of hugging and nuzzling broke out as 'farewells' were said and teary eyes were dried.

Bear considered the remaining males. 'We've got to assume the worst,' he said, his face darkening. 'We may have to fight again.'

'Torches are out,' said the returning pair of mice.

'Okay,' said Bear, nodding. 'Divide the tools.' He lit the hole again with his torch, straining an ear sideways. 'Are we clear?' he asked the darkness. *'Hello?'*

Bear leaned in to call again, but a whistling scream answered and a barrelling wind forced his eyes shut and his ears back – the torch in his paw wrenched free. It spun to the dirt where the flame danced and shrank before puffing out to an ember.

Eyes blinked in the dark, now thick and pressing, the acrid smell of the torch in their nostrils.

'Nobody move!' said Bear. *'Nobody move.* Remember where you're stood. He felt for the hole behind him. 'Touch is key now. Place a paw on the backs of those in front of you. I'll have nobody panicking.'

With their senses alive, each did as instructed and following Bear's voice they rose one by one into the tunnel. Bear stayed until last, helping the final mouse off.

With just himself to go, he pondered. Would the tunnel allow his escape? That thought disappeared with the sound of a tumbling wall.

Bear trod towards the sound, his useless eyes wide, his ears pricked. Shouting, cheering, laughter – all echoed down towards him. With paws out, he felt for the wall. Pulling himself in, he began to scrape up the tunnel, coins and torchlight on his tail.

Many paws heaved Bear from the hole into a blinding white light, his eyes forced shut, his face and fur sodden.

'Don't try to open those for a while,' said Morris, helping him up. 'It's whiter than white up here.'

Bear steadied himself on the mouse and creased open an eye. 'I'm probably more earthworm than bear now,' he conceded.

'The coast's clear up here,' said Morris. 'Take a few lungfuls, friend. We are once again free mice.'

With his sight adjusting, Bear straightened and breathed the cool, fresh air. He began to cast his eyes around. Above and all around were vast reaches of branch, woven with fingers of green.

Explosions of colour punctuated the darkness. The tree's lights. Mice were hurrying about the snowy ground, pointing, shouting; directing scampering rodents up to points among the branches where great baubles swung in the wind.

Morris broke Bear from his trance. 'Let's get this hole filled!' he said, harrying the mice around him. With Bear's help they dragged soil and stone and snow into the opening until it formed a tight plug in the gap.

'Our scouts have had a good look around,' he said to Bear. 'It seems we'll all be able to get away on baubles, and since we are so low in the tree, that is a fine piece of luck; they're normally scarce around here.'

Up above, a bauble sputtered into life and died. The pairing of mice aboard it tried again, and with a little coaxing it relented and started, grinding and knocking until it wound down to a gentle hum. They untied its mooring and pulled free of the branch, showering needles to the ground as they went.

'Most of these baubles haven't flown in a while,' offered Morris to Bear, as they watched its flight through the air. 'I'm sure they'll be just fine though.'

Much lower though, and beneath Bear's very paws, the ground shook. All struck still, their eyes roving the floor, crouched ready.

A boom like an underwater cannon sounded, splitting cracks through the snow. The mice hopped in fright. The young were gathered up. Another boom and the snowy floor visibly lifted. Every-mouse watched the ground backing off.

Thinking fast, Morris ordered a team over to where he stood, right on top of the plugged hole. The following force heaved and fractured the ground. Thrashing a paw at the air, Morris summoned down two commandeered baubles and then indicated the groups to leave first. Swooping, the baubles landed and began to take passengers.

A third was on its way, the fourth yet to be reached by a young mouse named Moriarty entrusted with the task, and still more than a few branches away.

'Get going!' yelled Morris to the pilots. 'Head for Treetops!'

The young pilots flicked salutes, did a quick head count and then sped off into the tree.

The third swung down and scuffed onto the floor before stopping in a drift. The pilot, flustered, raised a paw. He was okay.

The awaiting mice took the trailing rope and began scaling the baubles' side and with everyone aboard, they laboured up and away, buzzing and droning as they went.

All seemed quiet below now. Some stepped off to wave anxious farewells, others to survey the ground and its damage.

In the end it made no difference how many covered the hole, as nothing could have stopped the eruption that threw the party high and wide. The mice lay sprawled, twitching and groaning among the debris. From the fallout was silence. Just the tree's deep echo.

Bear rolled his eyes to the hole, as did all the others. Something lay partly out of their escape tunnel. Whatever it was (golden, but too large to be a coin) looked inanimate, perhaps dead. And then it moved.

Soil unsettled. It moved again. Mice began sitting up. Bear did the same. A hand shot from the earth and grabbed at the air. It twitched as though confused, and then drove back at the ground where it plunged again and again, craning dirt away like a robot mastering a series of movements.

Before long, the hand stopped. The hole was now open. The thing of gold then straightened upright and a dark line on its face tore open making an angry, neanderthal sound, causing all to leap with shock. Then two irregular eyes, one set higher than the other, flicked open.

There were gasps. They were the eyes of a woken giant, yet here they were, twisting, swivelling, in the head of this abomination. Though partly buried, its size was near triple that of a regular coin. Its armour was a patchwork of gold, obviously cobbled together in a hurry. From the temporary silence came a wailing, stricken yell.

The coin – or *mutant* coin – turned its head to the source to witness a skinny young mouse, driving through the snow, a tightly-packed snowball held in its paw.

'Die, you ugly, star-murdering scum!'

The ball launched. The mutant dumbly watched. It struck the thing hard square between its eyes before it dropped with a dull thud on the ground. It appeared to have no effect.

A slow chain of thought kicked in. It registered something. Probably pain. It became angry, much angrier than before, and with that it rose with incredible speed out of the ground, like the undead on fast forward. Ten mice and a bear shot to their feet.

Dirt and snow leapt as the mutant threw back its arms and roared, saliva torn across its mouth. Its eyes turned, one quicker than the other to the mouse who'd lobbed the snowball. The mouse, in turn, crumpled and fainted.

It started toward him, momentarily caught by its foot in the hole. With a snarl and a wrench it was free, and in that moment, Bear acted. Dropping, he scooped some snow, pressed it tight and threw it hard at the shambling coin's head. It missed.

A mouse closest to his comrade stepped in its path and planted. The mutant stopped and looked down at the obstruction. The mouse, shaking, was promptly lifted and torn in two, killing him instantly. The coin looked at the halves laid either side of him and decided they posed no further threat.

This time a snowball connected, striking its slower, lower eye and exploded. After a pause the mutant wheeled, bellowing rage and pain, swiping blindly at the air. He inhaled through a single, malformed nostril, trying to find the one who'd thrown it.

'Take the mouse now!' yelled Bear to one of the poised young, who quick as a whippet dove in and scooped the poor fellow from the ground, and with him limp over both arms ran back to the main group.

Morris looked up, agitated. 'Where *is* Moriarty?'

'There...' pointed one, and all eyes found a glittering scarlet ball ridden by a windswept rodent. A snarl from behind got everyone moving, hurrying to the bauble, now skidding to a halt on a bed of snow.

'Toss the line! *Toss the line!*' called Morris, running fast and low at the craft, his thin arms swimming through the air.

140

The exhilarated pilot, his fur ridden up from the breeze, was grinning. A frantic voice from below caught his attention. He turned his head, still breathless and smiling, and saw the abomination. His face dropped. He hurried the rope over the side and killed the engine.

A pair of paws appeared first, then Morris, frantically scampering up the rope.

'What are you doing? Start the damn engine!'

Snapped from his daze, Moriarty began stabbing a paw at the control panel, though it only served to shake the bauble, and with a wheezing bang the thing stalled.

The mice below fled, scattering away from the murderous, rampaging coin. With eyes only on the mutant, Moriarty was now punching the buttons; with luck, the bauble tremored and kicked and roared into life. He threw a lever forward and the craft began shifting off, showering snow from its great belly.

A mouse reached the overhanging line, leapt and scurried up, then another and four more, until just Bear and a single mouse were left down on the snowy floor, driving hard for the bauble.

The mutant had built to top speed now, pounding over the snow like a juggernaut.

Behind and much further back, coins were now piling out of the tunnel. It didn't take them long to locate the action – south-west of their position; soon they were all bunched on the hill of soil in a rabid pack, urging on their monster. Equal in voice were the mice atop the bauble, yelling and willing, some thumping the curved floor they clung to.

Moriarty turned from the scene, the quickening bauble rising and falling, scudding the ground as it went. Morris came low to an edge where he grabbed a line and abseiled down, just feet from the passing ground. 'Come on!' he yelled, a paw outstretched to Bear.

Plodding, panting, Bear took it and pulled himself up and over Morris, clambering breathless to join the frantic pack, all cheers and back-slapping. The mutant, its target now final, seemed to find another gear.

A mere swipe away, the coin grimaced and made a final grab. He got the mouse – its tail at least – but Morris had a paw. The bauble took off, taken on the wind as the mouse strained and stretched – and cried out as his tail tore off.

The mutant stomped to an eventual halt, the limp appendage in his hand. His face was wrung with rage as he followed the bauble up and up until it winked out in the heights.

Sitting ducks

F resh from escaping the mines and its army of coins, Bear and seven mice had spread themselves quite comfortably across the top of the broad bauble. Young Moriarty still piloted; it was agreed he had things in hand, although Jacob, a mouse with a keen nose, was helping aid navigation. Poor Lawrence was still blessed, as everyone kept reminding him, with the remainder of himself and his life.

The rest were exhausted. Some crouched or squatted, while others lay with their paws behind their heads, way down the sides of the bauble, held safe by its gravity field, enjoying their flight through the tree, but most of all their freedom.

There was no sign of the three baubles who'd taken flight before them; a good thing, they'd agreed, as they were probably already halfway to Treelights.

Bear meanwhile approached Morris, with the mouse squat, watching the tree unfold. He lowered to sit beside his friend and brought his voice to a whisper. 'Will the tree have enough to stop Phaedria?'

Morris sat too. He glanced around, then looked at Bear. 'Do you know what happened to your young master?'

'Henry?' said Bear. 'No. No, I'm afraid I don't.'

'Well,' said Morris, looking off. 'I wonder... wonder if Phaedria has used him for some purpose or other.'

The bauble gave a turbulent wobble as they rounded a broad hanging branch.

'You mentioned her eyes lit up at the sight of him?'

Bear narrowed his eyes in thought. 'They did, they did.'

'Well,' said Morris. 'I think she may use him. She may have him hostage or running an errand or something.'

Bear pulled his head away, as though he didn't want to hear any more.

'I'm quite sure he's alive,' said the mouse, placing a paw on his friend's shoulder. 'Personally, I think she'll have him find Lilly. To feed her false information, or...' He broke off. 'That's what I'd do anyway.' He gave Bear's

143

back a rub and settled to watch the tree again. 'In answer to your question,' he continued, 'we have the numbers to stop Phaedria. If we could all come together, then yes, we stand a chance, but-' His whiskers blew in the wind. 'They'd all need fair warning.'

Bear, his head low, spoke. 'I believe he's alive too.'

'The one place I reckon she's headed, coin army and all,' said Morris, raising to crouch, 'is Treelights. Control Treelights and you control the tree.'

Bear drew his legs up to his chest and cradled them. His eyes marbled with the tree's colours and wonderments, before they blinked and swam back to the present.

*

Young Moriarty and Jacob seemed to all to be a good pairing. This was evident in that most were laid out or asleep as the bauble wove a route up and through the tree. The only ones keeping a watch on them were Morris and Bear, between them quietly marvelling at the pairing.

Young Moriarty's piloting showed far greater experience than his young years, and with Jacob positioned at one o'clock, sniffing and pointing, harnessing scents on the tree's currents, so they too were at ease, though not completely off-guard.

At the back of the bauble, staggered over its edge, was another group of mice. They'd been responsible for most of the dirt-hauling.

Blackened and tired, the wind playing with their ears, they rested. One of the team was sat up, content to watch where they'd been rather than where they were going. It was this mouse, Junior, who'd spied something.

At first he thought it a bird, perhaps a star, as the dot way behind didn't warrant much more than a glance. But as the dot became larger and more prominent, Junior sat up and took note. He cupped an ear with his paw. He could hear a faint din travelling with it.

Junior leaned forward, creasing his eyes – and leapt in startlement.

'Every-mouse, every-mouse. Wake up!' he squeaked, scampering small circles. 'Up on your paws, now!'

Morris and Bear heard the fuss and rose with the others to see what the problem was. Junior said no more; he didn't need to. His companions followed his outstretched paw marking out something in their wake.

'Great snowballs! is that...?'

Bear came through to the back-most slope of the bauble. 'Morris, are you seeing this?'

'It appears,' said Morris, squinting, 'they only found the one.'

A bauble, laden with coins from the very top to the very bottom, was slicing its way toward them. A roar accompanied the rabble, all bristling and golden, waving fists and sticks and blades of pine, baying for the mice.

At the eye of their storm was the mutant. He was shoving his way around, grabbing and punching and whipping at coins indiscriminately, urging the bauble on.

Lawrence crooked his head. 'Is that my... tail?'

Moriarty didn't need to be told. He shouted a warning to the mice and with a fear-struck backward look he threw forward a lever. The bauble jumped and kicked up a gear, building up speed.

Onward they raced, swinging through the tree, ducking branches and crashing over boughs, with stars leaving dusty trails of light as they fled their path. As fast as they flew, they were still being closed upon.

'What class is that bauble?' gasped Lawrence.

Junior shielded his eyes from a passing star's glare. 'It's so overloaded I just can't tell. It's gotta be purple-'

'Or black,' piped up another. 'How fortunate for them.'

The coins' breakneck speed was due to the bauble being Purple-Classed, but also from the recklessness of its pilot – and at the expense of a few lives. The bauble veered sideways, skidding into branches and losing a coin or two, rising and falling onto boughs, crushing others, sending them spinning and screaming into the darkness.

It still wasn't fast enough for the mutant. He cleared a rough path to the pilot and lashed his whip-tail overhead, loosing the pilot's grip. A second coiled his leg, yanking him clean off the craft.

With a tearing roar the mutant slammed his arms onto the wheel, his irregular gaze fixed solely on his target. The coins made space for their new pilot, bracing as the mutant hefted a lever. The bauble shunted forward and the mob began braying once more.

Moriarty's paw was poised, shaking with indecision; below it was the speed stick and before that a slot – a space allowing one more shift. The mouse dragged a paw down his face, swerved to avoid a branch and pushed the lever forward.

Seven mice and a bear suddenly bent to the wind. The race was on. They flew into a bend, pitching and whining with each held as best they could. The bauble rolled over and over, grazing an overhang. The escapees were almost upside-down, dodging needles and twigs which joined their slipstream, showering their pursuers.

The coins followed along a deeper line, some painfully spiked from the fallout. With a cheer they shot out of the branch and into the open.

Down the mice went, every-paw to the bauble, battling wind and gravity to stay on the ride. So too did the coins, losing two to the downforce, spiralling off like ragdolls. Moriarty levelled sharply, flooring everyone – the coins shot past. One attempted to board, but he bounced off the side, bicycling his limbs in the air.

Then came a moment of brief relief as the coins were gone from view; their noise along with them. The mice breathed a little easier until a sharp-eyed passenger called out. Just over, charging on the wind came the Purple-Classer, but it was forced to slow as a patchwork of needles divided the craft.

Moriarty slowed the bauble to cruising speed. So too did the coins. Between passing holes in the greenery, the two parties eyed each other silently.

As the greenery thickened in places, so Morris instructed their best lookout foremost, along with a hasty line of their strongest to repel boarders along the near edge.

But Morris wasn't planning to engage. Instead he instructed the mouse to give a signal, just as soon as he could.

Both drifted like submarines running silent. A signal came back from the lookout. A breach in the greenery was approaching. But Moriarty did nothing.

He maintained his speed, his eyes forward. Movement came from the other bauble. They had seen it too.

The mutant grabbed a coin and pushed him roughly to the wheel. Swaggering to the edge, the mutant looked to the mice and made something like a smile. Some mice turned in disgust.

The tear in the wall approached. The coins jostled. The whip-tail uncoiled to the floor. With a clunk the Purple-Classer swung away before swinging straight back, headlong at the mice. They were sitting ducks.

At the last possible moment, Moriarty pushed a button. It read: *Bauble Gravitational Field – DO NOT USE UNLESS SAFELY DOCKED.*

Morris called: 'Now!' Seven mice and a bear dropped and clung to the bauble's line before dropping like stones. The coins missed. Some swiped as they passed, buzzing overhead.

A swarm of golden heads cursed and then turned to see what would kill more than half of them. A jutting, needled branch came over the top, impaled the front line and scythed a side clean. It spun the bauble a new course, losing even more as it did so.

Moriarty – flattened like a castaway clung to a raft – threw a paw again and again at the button. The bauble, falling fast, began to vibrate and shudder as it sought to reverse its aimless turning and level off.

With a great mechanical groan, the craft pulled up through a series of judders until it stopped once, twice, and finally just a few metres from any real danger.

Breathless and still prone, the troop muttered a silent *thank you* and looked up to see Moriarty peeling himself from the wheel. He was whiter than normal, but laughing.

'Now tell me,' he said, stumbling. 'Have you ever hitched a ride like that?'

Bear rose from the floor. 'Moriarty.' He slapped the mouse's back. 'You truly are a great pilot.'

The mouse beamed and leaned on the wheel.

'But,' said Bear with a slant, 'Please don't do that again; not while *I'm* a passenger.'

Laughter ran round the bauble, but only for a moment. The coin bauble was now flying headlong at them, listing badly and near bare of troops. There were just seconds for each to dive before it struck, shattering both baubles completely in a deafening crash of glass.

A diversion

There was a blur of falling, flailing, tearing through branches and a vacuumed *thwump* as many figures landed in a drift of snow. And then silence rang in waves.

Bear groaned and fought away the snow covering him. He gazed blankly around, his coat matted with dirt and ice. He began to make out shapes and movement. He trod downward to lift himself, only to send a paw clean through a branch and snow into thin air. But he managed to stay upright and hauled himself up to his waist. With great effort, he sat upon the rim of the opening he'd made.

Bear cast about between ragged breaths. His immediate surrounds were fresh snow, but it didn't stretch very far. Beyond its small horizon were distant stars and thick branches of pine. With a start, Bear realised himself to be delicately perched upon the extreme reach of a limb, a shelf of branch that had caught a snowfall. It was bouncing from the movements of his companions now surfacing. He acted and swung up his legs, rolling clear before the snowy covering slid away and over the edge.

Raising his head, he saw seven mice brushing snow from themselves; dazed, wondering where they were.

'Where are the other three?' Bear rose to his feet. 'Morris, Lawrence, and-'

'Junior,' said Jacob. He trod a circle, searching. 'They could be *anywhere*.'

'Here!' came a muffled cry. All eyes shot to a mound of slowly unsettling snow.

A paw, then more paws popped from the snow, reaching, and with help from the others they were heaved out. Morris and Lawrence lay catching breaths, shivering on the ground.

'Get them up,' said Bear.

'Junior?' asked Jacob, propping Morris up.

'Can't say I've seen him,' he panted. 'No sign?'

Bear frowned and began scanning the branches above them. 'Perhaps he's tangled up there somewhere.'

'Maybe he ain't,' came a gruff voice from over.

The party spun, startled. Three coins appeared from the shadows into the clearing, dragging the captive Junior limp and face down across the snow. He didn't look to be resisting – or even moving.

Emerging from the dark of an overhang behind them was the mutant, the weak light accentuating his beady, slow-swivelling eyes, his lopsided mouth quivering as though he were attempting to smile – something he had likely forgotten how to do. His size was still a shock to the band.

Morris broke forward, but Bear stopped him. A few paces away, the coins unloaded the mouse to the floor and stepped aside to let Phaedria's champion through. His breathing – mostly through one nostril – sounded lustful and rasping as his eyes pulled left to right, surveying the group.

Bear planted his paws and steeled his own. The mutant's gaze stopped upon the teddy and he snorted before reaching down to grab Junior's leg. Lumbering a couple of steps, the patchwork monster wheeled, releasing the mouse into the air and off into the dark void beyond the branch.

The mice squeaked terror and outrage as little paws clutched faces, clutched each other, and swore vengeance upon the coins. It was all too much for Lawrence who'd witnessed this open-mouthed and rooted; but now his brow furrowed, determined and angry, and he sprung off to attack the big monster. A soldier coin drew a pine blade. Stepping into his path, he slew the mouse with a slashing, downward cut.

It brought a frenzied excitement to the coins – a dark, eager edge to their eyes. The mutant came forward and gave a grudging sniff. He kicked the dead mouse, rolling him over, his blood staining the snow.

Bear held the line. They had to make this final stand together if they wanted to stand a chance. But his eyes were drawn to a bird alighting to the ground nearby. Its wingspan was far-reaching, its yellow eyes piercing and fierce.

The coins noticed this too, most notably the mutant, who turned slowly from the mouse on the floor, his curiosity pricked. The jayhawk clicked its beak and held its eyes upon the mutant, staring and unflinching. A soldier coin closest took a couple of steps away.

Every head was now turned to the bird, fearsomely large. The coins rearranged themselves to face it. Sensing a new challenge, the mutant stepped forward to present himself. His arms were parted and his hands open, daring the bird to come on.

There was a tense standoff. Breaths were held. It was broken by a piercing cry from the jayhawk. Its throat opened skyward, talons clawing at the ground, wings broad and flapping.

The bird brought them in, dashed at the mutant and launched, leading with sharp talons at the coin's chest, where they gripped at his casement, creasing and crushing, a peck from its great beak puncturing a hole in the golden armour, all shrieks and wings.

The mutant swiped and swung, staggering a half-circle before the bird released and flew clear.

'Who is this bird?' asked Morris to Bear, his eyes only on the battle.

'I... I don't know. But we need to be ready if needed.'

Coming round, he moved among the mice, ordering them to arm themselves, to grab anything that might double as a weapon – a piece of glass or a loose pine needle.

The mutant shook his head, his legs splayed, and began searching for the bird. The jayhawk landed across from the coin. It settled and stared. Incensed, the mutant made for the bird, stomping with arms outstretched. The jayhawk hopped sideways, taking brief flight.

The lumbering coin skidded to a stop. The pair faced each other. Both attacked then, spinning off one another, swapping places. A dark line sped across the coin's chest. He looked down, ran a finger through it and tasted the chocolate mixture. The mice grimaced.

With his other hand, the coin gripped the armour over his chest and pulled it closed, creasing gold over gold. He chose then to circle the bird, who followed and engaged the play, with little room between them. The jayhawk leapt, feigning attack; the mutant swung – missing clumsily. Again they circled.

The jayhawk twitched; the coin tensed. He twitched again, but followed in, clawing and gouging at the mutant's head. The coin roared in pain and frustration and flew blindly at the bird, chocolate streaking from his wounds, his arms windmilling.

The remaining coins stood alert with concern. They noted the mice and teddy bear were armed.

'Keep an eye on those three,' said Bear from the side of his mouth. 'They come at us, we go together. Got it?'

'Understood,' nodded Morris, 'though I'm not sure we'll need to. This bird looks useful.'

The space between the fighters had narrowed. The jayhawk pressed his advantage and sprung, flying at the hulk with sharp talons. The mutant was quick and turned. He grabbed the bird's wing and swung his opponent full into the ground.

A clubbed fist followed, missing the jayhawk's skull and sending up powder that clouded the battle for a few seconds. From the mist a moan sounded.

The bird bent and swiped his brown beak clean on the snow. But the mutant barely noticed its wound, a gaping triangular puncture. It seemed only to spur on its aggression.

With fists clenched, the coin came on, fuelled only by rage. His guard was down. With might, the bird launched. It attacked the golden armour, stabbing and tearing, again and again. The mutant continued evenly, his eyes guarded, a grim determination driving him.

The jayhawk paused, then lowered and launched. His fearsome beak snapped at the mutant but he reacted in time, surprising all with his speed and diverting his assailant to the ground with a well-aimed elbow.

With the bird stunned, the mutant straightened. His nostril flared and his uneven eyes watched, waiting for movement. He was in no hurry now.

He placed a foot on the bird's frame, gave a derisory snort and bent to lift a wingtip. A silence fell from both groups; one awed, the other horror-struck. The mutant studied the plumage with faraway eyes.

It seemed to dawn on the creature that he held his prize. He looked to Bear and then to the mice. There was no doubting they would be next. He managed a lopsided smile. That smile flashed to a fierce grimace as he gripped the wing by the joint and tore it forcefully off. The mice squeaked and hopped.

Bear raised a jagged shard of glass. His companions too raised weapons. Even Bernard, the oldest mouse of the group, stood ready.

The coins stepped up, their excitement barely contained. With a flick, the mutant tossed the bird's wing. It fluttered and turned on the breeze until it vanished over a snowy reach. But a light began to spark at his feet, and he brought his slow-moving eyes downward, confused.

A glow like a brilliant sun played on the mutant's face. At his feet a transformation was taking place. Both parties gawped in wonderment.

Once motionless, the jayhawk's limp body was now positively teeming with a metamorphosis of change; glittering feathers disappeared, reappeared and spun off; the great beak flashed and ghosted until it was gone, replaced by a face, bright and hard.

A rush of noise came and built, causing the mutant to stumble backward. On the floor, a coin sat up – minus an arm, drawing air and crying out. He fumbled at the stump and his eyes told of pain.

A shard of glass skidded to his side, tossed by Bear. Maybe the mutant hadn't seen it or perhaps it was shock, but when the bird-coin sprang up delivering blow upon blow, the mutant just took it. He rocked, sputtered and gurgled. His chest already awash with chocolate now fountained. He fell to his knees.

The remaining coins stood stunned. One began retching. The bird-coin stepped over the laid-out mutant to engage, but the fallen monster's hand swung out.

It might only have knocked him onto his behind, but it concealed a pine dagger. Sunk to the hilt, the mutant's fingers released and the dagger stuck home.

As though time had stalled, the bird-coin swayed. He mouthed disbelief and fell forward, stopping flat on the snow with a thud.

The mice ran over and raised him carefully to a knee; at the same time came the coins. Bear crouched, lifting a needle from the floor. He ran at the coins, all roaring noise and blazing eyes. It was enough to see them turn tail, bumping into one another as they fled for the darkness, shouting back threats as they left.

Bear returned to find the coin still down on one knee, his hand cradling the dagger's hilt, surrounded by mice. His breathing was ragged now.

He made no effort to pull the blade out of himself but looked fiercely around the mice until he found Bear, and his eyes stayed upon him. And then the coin did something unusual. He smiled. Bear's head inclined.

A grim air hung over the scene. Every-mouse could see this coin wouldn't make it.

Morris placed a paw on his casing. 'Who are you, coin?'

'I am... one of the Queen's guard,' he managed, blinking. His tongue ran slowly over his lips. 'Llorn. My name is... Llorn.'

Morris's paw went to the dagger. The coin growled.

'Never mind that. You... need to know what's... happening.'

His breaths quickened. A brown gush ran over his hand. Though his eyes glazed, they stayed upon Morris. 'The tree...' he continued, 'will soon be at war.'

Morris squeezed the coin's shoulder, halting him. 'Save your words. We know this. We were made to mine gold to make their armour; I'm afraid we had no choice. We managed to escape.'

Llorn coughed and looked slowly round the gathering, rolling his darkening eyes. 'No mean feat, but you... are far from safe.'

Bear came forward and crouched, his eyes level with Llorn's. 'We're on our way to Treelights-'

Llorn shook his head. He slumped a little, the lights dimming in his eyes. 'You must... detour.'

Morris moved forward, but Bear held him back. He knelt to prop the coin, his paws on both shoulders. 'To where?'

Llorn snatched at the air as though about to drown. 'The... Walnut Kingdom. It's in... the Glades.'

'And do what?' urged Bear, shaking him.

His sight now gone, Llorn whispered: 'They have to fight.'

'They will,' said Bear. 'They will. I give you my solemn promise.'

With his final breath, Llorn's arm fell limp to his side. He stayed in position, upon one knee in a pool of his own blood, ashen and statuesque.

His heart heavy, Bear leaned in to Llorn's ear. 'Thank you.'

All heads hung low.

Bear rose and blinked at the tree. 'We need a new bauble,' he announced after a time. 'We dig a shallow grave and we go.'

My wolves will find you

P haedria held out a hand. She turned it slowly, clenching, unclenching, feeling its strength, darkly marvelling at its return. It connected to an arm, fully-formed but to a body incomplete; her left side was still a polluted swimming darkness.

With her formed hand she adjusted the shield before her. She beheld her image in its polished golden sheen, something she'd been doing more and more frequently. Dull, black eyes followed her fulfilled side.

With her right hand she began tracing her outline with a fingertip, stopping here, passing there. The pointed finger stopped at her shoulder. Her eyes flickered. A black bead of moisture formed in the corners of her dark sockets and for a moment her eyes conveyed sadness. A blink, and it left.

The part that was once fairy, once feeling, was chased away. An inky blackness pooled in her eyes. Inclining her head, she met her image. Done, she veiled the makeshift mirror and left her quarters.

A coin guard had been waiting to speak with her. As she came closer he arched his back, puffed his chest up and saluted. He took a moment to see she wasn't stopping, returned his arm and hurriedly made after her.

'Speak quickly.'

'My lady,' he said, jogging at her side. 'Two of your Star Squads have returned.'

'Good,' she said, her voice suddenly underpinned by a bright fanfare, marking the squads' return. 'I hope for your sake that they bring a good number.' Her eyes lingered upon the coin, then left with her, leaving the guard in her wake with a new crease to his forehead.

A group of coins had gathered, attracted by the arrival of the two teams, but quickly dispersed upon seeing their queen.

She arrived like a ship of doom, parting wave upon wave of coin until finally she stopped, the arrival just before her. Just as waves rebound from river banks, so the crowd came slowly back.

Before Phaedria were nine coins. They looked as though they'd returned from a gruelling day's work. None saluted or even stood straight.

154

She angled her stark white face, peering over a steep chin, her eyes expectant. A dishevelled coin shuffled forward. He opened his mouth to speak but stopped, distracted. Reaching an arm to his rear he fumbled, cursing and straining to grip the offending splinter between his forefinger and thumb. 'Bloody needles!' he griped, tossing the splinter aside.

Two or more of his team applauded, laughing at his misfortune. He turned and bowed, rolling his hand royally before pulling up his sagging casing, and then turned to face Phaedria.

A wand was thrust directly under his nose.

'Name?'

'B-Baldock...'

'Good hunting?' she asked brightly.

The coin held his breath, almost cross-eyed. 'We... did manage to c... capture a couple of stars,' he stammered, addressing the wand as though it were a reared cobra.

'A *couple*,' echoed Phaedria. The wand remained unmoved. She turned her head. 'And your team?'

Nobody moved until a coin was shoved forward from the pack.

'Gimble,' he said, withering. 'We got four stars.'

'*Four*. I suppose,' Phaedria said with quick consideration, 'that four is better than a couple. Congratulations. You get to stick around a bit longer.'

Baldock's eyes followed the wand upward until it blasted him to pieces, showering his team.

Phaedria stepped carefully over what was left of her smouldering ex-Squad Leader and stopped just short of his team. Her hand went up, wand pointed. Instead of the violent ejection of a spell, it twisted awkwardly and shot back.

Phaedria cried out and came low, cradling her arm to her body, shaking slightly. She stayed silent and still, her head bowed.

Panicked, the four star-seekers came alive. They battled two choices. Stay or flee.

One made his decision. Leaping a corner of the crowd, the coin was off. He'd sprung well, tucked and landed nicely side-on, where he rolled at speed until falling to one side. He chased ever-decreasing circles before finally stopping flat – half-a-dozen twig spears in his side.

Phaedria stirred. Like a black flower in bloom she began to rise, opening slowly with her white face at the centre. Three hundred pairs of eyes watched her with fearful interest. She approached the team – now three – and counted with her eyes.

'I thought there were more of you,' she said, though her eyes had already passed to where the coin lay dead. The remaining coins looked unnerved.

But Phaedria looked distracted. Closing the incident, she spoke. 'Both teams. I want you back out and returning with at least a half-dozen stars each. And in half the time it took you to claim these.'

Eight of the coins wilted. She had effectively passed them a death sentence.

'Don't think to cut loose either,' she said evenly. 'My wolves will find you.'

The leader of the second squad wrestled with his thoughts. 'My lady,' he said, stepping forward, his head low and bowed, 'we tried our best out there. The stars are fast. We could use more help-'

He stopped. Had he asked too much? His dark-ringed eyes begged consideration. Phaedria said nothing; an uncharacteristic pause of thought.

'We could use the sprite, my lady,' he said, now rising a little. There was another pause of thought and a narrowing of eyes.

'Don't push your luck.' Phaedria crooked a smoky, tendrilled finger at him. 'But ever merciful, I hear your plea. Take another handful of troops with you. Fail this time and I'll smelt you all. Now GO!'

The coins upped and scuttled off as though Phaedria was an erupting volcano, her lava chasing at their heels.

Silence eventually settled. The coins were gone. Two nets lay, faded rainbows of colour escaping them. Their time had come.

Phaedria turned her attention to a part of her body hidden beneath her cloak. She passed a smoky hand into the space that was once her left ribcage and turned a finger within it, making it swirl like a potion in a cauldron. She withdrew her hand and passed to where the nets lay.

Producing a forefinger, she sliced bind by bind with a fingernail. Once it was wide enough, she plunged in a hand and retrieved a star with all the care a mother would show her newborn.

She laid it down in the snow, its faint oval eyes mournful. From a pocket she withdrew a corseted bag. Untying the string, it fell open, casting up a wondrous soft light. The light twinkled and played like tiny bubbles leaping from champagne.

Phaedria's features lit up; not from the glow that revealed her face as gaunt and aged, but from what she saw. Her eyes, wide and awed, told she was witness to something no other had seen, as though she was privilege to great secrets.

The star was brought to the bag's mouth and held in the light; the light came to life, turning and spiralling tiny motes, streaming delicate colourful fingers around the star. With her hold released, it shrank and withdrew until it was gone. This went on five more times. When all was done, Phaedria pulled the string closed and tucked the bag back into her cloak.

She raised her head, feeling change. Her left side had returned.

'I think it is time,' she said, raising an arm, 'that my pet returned.'

Her fingers contorted and pulled at the air. She brought her hand to her chest and breathed freely, her powers replenished.

'It's time for war.'

A new route

Somewhere in a dark part of the tree was a shadow. Its movements were quick – swifter than those of a coin – but they hadn't been of late. From an impossible leap, the figure bent a branch to its limits, unseating the snowy cover into the darkness below.

It stopped moving, invisible beneath the black boughs, troubled. Hands suddenly gripped its side – pain riddling the creature.

It shifted to where a pale sliver of light lanced the foliage. An ice-shapen face broke it, its yellow eyes rolling. Sprite lidded them and tamed the pain. A dark line of blood ran from his mouth. The worst of the hurt had passed.

His dirty yellow eyes grew. Falling forward, he leapt again and again, downward and across, skilfully directing his fall each time with the lightest of touches from his ice-white fingers. A leap away from an intended landing, Sprite's arms instead strapped his stomach, the subsequent fall not important, the immediate pain now everything.

The creature curled and crashed downward, branch over branch, plunged and spiked into needles, until lunging, he stopped.

He dropped from the branch to another, went to his haunches and coughed up blood. His wounds were seeping over spears of dark green. Sprite's eyes closed.

In time, they opened and rolled upward. They mapped a new route and he lumbered off.

*

Sprite's change in direction had brought him near to where he'd left the cavern via the long, upward tunnel. He slowed, favouring stealth. The going had been tough; he'd lost blood, but he'd been moving freely, the pain seemingly levelled. Close now, Sprite gained a vantage point. The Great Tree was still.

A clockwork *pat-pat* onto a needle below alerted him to a cut on his forearm.

He pulled it close, ran his long tongue over the wound and pinched it closed. Letting go, the wound stayed. It would do for now.

On the other side of a mish-mash of needles stood a pair of coin guards. They had just changed shift as they stood straight, dutiful and attentive. Neither was talking. They hadn't noticed the keen yellow dots watching them from somewhere dark and hidden.

One guard began another sweep with his eyes, the same sweep he'd been doing since being posted, guarding the entrance to one of four tunnels. They'd had very specific instructions: the war machine was nearly ready to roll out. Vigilance was the key now.

His eyes roved the green and relaxed. He took a swig from a gourd and turned to his opposite, but he wasn't there; just a blade and a dark streak on the snow in his place.

From a step, then another, the Coin saw the streak was chocolate, running zig-zagged through the snow, disappearing around the tunnel entrance.

Alert to the danger, he crouched, his spear ready, but a dark fluid spat from his mouth.

An ice-white hand was protruding from his chest.

He had strength only to turn and meet his killer before starting a fall forward that ended with his death on the snow.

Sprite unhooked the key from the Coin and shifted uneasily, his head shaking in fits, as though trying to rid itself of something. His darting pupils scanned the clearing.

He was alone. A clunk, then a squealing resounded through the tunnel as Sprite slipped in and closed the door again, creating instant, impenetrable darkness.

He crouched, attentive, allowing for his eyes to adjust. Blinking, he started off down the long, gouged tunnel, bounding gaily, running circles up walls and over the ceiling.

In time his faint yellow eyes came floating through the velvet darkness, wide and watchful, but they thinned with suspicion. A great thud made them swivel. They were forced shut as a crescent of light tore over them.

The light showed up a face, ice-white and startled, as the butt of a spear was brought into it. With the circular door open, the coin guard stepped in. Sprawled on the floor now, Sprite lay unconscious.

159

The guard, clutching his twig spear, came closer. His face registered no emotion. Then he saw Sprite's hand, stained a dark brown from his long, sharp fingertips to his elbow.

He drew a tremulous breath and brought the butt down again.

Old friends

W hen Sprite awoke, his head was lolling in rhythm to a hollow, rolling noise below him. His senses returned enough to find he was moving, a cave's ceiling passing high above, the odd crackle of a torch going by, and he winced at the pain from his head.

He could see he was stood atop a cart, his hands bound to an upright post behind him. Four misshapen wheels rolled him across a wooden bridge. On either side beyond the staked timber posts was endless darkness. Now his eyes began finding and counting the coin guards around him.

Two passed beneath a high torchlight ahead. One followed to his left. His eyes rolled right. Another passed out of the shadows into the light beside him. The guard held a twig spear, his armour fired gold in the flame. He watched the ice-creature unblinking.

Sprite let his head go limp and knock into the wood behind him. Approaching him was a great looming shape. Its base was wreathed in shadow, its top now apparent as logged battlements.

A guard called up. Somebody signalled down. A clunk and a clatter of chains sped a great portcullis up. Sprite was led inside. The chains, slinking and clacking, brought the fortress door closed.

Sprite peered groggily around. He was in a large wooden chamber. Beset in the walls were torches, lighting doors and walkways and ramps going upwards. Coins milled between them, hurrying with weapons and hefting contraptions and carts of heavy stone.

From the busy stream stepped three guards, led by one of Sprite's captors. The other two were larger, highly polished and with a look of authority. The lead coin stopped them before the cart, came forward and took Sprite's arm. He pointed out the stain of cracked, dried chocolate along its length. It was observed by both. One turned to the other, nodded, and left the way he came. Sprite fell unconscious.

It took a bucket of water to bring the creature round again. He reacted with a growl and snapped at the air. Someone moved forward. His eyes laboured to focus.

161

'So, you decided to come home at last,' said a casual voice.

He pushed his head up, straining hard against his binds. She came closer. Like a drunk roused, his head swayed, taking in the fort's courtyard. A cloud of dark smoke trailed from a fat smelting pot. Guards patrolled the logged walkways above. Coins were all around him.

And now in front of him stood his tormentor – his *master*. She reached out a hand, and to Sprite's surprise it touched him where once it couldn't and began to stroke his head. He indulged her – then tried to bite it clean off. But her wand held his head fixed, his mouth forced open.

'Sprite, my pet,' she said, 'haven't I been looking after you?'

The wand flicked subtly once, then twice, bringing his jaws even further apart before snapping them shut.

'Where, oh where have you been?'

He did nothing but watch her, his head hung heavy. She placed her wand beneath his chin, lifting it so she could see. Green blood streaked his cheeks like cracks of lightning, running from the corners of his mouth.

'I thought I might have killed you, calling you back.' She circled his face with her eyes. 'It looks as though I applied just the right amount of persuasion.' The wand pulled away and Sprite's head dropped, though his eyes stayed on his master.

In the foreground, background and walkways, coins observed with dark delight. Phaedria wandered a circle. She noticed the attention Sprite was receiving and slipped seamlessly into another of her offenses, toning down her manner.

She approached him slowly. 'You don't have many friends here, do you, Sprite?'

A pair of large yellow eyes flicked lazily left to right. She moved closer, taking one of his hands. 'My pet,' she said, stroking his long fingers, 'you mustn't play with the coins. They don't like it. I don't like it either.'

Her eyes rolled black as she came close to Sprite's ear. 'They want to tear you limb from limb.'

All eyes were upon him. Phaedria toyed with her wand tip. 'You were sorely missed, you know.'

Sprite could do nothing but watch and listen. Phaedria wandered the crowd's edge, trailing her cloak. 'I think we all missed you in a way. Did you know?' She stopped abruptly and faced him. 'That I tried to lay waste to more than half a Star Squad?' Sprite made no motion.

'It was quite embarrassing, really. They'd turned up, both teams, virtually empty-handed. Well,' she said with a reasoning tilt of her head and a pointed movement of her wand, 'i was naturally not in the best of moods.'

Phaedria stopped her wand with her other hand, holding it between her downturned fists like a cane, and continued. 'I was forced to smite them – at least I would have, had I enough power to do so, you see,' she said, halting. 'For all their skill and fleet-footedness they simply cannot catch a star quite like you.'

Her words hollowed and died. They seemed to have no effect. Her patience was done. She inclined her head. 'I'm afraid you must die now.'

The creature, bound and under the watchful eye of all, merely raised a breath and blew it out. Phaedria paused, assessing. 'There's no choice,' she said, holding a blackened finger aloft, 'but you may have a choice in the way you die. I thought I would afford you that luxury; after all, we have a history together.'

Now Sprite did look at her. She held his eyes, smiled, and then turned away, pacing another circle like a ringmaster feeding an audience. Some coin eyes followed her, though most stayed upon the ice-creature. All were silently willing her on.

A gap appeared in the crowd at floor level and through it padded two wolves, eager to see an old colleague meet his end. In unison they came around Phaedria, flanking her as though reinforcing that there were really only ever three of them.

The creature might've sneered, but he couldn't sum up the effort – or couldn't be bothered to.

She acknowledged them one, then the other, and then faced Sprite. 'How do you wish to die?'

The creature's eyes sharpened, though they looked away to the floor. 'The boy, the one you followed. Did he reach Treetops? Did he succeed? Tell me simply this and I shall ease your passing. The summon within shall destroy you from the inside out. You surely feel his claws around your heart? Perhaps for you there would be some honour in you dying at his hand.'

163

There was movement and disquiet among the gathered, but Phaedria threw up her arms to quell it. 'The other,' she mused darkly, 'would see you die at the hands of my beasts.'

The wolves' white eyes seemed to burn. A low hum built as torches popped and crackled and expectation grew. Chatter broke out among the crowds on the walkways, and as though she had the power to hold and still time, Phaedria cut through the air with her wand and silence fell. Her chin raised, her nostrils flared and Sprite's binds came undone. He fell to his knees and then off and over the cart.

'Which is it?' she said, stepping over him. 'Did the boy reach Treetops?'

Sorry and broken, Sprite fought his sinewy frame up onto all fours. His head, bloodied, twitched twice.

'Was that a *yes*?'

He fell onto his back and fixed her with his dirty, yellow eyes before nodding weakly. Her own eyes showed the merest glimmer of remorse before she lifted her wand and struck it at the air, doubling the ice-white creature.

All heads bent in. Twisting and bucking, clawing and turning, Sprite turned painfully, painting a circle of green blood on the floor.

The show didn't last long. Gurgling, his blade-like fingers at his chest, Sprite blinked and found Phaedria. She was watching him. He managed somehow to smile and then he stilled, his lids sliding shut.

There was silence. And then a cheer sprang from the mob of coins packing the walkways, feet and spears thumping the floors. Below the celebrations was a mess of a creature.

Phaedria stared at the heap, her eyes unfocused and glazed, and then as though her senses returned on a crashing wave she spun and threw her arms up. 'SIIILLEEEENCE!' she roared.

All instantly obeyed. Her eyes investigated for movement. There was none. She calmed and spoke. 'This creature had to die – I know, I killed him – but I will not be celebrating his death. He was no friend, but he did more than anyone here to help my return. Forcibly, I'll admit.'

She began to wander, bathed in the lapping torchlight, treading among the long shadows in between. She felt at her wand hand, taking the coins in. 'He caught me thirty-three stars.'

A hush fell.

'He was also brave. He could've been one of my greatest Captains, but he was also mad. And very stupid, and so-' She stopped abruptly, pointing her wand at Sprite. 'He couldn't be controlled. He had to go.'

Murmurs echoed around the chamber, the noise growing into the silence.

'He won't receive a burial,' Phaedria announced. 'Instead my wolves shall drag him from here and throw him from the highest limb or tear him to pieces – I don't know which and I don't care. What I do know,' she said sharply, 'is that I left you a task. *I... require... another... ten... stars*! We march. WE MARCH! Bring them to me along the way!'

With a swish of her cloak, she turned heel and parted the crowd, moving swiftly under a raucous and violent approval of noise.

A snake of gold

'Are you sure we're in the right spot?' asked Pluck for the umpteenth time. Henry didn't respond. His shiny, black robin eyes were fixed somewhere far back. He eventually answered with the same response as the one before, and the one before that: 'I don't know.'

Pluck joined Henry for a moment, searching the branches before tweeting irritably that it was all a waste of time. She peered out beyond his shoulder. 'He isn't coming,' she said. 'Or we are in the wrong place.'

'Fly here, carry on there,' said Henry, imitating Llorn, 'and I'll catch up with you as soon as I can. So,' said Henry reverting to himself, 'here we are waiting.' He threw up his wings. 'My guess is as good as yours.'

Pluck stepped around Henry, blocking his view. 'You have been to this part of the tree before, so your guess would in fact be better than mine.'

Henry huffed, giving Pluck his full, grudging attention. 'Don't you care that Llorn isn't here? Our guardian, our guide? The one picked to lead our mission?'

Pluck rolled her eyes and dropped her wings, keen to get away from the subject. She joined Henry at his side, finally coming round to the fact that Llorn was way overdue an appearance. 'Where *is* he, Henry?' she asked, suddenly concerned.

Henry wrapped a wing around the little robin. Together they watched and waited.

*

Tired and a little sleepy, the young robins were laid out on a branch. They'd cleared the snow from it and bunched some needles to create a barrier from the wind for warmth. Gabriel flew in from nowhere, scaring them witless.

'Great stars!' cried Pluck, a wing on her chest calming her heart. 'Where in Treelights did you come from?'

Gabriel didn't answer immediately. She was busy checking them over. 'I've been looking around,' she said, touching their heads with a wingtip, 'and I'm no closer to finding where we are. Are you both okay?'

166

Both nodded vigorously and then blurted something about Llorn at the same time, causing Gabriel's features to wring.

'Llorn isn't here yet,' said Pluck finally, and Gabriel's head rose instantly, looking out over their heads.

'How long has he been gone?'

'A long time.'

'Are you sure this is the meet point?'

'Well,' said Henry, recounting the instruction and star-grouping. 'We're pretty sure.'

'And he seemed okay to you?'

The robins turned to one another and nodded. 'Same grumpy old Llorn,' said Pluck.

'Then,' said Gabriel with growing concern, 'something is wrong.'

At that moment a fanfare sounded, startling the birds, distant but unmistakable. Gabriel swept across, hurrying them to cover. She told the birds to stay while she fluttered to a vantage point. What she saw made her tremble.

A glittering snake of gold – four coins wide – and as far back as her eyes could see, stretched out below her, winding and marching. A war machine in motion. Spear points jostled along its spine like some terrible creature's armour, as blades and slings and nets made up the gaps.

Along the edges were runners and scouts. They whipped in and out of the dense branch, hunting for spies or possibly stars. But any star would have fled this golden river coursing their land.

'By all the fairies...' said Pluck, joining Gabriel's side.

Henry had followed too. Gabriel didn't scold them. Too much was going through her mind, but she soon had them low and out of sight.

'Bear,' blurted Henry, suddenly clamouring to see, but Gabriel held him back. Instead she looked herself, slowly and carefully. Her expression didn't alter, and when she turned to Henry he already knew.

'I can't see a bear. He may be further ahead, or even right down at the back-'

'Then he's back at the fort,' cried Henry, as a wing was brought over his mouth.

'Quiet!' hissed Gabriel, peering around. 'That too is a possibility, but unlikely.'

Henry didn't calm until Gabriel shook him still. 'Will you be quiet?' After a pause and a nod, her wing was removed.

'Llorn,' said Henry, his voice hushed and emotional, 'is supposed to be here. To rescue him. The mice too. It was his job.'

Pluck watched Phaedria's army, entranced, her features lit a sun-kissed gold.

'Do you see him or any mice here?' asked Gabriel, running a wingtip. 'I don't.'

Henry remained unmoved.

'Henry,' sighed Gabriel, rolling her eyes, 'I would gladly offer myself to the task, but you can see what is down there. I have to hurry back and warn our Queen.'

'So let me try,' implored Henry. He knew from Gabriel's stern look that it wasn't an option.

Pluck came skipping over, diving between the pair. 'I've counted more than two hundred so far,' she whispered excitedly. As her head spun from Henry to Gabriel, she began to sense something was up. 'Is there a problem, other than the one below?'

'Gabriel was just leaving,' said Henry, glum. 'She needs to warn the Queen.'

Pluck's brain stalled but sparked with a thought.

She sauntered up to Henry and threw a wing around him. The other she pointed at Gabriel. 'You'd best be off then, but don't worry-'

'I won't be worrying,' said Gabriel, 'because I know you'll be watching after Henry very carefully and with absolutely no messing about, and you are going to get him, and yourself, in the opposite direction to this army.'

As they nodded – Henry a little reluctantly – she checked their eyes for sincerity and then quite unexpectedly broke from character and hugged them both. 'May the luck of Treelights go with you both,' she breathed, cradling their heads, 'and make sure to keep going. Don't stop. I'll send some angels to find and guide you as soon as I can.'

And with a flutter of wings she bade them farewell. Her show of concern left Henry wondering as he stood dumbly, until Pluck's wing clapped his back, taking him a step forward.

'Well, my fine young robin,' said Pluck with all the gusto of a pirate setting sail. 'We – that's you and me – are finally shot of that worrisome old bird, so whaddya say we tag along with this bunch, at a fair distance of course, and see what they're up to?'

She hung on Henry like a drunken madam awaiting his answer.

'Don't you ever listen?' said Henry, lifting Pluck off him. 'We've got to go-' Henry stopped as something jarred in his mind.

He stood and thought, and thought some more, and something like a smile crept onto Pluck's face. It were as though she were silently coaxing something from him.

'We could look for Bear,' said Henry, brightening.

'And the mice too,' said Pluck, filling in the gaps.

The pair shook wingtips and agreed to keep track of the marching army below – at a safe distance of course.

'Don't forget,' said Pluck, 'that we are birds, so don't go panicking if we are spotted somehow.'

The pair sprang off to follow with Henry searching, and with Pluck loving every dangerous minute.

*

The birds' enthusiasm as they winged through the tree was now fast disappearing. This army was huge. Bear just wasn't to be seen and invariably slipped from Henry's mind as the sheer size of Phaedria's forces began to awaken him to the very real possibility that soon there would be a war, and possibly no Treefolk thereafter.

Perhaps he'd been short-sighted. But what could he do? What could *they* do? Frustration ate at Henry as he hopelessly observed the golden line below. They would surely now have to follow orders.

With a swift turn of wing, he made after Pluck who'd landed on a bough and was hopping between the dark branches, spellbound by the show below.

'Pluck,' he said, tapping her shoulder with a wing. 'We've got to get out of here.'

But Pluck pushed it off. 'I've found its beginning,' she whispered. 'We're near to the front – *the very front.*'

Henry peered down, dazed. 'How far along?'

'Down there.'

Henry's head swam with indecision. Below, the dark branches hissed and snapped as someone pushed through them. A circular silhouette appeared. It turned slowly, stilled, then skipped on. The pair breathed again.

'It's too dangerous,' urged Henry. 'Let's get away... *that* way.' He motioned, throwing his wing behind him.

But Pluck just shook her head. 'How much longer do you think we'll stay as birds? We double back, maybe get lost. The tree, by the time we're back to our own forms, will be crawling with coins and then I doubt we'll ever get back. No. Our best chance is to get ahead, to follow their direction, which is almost certainly Treelights, and get clear.'

Henry listened and had to admit she was probably right. They were, after all, quite lost. And if they transformed? Well, that didn't bear thinking about.

'Okay,' agreed Henry, gazing down, gold and torchlight in his eyes, 'but we need to be quick and careful and-'

'You worry too much,' said Pluck, rubbing his feathery head. 'Come on, let's go.'

And from that point on they picked a route through the tree, high above Phaedria's army, quickly and quietly until Pluck's signal halted them. Down below, she pointed, was the spearhead of Phaedria's force. A line six-wide of large, brutish coins, scything foliage and snapping branches; smaller coins flitted off, like bees, searching and hunting.

Among all this was Phaedria, stood atop her sleigh, pulled by her slavering, padding wolves. Occasionally she'd throw up an arm, sending flare-like lights off into the tree, illuminating paths for the coins in their search for stars. Behind, her forces soldiered on.

Henry nudged Pluck and the pair slipped into shadow, off on their way, ever watchful for her scouts.

*

The confines of their dark surrounds had been steadily opening out for the two young robins, affording easier passage from one part of the tree to another. The light was stronger here, thrown up from the broadening snowy ground until they shot from the branch onto a bright, wintry plane.

With their eyes unaccustomed, they floundered and flapped before righting themselves and turned a slow circle, alighting onto a branch. Their eyes adjusted, they peered out.

The tree they perched in stood atop a long, snowy slope down to a jagged ravine, running sideways across the land. It spanned as far as they could see. Beyond it lay a barren expanse of snow before the thick green of the tree began again.

'Well,' said Pluck, adjusting her hold on the branch, 'I've never seen this before.'

'I might have,' said Henry, straining a look down its length. 'I think this is Winter's Cut, but the beginning maybe.'

Pluck frowned and turned to her friend. 'How do you know about that place?'

'Well... oh, it doesn't matter.'

'It's so still.' Pluck craned her head around. 'No wind, no movement in the trees.'

'I don't like it,' said Henry, his feathers bristling.

'Well, we've still got to cross it.' Pluck leapt from the branch, turning a few graceful twists before beating her wings to hover before Henry. 'We're running out of time, remember?'

The robins took off, gliding down the hillside to land before the precipice. They tiptoed up to its edge and gingerly looked in. Harsh, icy walls fell away on both sides to the snow-covered ground way below, its bed littered with boulders and branches – a dumping ground of sorts. Purple and blue streaked the icy faces.

'How wide do you think it is?' asked Henry, raising his head to the other side.

'Too far for the Fallen Fairy to cross,' said Pluck, following his line of sight. 'Just what is she playing at? How do they expect to get over this?'

Henry searched the ground, the walls, *anywhere*. 'There,' he said, extending a wing. 'Further along. Is that a bridge?'

Pluck screwed up her eyes. 'Maybe, maybe.' The robin leaned out to see. Tipping over to fall, she rode down the steep walls and banked off above the deep bed toward it. 'Come on,' she called back, the sound echoing through the pass.

Henry fell too, his stomach still not used to the sensation, and flapped to catch up. He caught up to Pluck, who was standing on the divide.

'It's a bridge, all right,' said Pluck, her beak pecking at the floor beneath her. 'Seems it's made of ice.'

Henry trod around. It was indeed ice, arcing up in the middle and spanning from edge to edge. The bridge was perhaps three coins wide and without sides.

'This is where they'll cross,' said Henry, drawing up. His eyes moved to the forest wall. 'She knows it's here.'

Pluck nodded agreement, though he paused. 'Would it be strong enough, for an army I mean?'

'If they went one at a time, perhaps.' Henry came low, looking closer at the ice.

Pluck launched and flew a few tight rings around the bridge before pulling up beside Henry. 'It does have some cracks, but I think it'll hold if they're careful.'

Both then spotted a light, orange and wavering, appearing on the edge of the forest. Beneath it stood a coin, his arm raising a flaming torch.

He spied the bridge and two birds taking flight, probably disturbed by his appearance, off and into the woodland beyond.

The coin thought nothing of them.

He grinned and nodded before heading back.

A bridge too far

Phaedria's forces arrived, preceded by the glow of fire and the splitting of timber.

More and more appeared, woven along the forest's edge, their demeanour excited, their eyes wide and roving. With a path clear for their master, she rode out of the darkness to the edge of the hill. Her eyes found the bridge, but she showed no sign of relief or joy, only blinking her dull, black eyes before raising her wand high.

A flare popped, rising high above the ravine and staining all with a deep red hue. Her wolves pulled on, sliding Phaedria atop her sleigh to the mouth of the bridge. Her coin forces poured after her and lined up, a fair distance from the steep edge.

The Fallen Fairy dismounted and trod to the bridge, but stopped short, her face stained by the downing flare. Memories rotated though her mind. One of her captains ran up to her side, offering apologies and brushing splinters from his person. 'We found it then,' he said, panting and looking around.

Phaedria ignored him and instead lowered to a knee to look across the span of ice.

'Will it hold us?' asked the coin.

'The question is will it allow us?'

Her Captain struck confused.

She rose to walk the edge of the ravine before stopping and turning. 'Bring me a scout.'

The Captain saluted and trotted off to a group of small coins. With one selected, they returned before her.

'Very good,' she said, her eyes only on the bridge. 'Off you go.'

The scout, processing the task, paused before he was shoved forward by his Captain. 'You heard,' he said, the back of his hand raised in warning. 'Go and get to the other side.'

Like a curious cat, the scout came low to the ground, his hands touching the snow as he approached the icy path. He put a foot forward, unhurried and cautious, followed by another – his beady, fearful eyes pulling side to side. As he approached the centre, his confidence grew, enough to rise and walk, but his senses stalled him and he stopped.

A wind had picked up. Snow tickled down the bridge past his feet. He turned to watch them past him, and noticed the golden army stood silent. A howl sounded through the pass, rising to a scream. It brought a flurry, then a storm before a blizzard came. The coin disappeared from view.

With the weather subsiding, the bridge came into focus, minus the scout. The Captain threw a hand to his mouth.

Phaedria gave a single nod. 'This is old magic. A parlour trick from an aged foe.' She strolled forward, stroking her wand. Her cloak trailed the uneven ground until she stood upon the edge of the chasm, her eyes searching below. Her Captain joined her search but found nothing new.

'Whom do you speak of, my Queen?'

'Winter,' she said.

'Who-' asked her Captain, his mouth a quizzical hole, 'is "Winter", my Queen?'

Throwing her cloak to her shoulder, Phaedria came closer to the sheer edge and peered in, just as a witch might gaze into a cauldron. 'I know who you are,' she whispered to the void. 'I have grown.'

Behind, her army of coins watched on. She stepped back and withdrew her wand. As if conducting an orchestra, Phaedria bounced her wand tip until her hand began to jump, pointing here and touching there, drawing circles in the air, her eyes tight shut. She finished with a slash, her arms splayed at her side. Phaedria's eyes opened. 'It's done.'

'Done?' asked her Captain, his face peeping over the edge.

'We can cross now.'

'We can?'

'*You* can. It's wiser to try the life of one coin than to risk an army of them.'

'I see,' said the coin, wringing his hands. 'I suppose it makes sense.'

Dazed, he marched away until he found himself staring across the long span of ice. Just moments ago, a scout had stood here. Where was he now? He stepped forward, trying to rebel against his fear; after all, he had no choice – and he was a Captain.

All eyes were on him, expectant, as the coin felt forward with his feet, easing his soles down, perhaps to avoid a possible trip or button that might alert this 'Winter' to his presence. But with each tender step, the coin appeared to grow in calm and confidence until a smile flickered upon his face as he found himself stood halfway. 'It's safe,' he laughed, motioning to the others. 'Come on!'

A murmur rippled through the coins.

Phaedria made no move though. She eyed the great cut instead. It was fortunate for Henry and Pluck, as when they appeared – flapping laboriously with the weight they carried – she didn't immediately notice them.

'Who are they?' the Captain demanded. Phaedria threw her head back. Her expression was urgent, her black eyes darting.

It was too late for her wand to take a clean shot. Two pulses of light shot past the birds and still their path didn't falter. Scarlet and jade exploded in the branches behind them, silhouetting the birds as they dropped their heavy payload – a frozen pinecone – carried by a broad twig it once hung from, straight at the bridge and straight at the Captain, his face streaked with indecision.

'Catch it! CATCH IT!' screamed Phaedria. At the last possible moment, the coin attempted to, his shaking hands ready, but it only served to kill him. He was crushed outright and carried with the cone, clean through the bridge and into the abyss.

'NO!' Phaedria twisted her hand as though trying to reverse the action, but nothing came of it.

A finger of ice held the last of the bridge, but with a 'ping' the joint spun into the air before following the bridge down, spinning and crashing off the walls. She stared disbelieving; then her eyes found the birds who'd done this – turning tail in the opposite direction – and they magnified with outrage.

She contorted with anger, firing wild bursts of light after them, but in her shaking rage none found their targets and only served to light fires in the trees beyond. The birds were now gone, diving out through a hole in the branch.

Phaedria stepped forward onto the broken mouth of what was once the bridge and looked in. For a moment she did nothing, and then her shoulders began to rise as she drew upon a seemingly endless intake of breath. Her army shrank back as she turned looking murderous.

*

175

Phaedria's subsequent outburst concluded with a pile of buckled and melted coins. Some were fixed in their last act of defence – hands uselessly raised against the force that had met them. For the rest of the coins it was good news.

Her anger had subsided.

She paced in thought, fingering her wand. Halting, she looked up, her thinking done. 'Form a line of twenty-eight... no, twenty-six coins. My strongest, fittest and most flexible.'

The coin army looked among themselves. Some stepped forward. As they lined up, Phaedria surveyed them.

'Put down your weapons or anything you carry. Now.'

The group did as she said and made a pile of blades, spears and nets. One newly-elected Captain later and her plan took shape; one that would test the very fibres of her chosen band.

Balanced like circus acrobats, stood one on top of the other, two towering lines swayed. Each were thirteen coins high. They pitched and staggered with the broadest of coins at the bottom of each, huffing and puffing and shuffling around.

Most of Phaedria's army – heads back, eyes up – were grinning. The order, as bellowed up by the new Captain, was to join the two lines by linking arms.

All eyes watched the towers of gold totter into place upon the very edge of the chasm. Arms were linked, the towers locked side by side. Phaedria screamed her final demands and the coins fell forward as one.

The topmost, their eyes fearfully large, threw out their arms and grabbed for the lip – crying out as they landed. Hands held fast, straining and heaving as the weight was taken. Woven like chainmail, the coin bridge groaned collectively, swinging like a hammock.

Cheers and laughter rang out from the remaining coin forces, cut short by a stare from their Queen. 'Captain! Ten of your coins. Round them up fast and cross. Do it now!'

Falling over himself, he brought the coins forward and prodded them, much to their annoyance, across to the double-line of coins, each linked face down, gently swaying.

'Go on,' barked the Captain, shoving the last in the back. 'Get going!'

The ten trod across the backs of their moaning comrades and reached the other side. The bridge, however, had suffered. Cries of 'hurry up!' and 'get moving!' sounded up from the deep cut.

Prompted by a wand, the Captain made a line of the rest and began to order them over when a problem occurred. One of the coin links was blubbing, saying this wasn't what he'd signed up for and that he was growing weaker by the second. Receiving a quiet nod, the Captain swung a small stick he'd fashioned as a baton up and under his arm and proceeded over. Below him and two links ahead was the coin.

A boot in his back silenced him, and then another forever as his fellow links let go, not wanting to go with him. He made no sound as he spun free.

'Another coin!' called the Captain, having to shout over the groans that had intensified upon being a link down. None came forward. He drew breath to repeat the order, but he caught Phaedria's eye. She motioned for him to fill the space. Cursing under his breath, he clambered flat and into place.

'Six at a time!' yelled Phaedria as she climbed into her carriage; her wolves pulled forward and slid over the bridge, followed by quick-marching pockets of coins, giving the golden causeway good reason to cry out.

It took the horde only a short time to cross, though to the twenty-six it felt an eternity. Shallow breaths and grunts were the only noises now.

Phaedria stepped to the ravine's edge. 'Well done,' she applauded, 'well done.' Now hold tight all of you.'

Twenty-six coins, previously groaning, choked a collective breath as Phaedria pulled her wand. Crackling fingers of white lightning leapt from it and danced upon the opposite ridge. Twenty-six eyes bulged as the far wall cracked away, falling like a silent tombstone, taking the back four with it.

Too tensed to cry out, the chain – still clinging to the near edge – swung and clattered into the icy wall.

Phaedria stepped forward and peered over. 'Let's not hang about,' she called down. 'We've got a tree to take.'

A curious sensation

S omewhere around mid-tree, just north of the cut, Henry and Pluck were still flapping, their slapping wingtips broadcasting their whereabouts.

The sound didn't travel far, as the tree here was dense with thick, healthy green, though wide enough in places for a pair of fast-travelling birds. Also thick here was a pressing gloom; there seemed to be an absence of light from the stars, perhaps an absence of stars themselves.

In the closing darkness they began to slow until one of the birds touched clumsily down onto a thin branch. The other landed by its side.

Henry looked back to where they'd come from. 'We seem clear now.'

There were no sounds of pursuit, no sound at all other than their small, laboured breaths.

'You think she has the power to transform coins to birds?' asked Henry.

'Perhaps,' said Pluck, rolling her aching wings, 'though we'd have seen or heard if she had.'

'Well, she didn't look happy. Let's not hang around.'

'Agreed,' said Pluck. 'It's lucky we're bird-form as I think she'd probably have us by now, although-' She winced. 'I am looking forward to getting back to my angelic self.'

'Okay?' asked Henry. He noticed that Pluck looked pained.

'Yeah. Just feeling a bit odd.'

Curiously, Henry felt his own stomach lurch sideways. 'Oh-' he said, his head beginning to swim, 'now you say it.'

Pluck wasn't listening. She was clutching her feathered chest with a wing, looking sick. Henry saw her arch. She squawked and exploded in a puff of feathers. Henry stared, beak agape.

Through the falling plume, Henry could see Pluck half-buried in a snowy drift below. He jumped to fly after her but he plummeted instead, his mass doubling, tripling until he landed deep in the snow, exploding feathers himself. Pluck hauled herself up, groaning and dizzy, her fingers feeling at her face.

'Henry. Henry?'

The boy popped his head up. Pluck screamed.

Henry had a tiny beak where his mouth was. Trying to speak, he emitted a piercing whistle, deafening the girl until it suddenly fell off and his mouth grew back. 'Sorry about that,' he said, feeling at his lips.

Henry pulled himself out of the snow, relieved to find himself still clothed, just as Lilly had promised. 'I think I'm okay,' he said, patting snow from himself. 'You?'

Pluck looked herself up and down. With her arms extended, she turned a full circle.

'Don't worry,' said Henry. 'I don't see any feathers, other than your wings of course.'

'Good,' said Pluck. She flapped them, shaking off the last of the snow, and scrutinised their surroundings. 'Well, I guess we're walking now.'

Henry adjusted his dressing gown and doubled the knot at his waist. 'Know which way we are going?'

Pluck nodded forward. 'I think it's *that* way.'

The pair wandered off, recounting their short lives as birds, laughing as they went.

*

Not far away, a wolf's head cocked to the air. He'd failed to pick up a scent, but he had heard a strange whistle. The beast narrowed its eyes of white fire and padded off in its direction.

Twin moons

Lilly stood within Treetops gazing up to the mountains, to the castle carved in stone. The only movement she made was the fretful steps of her fingers, up and down her wand.

A coin guard approached but paused short, looking a little awkward. She was alone. He'd noticed his Queen's absent look; it made her look like a little girl lost, but he wasn't about to remark so. As she hadn't noticed him, he took a step forward and coughed lightly. Her glassy eyes flickered but drew focus as she turned.

'Julius,' she said, her view returning to the castle.

'My lady,' he said smartly. The coin kept his eyes forward, awaiting questioning. The air only swelled with silence. Eventually his Queen lowered her wand. She tilted her head toward him though her gaze remained on the mountain. 'How many of our envoys have returned?'

The coin glanced at her before answering. 'Of the seven who went out, four have returned.'

'How many,' she asked, as though cautious of eavesdroppers, 'will rally?'

'Not nearly enough, my Lady.'

Lilly digested this news and straightened, nodding slowly, distant. 'Not nearly enough...' she repeated, fingering her wand. 'Any news from Llorn's party?'

Julius, still stood to attention, answered. 'None as yet, my Lady.'

Lilly muttered something, too quiet to hear. The coin at her side flashed a look of concern. He rearranged his footing and drew breath to speak, thought better of it, but spoke anyway. 'Is everything okay, my Lady?'

She didn't answer straight away. He watched the absent turning of her wand.

'You know,' she said, thinking aloud. 'I've never felt that that castle had a place here.'

Julius listened.

'I can enter the main doors, but none of the rooms,' said Lilly, half-laughing.

The coin looked to the castle, his brow creased. He looked glumly around the mountain line.

'Enchantments,' she said, tapping memories. '*Powerful* enchantments.'

She flicked her eyes sideways. 'Took a great effort to oust her. Luck too.'

She rolled her eyes back to the mountain, her face darkening. 'We shouldn't have won, you know.'

The coin's eyes dulled. He seemed to be elsewhere, turning over thoughts.

'Would we be so fortunate this time?' She tailed off and looked up to the star. Julius followed her line of sight.

She placed a hand upon her guard. 'We shall certainly try.'

Julius smiled. He firmed a grip on his staff and looked up to his Queen.

'I can't chance our fate,' she said finally. 'I'll go out, gather our tree's numbers. We'll make a stand.'

Her hand left the coin as she turned to him, her mood brightening. 'This will mean that there will be great responsibility upon your broad golden shoulders. I will leave you to muster what army we have here. Mobilise *everyone*.'

Julius gripped his staff resolutely and thumped it into the floor. 'It shall be done.'

'Then there is no time to waste.' Closing her eyes, she clapped her hands. 'We must be ready.'

As Julius saluted, an old bauble lined with a tatty red velvet arrived. She leapt up to grab its trailing line.

Lilly looked down to her guard and smiled. 'May we borrow again from the luck that brought us back from the darkness.'

With that, she threw back her head and was gone.

*

'And now?'

Pluck looked up. The tree had become heavy with darkness and silence, the dull glow of snow beneath their feet providing the only light.

Henry and Pluck had been walking, climbing and trudging in the direction of Treelights, at least they hoped so. Where they'd begun jolly and optimistic, it now felt like they'd been abandoned.

Pluck rubbed her neck. 'I'm not sure,' she said limply.

The boy sighed with impatience. 'Any idea?'

'Henry,' said Pluck halting, 'there are no stars here and haven't been for quite a while. I'd normally be able to navigate by them, and so right at this moment, and in almost complete darkness, it's nearly impossible to tell where we are.'

'Okay, okay.' Henry kicked up snow and stopped, gazing up. Deciding they may as well be blindfolded, he dropped onto an upended log. 'We might as well rest,' he said, patting a space behind him. 'Come on Pluck, sit down.'

Pluck's wings fell behind her shoulders as she dragged herself over and slumped down. 'I feel useless at the moment,' she said, rubbing a sore foot. Henry thought in that moment she might cry.

'Useless?' he laughed, pulling her into his shoulder. 'Is this the same young robin that brought Phaedria's army to a grinding halt?'

Pluck sniffed, looking sorry for herself, and then laughed against her will. 'Well of course I've been useful. That's why Lilly sent me.'

Henry gave a half-smile and tried another look up into the tree. A silence grew.

'Tell me about yourself,' said the boy, resting down to an elbow.

Pluck pondered the question as though it were a very strange thing to ask. 'What do you want to know?'

'Oh, I don't know... how old are you?'

'Eight.'

'And you?'

'Same,' Henry nodded.

Pluck scratched her arm.

'Your parents?' Henry ventured.

'What about them?'

'Where are they?'

'They're dead.'

'Oh,' said Henry, rising. 'I'm sorry. What happened?'

'Phaedria,' said Pluck, her eyes dull.

'Phaedria? The Fallen Fairy?'

'Yes, Phaedria the Fallen Fairy,' said the angel, her patience done.

Henry regretted the question. 'I'm-'

'Don't worry,' Pluck cut over him. 'It was back when she turned bad, went mad – I don't know. Anyway, I was very small at the time.'

Silence crept up again. Pluck looked off, reflecting. Henry leaned forward, kicking his heels into the log they sat on.

'What about you? How'd a human young end up in the tree?'

Henry looked blank, asking himself the same question. 'It seems like such a long time ago now, I'm not sure.'

'How can you not know how you got inside the tree?' Pluck was suddenly animated. 'Let's start from the beginning. Where are you from?'

'Well.' Henry rubbed his chin as though the question were tricky. 'I'm from the lounge – I mean, the lounge in my house which... which is in London.'

Pluck spun on the log and sat hugging her legs. 'Describe "lounge" for me.'

'Lounge?' Henry was bemused. 'Well, a lounge is a living area.'

'You mean living like a forest full of plants?'

'No. Well, there are plants, but not too many,' he said, turning to Pluck. 'It's certainly not a forest. There's a settee, a sofa and a T.V. and-'

'T.V.?' Pluck swatted the air. 'It all sounds a bit confusing really. Can't you just skip to the bit about how you entered the tree?'

Henry stood and shuffled a circle. 'This tree, this actual tree we are in...' Henry groped for a better explanation. 'Is sitting in my lounge at home.'

Pluck did nothing for a moment and then rocked backward laughing.

'This tree? This great, enormous tree is in the place you call a lounge? Just how big,' she scorned, 'is this lounge of yours?'

Henry hopped off the log and took a stick from the ground. He walked something of a square, dragging a line as he went, before tossing it away. Pluck followed the line with her eyes and looked ready to start laughing again. 'Are you all right?' She took Henry's head in her hands and rolled it around to examine it.

Henry batted her away. 'Yes, yes, I'm all right!'

She folded her arms, a little crossly.

'Henry,' she said, reasoning, 'how can that be? Look at the size of your little square, and look at the size of this tree. Your square would fit inside it a gazillion times or more.'

Henry sighed. 'I know, I can't explain it, but this tree at home is probably...' He hopped onto the log and held his arm high, his feet tiptoed. 'This high, I would say.'

Pluck looked curious. She could see Henry wasn't joking and believed that in his mind at least he told the truth. She became serious for a moment. 'Tell me how,' she said, folding her arms, 'you came to own the tree.'

Henry looked blank for a moment. 'We bought it.'

Pluck poked her head forward. 'You bought it,' she echoed.

'Yes, every year,' said Henry, now walking a circle in the dark, 'me and my father go out and choose a Christmas tree. We buy one, the best looking one, and tie it to the top of his car and we plant it in a red bucket and we decorate it.'

Pluck was trying to listen, but it was all too much, like she'd been following directions to some faraway place that had too many twists and turns in it.

In the end she shook her head to clear the confusion. 'I think when you switched back from being a robin,' she said, her eyes wandering to his forehead, 'your brain didn't quite make it back.'

'I'm telling the truth.'

Pluck could see the appeal in Henry's eyes but her own didn't soften. 'So where did I come from? And all the other Treefolk?'

Henry stifled a laugh. Pluck gave a quarter-turn of her head to hear clearly. He looked at the young angel with a measure of guilt. 'We keep you all in a cardboard box in the loft.'

'A box?' she said, turning her head a little more.

'Yes, a box with balls of newspaper to stop anything breaking.'

Pluck said nothing. Henry shrugged.

'You're deluded, Henry,' she decided. 'Perhaps Lilly can give your head a tap with her wand.' She turned a finger. 'To get your mind working again.'

'Suit yourself,' said Henry, hopping back onto the log. 'But I'm telling you-'

Something growled. Henry and Pluck froze, their breaths held, their hearts thumping. All around them was darkness and shadow.

Henry began moving his widening eyes around the dark clearing. Nothing could be seen. The sound had been unmistakable.

Henry risked a movement by looking to Pluck, his hand cupped to his mouth. *'What do we do?'*

'Start by shutting up and staying still!' she hissed back.

184

The pair gawped at the gloom around them, their mouths open. Twin moons came out of the darkness. They hung there, unblinking, staring. Another growl. Slower. Guttural.

Pluck threw her hands to her mouth, but the gasp had already escaped it. Henry spoke in ragged breaths. He could make no sense. The lamps of white fire thinned, their intent clear.

'Run!' screamed Pluck, grabbing up the folds of her dress and spinning in the snow. 'Right now, Henry, right now!'

Henry didn't follow for a moment, transfixed by the eyes of something he couldn't see. Then he turned, stricken, and leapt away.

Henry pistoned his legs, his adrenaline pumping. He caught up to Pluck, ducking her way through the branches. Her desperation was evident in her whimpering breaths, and between them they fought and tumbled over the snow and brush, trying to escape.

The wolf made no move. It could travel swiftly over this ground, this terrain. It could hear every breath of its prey and the thin pine air was thick with the scent of young.

The wolf might have drawn it out, made a sport of it, but he had a master now; one he felt compelled to obey. He had a job to do. He set off, building speed, panting lustfully, muscular haunches now powering into the snow, his massive black outline visible every now and then through the gloom. He would soon be upon them.

A short way ahead, the boy and the angel stumbled on. Their faces were scratched by the low branch, their legs caked in snow. Then with a cry of pain, Pluck was pulled backwards.

'Pluck!'

Henry stopped and staggered back through the dark to where Pluck hung helpless and exhausted, snagged badly on a branch by her wing.

'Oh Henry!' she cried. 'I can't get free. *I can't get free!*'

Henry untangled her, his fingers fighting feather and needle, but he felt the hammering of paws and heard the breaths that told of widening jaws.

'Close your eyes!' came a voice. Henry held Pluck, confused, but he did as he was told. A light, brilliant-white burnt fierce upon Henry's lids. He wondered if he was dead. He came round to Pluck clawing at his arm. Noises travelled to his ears. The same voice as before, along with others, was urging something away.

'Come back,' said Pluck into his ear.

Henry tumbled to the floor, still clutching the angel, and he felt the shock of the cold snow. His eyes flicked open. The wolf, dark and huge before him, recoiled from an intense but pleasant light – a light from a hovering star. Three portly Christmas puddings stood below it brandishing weapons. They advanced step-by-step onto the beast, jabbing spears at it, ordering it low, ordering it to leave.

Snarling and biting at the weapons, the wolf eventually cowered and turned tail, its eyes almost closed to the fierce light.

'Easy now,' said a pudding to the star. 'You did good, you did good.'

Butter-brandy topped and strapped with weapons, the pudding reached out and brought the star close. The star stuttered and blinked, its features returned, the job done. It gradually morphed back to a comfortable glow.

'There's a lad,' said another pudding, walking over to drive the butt of a spear into the snow. He came close, marvelling at the light, admiring the spirit of the little fellow.

'It's no wonder these are being stolen by the Dark Witch,' said a third pudding, his eyes pulling from the light to the young pair on the ground, 'but I'll bet she had her beady sights set on these unfortunates.' He lowered, bringing his hands to his knees. 'Are you two okay?'

Still in shock, Henry gazed up as all three puddings looked to him, their shiny black eyes on Pluck for a moment but then returning to Henry, wide and glistening.

'Is that a human?'

Henry coughed. A pungent smell of spirit hung thick in the air, but he said nothing and rose to present himself.

'Henry,' he said, brushing his palms free of snow and offering a hand.

'Pleased to meet you,' said the pudding, his voice tinged with amusement.

'Thanks,' said Henry. 'For saving us, that is.'

'Oh, don't worry,' said the first pudding, releasing the faint star into the air. 'It wasn't any bother. We were in the area anyway.'

'I'm McDonald, this here's McHooten and lastly,' the Pudding threw a thumb backward, 'that's McPud.'

186

McPud looked to be thinking. He stirred out of his wonder and suddenly pushed between the puddings, pointing an accusatory finger at Henry. 'I've heard, of all things, that these humans quite like to eat a bit of pudding.'

'Will you just ease down there, McPud,' said McDonald.

'Aye,' said McHooten on the other side, having to hold back his animated friend.

'I think all that brandy you're soaked in has finally gone to your head.'

'It's the truth, I'm telling you. Just ask the boy – *ask the boy*!'

By now, Pluck had risen to her feet to get involved, but Henry pulled her back.

'It is true,' he said.

'True?' said McHooten, as though he had a bad taste in his mouth.

McPud had stopped wriggling and was looking wide-eyed at McDonald.

'You see? You see? *True.*'

McDonald turned to Henry. 'Is that so?'

'Some humans do,' said Henry, his hands open. 'At Christmas, that is.'

McPud re-doubled his efforts to reach the lad, but McDonald held him.

'At Christmas-time too!' cried McPud, his body arched in outrage. 'The monsters!'

'But they're not real – the puddings we eat, I mean.' Henry looked between them. 'They only *look* like you.'

'Lies! Lies!'

'Will you quit it'?' McDonald grabbed McPud and shook him. 'He's only a wee lad, not a monster, you big daft Pud.'

'Only pretend Puds? Not real live Puds?' asked McHooten.

'Only pretend Puds, and I'd know; my dad makes them.'

'Well,' said McDonald, releasing his friend, 'that's good enough for me.'

McPud felt all eyes upon him.

'Okay, okay,' he said, throwing his arms up. 'I can see the wee chap is no threat to us and probably not a monster.'

'Then the lad and his angel can be called friends,' said McHooten, his arms open in a welcoming gesture.

Pluck folded her arms. 'I am not *his* angel.'

McPud came over and ruffled the angel's hair. 'Whatever you say, Missy. Whatever you say.'

Pluck pulled away, incensed. 'Aren't you lot a Star Squad?'

'Oh aye,' said McDonald, plucking his spear from the ground.

'Well, aren't you supposed to be finding stars?'

'This,' said McHooten, turning, 'is the very last one in these parts.'

'Well, then we'd better get going,' said Pluck. 'Phaedria and her army are heading this way right now.'

'Phaedria? That witch? I've a bone to pick with her,' said McPud, inflating and about to march. A cuff around his ear stopped him.

'Are you a fool, McPud?' said McDonald. 'You may be handy and all, but to try Phaedria on your own? Bah! You'd be a mad-Pud to try such a thing.'

'Pluck's right,' said Henry. 'We've got to go. I don't mean to sound rude, but she's right behind us. We have to get to Treelights.'

'Aye,' agreed McHooten, looking to the darkness beyond them. 'I suppose you're right.' The pudding shouldered a bag and took some bearings. 'It'll be quicker this way.'

The young pair now had company. Afforded the luxury of starlight, they made off after the three.

*

Fresh from pushing the last of the snow over Llorn, Morris cast about for transport. His grave wasn't particularly deep, but it would veil him for some seasons. Two mice were already ahead of him, scampering off to a branch, bent double from the weight of a bauble.

'It's golden,' noted Bear, appearing beside him. 'Does that mean it's quick?'

Morris gave a little laugh. 'Friend, it's a cruiser, but we'll take it.'

Both looked up to see the ball, skimming on the air down to them, the pairing of Moriarty and Jacob at the helm, both looking happy to be reunited.

They cleared the remaining mice from the snowy floor by skidding round to a halt. The line was tossed. The remaining mice clambered up, clapping the backs of the pair before turning to Morris and Bear.

'Are we really going to The Glades?' asked Bear to his friend.

'I'm afraid so,' said Morris, leading the teddy onward.

Seize them!

The journey so far had passed uneventfully.

It gave the passengers a chance to rest, tend to their wounds and with a comforting knock coming from the bauble's inner workings, it allowed some to ease into sleep.

The tree wound past like clockwork, as branch upon branch seemed to part to allow passage, like arms swung low, revealing the way.

It occurred to Bear that the tree's beauty never diminished. As he sat in silence, the winds tousling his fur, he gazed in quiet wonder at the sights that passed by.

Heavy boughs of snow sometimes gave, dusting them all in crystal white, while branches seemingly as thick as the tree's very trunk snaked off into the heights with stars coiling their length like flexes of neon disco lights. Great beds of deep green made patterns everywhere.

Bear's marvelling eyes were becoming heavy, but before he could finish the sequence of nods that would take him to sleep, he was prodded in his chest by an old wooden pipe.

His eyes fell upon the oldest mouse in the group, Bernard, settling in front of him. 'Where on earth did you get that?' asked Bear.

The old mouse gave him a knowing look. 'Found it under the wheel. Why not? I'll probably be dead soon, anyway.'

He began stuffing tobacco into it as he fixed Bear with an unwavering gaze. Bear settled, resigning himself to the impending conversation.

A downturned flame struck from a flint was already furnacing red and gold embers, and from small sucking noises the old mouse puffed clouds from the side of his mouth that dallied, before catching the wind, forming a faint dotted trail.

'These walnuts,' he said as though picking up the threads of a conversation they'd once had, 'are a tricky lot.'

Bear gave a slow, single nod.

'Consider themselves above all others, y'know,' said the mouse, poking his pipe Bear's way again. 'Oh yes,' he said, puffing, 'they are all high and

189

mighty these days. A shame. They were good company at one time: funny, adventurous, and damn good drinkers.'

The memory brought a smile to Bernard, though it crumpled into mutterings and grumbles as he sunk into himself. 'One thing I will say is that they are a clever bunch. Perhaps,' he wondered, 'they don't think the rest of us are suitable company.'

Bear raised his brow and rocked gently back and forth as he digested all he was being told. Finishing the conversation, the mouse hauled himself from the floor and tapped out his pipe into the passing wind. 'Whatever you are planning,' he said, 'make it good. You've got a promise to keep.'

Bear mulled the conversation over as he watched Bernard shuffle off. Perhaps in that moment, he realised the weight of his words, for he looked about the mice and buried his head between his cradled legs.

*

The Glades appeared quietly, announcing their arrival only through subtle changes in the green and the light reeding through them. Moriarty woke the band by wiggling the craft, causing sleeping heads to slide side to side until they were all awake, much to the amusement of Jacob. Paws rubbed eye sockets until eyes stared in wonder. It took a while for their fellows to rise.

By now, the dark, fitfully-lit tree was behind them with a new world, like an underwater Eden appearing in its place.

In here, the tree's wood seemed to have almost vanished, although from a closer look it had been cleverly concealed by pale green leaf and brush, wrapping it entirely in long tendrils like vines.

In came rays of crisp bright lines from pale stars, finding ways through the broad leaves. The passengers marvelled at the change in scenery, as the usually dark blades of green were now light, elongated and tropical looking. They putt-putted in and out of them, finding their way further in.

Great fans of leaves draped lazily across their path as they pushed on. Jacob pointed, excited. Staring down at them was a walnut.

It was held in a harness, supported by a thin rope that hung from somewhere way up. It observed the craft from over the rims of some spectacles it wore, with eyes dark and raisin-like.

As the bauble passed by, they could see now that the walnut sat in a tan, leathery pouch lined with pockets, tending to some plant life, its little legs dangled through holes. The craft pushed on into another area, all eyes following the nut, and its own following them. There were a flurry of hushed questions.

'Did you see?'

'Whoever was that?'

'Why didn't he talk?'

'What a strange place,' said Morris.

'Agreed,' said Bear.

The baubles' gentle knocking was suddenly drowned out by a zipping, speeding sound as something fell from the heights. A brown parcel appeared before the craft.

It was another walnut, a leathery harness cradling its lower half, the protruding legs painfully thin. The eyes this time had a look of suspicion.

A signal was given and the craft idled into a bough, tied up and shut off. Weapons were raised, but Bear ordered them down.

'Announce yourselves and state your business,' said the walnut in an impeccable accent, dangling before them.

'I am known simply as Bear, and this band are my friends.'

'And tell me, why have you entered the Glades without invitation?'

'We don't mean to trespass,' said Bear. 'We were hoping to speak to someone.'

The walnut rubbed his equivalent of a chin, his shell lined with woody wrinkles, his mouth broad and thin. 'I assume your appearance is unannounced?'

'I guess so.'

Morris stepped forward to enter the conversation. 'We come on behalf of the Treefolk and all its occupants. We are seeking-'

'And who are you to speak out of turn, rodent?' The walnut wriggled his legs to turn. 'I was conversing with the hairy fellow here.'

Morris, bemused, went to speak again, but his friend held him with a paw.

'You, "Bear", continue.'

Bear wrung his paws in appeal. 'We come on behalf of our governing fairy Lilly, for the Treefolk too, as my good friend was saying-'

The nut raised a hand, calling a halt.

'We've had all that nonsense round here before,' he muttered irritably, adjusting his seating. 'I've given you far too much of my time. I fear you will all land me in real trouble. Now I suggest you leave.'

'But-'

'That's an order. Start your craft and head out, and be jolly careful about it. These plants have been nurtured with love and care for many a year, so just mind how you go.'

Much huffing and puffing went on. Some drew breath to speak, but they held dutifully, waiting on Bear. Unable to contain himself, Morris voiced his feelings.

'Now listen up, you fool,' he said, shaking a paw. 'There's a war about to start and we are all involved. We're heavily outnumbered and we must have your help.'

Morris's speech backfired as the walnut began bouncing in his pouch, his raisin eyes creasing with anger. 'Get out!' he blasted. 'Out! Out! OUT!'

Initially shocked, the mice deflated. There seemed no way around the cantankerous old nut; even Bear turned resigned to Moriarty.

'Start her up,' he said, his shoulders low.

Jacob hopped up as the bauble fired, untying them from their docking point. As they droned away, the walnut followed their course, taking calming breaths, nodding.

Bear looked around the mice. Their eyes told of disappointment. Even Moriarty looked beat, slumped sullenly over the wheel.

'Let me give you a break,' said the teddy bear, easing the mouse's grip. 'You've hardly slept. Here, let me take a turn.'

Moriarty laughed. 'It's appreciated, but no. It takes time to qualify as a pilot. You can't just-'

Bear shoved the mouse sideways. He spun the wheel a circle and threw a lever forward. Every-mouse began skidding backward as the craft clunked and jumped, building speed into a long banking turn. The walnut, still nodding, halted.

Bear and his party were increasing speed. Something was wrong. The bauble bombed an erratic circle and straightened, fizzing and swerving headlong at the dangling walnut.

A nobbled hand sprung from his pouch and reached, then reached again, until a chord was found and urgently yanked. With the line squealing, the nut shot upward just clear of the careering bauble before it crashed through the greenery.

Moriarty's eyes popped out of his head. 'Bear, you lunatic! What are you doing?'

Bear wasn't listening. He was trailing great lengths of leaf and vine like a kite's tail turning circles, ploughing new and unwanted paths through the Glades. The walnut hung stunned.

He looked down from his vantage point, his mouth quivering, following the buzzing, whipping ball, and then with a strangled moan he exploded with rage.

'Seize them! SEIZE THEM!' he hollered, running the pull-chord between his fingers, bringing him swiftly up through the heights. His call was quickly answered by the stirring of many walnuts.

Bear, meanwhile, was on a wrecking spree. He whooped and cheered every time they tangled through a neat wall of foliage and 'hoorayed' every new addition to the tail they streamed behind them. Morris, his eyes twitching and streaming, managed to reach Bear and clamp his paws around his wrists.

'What in Treelights do you think you're doing?' he shouted above the swish and whip of leaf. 'Are you trying to kill us?'

Before he could answer, a brief scream of glass filled their ears. The party began to fall. They plummeted – clawing at the rushing air.

*

Somewhere deep within the tree, not far from Treelights, Phaedria's army marched. Torches blazed along its immeasurable length, lighting each and every coin beneath in molten gold, their dark lidded eyes fixed front, their legs pistoning through the snow.

Their pace had quickened now. All the scouts had returned. Only one pale star had been caught. Phaedria knew as it sank into her bag that continuing to search would be fruitless. They'd all been called in. They were expecting her.

As her sled thundered over the ground beneath the dark green reaches, the light all but gone, she smiled. This would be something like the tree to come. With sudden force, she yanked at the reins, pulling her wolf up.

The other wolf, absent, had been replaced by a pair of 'volunteer' coins who were both harnessed. With the reins now slack, the pair were able to loosen their binds and wretch.

Phaedria watched the snow-steeped ground ahead. From out of the darkness came a low, black figure – a creeping shadow. It had eyes of depthless white. Nearer, now visible, it padded to the sleigh. Neither wolf acknowledged the other.

'Oh,' blew the first reined coin, a hand at his chest. 'Thank the stars... our relief has come.'

'And not a moment too soon,' gasped the other. 'My casing is almost worn through.'

Leather rolled, biting their backs. 'Unstrap yourselves!'

The coins released themselves and trudged back to join the line.

'If I catch you slacking...'

Both hurried on, looking sick. Phaedria seated the reins and stepped from the sleigh to meet the wolf who'd stopped short. Their eyes met, with her own black liquid, the wolf's pale fire. The connection was broken. The beast slid into the harness, aided by a coin alongside her brother.

Phaedria climbed back aboard and took the reins. 'The boy,' she said, rolling the leather, '*survived.*'

They were off again.

A fresh entanglement

T he demise of the mice and Bear never came. Instead they met with what the walnuts had installed as a precaution: a safety net – broad and strung with rope. It had knocked the wind from them as it creaked, gave and bounced, with many now sporting cuts and bruises, flayed by the branch as they fell.

They rolled around, steadying themselves, as shards of glass and leaf rained down. Morris sat up and did a quick head count.

From the groans of bewilderment came the voice of Bernard. 'What in the blazes were you thinking?'

'Never mind that now,' said Jacob, rubbing a paw over a bump on his little white head. 'I'm sure the furry fellow had a plan – and if he didn't? Well, there was fun to be had at least.'

'Fun?' said the old mouse. 'The toy is a buffoon.'

A paw was placed upon Bernard's shoulder. Heads turned to Bear for an explanation.

He sat up, shrugged, and appealed with open paws. 'I'm sorry, really. But there was only one way for us to gain an audience with these pompous hard-shells-'

'And that,' said Morris, arms crossed, 'was to wreck their precious gardens.'

A thrum of squealing strings cut the air as a troop of walnuts descended from the canopy above, their legs straight out in front. They landed, encircling the untidy mob.

A leaf-strewn Bear stood ready to explain himself, but a staff swung from behind and levelled him. Bear staggered up again, fluffing his head back into shape. A long dent had appeared between his ears. He felt round for a tear as another swish sounded, but the blow never came.

'That'll do.'

Bear turned to see a large walnut, his hand holding the staff – preventing a second strike from a comrade. His would-be assailant shouldered the weapon and creased his raisin-like eyes hatefully.

'We are not barbarians,' he continued, his wood-like fingers turned open-handed to those present.

The mice huddled together.

'My name is Greatshell,' said the large nut, his voice clear and eloquent, 'and I am in charge here.'

His eyes took in Bear and the mixture of mice, stopping briefly on each. A dark crag opened across his round face. 'I advise you not to try anything.'

There were no protests from the group.

'Good,' said Greatshell, bringing his fingers together. 'I am placing you all under arrest and you shall be brought to trial. And as you have damaged our most sacred sanctuary, I do not favour your chances in front of the Great Grand Walnut.'

At this, the assembled nuts bowed.

'But we only wanted-' said Jacob, trying to right himself on the netting before a walnut came forward and slapped him flat.

Up jumped Lawrence, who swung a beautiful left hook – landing square on the walnut – before dropping to a foetal position to cradle his paw. The nut stepped away, expressionless.

'You frightful bullies,' said Bernard, hurrying to the injured mouse's aid.

'Are we done?' said Greatshell to the rest.

An eventual nodding of heads followed.

'Excellent. Then I shall see you all up top.'

The hanging lines around each nut pulled taut, squealing as they lifted the group's captors up and out of sight.

'Oh, Bear,' said Morris, his head in his paws. 'What have you done?'

A mechanical clanking broke the silence from above, as the net's outer edges began to rise, guiding them all to the centre to tumble over one another, forcing them into the ropes' bindings.

They began to rise themselves, bagged and wriggling, bulging the creaking rope all around them. With the net drawn so tightly, none could move. It pulled them steadily upward, jerking every so often bringing moans and groans from the captives.

'Nice going, Bear,' griped Lawrence, still partly blackened from the mines. 'We're trussed up good and proper for your moment of madness.'

'Hush,' mumbled a mouse beneath him. 'At least you're not swinging a pickaxe anymore.'

'Ah, from the frying pan into the fire,' said Lawrence, pushing a paw from his face. 'I guess we should all be grateful.'

Bear, however, hadn't seemed to have heard. He gazed out through the net, his face preoccupied with thought, looking beyond to nothing in particular. A call came down from the top of the net to break up the bickering.

'I see something ahead,' said Jacob, topmost.

The net slowed, turning and straining. Starlight lit them up for a moment. The twinkle of light in Bear's eyes was snuffed out by a looming octagonal shape bearing down on them from above. Eyes rolled upward and paws gripped rope binds as each hoped to catch a glimpse.

A trapdoor was thrown back and the party were brought through, hefted sideways and dropped to a log floor, spilling them wide. Some received a welcome kick from the walnut guards who were stood around the opening.

'Untangle yourselves and get into a line,' said one.

The band hurried upright and shuffled into place. Their eyes moved from the guards to the walls, to the ceiling, all built from timber logging. Beyond was a broad corridor staked with torches.

A large walnut stepped forward. My name is 'Knarl,' he said. 'Remember it.' He paused, awaiting dissent. None came. 'You will now listen to me.'

He unrolled a piece of parchment and read it aloud. 'You are now residing within the Walnut Kingdom. As such, you are the subjects of the Great Grand Walnut and are thusly under his rule.'

The party made no comment, other than the twitch of a nose or a cough. The walnut swept his eyes over the captives before rolling the parchment and strode off, with the band herded after him.

They were led up the corridor which dog-legged here and there, a spear at their backs, the crackle of fire in their ears.

A warmth had built – initially pleasant, given their time atop the baubles – but it began to bloom into an aggressive heat until it became quite uncomfortable, making them at first a little sleepy, then sweaty.

'Saints alive,' said Moriarty, plodding the walkway, pawing sweat from his eyes. 'They've got to be roasting in their shells.'

'Ugh,' said Bernard, stopping. 'Can we please take a break?'

The butt of a spear got him moving again. Before long they'd reached the corridor's end and a vast room presented itself; its ceiling was high and airy, so high that mist-like clouds hung there. All along the walls, from top to bottom, hung vines, plants and even flowers – covering it completely.

Bear trod his paws up and down. 'They've even got grass in here.'

Their eyes were so drawn to the rest of the room, they hadn't even noticed.

'I could live here,' said Jacob, his head swivelling to take it all in.

'Don't get too comfortable,' said a walnut guard. 'You're going straight to the cells to await trial.'

Knarl motioned a hand and the party got moving again, following the chief guard over the grass and around a fountain central to the room – comprised of half a tree trunk. Water spilled from its open top, cascading down its sides to a crystal-clear pool. The Kingdom's gardeners rode lines up and down the walls, trimming and pruning.

Knarl led them into another corridor, tighter and darker than the one before, until he finally stopped before the cells. 'Your new home,' he announced.

The mice in line lifted their heads to see a wall of wooden stakes, floor to ceiling, a small gap between each. A nut guard stepped up, unlocked a door and swung it open. 'In you go,' he said, waving his hand.

The mice, sniffing and touching, felt their way up to the door with each casting a backwards look as they went in, their bodies trembling. Bear hung back, the last to go, and asked Knarl for a quick word.

The guard gave the teddy a curious look, then a malicious grin. They stepped into a darkened corner.

'Knarl, right? That's your name?'

'What do you want?' The nut frowned.

'Look, I understand we're in a whole heap of trouble and that we're due to be tried, okay?'

'Correct,' said Knarl.

'In a courtroom?'

'Right again.'

'By a judge. The judge being the Great-'

'Grand Walnut,' Knarl finished.

'Okay, okay, I've got that,' said Bear, shifting between paws. 'Now, is it possible to find out exactly when that will happen?'

Knarl's eyes thinned. 'Could be next week, could be next month. The fact is that the Great Grand Walnut has a lot of cases to get through. You see, we get a lot of visitors up here.' He leaned forward. '*Unwelcome* visitors. We even found an elf naked in the fountain one morning, swimming circles.'

'Really?' said Bear, tutting.

The guard folded his arms. 'Really.'

'It's just that – now, hear me out please – I'm sure a lot of these cases are minor offences-'

Knarl grabbed Bear by his fur, bringing their faces close. 'We *drink* that water.'

'Oh,' said Bear, screwing his face up. 'That's disgusting.'

The chief guard released his hold on the teddy.

'But I'm sure that what we've done, the mice and myself, far outweighs them all, agreed?'

Knarl considered the conversation.

'I'm guessing, and I can only guess, mind, that the Great Grand Walnut would be annoyed – no, *furious* – to learn that our case wasn't brought straight before him, rather than sitting all the way back at the end of a line.'

The nut guard by the door had grown impatient. 'Knarl,' he said, running the door back and forth. 'What's the hold up?'

The chief guard ignored him.

'Imagine,' said Bear, his paw travelling sideways, an arm around the guard's shoulder. 'The Great Grand Walnut hops a ride on a bauble, off to see his precious Glades, and what does he find?'

Knarl could almost be seen picturing it.

'Well,' said Bear, shaking his furry head. 'I wouldn't want to be the nut who'd led the offenders to their cells, not having gone straight to him first.'

The chief guard looked to be doing a lot of thinking.

'Knarl?' came the call from the door.

'Shut up, a moment. Just shut up.' He began pacing, his eyes on the floor, his hands joined behind his back. Bear stood waiting.

'Lock this one up with the others,' said Knarl, done. He shoved the teddy bear forward to the cell. The door guard chased it closed behind him, whistling a tune as he did so. He gave the captives a smile before joining his chief guard out of a side door, lifting a torch from the wall as they went.

199

'Making friends?' asked Bernard, removing his pipe and tobacco from the depths of his ear.

Bear parked onto a bench beside Morris, his face lined with troubles.

'What's going on?' asked his friend.

'Nothing,' said Bear, taking a pebble from the floor and throwing it. 'Nothing at all.'

Furry little outlaws

'Back on your paws,' said a nut guard from the other side of the bars. Bear and the mice were laid around the cell. They peeled themselves up and stood dishevelled before him.

'Got a busy day ahead of you,' he said cheerfully, dragging the butt of his spear backward and forward across the bars, paining their ears. 'Tell 'em,' he said, leaning back. 'Come and tell 'em.'

Another nut guard appeared. 'Well, some of us appear to be in a lot of trouble,' he said, his fingers rolling a grip around the timber bars, his face coming up to them.

'Is it us? Are we in trouble?' asked the first guard, a hand on his opposite number.

'Us? No, no,' said the second, his head turning slow disagreement. 'It's these furry little outlaws.'

'Oh, that's great news,' said Bear, clapping his paws together, his big amber eyes bright. The guards shared a look.

'Think you're going for a stroll around the gardens?' said the second.

'Gonna be up before the Great Grand Walnut,' said the first.

The mice looked unsettled.

'Though a trip to meet the gardeners might be a better idea,' said the second, his eyes picking out each of their faces. 'I'm not sure they agree with your rearrangements.'

'A bit sweeping,' said the first. 'The changes, I mean. Took 'em years, apparently.'

Knarl appeared from the door behind them. The guards pulled aside.

'Open the door.'

The chief guard stepped in. He wore a blue cape with a golden brooch adorning one breast. He gave Bear a measured look before assessing them all. 'Your time has come,' he said. 'Follow me.'

The band left the cell on the heels of Knarl with the guards dropping in behind.

They shuffled single file through the door and into a tunnel, the walls and ceiling wooded like roots growing up and over them.

Morris tugged at Bear's fur on the way. 'I do hope you have a plan,' he whispered, his eyes rolling up to his friend. 'Or we are done for.'

Bear glanced over his shoulder. 'We'll have to see what we're dealing with.'

They walked onward. Every now and then walnut guards stepped from breaks in the wall to flank them with torches held high, the flames making long shadows of the captives.

Warmth was coming through. A stifling closeness. Noise too, in the near distance. Chatter, like a theatre crowd awaiting a performance. Knarl reached the tunnel's end, and the party – now sided by eight guards – followed him out.

Rubbing a paw on his neck, Bear walked on until they were halted. His big eyes looked up and rolled around. The courtroom, if it could be called such, appeared as something like a cave with a ceiling that rose way above them, but instead of stone the walls and ceiling were gnarled, woody lines running in all directions. Walnuts sat high up in them, in snug, pod-like openings, circling them with their legs dangling over the edges.

The chatter, passing from nut to nut, began to fall away, replaced by an awed silence. The eight guards split off, taking positions by the walls, their feet crunching on the dusty floor. They seated their torches in the walls.

Knarl stepped up to a large, upturned log. It was laid out on the ground, side-on, facing the group. As time went by, whispers ran around from up high, as a small marching walnut appeared from an opening, trailing a brown cape on the floor in its wake.

Drawing breath, the little nut arched backward. 'Silence in the court, silence,' she called. She followed the walls with her eyes until satisfied. 'All present and able, be upstanding for your greatness, the Great Grand Walnut.'

The guards rearranged themselves and stood straight. She walked off to a chair and table, bringing her cloak aside and sat down. Taking up some papers, she tapped them into order and brought her seat in.

The party's eyes went to the opening to witness a broad walnut, stepping slowly into the courtroom – each foot sliding forward, then pausing, with the other following suit.

The walnut's arms went up to a 'V' and cheers rained down from the pods as the nuts banged their heels on the walls and whooped and clapped his arrival. Then his arms lowered to bring silence until only the crackle of flame could be heard.

His head turned to the long trail of cape he wore, a full, purple velvet, his eyes searching the opening, until a small pair of walnuts ran through. With each lifting a corner from the floor, he continued up to the log, laboured up a small ladder and took a seat within its hollowed-out centre.

'Am I seeing this right?' said Morris quietly to Bear, as he and the mice all gawped and stared at the 'great' nut.

The main difference between this walnut and all the others was the fact that he was missing a large portion of his shell – the top – revealing the pale brown walnut inside.

His raisin eyes just beneath looked out over the captives as he made himself comfortable. His two assistants suddenly appeared either side of him. One hurried a white wig onto his head, curled at the sides, as the other poured a drink from a jug into an ornate wooden cup. He raised it to his mouth, taking time to assess the accused.

'Now tell me,' he said, bringing the cup from his mouth, 'exactly who this cute little lot are.'

Knarl dropped his head and paused before speaking. 'This "cute little lot" are up on the charges of vandalism and attempted murder, your honour.'

'Really?' said the Great Nut, his broad mouth now a hole. 'Are you being serious?' Casting around, he asked the same question.

'Very much so,' said the chief guard as he turned to face Bear. 'This one's as villainous as he is furry.'

'Oh, come on,' said the Great Nut, declining an offer of a top-up from his assistant. 'Are you putting me on?'

'I'm afraid not, your honour.'

The walnut's other assistant took a bowl of food passed up from the floor, then reached down to produce a bottle. He began drizzling something like oil across the top and seasoned from a height, before sliding it carefully in front of his master. The Great Grand Walnut absently lifted a slice of something from it and began to eat, trying to comprehend all he was hearing.

Knarl rearranged his feet and fumbled his fingers. 'The Glades have been wrecked, your honour.'

The Great Nut's mouth, slowly turning, stopped. He mumbled something, stood to spit it out and threw his hands onto the log's lip. 'My Glades,' he bellowed. 'My precious Glades, wrecked?'

The chief guard nodded. The gallery gasped.

'But, how?' The walnut steadied himself, his assistants standing to support him.

'It was a bauble, your honour,' said Bear, stepping forward into torchlight. 'But my friends here were no part of it. I was the pilot.'

'A bauble? said the nut, shooing his assistants away. 'Was it an accident? Tell me it was an accident.'

'No accident,' said Bear. 'And I'd have brought the whole lot down, were we not stopped.'

The Great Grand Walnut slumped back into his seat. He began thumping the hollow wall of the log. He slowly rose, a dark expression on his face.

'Why?' he asked, stamping a foot. 'Why? Why? *Why*?'

'To be brought before you,' said Bear, his arms wide. 'To ask for your help.'

'Then why didn't you ask to see me?'

'We did,' said Morris, piping up. 'We were told to go away.'

The walnut blew a long breath. He looked done. 'Let me entertain this nonsense for a moment.' He adjusted his wig and sat down. 'What *help* exactly were you after?'

Bear raised his head and looked all around. 'Phaedria, the Fallen Fairy,' he said. She's on her way to Treelights. To war.'

The Great Grand Walnut struck dumb for a moment. But he leaned forward, took a slice of something and motioned his assistant to pour another drink.

'Did you hear me?' said Bear.

'Oh, I heard you,' said the nut, his mouth working the food over. 'We had a recent visit. Asked us to stay out of any disagreements her and the Treefolk might be having.' He levelled the food in his hand at Bear. 'It has nothing to do with us.'

'What did she promise you in return?' asked Morris, coming forward.

A walnut guard stepped up, halting him. The Great Grand Walnut had to lean forward to see the mouse. 'We simply promised not to intervene.'

Morris brought a paw to his chin in thought. 'The expansion of the Glades,' he laughed suddenly, nodding his head. 'Of course.'

The Great Grand Walnut put his food down. An assistant wiped his mouth. 'That's none of your business, vandal.'

'I've seen different plans,' said Bear, raising his voice.

'Oh?' said the nut, raising his cup. 'Well, let's hear them.'

Bear looked around. 'I'd have to show you. We'd need materials – timber, namely – but we don't have time.'

'Ah, we have time,' said the Great Grand Walnut, settling into his seat. He raised a hand and clicked his fingers. A nut appeared below and looked up.

'Bring more food.'

A graphic demonstration

At the top of the tree, preparations were being made. Lilly had returned, touching down to the snowy plains of Treetops aboard her red velvet bauble. She fluttered down, barefoot, her hair bedraggled.

Before her were six different Treefolk: chosen representatives of each kind.

'Do we have the young safe?' she asked, striding towards them.

'The last are being ferried from Treelights as we speak, good lady,' assured Athena. Her hair was white gold, lit from the soft light from her halo.

Lilly stopped before them. 'And with the highest protection?'

'We have our best angels, coins and elves escorting them,' said a robust looking elf by the name of Connell. 'We can do no more than we have.'

'What about the shelters within Treetops?' Lilly asked a toy soldier stood close by. 'Are they stocked and well-guarded?'

A peaked black hat raised. 'Ready for a season's siege,' he said, throwing out his chest and raising his hand to salute.

'Well, let's hope it doesn't last that long.' Lilly dragged the hair out of her eyes. 'Before our forces are deployed, however,' she said, all able to see her face, 'we have a more pressing matter than Phaedria's army. Two young are missing. An angel named Pluck, and the other a human young called Henry.'

Lilly's eyes passed between them. 'They are overdue.'

All heads nodded in understanding.

'Gabriel was with them. Llorn too, though the angel has reported him missing.'

'Don't worry about our brother,' said a coin, beating a hand on his chest. 'He's one of our best.'

'Even so,' said Lilly. 'I'm just making you aware.'

'Gabriel came swiftly back to inform us, and thankfully we know the timing and whereabouts of her approach.'

Lilly again swiped at her hair, feeling the mess was a mere irritant. 'She left the pair with instruction to fly a route she deemed safe, though they are yet to arrive. Gabriel has since led a search team back out. Please,' she said, looking among them, 'keep your eyes and ears open.'

The soldier stepped to attention and saluted again.

'By the way,' said Lilly to the soldier, his eyes now shaded. 'Where are the armed guard? Have they arrived back at Treelights?'

'They should be there already, my lady. I'll go with your permission to find them.'

Lilly nodded. The soldier spun on his heel and left. She watched after him.

'Elf, snowman,' she said, returning. 'Keep half of your armies here in Treetops along with two of my coins. We can't rule out an attack here. The rest shall follow me to Treelights to join our forces. Tell all Star Retrieval Squads to finish up and get back.'

Before she left, Lilly stood squarely to the folk.' We are now unfortunately at war, and if it's a war Phaedria wants,' said Lilly, her voice now low, 'then a war she shall give her. All those to Treelights with me.'

The departing were wished luck as they ran towards baubles. Like a whirring caterpillar, they curved away from the snowy floor and headed clear for the mountains.

*

Bear and the mice were allowed basic tools. Even basic food and drink was provided for them. Under the watchful eyes of every walnut present – including the galleries above – the mice hefted the bulk of Phaedria's plan into the courtroom's centre, with help from a pair of grudging nut guards.

Two long timbers were brought to meet at one end, and under Bear's instruction – and some skilled chiselling from Lawrence – a dowelled joint was made.

Bear nodded and turned to the Great Grand Walnut, who'd watched so far with interest, largely ignoring his assistants' attempts to tempt him with food and drink.

'We've got a basic working model,' said Bear, rolling up a drawing, 'but to demonstrate what it does we'll need a shell.' He looked up at the galleries. 'Don't worry – it should be empty, but as strong as a live walnut.'

Motioned by the Great Grand Walnut, four guards left the courtroom and returned moments later with two equal empty halves.

'Bring them just over here,' said Bear, pointing to the timber's pivot, 'and place them together between the beams.'

Once in place, the Great Grand Walnut rose, transfixed. The whole gallery leaned as far out as they could to see; even the nut guards' composure had slackened.

'And now,' said Bear with a showman's touch, 'I shall require the help of just two walnut guards.'

The Great Grand Walnut singled out a pair on the wall. He flicked a finger towards Bear. They looked up to him as they passed and he waved them eagerly on. Bear guided them to the timber's far ends.

'You, stand here and place your hands. And your friend can take the other side.'

He walked back to the mice and ushered them away.

'Okay...' Bear rubbed his paws and walked its length. 'I think it's ready.'

He looked to the Great Grand Walnut, now flanked by his assistants, their duties forgotten. 'Can we proceed?'

The nut nodded.

'Everyone watch their eyes,' said Bear, 'and push!'

The two guards, unremarkable in their size, walked the beams toward each other. They tensed and the nut creaked, then exploded, showering anyone within range in broken nutshell.

Screams rang out; others choked with panic. The Great Grand Walnut was leant over his log, eyes wide with disbelief, his assistants gripping his sides. The two guards on the floor shook their heads.

'It's only a rough model,' said Bear, flicking a piece of shell from his shoulder,

'but it gives you the idea.'

The Great Grand Walnut was trying to pry his assistants from him. 'Yes, yes,' he said, wild-eyed. 'Quite a graphic demonstration. And you say you have seen these-'

'Walnut Destroyers,' said Bear, his hands on his hips. 'Oh, yes. Phaedria has many of these, and far more efficient than this cobbled-together model.'

The nut gripped his mouth. 'The barbaric, double-crossing witch!' he muttered. 'She is planning to cleanse us from the tree!'

Bear looked to Morris. They shared the tiniest of smiles.

'Bear,' said the Great Grand Walnut, rising to stand. 'All charges against you are hereby dropped. You also have my firm allegiance.'

A great roar went up the walls as the mice mobbed Bear.

'Walnuts!' bellowed the Great Grand Walnut, his deep crag of a mouth quivering. 'Prepare for war!'

Severe problems

P haedria had driven her wolves hard. Her army had maintained the pace for the most part. It had been easy for them: keep up or be slain where you fell. It was enforced by a select gang of coins running a line back and forth, and while they'd only dispatched one – a previously harnessed coin – the other had remained doggedly upright.

Phaedria's eyes roved around the dark shapes of the tree. She was close now. There was someone ahead. Slackening the reins, the sleigh slid to a halt. Her coin forces pulled up; heaving, breathing, hands on knees. Her Captain jogged up to the sleigh's side.

'Stay here,' she said, her eyes fixed forward as she stepped down from the carriage. The coin clicked his heels smartly, though he couldn't resist following Phaedria's line of sight off to somewhere in the dark. Within moments, she'd gone, melding into the shadows.

Phaedria drew her wand, alone now. A column loomed out of the murk, daunting in its mass – the tree's trunk. Phaedria stepped forward, stowing her wand. 'Have you been seen?'

A toy soldier raised his rifle, startled. 'My lady.' He lowered it. 'You... no,' he said, remembering the question. 'I've not been seen.'

'Are you sure?' she asked silkily, a hand stroking the tree's bark.

'Quite certain,' said the soldier. Her preoccupation allowed him to study her.

'Then my army is ready,' she said, turning. 'I trust you have the numbers?'

'Enough to present a problem,' said the soldier.

'I want you creating *severe* problems.' Phaedria circled him. 'Can you do that?'

The soldier straightened. 'As you wish.'

'Then get your troops up off the floor. Be quick.'

The rifle's butt was brought into the floor three times. Snow-covered ground began lifting as scores of uniformed soldiers rose up all around them. Phaedria's attention, though, was on the trunk before her. She traced her wand through the air – her words foreign to the soldiers – and stood back.

A deep lilac burnt into the trunk, a door's outline in its wake. The soldier watched intently. He turned to Phaedria, but she knew his question already.

'I once ruled this tree. Do you really think I'd forgotten its secrets?'

The soldier's face tightened. 'No, my lady. Of course not.'

Phaedria took a step back, allowing a door of thick wood to swing open. A lavender glow within lit the eyes of the hundred or so soldiers.

She stepped in, feeling around the doorway and peering upward. 'Climb quickly,' she said, her voice rebounding around the circular walls, 'and look for my signal.'

The soldier saluted, turned on his heel and looked to his seconds. He turned again to Phaedria, but she was gone. 'Lose any excess you are carrying,' he announced. 'We travel light and fast. Make no noise.'

*

The head of each kind had their orders. The young were gathered. Treelights was as prepared as it could be. Lilly had returned to Treetops, and other than the milling and noise of the encampment on the other side of the mountains, all was quiet. Unnaturally so. Nothing moved, nothing ran, no one sang.

She cast around, surveying the empty land. The forests. The lake. From where she stood, beside her weather-aged cabin, she looked down from the mountain. She could see almost all of Treetops. It was a view she had never grown used to, had never taken for granted.

Had she seen it alive with Treefolk for the last time? It were as though she were visiting a ghost of Treetops, one that had been recreated in another place, a perfect replica though unpopulated.

Lilly noticed the wand in her hand. It looked no more than a crooked stick. Other fairies had come and gone. Their wands had all been special, crafted straight as a conductor's baton, to be held between forefinger and thumb and swished delicately. Or a wand, long and light, that would glow like the sun on a white flower, its good magic felt before one had even touched it.

There were others equally remarkable. Herself, she noticed, was also remarkable. Bedraggled hair, barefooted, wearing a dress like an overcast sky. Perhaps she should've wrapped herself in silk or satin, behaved more lady-like, created a distance, a mystique. But that would not have been her. That would have been folly.

She was merely one of the Treefolk – just one with greater responsibility. She had no love of power, no will to dominate. She loved the simpler life, the simpler things. But she would have to put all that aside.

That gentle fairy would be gone for a while. Lilly's eyes moved slowly across the mountain tops, as if reading a plan of what she must do. Phaedria's magic was once strong. Could it now be stronger?

Lilly knew what she must do, the only thing she could. She drew upon her magical pool, near depleting it, and closed an impenetrable, invisible seal around Treetops.

Nothing could now get in – not even Phaedria, at least so long as Lilly lived. In this way, she had forced the battle to Treelights, but Phaedria would know this. It was simply an insurance.

She boarded her bauble, climbed away, and didn't look back. Her features were hard-set.

Preparations

Henry, along with a still grumpy Pluck and three puddings who'd been quite excellent company, wound his way down the hillside. His heart gave a little leap at seeing Treelights again. It had the look of a miniature village, a picture-postcard of all that was Christmas before him. There were overly tall houses hunched over the crooked streets, the clock and its spire, the Trunk Hotel still with its gap-toothed golden windows and a seemingly eternal snowfall. It would have been perfect were it not about to see war.

Henry had absolutely insisted on being part of the effort, and so they had reluctantly – if not a little gladly – promised to kit-out the young human in battle gear. He felt that perhaps this had contributed to Pluck's dark mood.

'It's strange to see no smoke from the chimneys,' said McPud, clumping heavily through the snow.

'Aye, so it is,' replied McDonald. 'There's something eerie about it.'

'It's a shame you can't see it in all its bustlin' glory,' said McHooten, taking the boy a step forward with a slap on his back.

'I did,' said Henry, looking up. 'I did once, with a friend.' His voice lowered. 'Though we didn't stay very long.'

They passed through the wood and into a furrowed path that led downward and into Treelights. The trees had disappeared now, the ground opening out before them. Houses and Treefolk presented, busying along, carrying boxes and possessions with an air of urgency.

They were stood in a street now. Above the painted signs that hung from pubs and shops telling of *Treelights' Finest Ales* to *Walnut Repairs and Polishing* were stationed lookouts stood on thatched and tiled roofs. They commandeered stars; lighting them up, they swung them up and over the tree's dark ceiling.

Hammers swung, boarding windows. Candlelit lamps were snuffed out. Weapons were passed out from makeshift munitions depots.

Henry, Pluck and the puddings were stopped abruptly, appearing before a wall of linked holly that halted their progress.

213

'State names and folk-type,' said an angel, fluttering down from a roof with a clipboard in his hand.

'McHooten, McPud and a star. One of your angel young, Pluck, and myself,' said McDonald, hopping a finger between heads. 'Oh, and a human young by the name of Henry.'

Running a quill down his list, the angel paused at Pluck's mention, then his eyes rose at the naming of Henry.

The boy was considered very carefully. 'I've had warning of your arrival,' said the angel, his face cast solemn. Henry's colour drained. He had unwittingly caused a lot of bother when last here with Bear. He raised fearful eyes.

'Welcome,' said the angel, his face creasing a warm smile. 'You and Pluck have given us quite the scare.' He ticked the quill twice on his paper and looked to the puddings. 'Well done.' He opened a holly-leaf gate and the troupe passed through to join a throng of criss-crossing Treefolk preparing for war.

'Let's get you fitted out in something protective,' said McDonald, guiding Henry and Pluck up another street. 'McPud, McHooten. Go and report that star in.'

The group parted ways. The pudding, boy and angel walked on. They were bathed in the glow of passing lanterns as they went, bobbing high atop poles, carried past by hurrying folk. Stalls were dragged inside or upturned for barricading. Treefolk clambered up ladders and over roofs, setting up defences.

Side-stepping a line of hopping candy canes passing the corner house, Henry recognised it was where he and Bear had enjoyed their fill of pastries and cakes.

It had been welcoming then; the smell of cinnamon and apple and hot, spiced juice. Now it was a dark shell, shuttered and deserted.

'Here we are,' said McDonald, guiding Henry and Pluck to an old timber door.

The pudding thumped a fist twice on it. Henry recognised it as the *Butter-Brandy Topping Parlour*.

A pair of large, dark eyes appeared from behind a letterbox-sized hole in the timber. They shifted left and right before disappearing. There was a sound of bolts being dragged back and the door creaked open.

'Good fishing?' asked a pudding, filling the doorway.

McDonald gathered Henry and Pluck before him. 'Only the one star. Saved the lives of these two, she did.'

The pudding held a candle high. 'Is that a human young?'

'His name's Henry. You might know Pluck already,' said McDonald.

'Pluck...' said the pudding, his free hand rubbing a little chin. 'Aye, I do. A cheeky, young scamp as I remember, but tell me: where did a human young come from?'

'Let us in you big dolt and we might be able to tell you,' said McDonald, pushing his friend out of the way. 'Close to starving, we are.'

The three hurried in from the street through the narrow side door. They were led by candlelight up a corridor. A door ahead was framed with light. A muffled flow of conversation could be head behind it. As the door opened, sound flooded out.

McDonald staggered in holding his gut. His face grimaced with pain; he turned slowly on his heel and keeled over. Many puddings were upon him; he was kicked several times until he leapt up with a roar, laughing. After much back-slapping, jeering and cheering, McDonald waved the noise down and went back to the doorway to pull Pluck and Henry inside.

'Presenting a fine pair o' young warriors,' he announced. 'Pluck, some of you will already know, an' a strapping human young by the name of Henry.'

'A human young?' asked one pudding, mystified. 'How's a human-'

'Well, I'll be...' muttered another, a pipe hung from his mouth.

Pluck's expression turned to an outright scowl at all the attention Henry was receiving. She stood as tall as she could and smiled, but all she got was a friendly ruffling of her hair.

McDonald steered the pair to a table where he sat them down and ordered some food over with his hand. Before long, the pair were tucking ravenously into thick soup and torn bread.

'Let 'em have some peace while they eat,' said McDonald, grabbing up a bottle and glass from the table. He poured a measure, drained it and fell into a chair – all in one seamless motion. 'I think these two have already seen a lot of action.'

'Action?' said a pudding, shifting forward in his chair. 'What kind of action has a wee baby angel an' a human young seen, eh?'

Henry didn't hear. His face was buried in his soup. But Pluck was listening, a mess of the stuff around her chops.

'We've seen more action than you ever will, you big sherry-head!' she raged indignantly, threating him with a spoon.

'Whoa there, lassie,' said the pudding, hands raised in defence. 'I was merely asking is all. No need to get your little wings in a twist.'

Pluck lowered the spoon but kept her fierce eyes upon him.

The pudding leaned close to his neighbour. 'I'll have the wee miss besides me in battle,' he laughed.

Pluck returned to her food as Henry tore into the bread unaware. The lively chat they'd first heard struck up again, until it became a constant wash of noise. Henry, plump around his belly and warmed to his bones, pushed his plate away. He slumped and sighed as he took the scene in. His eyes began to blink more and more.

'You can sleep all you want after the battle, young Henry,' said McDonald, giving him a friendly shake, 'but not right now. Here, come and help me sort some armour for the puds. We can find something for you two as well.'

There was a brief respite in the chatter as Henry, Pluck and McDonald went out and up some stairs to a door. Here, in the low-beamed room was a positive war-chest of armour and weapons, as though they'd stumbled upon the lost burial chamber of some great war chief. Henry and Pluck lit up.

'No one makes better battle armour than the Puds o' the Great Tree,' said McDonald, walking among the weaponry. He eased a blade from a pile of dull breast plates and stood examining its steel edge for a moment. To Henry it appeared almost comical, the sight of this big pudding going all misty-eyed over the weapon before him, but he didn't dare laugh.

'Some prefer the hardened pine blade,' continued McDonald, turning the blade in his hand. 'Light and fast, no doubt, but us puds'll never settle for anything other than forged steel, made by our wonderful smiths.'

McDonald glanced sideways to a candle – the only light in the room – and the pudding spun. The blade flashed – and there was darkness.

A flint struck and the pudding reappeared in the candlelight, the thrum of the blade still audible. McDonald replaced the blade as though handling a new-born. Henry flushed a little red. Pluck asked the purpose of some smaller blades in a basket, shaped like daggers.

'The two of you will be claiming one each. Here,' he said, lowering to take up one in each hand, 'get a feel of them. And their purpose? Well, they're for getting up close and personal.'

Henry weighed the weapon in his hand, his legs splayed, and waved it though the air. McDonald gave a wry smile and turned to open a chest. After tossing most of the contents, he produced a pair of chainmail vests.

'Here,' he said, throwing them. 'These should fit.'

Pluck caught hers and held it out in front of her. 'I have wings?' she said, and dropped it to the floor.

Henry, meanwhile, stood his blade against a wall, removed his dressing gown, and wriggled into the vest. 'I thought it would be heavy,' he said, looking it up and down.

'I told you,' said McDonald, walking round him. 'Our smiths are the finest in the tree.'

The pudding swiped Pluck's up from the floor, shooting her a look as he did so.

'They'd have no problem tailoring-'

'I won't be wearing it,' said the little angel.

McDonald walked to the blade and put it firmly in her hand. 'You think this is all a big game?'

Pluck looked up to the pudding, unmoved. 'I *won't.*'

The pair had a brief, silent stand-off before McDonald turned and walked to the door. 'You'll be using that blade, though,' he said over his shoulder. 'Otherwise, it'll be a trip on a bauble to Treetops. You can wait there with the other babies,' he said, treading down the stairs.

A reunion of sorts

B ack in the buttering parlour, the noise had reached a new level. Henry and Pluck stepped between dark, round bodies until they found a pair of empty seats by a wall. They parked up, with Henry coughing.

Smoke turned slowly out of pipes, creating a bank of cloud above them as puddings chatted, nodding, laughing and drinking. Over the intertwining chatter and the clinking of tankards came McDonald's voice.

He'd stood on a table to be seen, the top of his head lost in fog, and held up his arms.

'Puddings,' he shouted. 'Puddings of the Great Tree!'

The noise wound down as butter brandy-topped heads turned his way.

'Savour this moment, for today we look to stain our blades with the blood of our enemy!'

Fists punched the air and a great cheer went up.

'Lilly has asked, and the puddings have answered with our numbers!' McDonald raised his drink.

A pair of tankards were brought before Henry and Pluck.

'It's nearly time for us to get out there, but before we do, I ask that each follow me first by raising a toast and taking a drink.'

A pudding beckoned Henry and Pluck up to their feet and nodded at the tankards before them. The pair took them; Henry sniffed at the foaming top.

'To the brave, good fortune,' said McDonald, turning and nodding.

'An' the swift demise of the witch!' cried another.

A harmony of raucous cheers sounded. Henry and Pluck faced each other.

'Good luck,' said the boy, knocking his tankard into Pluck's. 'I'm sure we'll be okay.'

'Good luck, Henry.'

The pair pinched their nostrils and drank. The angel's eyes grew wide, her cheeks full, and with a great, rasping spray, she covered the back of a pudding with strong, brown ale. Henry swallowed hard and placed the drink down, gasping for air. The pudding hadn't noticed.

Henry's ears rang. The room was swimming, but a feeling of strength coursed through him.

McDonald dragged a hand across his mouth, his head back, and tossed the tankard aside. 'Victory will be ours!'

*

Before long, every pudding was fitted out with battle gear. Dull steel plates encased their bodies, front to back; curved metal caps topped their heads. Some shouldered the forged blades that McDonald had swung, while others held chained maces; spiked steel balls hung from chains. A few, Henry noted, wore no armour. Those puddings appeared darker than the rest, as though stained with a black ink, their weaponry an assortment of short blades and knives tucked into belts around their waists. They were shown quietly out through a door at the back, a brief, chill wind meeting them.

The last to appear from the stairs wore the heaviest armour of all. Each plating looked double-strength, with arms and legs protected too.

They took up shields, tall and rectangular, and selected pikes stood along a wall – long pointed spears that scraped the ceiling.

They reminded Henry of a London pillar-box back home. They lumbered through the crowd of puddings, their large breadths making progress slow, until the team of around three-dozen divided off; one line to the front door, the other to the back. There was no talking, barring low-spoken commands, save for the heavy footfalls on the wooden boards and the clunking of meeting armour.

With everyone in position, Henry and Pluck felt a pair of hands on their shoulders; those of a pudding by the name of McBride now tasked with their safety, selected by McDonald.

All awaited their commander's word. Central to the packed room, McDonald turned his armoured head left and right, before raising a hand, signalling both directions. Two doors were flung open, the front, then back, and a howl of wind channelled the room, vanquishing the smoky cloud bank in an instant.

Lines of Christmas puddings began bouncing out of the doorways into the dark streets beyond, the exit flow constant, the movement and co-ordination seamless. The biting night air heightened the beat of Henry's heart.

His hand trembled upon the blade in his hand, and then from a firming of a grip on their shoulders, Henry and Pluck were led out last as part of a pudding team.

They hugged the shadowed streets, as the more heavily-armoured barrelled straight down the middle. Puddings streamed out of shop fronts along the way, other units joining the effort. They ran without word over the snow-draped cobbles, passing boarded shops and houses.

Looking up, Henry saw star-beams lancing the flurries as Treefolk swung them round, their fronts lit with the glow from each.

The streets were widening now. Angels bearing lanterns, boxed orange glows bobbing on the ends of long poles, provided the only source of light as more and more Treefolk joined the numbers heading off to the town's outskirts.

A congestion of snowmen, canes, dates and elves were ahead.

'Stay close,' said McBride.

Each kind were divided and sent to their positions by angels bearing clipboards. McDonald was spotted by one stood on a soapbox, and ushered straight through the crowds to the front line; the heavily-armoured puddings pushed through and divided left and right to take their places at the front.

Henry and Pluck were held. 'That's far enough for you two,' said McBride, guiding them sideways. He walked them nearer the back to a snowy bank, affording them safety and a view.

The standards of the various folk interspersed the air. Beyond the battle lines was a holly fence, spanning east to west, the first line of defence for Treelights, and after that a white expanse of snowy ground. It led to the foot of a hill; at its peak a forest.

The initial tension began to ease as their numbers were considered. Perhaps, some reasoned, Phaedria might glimpse their army and turn tail. It was fast becoming a reunion of sorts, and their collective composures began to slacken.

The pudding phalanx remained steadfast, their eyes watching the far hill and the forest topping it from beneath their cradle-capped helmets. Their gaze was drawn by a dark bird flying from the hilltop. It flapped low through the downing snow and flew a broad circle around the armies before heading back the way it came.

'She's almost here,' said McDonald to the line.

By now, many Treefolk had staked their weapons in the ground to receive hot drinks. Food, too, was passed round. Gossip was caught up on; some were even laughing. Star beams still crossed the snowflakes. The chatter wound down as the lights began to urgently skirt the edge of the far forest: one point in particular.

Something was there. A silence fell as though the Treefolk strained to hear the very sound of snowflakes meeting the floor.

A figure was coming down the hillside. McDonald gripped his pike and leaned forward. 'Take this,' he said. 'I'll deal with it myself.'

The pudding eased himself over the holly and headed to meet the figure. Star-beams divided to light up the two figures, creating a kaleidoscope of colours as they crossed, until the pair stood opposite from one another.

The Great Grand Walnut tossed his cloak over a rounded shoulder. They considered each other for a moment.

The nut spoke first, looking pained to do so. 'It's been too long,' he said.

'Aye,' said McDonald, rocking back. 'It's been a while.'

A silence grew.

'What are you doing here?' said the pudding, frowning. 'If you're needing fertiliser for your precious plants, then I've got to say – it's a bad time.'

The walnut looked past McDonald to the swarms of Treefolk. 'I see you have company.'

'Yep,' said McDonald, glancing back. 'Just a few, you know.'

'Expecting someone?'

'Aye, any minute now.'

'Funny, we were looking to meet someone here too,' said the nut, casting around. 'Mind if we wait with you?'

'Not at all, not at all.' McDonald stepped aside to present the ground before them. 'You and your band are most welcome.'

The walnut wrung his hands. 'Thanks,' he muttered, and stepped on a few paces.

McDonald watched the nut stop and turn. He raised a gnarled wooded hand.

'Well?' he cried, his voice carrying up the hillside. 'What are you all waiting for?'

221

At once, a broad line of walnuts came from the trees and onto the hills. Two small walnuts scurried before them, hurrying to their chief to bring his trailing cape from the floor.

McDonald allowed himself a little smile and followed, ambling behind with his thumbs tucked behind his breastplate. The walnuts integrated among the Treefolk, bringing weapons, slings and long straps.

Henry saw one stood out. Before Pluck or McBride could react, he'd made a dash down the small hill they stood on. He discarded his blade and with his heels kicking up snow, he ran into the back of the crowd, pushing blindly through.

'Bear!' called Henry, jumping forward and trying to get clear, upsetting many patrons of the tree as he went.

'By all the bleak winters!' said an ashen-faced angel, her hand to her heart. 'I thought we'd been flanked!'

'Steady on!' said a parcel spun a circle.

And then Henry finally tripped and fell onto a pyramid of ice-blue snowballs as they flattened in all directions.

Henry heard the stunned silence, feeling the cold points of ice beneath him. Someone grabbed the front of his dressing gown, hoisting him upward.

Henry tensed, eyes shut, but he was pulled tight into a familiar furry chest.

'Henry, oh, Henry! I thought... I thought...'

The boy's eyes blinked open.

'Bear... you're safe!' said the boy, catching his breath.

The big teddy released his friend and they stood a pace apart.

'Where on earth-' but Henry paused, distracted. 'You're looking a bit... shabby.'

'Nothing a few stitches and a spin in the washing machine won't sort,' laughed Bear.

The boy smiled. 'Been hanging around with walnuts?' He nodded towards them. 'Forgotten your old mate?'

Bear glanced over at his comrades. 'Good company, these lads. A solid bunch.'

Henry's face split into a smile. 'Good to see you again.' He stepped into Bear and hugged him.

'Likewise,' said the teddy, ruffing up the boy's head.

Something cold pawed Henry's shoulder and he turned to meet with a snowman. The neat stack of ammo Henry had levelled was his.

'Hey, jack-in-a-box,' said the snowman, removing his top hat. He was near twice Henry's height. 'You know how long it took my feeder elf to make this stockpile?'

About to reply, Henry was eclipsed by Bear. His teddy stood square in front of him, but an armoured pudding stole into the gap again. Now the pudding and the snowman were stood face to face.

'Is there a problem here?' asked McBride.

'No, no,' said Henry, stepping back into view before the snowman could respond. His feeder elf had disappeared. 'I was just helping tidy up some snowballs.'

'And so was I,' added Bear, crouching beside Henry and bringing some into his arms.

'Well, if everything's okay...' The pudding clapped his breast plate and gave the snowman a curt nod. 'Don't be too long.'

'I see you've been making some friends,' said Bear.

'You too,' said Henry.

'More than you have at home,' reflected Bear.

'Probably,' said Henry, rolling a snowball in his hand.

'Can we have a little less chat?' The snowman's arms were folded in impatience.

The three had eventually made a pile, and as Henry and Bear walked away they heard the snowman cursing the whereabouts of his elf.

'Are you missing home?' said Bear as they made for the little hill.

'My dad, mostly.' Henry had his hands in his pockets, his chin nuzzling his chest. 'As much as this is the most wonderful and dangerous adventure I've ever been on, I do miss him.'

Bear slung an arm around the boy's shoulder. 'We'll get home,' he said, consoling his friend. 'But I fear we've got to get through this first.'

McBride and Pluck were stood waiting.

'What in Treelights is that?' laughed the young Angel at Bear's approach.

'That's Pluck,' said Henry, shaking his head. 'I wish Lilly would change you back to a bird forever,' he said to her now sour face.

'McBride,' said the pudding, extending a hand to the Bear. 'And Henry,' he said, watching the boy take his place. 'Don't do that again.'

A bugle sounded a long, wavering note. The Treefolk looked to the battlefield, then the air, as a number of objects flew toward them.

They fell a few feet short of the frontline, *falomping* into the snow at their feet. McDonald cleared the snow from around one of the holes and put his hand in, retrieving a large snowball. It had a jagged, brown etching scratched into the icy ball.

Eight snowballs were taken up into the hands of eight Treefolk along the line. Each bore the same message: *I am the one true Fairy. The Tree is mine.*

Eyes rose to the woods. McDonald seemed to break the spell that had stolen over them all. From a padding of feet, he launched the ball back with a hiss through the air.

Seven more followed. Someone shouted, then another; a show of defiance that spread like wildfire until every one of the Treefolk were shouting themselves hoarse.

The sound was broken by a drum; a slow, deliberate beat, echoing down the hill. Eyes began to widen. A flame sparked in the dark of the woods.

The drumming steadily increased in volume and quickened, becoming a lively, incessant noise; the flame became one of many – a searing forest fire along its edge. Beneath stood coin upon coin, half-cast in shadow, their faces golden, eager and hateful.

Some Treefolk began pointing, their mouths hanging open. The falling snow had the pinky hue of spring blossom. The coins came on a step and the flaming line jumped, the drumming a constant noise.

'Hold the line!' shouted McDonald to each side. 'Hold the line!'

The torches were tossed and the coin army took off, running down the hill towards them.

Few noticed the snowfall was now a deep red. Some Treefolk froze with fright while others ran around panicked, pushing back towards the town. The gap was closing and the Treefolk scattered until a low, buzzing drone stopped them.

A red velvet bauble flew above them, bumped and buffeted by the wind. It dipped, then dove. Lilly rolled into view, gripping the wheel, her hair and dress chased back from the downdraught. Hats and capes whipped up as she shot over the heads of the Treefolk and a cheer went up.

Lines began re-organising and weapons were raised. Banking a low turn over the oncoming coins, she brought the craft down, just clearing the holly, and scuffed and rolled the bauble on the snow, spilling her. She got up and ran to the Treefolk.

'Beware the toy soldiers!' she shouted. 'They fight for Phaedria now. Slay any you find!'

Heads turned and murmured. Most, it seemed, had overlooked their absence.

Lilly reached the puddings, received a thin blade and walked the edge of the front line.

'Steel yourselves!' she said. 'Fight for your young, fight for each other. Do not let this tree pass into darkness!'

The gold swarm was little more than a field away, but all eyes held on Lilly. She looked over the masses present; some wondered if she were taking them in for the last time. But there was no sadness in her eyes. They blazed.

A stampede of feet thundered, noise rising from their mouths. The coins were here.

'For the tree!' said Lilly, punching an arm upward. The Treefolk sang their intention as Lilly ran back to her bauble.

She took off low for the coins, rolling the craft to slay one as she went before shooting up and away.

Those remaining drew pine needles. The pudding phalanx steadied. Walnuts were pulled back into bands looped over stakes. Elves readied snowballs.

McDonald raised his pike, and brought it forward. 'FIRE!'

A whoosh and a twang saw twenty walnuts loosed at the coins, clearing the holly. They bounced twice as they smashed successfully through the front line.

Snowmen hurled volleys of balls – a *zip-zip* sounding – felling some and blinding others, as the coins hurdled the fence, some caught and wasted on the phalanx front line.

Gaps appeared and through them stepped puddings bearing blades, finishing the floored coins. Dazed walnuts began tumbling back to the Treefolk as hands pulled the retrieval chords tied around their waists.

A new coin line appeared, and another, their numbers greater this time – all blades and noise, charging down the hillside.

The holly barrier had opened a little and gold poured through, leaping and slashing at the puddings. Their line bowed with the strain, but they held and again dispatched at will. Some, though, had fallen. They were pulled back through the crowds as the pudding front line shuffled around to fill the voids.

Henry stood at the top of the small hill, wilting. He could never have imagined such a sight. Pluck, though, bounced up and down, the blade following in her hand, watching with keen anticipation.

The next wave came bearing torches – with the line staggered – as coins appeared randomly from the wood at their backs to join the glittering, shimmering mass.

The phalanx again braced, facing their greatest number yet as flames spun over their heads and the enemy leapt at them, bringing down blades.

Fires took among the Treefolk as random groups fled the flames, the worst of the casualties being the gift boxes who ran around on fire before being heaped with snow by their fellows.

With the front line partly breached, pockets of coins fought Treefolk, claiming a small number before being mobbed. As the fighting died down, all eyes went to the far woods. Nothing was there. Someone cheered. Before long, they all did, jumping and shouting and punching the air.

McDonald counted heads at the front. Passing over his shield, he told McPud to keep everyone where they were and to pass the message on. He strode out into the open and turned. Tiptoeing, he waved hands in different directions toward him.

In time, McDonald was met with varying Treefolk. 'It's not over,' he said, staking his pike into the ground. 'That was merely to soften us up.'

The assembled folk sounded surprised.

'You think there are more?' said the Great Grand Walnut, yanking his cloak from his assistants and pointing them off.

The pudding's shaded eyes pulled to the woods. 'Have you seen Phaedria? The most powerful fairy that ever governed?'

'I don't know,' said a snowman by the name of Bjorn. 'Just how many does she command?'

226

'She knows our numbers, our capabilities,' said Halder the elf, slapping the back of his hand into his palm. 'You think there's more to come?'

McDonald unseated his pike. 'We have to expect it.' He starting walking towards the front line. 'Get everyone into position.'

Fearful eyes watched them as the pudding and the group finished their meeting. McDonald took his shield back and checked his armour as he rejoined the ranks.

A single drumbeat sounded. It beat out from the woodland, devoid of melody.

'Here we go,' said the pudding.

Assassins

The puddings Jameson, Doon and McAvoy halted, stunned; their breaths stolen away by the sheer din that escalated around them. The drumming had begun again, as had the noise from the coins. They'd heard nothing like it before, as the very needles of the branches they sat in trembled. They melted into their surrounds, only their eyes moving.

They had miscalculated their position a little. McAvoy adjusted his backpack. Jameson glanced through a break in the greenery. All he saw was fire and gold.

He ghosted back to hiding. The smell of tar and smoke filled his lungs, and his eyes ran. He didn't need to word caution.

Through the tight branch they continued, making sure their weapons were stowed securely. If something were to fall, then the game was up. There would be no escape. There probably wasn't a chance anyway – they knew that – but they at least wanted a shot.

Jameson stopped. The foliage ahead was darker, meaning it was too dense. To pass through it would be slow, maybe noisy. They would have to climb lower. Jameson looked to his team, raising a question with his look. They both nodded, happy to go on.

Like leopards, the three slunk downwards as tiny pinpoint shafts of gold penetrated their cover. They kept to the shadows as best they could as sounds of an army preparing for war carried up all around them.

If discovered, Jameson reasoned, he'd have the backing of two excellent puddings. They'd take a few coins with them. The sound of a horn blitzed the air. There was another, then one further over. It was the signal to march. The final wave.

The three moved deftly to vantage points, peering below. No snow could be seen. It lay beneath rippling waves of gold and firelight for the coins seemed as one as they trod to the sound of the drum.

The situation allowed the three to move more freely. Jameson brought his eyes from the scene below and pointed off. The team disappeared into the dark.

*

The three puddings had stopped. They peered down onto a band of five coins on the snow-covered ground. Phaedria was nowhere to be seen. Doon suggested asking them.

The five, they guessed, were a token resistance; an alarm. A small measure of security just in case a band of assassins were to somehow infiltrate. The coins below didn't seem to be taking the threat of all that too seriously.

Phaedria's guard were either chatting, leant on spears or tossing snowballs. If they had been paying attention, it would still have done them no good – the three were out of sight. Their dark, moist bodies blended seamlessly with the darkness.

Jameson pointed a finger up. Doon rose and climbed off without sound. The remaining puddings continued watching. The troupe below, bathed gladly in the light of a staked torch, seemed to be rather enjoying the war.

Their selection to stand guard appeared a privileged one, and one that perhaps held them in good favour with their master. They laughed and joked, carefree.

'FIRE!' yelled the largest of the coins suddenly – and then laughed, mocking the attempt of the smallest of his squad's efforts to nail a low-slung branch with a snowball.

The others laughed at the effort, watching the ball sail off into the darkness, missing the timber by a good two feet.

'Lemme try again!' said the coin, lowering to scoop another handful, but the largest coin – Warchief – planted a foot into his behind, sprawling him flat out on the snow. 'Not today, little Nugget.' He turned to click and point a finger. 'You're up next.'

The chosen coin, squat and misshapen, resembled the shape of a pear. It had cost those who mocked him their pride, at worst an eye.

He stooped to crouch, but side-footed some snow into the face of Nugget, still finding his way up from the ground. 'Fat lot of good you are,' said Pear, kneeling to press a snowball together. 'Take a look how it's done.'

Nugget swiped his face and rose to go for Pear, but a spear butt blocked his way.

'Settle this later,' growled Warchief. 'I'll even referee it myself, but keep it down for now. If she finds us fightin' instead o' guardin' then we'll all be dead.' He swept the tree with his eyes. 'Now make this throw your last.'

Pear brought his eyes from Nugget to the target. He cupped the ball, wound back and released, but although he'd heard the snowball crack off the branch, he didn't see it.

A Christmas pudding had landed from nowhere, four paces in front of him. Four coins flashed weapons. Pear, at first surprised, laughed. Nugget, still prone, didn't seem to have noticed.

Pear swaggered a step forward. 'What's this?'

Doon remained still, but poised, his eyes on those he thought a threat.

'I reckon this pudding is lost.' Pear's head inclined. 'Are you lost?'

Warchief pushed through the troupe to make himself known and assessed the stranger. 'Looks good enough to eat, I'd say.'

Doon's eyes passed between Pear and Warchief, though he was aware of another coin edging forward.

'Aren't you supposed to be back at Treelights?' Pear took a slow step forward.

'Maybe he's a deserter,' said Warchief, his knuckles rolling on the hilt of his blade.

Doon stepped back. Five coins followed.

'Hey,' said Pear, stopping. 'Where ya goin'? We only wanna be friends.'

'Yeah,' said another coin, following, though Doon didn't observe him. 'We're all good guys here.'

Doon retreated another step. Warchief brought his arms out to halt them all. 'Don't worry,' he said, his eyes scanning the clearing. 'I think this one is alone. He's got nowhere to go.'

Pear's eyes flashed with menace. 'Let's have some fun.' He raised his blade. 'After all, this is probably the only action we'll see-'

Pear slashed at the pudding but Doon side-stepped the attack - the blade missing his eye by a whisker. Pulling the staked torch from the floor, he swung it hard into Pear's head. Embers of red exploded.

A flame leapt across the coin's casement as he reeled, pained and dizzy. Darkness dispelled the light, so black, the air seemed suddenly solid. Pear hit the floor, pulling snow onto his head.

The rest of the coins waited, eyes wide, adjusting; Pear's snarling and whimpering the only sound.

One of the back line ran forward then – yelling for Phaedria with his blade raised. His yell became a yelp as the torch butt floored him.

The three coins, still standing, knew then of their target's whereabouts from the noise as well as the dark silhouette he'd become, their eyes now accustomed. They moved to go in, but something had landed behind them.

The coin furthest back hurtled forward, making a gurgling noise as he went. Whirling, the coins saw two black outlines. Blades were raised. Breaths quickened.

Warchief moved first, though not at his own peril. He shoved his fellow coins at the puddings, knocking them apart, then followed fully into Jameson who went over into a drift.

Warchief pulled his blade and McAvoy his, their dark outlines circling one another. The pair clashed. The pudding's blade spun free, its size no match for the long needle. The large coin spun the blade's hilt in his palm, his opponent unarmed. 'If only I had light to watch you die.'

The coin's silhouette grew in height, his blade raised, but the killing blow never came. Warchief upended, falling to a heap.

Regaining his senses, McAvoy reached into his backpack and brought a star from it. Slow to start, the star pulsed until a pale blue finally emitted, throwing out a beacon of light.

McAvoy saw Warchief on the ground, a blade's work near cleaving him in two. Behind him was Jameson, finishing the coin they'd used as leverage, now laid out in a brown pool.

He raised the star to light up Nugget, rising from the body of Pear, and running headlong for the darkness.

'Let him go,' said Jameson, wiping his blade clean on his thigh. He looked to Pear on the floor, his hands clutching his throat, legs kicking, paying dearly for his earlier actions.

The puddings wandered over. Doon stood over him, eyeing the tip of the dagger in his hand. 'Just tell us where she is and I'll ease your passing.'

Chocolate rose up from his mouth and gurgled over his flat golden face. Doon lowered to one knee, his weapon held out for the coin to see. 'I can end it. Just tell us.'

Pear's eyelids fluttered, fighting to focus on Doon. He looked to be trying to speak. The Pudding brought his head low to hear.

With immense effort, Pear formed his mouth to a small hole, his chest convulsing, and spat a spray of dark spittle at the Pudding's face - a sickly smile his parting expression.

Doon wiped his cheek, stowed the dagger and stood. 'Fat lot of good he was.'

'Well, she must be close,' said McAvoy, looking over his shoulder, 'though the little one might raise the alarm.'

'You think he'd be welcome back after what he'd done?' Jameson looked over to the fleeing coin's footprints. 'He won't be running back to her. I'd guess that she's in the opposite direction.'

Doon nodded. 'Makes sense.'

McAvoy brought the star before him in both hands, his face lit a pale blue. 'It's time we let this one go.' The star's faint, oval eyes appeared to sadden.

'Go hide little one, go and hide, understand? Shut out your light and find somewhere far away,' said the pudding, his eyes crossing the dark boughs above them. 'Somewhere safe, okay?'

The star made a mournful sound and blinked slowly, dimming a little. 'That's it,' said McAvoy, 'that's it.' He raised the star up and gently released it to the air and the light floated above them. It turned as though deciding, then drifted off. Its glow of colour was gone, a translucent shape disappearing into the gloom. McAvoy pulled a long face, his arms hung by his side.

'You can have a good cry once we've killed Phaedria,' said Doon, shaking the pudding's shoulder then leading him away. 'Come on. She won't take us seriously if you've turned up with tears in your eyes.'

*

Jameson, McAvoy and Doon halted. Having left the snowy floor, and again taken to the branches, the trio waited in silence. Ahead of them were noises, interspersed with voices. There was also light – an orange-fingered bloom through the foliage, perhaps denoting the position of a camp.

The puddings remained in darkness, though their eyes scoured for openings in the greenery. Jameson pulled his brothers close, guiding their eyes to a pair of coins, just visible. The pudding captain signalled a route over and the three crept from their perch.

Though the coins were immediately ahead, the group's attention was drawn to the light and a scene playing out on the snowy floor in a clearing just off to their right. They strained to see and hear what was going on.

Jameson, meanwhile, found a blade at his throat. A coin from behind leaned slowly over his shoulder. 'Quietly, now,' he said, his voice low.

McAvoy instinctively drew a dagger. Doon fumbled for his and nearly fell. Jameson smiled and eased the weapon away. 'How long have you been following us, Bravus?' he whispered.

The coin squeezed between them, craning for a view of what was going on in the light ahead.

Doon and McAvoy settled, ignoring the coin.

'Back at your own little show,' breathed Bravus. 'You puddings are sloppy.' Jameson smiled. 'Let's get closer.'

The voices rose again. There was shouting too. The four used the noise to move quickly and based themselves at clear vantage points. A log fire burned in the clearing.

Below them, a scene was playing out. Three coins were bound and tied around a large table-top tree stump.

One protested at something, wriggled, and received a volley of abuse from a pacing coin guard. Another made to speak and received a kick. The four in the branch darted their eyes.

'Can you see her?' hissed McAvoy.

None of them answered.

'Who are the three coins?' said Jameson, leaning over to Bravus.

'Survivors of the first wave. Thought their part in the war was done.'

Down below, things were progressing. Another pair of guards appeared in the clearing, discussed something, and pointed out one of those bound to the stump. The original guard confirmed their choice and reached down to untie the coin. The captive felt at his wrists, looking confused, and was shoved away. One of the guard pair lowered something in his hand: a sling.

The untied coin began to stumble, then jog until running out of view. The sling-coin looked around the floor. He lifted a small rock and loaded it, began to rotate it above his head – a *whoom-whoom* sound – and released.

A thud was heard. The guard pair turned back to the stump, conversing. The original guard stood waiting.

'One less, I suppose,' whispered Jameson.

The sling-guard – arms folded, a hand at his chin – had decided. He pointed a finger. The original guard came low to the bound coin but startled at something out of view. He straightened and animated, talking quickly, but shot back from a red blast.

The coin guard pair turned, surprised, and suffered the same fate. The remaining bound coins could only watch, eyes wide at someone's approach. With a cry they lowered their heads; as a blast momentarily blinded the four, each grabbed a hold on the branch they hid in. They opened them to reveal two smouldering, blackened casements, still curling from the heat.

A dark figure came into view. She assessed the wreckage, back turned to the four, and looked to the fire. The hidden silently drew weapons.

Phaedria's head cocked and the four froze. She wandered to the fire and raised a hand. The flames died to nothing. The assassins held in complete darkness.

'Spread out, brothers,' said Jameson, 'and strike fast. She knows we're here. May the luck of the tree be with us.'

The fire's embers now provided a weak, tinder-light, and from it plumed a smoke. It bloomed unnaturally and began coursing the air the air around them, their view of the clearing gone.

Doon found a new position, his eyes watery and blinking from the acrid fumes. He strained but could see nothing. A light flashed and the smoke lit up like a crack of lightning through a storm cloud. Another flash.

The coin heard one of his fellows cry 'for Lilly!' before another blinding light. Doon was almost panting. He took a dagger up in each hand and whispered prayer. The pudding stood, blades raised, and leapt forward. The four were never seen again.

A final stand

T reelights rallied. The drumbeats wore on, but hadn't quickened. The woods were just a dark line.

The Great Grand Walnut found McDonald, the pudding's eyes fixed to the top of the hill. 'Christmas pudding,' he said, his hands holding his big, rounded belly. 'What do you see?'

McDonald's eyes flickered, brought out of a trance. 'Nothing.'

'You said something about Phaedria commanding more numbers. Do you know how many?'

'We'll find out soon enough.' The pudding watched an elf hurry past the front line carrying a badly burnt giftbox.

The nut watched, too. As he turned, his assistants followed, shuffling around with his cape.

'You know,' said the Great Grand Walnut, his attention back on McDonald. 'We were about to invite you all up to see what we'd done with the Glades. A party of sorts, I suppose.'

The pudding said nothing.

'Perhaps we could start,' continued the walnuts' leader, 'by re-opening your great drinking houses first.' He leaned in close. 'You know, for a bit of lubrication, and perhaps some of the town's fine food – once all of this is over, of course.' He laughed.

'We'll always be grateful for your returning here today,' said McDonald, now meeting the nut's eyes. You command a great army. The Treefolk and Lilly are heartened by your return.'

'Speaking of our fairy,' said the walnut, rolling his head around to scour the heights, 'have you seen her?'

McDonald straightened his pike. 'I'm sure she'll return soon.'

'Well,' said the nut, casting his eyes over the many assembled. 'I hope she's not fashionably late. We can't just wait around forever.'

'Don't you have your nut lines to organise?' said the pudding, his eyes tracing the hill left to right.

The Great Grand Walnut stared at the pudding captain. 'As Lilly is so relaxed about a spot of warfare, then I might as well be.'

He turned to leave as the drum became many, their noise five-fold, ten-fold, and quickened. The walnut hurried off.

'Same as before, troops,' said McDonald, his expression unchanged. 'Same as before.'

*

Gabriel touched down to Henry's side, bringing the boy from his stupor. 'Okay?'

Henry pulled his blade to his body. 'I'm not hurt or anything.'

The angel looked to McBride and received a nod. 'Teddy bear,' she said, turning to Henry's friend. 'We could use someone as big and strong as yourself in the coming battle, and don't worry.' She dropped a hand onto McBride's shoulder. 'This pudding has been decorated many times. He'll look after both young.'

Bear looked to Henry and the boy nodded vigorously. 'I need a weapon,' he said. 'Something big.'

Gabriel pulled Bear in and pointed someone out in the crowds. 'Henry,' she said. 'Come back a little. I want a very quick word.' The angel guided Henry away, down the back of the hill in the town's direction. She turned his shoulders to face her and lowered to his level.

Henry looked as though he thought he might be in trouble.

'I know you'll be okay,' she said, searching his eyes. 'Henry, I think you're here for a reason.'

Henry frowned, confused. 'I don't think so.'

'It might be small, whatever it is, but I think you were called here. Perhaps-' She looked up through the falling red snow. 'By the Tree's Great Star itself.'

'I think you might be wrong.'

Gabriel beamed warmly. 'Don't be afraid, human young.' She stood and brought her gaze back to the masses of Treefolk. 'Stay by McBride's side,' she said, guiding a hand behind his back. 'Hurry.'

*

Bear had claimed a mace from one of the puddings. He nodded thanks and walked back through the crowd, feeling the weight of the spiked ball on the end of the wooden shaft. He found himself stood among some elves and he stopped.

They nodded among themselves and puffed their chests out, appearing galvanised at the large teddy bear stood central to their midst, now rolling out his shoulders, his eyes on the battlefield.

The incessant drumming stopped. An instant hush fell. From the dark woods, a flaming line blazed from right to left – like a fuse lit, eclipsing the treeline with flame. Each coin before it, their numbers greater, was burned molten.

The drumming began again, running now – a galloping beat – and it brought the coins on as one down the hillside. There were no shouts from them this time.

Pluck buzzed her little wings to fly to the front line before her dress was yanked by McBride. The pudding phalanx held for the charge as the coins thundered over the ground, treading over their fallen compatriots, the holly barrier now close to useless as too many came.

Angels flew out to meet them, spiking coins with arrows from bows, but some flew too low. Nets were thrown, ensnaring some to be mobbed like ants upon something sweet.

Close enough to see their eyes, now, McDonald gave the order. The long, lancing pikes were lowered to skewer the first among them; the most eager, or enraged perhaps. The puddings holding them slid back as coins found themselves impaled upon their lengths.

The front line strained with a great crashing noise, arcing with the pressure as the Treefolk crushed with the charge, some too bunched to draw weapons, some face to face with the coin enemy.

The embattled fought to free themselves. Bear, though, found a gap. He ran and leapt through it, bringing his mace down from behind him. His target followed its downward arc with lidless, saucer-like eyes, caving the top of a golden head.

Phaedria's forces – frenzied, slashing, hacking – bought themselves space. The Treefolk engaged, swinging their own weapons – some home-made – until they eventually fell, though not before claiming some themselves.

237

The coin numbers seemed constant, the front line fragmented as pikes were abandoned and blades were pulled.

McDonald impaled one coming, withdrew to spin and halved another before visually assessing the line. 'The middle! Defend the middle! They're all-' He broke to bury a dagger in a coin's eye. 'Pouring through the gap!'

Orders from both sides were largely ignored or unheard now within the free-for-all. A unit of giftboxes had balanced into a pyramid and fell upon a band of five back-to-back coins, holding off the surrounding Treefolk, scratching and biting as they fell. The five were routed and finished.

Feeder elves moved in a blur, furiously packing icy snowballs to top up reducing piles as their snowman picked off any coins getting too near with high-velocity shots.

One such elf – young Finn – found his stockpile growing. He looked up to find his snowman's head missing.

The starlights sweeping the battle had been abandoned as their directors had joined the fray, realising they were needed.

Oddly, a bugle sounded from Treelights. It cut through the noise at the top of the hill, blowing a long, wavering note. It slowed the oncoming coins as they awoke to the Treefolk, parting to allow a carriage-load of elves and one Bear to power through the gap, the reindeer's hooves drumming in unison ahead of them.

The elves swung candy canes, hung over the sides, as Bear topped golden heads as they went, ploughing a broad furrow straight for the hill.

The Great Grand Walnut saw a chance. He instructed several nuts to follow. Forming an arrowhead, the walnut team followed through, snow-ploughing dazed coins in the sleigh's wake with the Treefolk following after up the slope.

An oncoming wave from the wood staggered on the hillside, torn between engaging or avoiding. The Treefolk formed an arrowpoint, dividing the golden forces.

With the sleigh too heavy, the hill too steep, the reindeer halted, snorting jets of hot air. Bear dismounted from the carriage with the elves piling after, joining the river of Treefolk, all whooping and shouting, trying to overwhelm the enemy. The rattled coin forces had to swing down from each side to meet them.

238

The battleground had moved. Bodies lay strewn about the hill. Phaedria appeared at the forest's edge. She looked at the carnage with irritation. Reaching into her cloak, she withdrew a black stone.

She tossed it among the Treefolk and brought her wand out, blasting an elf running at her to pieces. McDonald had seen it. He ran to the small hole in the snow and buried a hand to find it. Red snow exploded, throwing him back onto the ground. The Treefolk pulled him up and gave the growing black shape room.

*

A dark underbelly of something travelled through the tree. It was visible, here and there, skimming over needle and branch. The dark shape was joined by three baubles, whipping and rolling through the near darkness; a low, buzzing following them.

The four traversed and dove, then shot out into the air above Treelights. The mice aboard blinked, then struck confused.

Moriarty held out an arm, stopping flakes in his paw. 'Why is the snow red, Lilly?' he shouted to his side.

Lilly didn't need to swipe her hair from her eyes; it was flowing back on the wind. 'It's harmless,' she said, looking down at the scene below. 'Just Phaedria trying to spook us.'

The craft formed a line with Moriarty leading them. The mouse pilot circled the littered landscape with the rodents aboard each bauble awed and horror-struck at what they saw.

'By all the Great Stars,' said Jacob, leaning over the edge. 'Get the slings loaded!' He signalled a paw to his fellow pilots and in turn to each of their crew. Rocks upon each were passed out from tethered bags.

Moriarty brought the craft low. With a great thrumming sound, they peppered the coin wave, hammering them like great hailstones and felling a good number. Some used others as shields.

Phaedria watched the baubles finish their run and struck her wand at the air. A green flare popped from it to sail high over the battle.

Bears and spiders

The toy soldiers waited on the outskirts of Treelights. Upon seeing the signal, they marched out with ranks crossing, joining, finding their places. From the call of their Sergeant, they raised a final exaggerated leg and ended the advance with a stomping halt.

Chests went out upon immaculate red uniforms. Eyes looked vacantly forward, chins raised. The Treefolk furthest back from the battle slowly rose from organising ammo or tending wounded to stand open-mouthed. For most, this was a joke. They'd had warning, of course, but to be confronted with this strange reality was too much.

The Sergeant gave another order and the first line lowered to one knee with their rifles raised. The soldiers stood behind aimed their guns too. A sword raised from their midst and fell. Sporadic cracks sounded, and Treefolk randomly fell too. Rifles were brought back upright and gunpowder was poured. They had no defence.

The Sergeant swept his eyes across the masses and thought it a mere matter of time. His ears, though, awoke to the sound of a hum. Its low note began to rise and his peaked eyes found a line of four baubles coming over the heads of the Treefolk. They broke formation to attack.

The Sergeant stumbled backward – his robotic manner broken – to urge his units to finish ram-rodding and to aim for the new targets. Shaded eyes flitted from gun barrel to bauble. Some broke rank and ran while others took aim. The more panicked still had rods in the ends of rifles.

Moriarty flew a low line, followed by the others, clattering the soldier's lines as they scuffed down, turning and sliding into them, crushing their numbers. Only two mice fell from the shots while others' guns exploded.

Lilly took the wheel from him as the mice leapt down along with the others, finishing any stragglers. She took off alone, punched the lever forward and made for the battle.

*

Most of the coins were having fun now. They hopped and cheered gleefully as they watched two puddings and three walnuts attempts to deal with a ball spider. The creeping black presence had divided the two armies.

The Great Grand Walnut walked to and fro, coaching, encouraging and advising.

Phaedria, too, screamed for the spider to attack. Her magical pool was low now; her left side had turned to smoke. Otherwise, she might have skewed the odds a little in their favour. Besides, Lilly was bound to show up. She had just enough left for her.

A familiar sound came down on the air. The fairy was coming for her. She stepped off to the side, aimed her wand carefully, and shot a rippling blast at the craft. Lilly pulled at the wheel as the bauble's undercarriage shot out, causing it to list and whine into a spiral.

She dove, plummeting, then brought her wings wide until she landed and made towards the Fallen Fairy, all in a seamless motion. She wasn't holding a wand, just a mere blade.

Phaedria breathed in the moment and filled her lungs. Lilly's free hand flew sideways to discard something and took up her blade with both hands.

Close now, her eyes fixed on the Fallen Fairy. She slew one coin, then another, trying to protect their master. It was the spider that halted her, skittering into her path with a pudding hung from its mouth by a leg.

The spider twisted and flung the creature at Lilly, covering her in a black, papery ash. McDonald stepped in and pierced the swollen black gut with his pike and leapt clear of the resultant lunge.

The spider came low, screaming shrilly at the pain. It rose incensed, but a dull boom and a shower of snow drew its attention along with everyone else's. A crystal-tinged mist rolled out from it, eclipsing everyone in a fog. A deep roar rent the air, hoarse and wild.

A coin appeared from the fog, fleeing the sound, but it ran into a pair of walnuts. The coin staggered, confused, and slumped to the floor, a blade deep in his gut.

With the chill air thinning the mist, a great white figure could be seen. It reared up onto its paws, revealing a giant polar bear. Its sheer size drew gasps. The bear swiped a paw sideways, taking two coins from their feet into the woods. The rest took backward steps, though one golden soldier stood before it paralysed in fear, his mouth hung. He bore witness to the beast rearing up. He tossed his sword, done, and was crushed by the bear's forepaws, flattening him.

Phaedria screamed for her forces to attack. With none coming forward, she drew a blade from a coin's belt and pushed it through him.

Some came forward, then more and more until the bear wore a glittering golden coat. Weapons were drawn, but the beast brought itself up and the coins cascaded from it like a waterfall.

The Treefolk took up arms again and picked off the fallen where they lay. With the polar bear turning, swiping and swatting at the golden sea, the spider took its chance.

It scuttled, small, dodging the falling coins and brought many feet up to cling to the underside of the beast. The bear, feeling this, looked down to see two black fangs puncture it – a low, mournful sound escaping the beast.

The great bear fell on top of cowering coins, its belly heaving final breaths. Phaedria laughed at the sight with one hand to her mouth, the other limply holding the wand.

The Great Grand Walnut narrowed his raisin-like eyes. He tore off his cape and went for the stick, side-charging coins from his path. But he too was mobbed and eventually broken apart, a golden heap smothering him.

Two small nuts who were clear of the battle clutched each other, their mouths wide. As they hugged, sobbing, fifteen mice scampered past them. They hopped over the bodies of the dead, padding up the hill to find Lilly's side.

They saw the polar bear and the coins jumping on it. They saw the Treefolk battling the coins. They saw the futility of it all.

One mouse lowered a sling, weighty with the rock inside. The other mice followed suit.

The Fallen Fairy awoke to the threat. She stabbed her wand at them, cursing, claiming one rodent, but her hand clutched the other. She reeled in agony and brought her hand to her cheek. It was hollow.

The spider, now missing two leg tips, raised eight darting eyes to a rhythmic sound. It dropped its body low to hide, but each rock found it. The spider convulsed and shuddered, its life ended.

Phaedria brought a weary face from the battle and looked beyond to the woods. She found Lilly's eyes, made the invitation, and walked from it.

Call them off!

The fires had died away now. The sounds of battle subsided. She could hear the compression of snow beneath her feet again. As she trod on in the darkness, her mind rolled back. She'd wandered like this before, aimlessly, not even knowing her own name.

Up ahead was a broad clearing. She picked through the gloom, side-stepping branches until she found herself stood within it. This, she thought, would do. The snap of a twig brought her round.

Lilly's silhouette stood on the boundary, a thin blade brought up before her. Phaedria's eyes blinked. 'Reduced to a basic weapon,' she tutted. 'What do you hope to do with that?'

Lilly advanced slowly, the tip pointed straight at her foe. 'Kill you, if I can.'

Phaedria smiled and produced her wand. 'I'm depleted, I'll admit. We both know it, but...' She tapped its end. 'I've still enough for you.'

The blade wavered, betraying Lilly's fear. 'You'll have to be quick,' said the Fallen Fairy. 'This isn't a coin you're dealing with. I'd only have to raise my wand and...' She brought her arm high to demonstrate. A flare popped from the tip.

Lilly ran and lunged desperately at Phaedria, but her dress snagged and pulled her back. With the clearing lit, the fairy brought her arm back to cut the bind, but she found her wrist in a wolf's mouth. Her other arm was caught too, taken between the teeth of its sister. Dropping her blade, she was dragged away and held on the cold ground. She fought, near whimpering, her hair blown from the wolves' panting.

Phaedria approached and stood over her. 'Look what you've become,' she said, inclining her head. 'A dress, tattered and torn. A crooked stick for a wand, and-' She laughed. 'What have you done with your hair?'

'The tree will go on!' cried Lilly, kicking her legs. 'They'll kill you before they follow you.'

'Kill me?' Phaedria crooked a smile. 'My dear, they won't be able to find me. The lights,' she said, raising a fist then extending her fingers, 'will all go

244

out.' She raised her head to look around, as though imagining the darkness to come. 'Anyway. I've got some Treefolk to slaughter, so first things first.'

Phaedria brought her wand high and angled her wrist, but her wand spun from it to land somewhere behind her in the snow. She turned to find Henry panting, his arm still outstretched from the snowball he'd thrown. He'd missed the Fallen Fairy, but he'd at least caught her wand. 'Leave her alone!' he cried, weakly.

The rage in Phaedria quelled. 'I'm almost finished,' she said, raising a finger and casting around on the snowy ground, 'just as soon as I find my wand...'

But it didn't appear where she'd expected it to. In fact, it didn't appear anywhere at all.

She fell to her knees and began to feel frantically around. 'A change of plan,' she said, her head twisting sideways. 'I'll be seeing to you-'

Something moved in the corner of her eye. She raised her head, breathless to what she saw. Her wand appeared to be floating off. In fact, it was being carried away – held by a miniature summon which was grinning and leaping from the small snowy drifts.

Phaedria clawed the snow through her fingers and followed the thing, staggering and stooping, threatening and pleading as she went, but a thought then slowed her.

And then the sound came, something in the dark branch above her. She stopped and brought her head back to find a pair of dirty yellow eyes, narrowed with menace, looking straight at her.

'No,' she moaned, as a white hand came forward with creeping icicled fingers. She expected it to grab her, but it turned, palm down, and a familiar combusting chime began to sound.

Summons fell from it to land upon her. Scratching, tearing and biting, they swarmed Phaedria as she spun and cursed, swatting and swiping.

She fell to the ground. 'Call them off, Sprite! Call them off!' she screamed, kicking and clawing.

The wolves released their hold on Lilly to power over the ground. They leaped in turn, biting and snarling, as Sprite mocked and smiled, just out of reach. It would be their turn now.

Summons fell from his hand, coating the wolves. With the ice-creature forgotten, they snapped at the vicious little things between their teeth until they too lay on the ground, writhing and biting and howling.

Sprite dropped gently to the floor. He ambled past his former familiars to where Phaedria lay and waited. The summons stopped their attack – they shook and vibrated before shattering, covering Phaedria in broken shards.

She lay bloodied and groaning. The air caught in her throat. Sprite's icy hand gripped her neck.

He brought his face close to hers, his breath dank, his eyes all-encompassing. She could see nothing else. Sprite's pupils appeared to wash away. She saw only a dirty yellow. A sea of it.

Blurred visions came to her, like chapters, and in her mind, she went away.

She saw the summon, turned, entering Sprite's mouth
Saw him follow the boy
A hand, her hand, commanding his return
A leap from a high branch into another, near killing him
A hand – Sprite's hand – conjuring a summon
Enters his mouth, kills the stunned creature within
His return to her
His deception

Phaedria spun away from Sprite – from his eyes, from his mind – and gasped for air. Sprite straddled her chest. While one hand still held her throat, the other was drawn back – fingers curled to hooks.

'Sprite, my pet...' Her voice was a strangled whisper. The wind built then, scattering her final words. The creature's hand shook and his face darkened.

He brought his rage but a wind blew him clear, clean off Phaedria. A powerful, rushing gust sent him tumbling over the ground.

He shook his head clean of snow, thought better of it, and leapt up into an overhanging bough.

Phaedria knew who'd come to claim her. She rolled her head to see a small, wizard-like character approaching, with an elaborate looping beard and piercing blue eyes.

A gathering wind built around Phaedria, whipping flecks of snow from the ground until it built to a maelstrom of noise, flapping her cloak and lifting her from the floor. She hung, suspended, as a storm whirled around her, tinkling and cracking, as ice began to form and solidify.

Phaedria turned with it too – until she became encased in a block of ice, spinning weightless in the air.

Henry watched dumbly as wispy streams coursed down through the branches to streak at speed around her. Winter summoned one to him. It came low and the little wizard stepped upon it to fly up, blasting a great wind from his mouth before him, and a gaping hole in the foliage.

Phaedria spun out after him.

*

The warring appeared to pause. The falling snow wasn't a deep red anymore. With all eyes on the spinning block of ice flying high overhead, the coins were in no doubt. Their Queen was inside it. They were leaderless; their fanaticism quickly evaporated.

There were no new lines appearing; they retreated back into the woods. Coins began to find themselves alone on the battlefield. Some escaped.

The Treefolk came together, as one, to rout them from the battlefield. Even the tiny giftboxes.

*

Two broken, bloodied beasts rose slowly. Their trembling legs were staked wide. Both wondered where they were.

One came to the other and began to lick its face clean. A human, close by, startled them. Mere wolves once more, free of Phaedria's spell, they limped off into the safety of the tree.

Henry came to Lilly's side and dropped to his knees. He looked upon her face, barely visible beneath all her hair, and raised each arm in turn to inspect them.

Lastly, he placed an ear to her chest.

'What are you doing?' said Lilly, her eyes fluttering.

Henry straightened and took one of her hands. 'By all the luck in Treelights!' he said, smiling.

Lilly blew the bedraggled hair from her face. She was grinning.

A debt of gratitude

It was to rapturous applause that Lilly and Henry returned, not only for their fairy and the boy, but for one another. Treelights had been waiting in the streets. Much of it came Henry's way, but it washed over him.

He broke from Lilly's side to push through puddings and walnuts and candy canes, to gingerbread men and gift-wrapped boxes, all slapping his back and ruffling his hair until he met square with his friend.

The pair hugged. Henry took a step back and looked his teddy up and down, namely his battle-gear.

Daggers were sheathed in a belt around his waist. His paw held a steel blade. The other raised a golden shield; buckled and dented, its owner's face still apparent. His head wore a metal cradle-cap helmet, strapped beneath his chin.

'What happened to you?' said Henry, incredulous.

An elf sidled up to Henry and threw an arm around his shoulder. The other hand pointed at Bear. 'He was into everything,' he explained. 'I saw him here, then the next moment I saw him there.'

'Is that true?' Henry smiled broadly.

'With the stars as my witness, so it is. We'd be glad to count him among our number.'

Bear just smiled through those amber-flecked eyes. 'I'm glad you made it back, Henry.'

A fanfare of startling clarity sounded, breaking up the reunion. Lilly had been raised up upon a platform of proud looking giftboxes. She was almost lifted again by the resultant cheer, but she eventually brought quiet.

'First things first,' said Lilly, brightly, and she brought before her what looked like a dark, silken, draw-stringed bag.

She pinched its collar and opened it wide, far wider than such a bag should allow. A beam of otherworldly light shot from it to strike the darkest heights of Treelights' Grand Hollow.

The assembled gasped as the light shimmered and rippled like a light shone beneath liquid, banding and swaying and breathing; phantom streams began tailing upward like ghosts, entangled with hundreds of brilliant motes – rapidly expanding shapes of numerous, glorious colours.

'The stars!' cried one, as the others began to clap and cheer and jump. Like an expanding galaxy, the stars flowered off into the heights, remapping the system they had for so long inhabited. And with them they brought back their song, the faint song of the stars. It filled everyone up and replaced the thing that had been missing; so subtle that no one had realised it gone.

The tree was as it once was.

*

The drinking houses of Treelights did a roaring trade that evening; even the young, now perfectly safe, were allowed to run around the establishments' worn wooden floors, mimicking the locals' heroics. Even the grumpiest of Tree-dwellers - though very few in number - laughed and cheered at their running battles.

Glasses were charged above swollen bellies, telling of the fill each had had of the tree's finest foodstuffs and ales.

Numerous toasts, in turn, and to each and everyone, rendered a great number hoarse. Traditional songs were sung and dances were danced, with each brand of Treefolk bringing something different.

Henry was sat upon a stool by an open fire. He too had a perfectly round stomach, straining at the elven costume he had happily accepted. Bear had quietly informed him that he stank. His pyjamas and dressing gown would be clean for the morning, he was assured.

To his right, and seated like the king-who-had-everything, was Bear. He seemed a part of the very lining of the high-backed chair he was slumped in. Something would appear at his paw every so often from the Mice; a tankard of local ale or another slice of something, to which he'd politely decline, then usually submit to.

Across from Bear and Henry was one of the walnut captains, sat close to the hot fire, his thin little legs splayed. He winked at them as he stroked his belly, absorbing the heat gladly into his battle-scarred shell.

Pluck squeezed her way through a number of folk to stand before Henry. She was eating a sausage and holding a glass of something fizzy. 'A few of us are heading out to a party later,' she said absently, working the food round her mouth. 'Want to join us?'

Bear pretended he was dozing. Henry frowned at the drink. 'What's that?'

'Well, it's better than the slop the puddings drink,' she said, raising the glass and swaying. 'We've managed to grab a few bottles.' She came close to whisper, but forgot to. 'They're buried in the snow outside!'

'I think I'll stay here,' said Henry, settling into his seat. 'Does Lilly know?'

'*Does Lilly know*?' said Pluck, mimicking.

'Does Lilly know what?' said Lilly, suddenly appearing.

Pluck tossed her drink at the fire, drenching the back of the walnut. She slipped between a pair of dancing dates, leaving the walnut to watch after her, his raisin-like eyes still wide with surprise.

Lilly looked stunning in a silky-silver dress, a world apart from her usual wild self. Her hair was brushed and tied flat across her head, blooming in curled bunches lain just above her shoulders. Her face too had been made up.

Her lips were wet-pink, her lashes black and long, with rouge upon her cheeks.

With a brief nod she greeted her friends. Someone offered her their seat. She accepted graciously and pulled it up close to Henry and Bear, who was fighting to sit upright. Henry watched him, amused.

'By all the stars of the tree!' said Lilly, breathless from the laugh escaping her. 'Last I saw, you were both lean and hungry.'

She leaned forward to poke Bear's midriff. 'My dearest Bear, you are almost a walnut!'

The nut captain by the fire paused wiping himself, confused.

'I see you have also made yourself most comfortable. Good for you both, but before I go and make a merry fool of myself on this establishment's dancefloor, I must thank you.'

And with that, she took a small hand and a Bear's paw and dropped to one knee before them. It was with an aching sincerity that Lilly looked upon them.

'What would our world have become without you?' she said, her eyes wet.

'We all owe you both a great debt of gratitude. And perhaps one absent ice-creature too. We owe you each...' she said looking between them. 'Our lives.'

Lilly's emotional outburst had startled them, bringing home the reality of what they'd all just endured. She rose then and began tapping a foot to a *tok-tok-tok*, played on a hollowed-out log.

'I don't know where home is for you both,' she called over the latest song to strike-up, 'but you are most welcome to stay here if you wish.'

She slipped away and danced off into the melee, but not before hoisting the walnut's tankard away with her before he could protest.

Henry and Bear looked at each other. They sat by the open fire and wondered.

*

Sleep eventually took hold of everyone that night; even the winding narrow streets of Treelights were rendered silent. Henry was among the first to see in the new morning, stretching and yawning from his bed within a quaint and comfortable room. It took him a while to get his bearings.

He had stayed at a pudding's house. A snoring Bear was laid out on another bed by a window, tangled up in his bedsheet. He smiled at the size of him. To think they shared a bed at home!

Henry rubbed his neck and looked up to the ancient, twisted beams, his mind elsewhere. He'd once made a promise to his mother. He thought of his father then, and he blinked – still dazed by it all. Memories rolled over and over like a cinema reel in his mind. They were only the good ones.

Henry's eyes eventually focused. He groaned. His father would be worried sick. He had to go home – *if he could* – and with a nod he affirmed he would go to see Lilly. He took a rolled-up sock from the floor and threw it at Bear. It bounced from his furry head, only serving to increase the noise coming from his mouth. The next hit him square between his eyes, making him blink.

'Ugh!' Bear ground his paws into his eye sockets. 'No more drink, and definitely no more food.'

'Bear,' said Henry, sitting up. 'You're not in the pub anymore.'

The big teddy pulled his paws away and looked around.

'I have to go home, Bear,' said Henry. 'I have to go home.'

The drowsiness left Bear's eyes. He looked at Henry. Henry looked back.

A smile and a wave

T he boy had done his best to refuse breakfast and get on, but their
generous host's spread and a ravenous Bear had seen him grudgingly
pull up a stool and place some preserved fruit and berries onto a plate. Along
with a hot berry juice, Henry cleared near everything in front of him.

During the morning meal, they'd recounted the night's celebrations.
Bear tilted back on his chair, very much at ease; Henry's head rose and fell
with laughter at his stories, especially the one involving a date getting
stuck in his fur.

But as they drank down their hot drinks, a silence grew between them. Bear
brought his seat level and cradled his drink. His big amber eyes rose from the
table to Henry. He looked about to say something but thought better of it, and
his eyes returned to his mug.

Henry pushed a berry round his plate. He too went to speak, but there was a
smart rap at the door. It brought their pudding host from another room, untying
an apron as she went. Hinges squealed and the wind chased in.

Henry and Bear turned to see Lilly stood framed in the doorway, stamping
the snow from her bare feet. She leaned in and hugged the pudding. The pair
shared a quiet word as the door was eased shut, and then her eyes found the
pair at the table.

'By all the stars,' she said, stepping into the room. 'Do you two ever stop
eating?'

They noted she was back in her off-white dress, her hair wild and tangled,
her feet bare. Bear looked to his empty plate and shrugged. Henry placed his
fork down and looked up at her. Her face mirrored his look of earnest.

'Lilly-'

'I know,' she said, coming close and placating him with a smile. 'I know
you have to go. I won't stop you.'

At this, their pudding host wrung her apron and headed into the kitchen.
One or two sobs were heard. Lilly wriggled her toes. 'Won't you join us all for
lunch, at least? They'd love to say goodbye.'

'I'd rather leave quietly if you don't mind,' said Henry, his eyes apologetic.

She placed a hand upon his shoulder. 'I understand. I'll be waiting in the kitchen.'

The pair went upstairs to make their beds, giving the room one last look.

Lilly dabbed the pudding's eyes with her apron as they entered the kitchen. She broke to hug them both and eventually followed them all to the door to wave them off.

Outside, a tatty red bauble idled. Tossing a line, Lilly helped them aboard. 'Most are still in bed,' she observed, pushing a gear forward and spinning the wheel. 'Ready to go?'

Henry nodded, Bear too, and off they went, whirring and clunking into the star-lit heights of Treelights.

As the snow-steeped rooftops pulled away, Henry spied the drinking house below. An elf was footing a ladder to its side while another hooked a wooden sign high, its painted face depicting the Great Grand Walnut stood proud beneath his name.

They waved up at the craft and the pair waved back. Away went the maze of narrow streets and the firelight from the streetlamps, and away went Treelights, lost in the closing flurries of snow.

The last they saw was the great trunk with its gap-toothed windows, lit like a pumpkin, before dark brushes of pine enclosed them, bringing with them their sweet sappy aroma, and the snow was no more.

The tree was dark and silent, save of course for the *clack-clack-clack* of their craft. At pleasant intervals on their way down through the tree, dark hues were broken up by starlight. Bear would tap at Henry's shoulder and they'd swing round to see soft, blissful lights staining the deep green, and hear the faint song of the stars as they passed by. And pass many they did.

The tree was repopulated. Lilly navigated them back down to the edges of the storm ring they'd passed through to get into the tree. It seemed so long ago.

It was here, windswept and fresh, that the three touched onto a mound of virgin snow and hopped down to the ground. The ground here was eerie. It breathed and glowed with a faint luminescence as the noise of the storm ring rushed past them.

Lilly spoke, having to hold her dress as she came closer. 'Are you ready?' she shouted.

Henry looked from the stormy blur to Lilly, then to Bear. 'Ready.'

Bear looked back to the tree longingly, then nodded.

'Very well,' said Lilly over the noise. She lunged forward and hugged them fiercely. 'Go well,' she cried, her hair sideways across her face, 'and again, thank you!'

They hugged her until it was time; then hand in paw, they walked off towards the storm and its relentless, chaotic noise.

They looked back as they went, but Lilly was now out of sight. Streaking bands of white and grey encircled them. Henry fought the gusts and staggered, unsure of the way, but Bear – although larger and stronger – seemed to be finding the going harder.

He fell once or twice, toppled by the wind; or perhaps his heart wasn't quite in it. Bear brought his paw from the ground to grab his friend's hand, but Henry didn't offer it.

Henry's eyes, creased to the wind, were softly smiling. He looked to his teddy, gave a small wave, and disappeared into the storm.

Bear called out for him, and again, but Henry wasn't there to hear it. He scrambled up, fell and rounded on the ground, trying to get his bearings. A dark outline of something lay ahead. He stooped and trod until the winds lessened, before stumbling to the snowy ground. He raised his head to find a pair of bare feet.

'Lilly,' he gasped, his face caked with snow. 'I've lost him. *I've lost him.*'

She helped him up and brought him away, looking wholly unconcerned. 'He's left you, Great Bear,' she said, brushing the snow from his head. Bear looked to the storm ring, perplexed. 'What do you mean?'

'Last night in the drinking house,' she said, a hand going to his shoulder. 'We had a chat.'

Bear cocked an ear, trying to snatch some sense from what he was being told. 'He thought you liked living here. Thought you had more friends; more of your own kind, in a way.'

'He... told you all this?' Bear's eyes were large and searching.

'His mind,' she said smiling, 'was made up.'

The teddy dropped his head then turned it toward to the storm. 'But who'll look after him?'

'He's shown a resilience beyond his years. I think he will cope. I believe,' she said, turning him toward the tree, 'that he has a father.'

Bear huffed at the word.

'Come on,' she said, guiding him back to the bauble, an arm thrown around him. 'I believe the Treefolk will be happy to see you back.'

*

Henry cleared the storm ring. He patted himself free of snow, took off his hat, and ran a hand through his curly, brown mop. The boy looked out across a barren landscape, his breath misting before him. Hills and snowy drifts as far as the eye could see.

He wriggled into his dressing gown and plodded off, his eyes looking to the diamond-white pinpoints of stars above him. Colours dappled the snow before him.

He turned to look upon the tree and was again awed by its size and majesty. How much had he seen of it? Had he done the right thing leaving Bear? As his eyes glazed with wonder, he smiled. Of that, he was sure.

Henry looked to the furthest horizons of the snow-covered prairie and found the waypoint. He turned up his gown's collar and padded off into nowhere, a trail of slippered footprints left behind him.

*

Henry was cold. He stood at the fir tree, clapped his hands together, and spied the ravine. He nodded and set off for it, his pace quicker now, and took the long downward slope into it.

Icy blue walls crept up either side of him. Gazing up, he found a strip of night sky where the curving walls didn't quite meet. Countless stars hung there.

The floor had levelled now. He removed his hat, tossed his gloves, and turned a small circle with his eyes upward.

Many stars ebbed and winked, but one remarkably so. It grew, doubling – no, tripling in size – and lit the ravine heaven-white as it hit.

*

Henry stood within a white, sterile room. He didn't know the space. His eyes wandered the walls and he felt warmth. There was carpet beneath his feet, he noticed.

Long shadows appeared and took the form of objects – objects he knew. There were seats in this room. A lamp too. Behind him was a chair. A figure was slumped into it. Sound came to his ears – a conversation.

255

'I'm off now,' said the voice. 'Be sure to take good care of Henry. Look after yourself too. Merry Christmas, Harold.'

A door clicked shut and Henry realised he was home. He walked to the seat and found his father. He was falling asleep. Henry took his hand and cried.

*

The boy had tucked a blanket around his father. He kissed his forehead and walked to the foot of the stairs. Their tree was still lit resplendently. 'Good night, Bear,' he said, and took the steps up to bed.

*

Henry tossed and turned. Nightmares plagued his sleep. He dreamed of Phaedria. He was stood before the Fallen Fairy, still trapped in her tomb of ice, her eyes shut. Henry came closer to touch it.

Phaedria was smiling. Her eyes flicked open.

*

The dream brought Henry from sleep. He sat bolt upright, clutching at his bedsheets and gasping. A hand came from the dark. It found Henry's chest and eased him back.

His father was beside him, silhouetted by the light from the hall. 'Easy now, son,' he whispered.

Henry's breath held, then released, and he lay still. It took a while for the boy to calm. His Bear, usually in his arms, wasn't there.

'You okay?'

Henry rolled his eyes to his father and nodded. It must be close to morning, he thought, as his father appeared almost sober. His eyes adjusted enough to see the faint whites of his eyes. They looked upon him with concern.

He took Henry's hand in his own. 'You've been looking after me for a while now,' he said, his voice tremulous. Henry heard the words pain him. 'But it should have been me looking after you.'

His hand tensed around Henry's, and he shook his head to himself. 'Your mother... your mother leaving us almost broke me. I got lost in the drink. Took no notice of what it was doing to you.'

Henry tried to rise, but his father held him.

'For one thing,' he smiled, tears forming in his eyes, 'it made you strong. Resourceful. But I should've taught you that, not have it forced upon you.'

Henry listened, impassive. His father again gripped his hand. 'Things are gonna change. I ain't gonna-' His voice cracked. 'I ain't gonna drink no more,' he hissed through gritted teeth. Henry blinked. His face leapt a little in the pale light.

'First things first, we're gonna have a great Christmas, like when there were the three of us, right?' He patted Henry's chest. 'You can open your presents, as early as you like, and I'll cook us a huge dinner. Sound good?' Henry nodded and smiled. 'Until then, get back to sleep.' And with that, they hugged in the dark, father and son.

Harold went to the door and stopped in the light. 'I feel like you've been away for a long time,' he said, looking down at his feet. 'It's good to have you back.' He gave Henry a wink and eased the door shut.

Henry had lost a friend in Bear, but he had now regained a father, and sleep took him easily and happily away.

9 781912 031191